EVEN IF IT HURTS

SAM MARIANO

EVEN IF IT HURTS

COASTAL ELITE, #1

SAM MARIANO

DEDICATION

Jacob Elordi,
For inspiring me.
You're one hell of an actor.

PLAYLIST

SWEET LITTLE LIES - BÜLO

SHAMELESS - **CAMILA CABELLO**

HONESTLY - **GABBIE HANNA**

JUST THE SAME - **CHARLOTTE LAWRENCE**

JOKE'S ON YOU - **CHARLOTTE LAWRENCE**

TOXIC - **BRITNEY SPEARS**

PLOT LINE - EMLYN

BORED - **BILLIE EILISH**

BOYFRIEND - **DOVE CAMERON**

AUTHOR'S NOTE

Before we dive in, I figure I should get some warnings out of the way.

If you're here for a lovely, upstanding hero, you have come to the wrong place. This isn't the book for you. This one's a real bastard. He's manipulative and spoiled. He's fickle and controlling. He does what he has to do to get his way. He will do shit you will not like. This is not a healthy relationship. I do not condone these things in real life (IRL, I'm actually a pretty big stickler for being a good human), and if you meet a Dare in the real world, you should run like the wind.

This is not real life, it is fiction where we are totally free to safely (and without guilt) have experiences outside of our own and enjoy the thrilling ride of being with batshit crazy heroes we would actually throat-punch and/or call the cops on in the real world. I write a lot of bad guys, but this one really sneaks up on you. It's sinister the way things unfold. Is it romance? Not in the traditional sense. This is a *very* dangerous, toxic relationship. But I love dark romance, and I feel like the bully genre lends itself to a bit of dark romance. I will never apologize for writing bad guys. It's fun to dream up psychos, and I write to entertain—myself and you. I write for adults who I expect to have their own good judgment and not use my books as relationship manuals (and that is *especially* true with this one). Want to know what it's like to bang a villain? Get it, girl. No harm done. None of these people are real, so they can't cause any real damage unless you have triggers.

So, let's talk triggers. **If you don't want any spoilers, skip the rest of this note.**

YES. There are triggers. A grocery list if I itemized them all, but let's suffice it to say shit in here is DUBIOUS, twisted, toxic, disturbing, occasionally violent/abusive, and morally sketchy at best. I'll add a TW in this one you don't usually see in my books because even for one of my manipulative heroes, Dare is… a lot. If you have been in an abusive relationship with someone who teeters on the brink of violence and find reading about them triggering, please skip this book. Is there cheating? Kinda, but not really. There's a big asterisk next to it which I won't explain because it's part of the plot. There is no cheating between the hero and heroine. I do not personally like cheating between the hero and heroine in books. I like my hero willing to do anything for his heroine, not out there betraying her. If the "cheating" in this book made you want to throw your kindle, I would be quite surprised. That said, there are plenty of other things that might make you want to throw your kindle! This is *not* a story for the safety squad. Like I said, this hero isn't a nice person, and he does some pretty ruthless stuff.

This book is intended for a mature, adult audience. I hope you enjoy!

PROLOGUE
AUBREY

THIS IS the story of an absolute psycho.

A pair of them, actually.

It all started one day while I was at work, and the school mean girl Anae came in with a return I couldn't process.

The article she brought in wasn't even from our store. I turned over the fuchsia top and looked for a tag anyway, but there wasn't one. The top had clearly been worn, too. There were faint pit stains underneath each arm.

Pushing the mound of material back across the counter, I told her politely, "I'm sorry, this item isn't eligible for return."

She had been talking to her entourage while I did my thing, but when I effectively told her she couldn't have her way, she turned, her glossy strawberry blonde locks catching the light, and stared at me as if I were a lower life form. "Excuse me?"

I offered an apologetic look. "I can't give you a refund for this."

"Why?"

"It wasn't purchased here."

"Yes, it was."

"No, it wasn't."

Her eyes narrowed at me. "Are you calling me a liar?"

"Of course not," I said, equipped with my best customer service smile. "Maybe you bought a lot of things that day and some were from here, but this wasn't. We've never carried this top before. And without tags or a receipt, a return is pretty much impossible. I'm sorry."

She didn't touch the lump of material on the counter. She continued to glare at me coolly before saying, "You go to our school, don't you?"

Anae has never spoken to me before, so I was honestly surprised she even knew that. "Yes."

"Then you know who I am."

"I do."

"Is that why you won't put through my return? Is this some sort of pathetic jealousy thing?"

"No," I said, hating life and my need for a job. Why couldn't I have just been born rich so I could live large on Mommy and Daddy's dime like she did?

That was the most insane part of all of it. Anae's rich! She didn't *need* to return the top, yet she made such a big deal about it.

"I want to speak to the manager."

"The manager isn't in right now," I told her. "But if she were, she would tell you the same thing. We can't return a shirt that wasn't purchased at this store. We literally cannot do it. If you take the top back to the store you did buy it from, maybe you can return it there."

Pushing the material back across the counter without breaking my gaze, she said, "Put my fucking return through so I can leave this crappy little boutique and never come back."

"I literally can't."

"If you don't, there will be consequences."

What does that even mean? "Look, if you want to call

back later and talk to the manager, you can, but no one will give you a different answer than I have. If I could do this return for you, I would. If I possessed a time machine and I could only use it once, I would use it to go back in time and stock this shirt at this store *just* so I could do this return for you now, but alas, I cannot. There is *nothing* I can do for you." I glanced behind her pointedly to a woman with a few articles of clothing draped over her arm, waiting to check out. "Now, if you'll please step aside so I can help the next customer, that would be amazing."

Anae's cold glare could save the polar ice caps if she used her powers for good instead of evil. "Remember this day, *Aubrey*," she said, her gaze flickering to my nametag. "Because it's the day you put yourself on my shit list, and trust me—that is *not* a place you want to be."

I wasn't really sorry she wasn't getting her way for once in her whole life, but I flashed her sympathetic eyes and lied like any good retail worker would have. "I'm really sorry."

She snatched her blouse off the counter. "You will be."

Anae tossed her hair and turned around, dismissing me and storming away in one fluid motion, her two minions right on her undoubtedly expensive heels.

I sighed, knowing she's exactly the type of person who would call my boss and try to get me in trouble even though I did nothing wrong.

"I love my job," I muttered sarcastically to myself.

The next woman in line smiled sympathetically as she placed her items on the counter.

"Did you find everything you were looking for today?" I asked her cheerfully.

"Yes, thank you."

Her manners felt nice after Mean Girl Barbie lashed out over nothing.

As the sane customer thanked me and started toward the

door with her shopping bag, I decided to text my boss. I needed to tell her what had happened so I could get ahead of it. If I waited until after Anae called with her version of the story, it would be harder to feasibly explain mine. I mean, aside from the seriously unhinged, who would actually try to get a person in trouble for not refunding a top that wasn't purchased at our store?

But when people do shit that crazy and you have to try to respond to it, more often than not, you come off looking like the crazy one.

IT'S days later at school when one of Satan's little helpers approaches me.

I'm standing in the cafeteria line. I blink a few times when I realize the girl who stopped in front of me isn't just waiting for a crowd to ease so she can sneak past—she approached me on purpose and is waiting for me to look at her.

So I do. We've never spoken, but I know her name is Mallory Cantrell. She's pretty, her curly hair tied up in a high pony, her Easter green top showcasing her cleavage even though it's against the school dress code.

"Hey. Aubrey, right?"

Cautious, I nod.

She smiles, her straight white teeth standing out against her dark complexion. "I thought so. I'm Mallory."

"I know."

"Right." She doesn't pretend to be surprised that I'm sure of her name, but she wasn't sure of mine. "We met at the store the other day. Kind of. I was there with Anae."

The line moves ahead of me so I take a step forward.

She moves with me. "Anyway, I wanted to say sorry about her whole demonstration of psycho bitchiness."

I crack a smile since she's being nice. If I were in her shoes, I'd be embarrassed, too. Of course, if I were in her shoes, I would have said something at the store when my friend was in desperate need of a Snickers. "It's okay, not your fault."

"She's really used to getting her way, so when she doesn't, she has no clue how to deal with it."

"Her parents clearly haven't done the world any favors there."

Mallory smiles, dropping her gaze. "Yeah, so I thought I'd extend an olive branch. Tomorrow night, we're all meeting up at Anae's boyfriend's house for a party. You should come. Bring a friend. It'll be fun. There will be drinks and pizza and lots of cool people. He has a killer pool, so bring a bikini."

That's definitely not going to happen, but just in case Mallory also isn't accustomed to being told no, I flash her a smile. "Thanks. I'll see if I'm free, maybe I'll stop by."

She blinks. "Oh." Momentarily lost for words, she looks around as if for some cue from a stage manager on what she's supposed to do next. Poor thing, she's a marionette with no puppet master.

"Was there something else?" I ask.

Her gaze snaps back to me, her pretty face set in a frown. "I don't know. I don't feel like we're cool. Maybe you could sit with us today."

"No, thanks." I say it with a smile so she's not offended, but I can't imagine anything less enjoyable than sitting with our school's answer to The Plastics. Besides, I have more important stuff to do.

Her frown deepens with annoyance and confusion. "Are you serious?"

"Yeah. No offense. I appreciate the invite, I just kinda like having my lunch break to decompress and eat my food. I don't like sitting with people."

"That's… so weird."

The line moves, so I step forward and shrug. "I guess."

She looks back over her shoulder. This time, I follow her gaze and see she's looking to Anae for some clue as to what she should do next.

Anae's eyes bulge at her with wordless reprimand, as if she's gone off-script and Anae isn't happy about it.

That's not suspicious at all.

Mallory turns back to me, opens her mouth like she's going to say something else, then promptly turns and walks back to her table without another word.

"Poor thing short-circuited." I shake my head, amused at my own commentary, and shift my focus to the food behind the counter. I haven't decided what I want to eat yet, but I'm starving, so I really wish this line would hurry up.

When the school day ends, I make my way home as quickly as possible.

I have a lot to do tonight. So much that just *thinking* about it exhausts me, but I suck it up and paint a smile on my face as I head inside with my school bag slung over my shoulder.

Mom is sitting on her recliner in the living room. I flash her my brightest smile. "Hey, Mom."

"Hey, honey. How was school today?"

"School was good," I tell her.

I consider letting her know I was invited to a party just so she has the impression my peers like me, but I decide not to. Knowing her, she would tell me to go and have fun, and there's no way I'm going to that party. I'd rather spend my weekend with her doing what we already planned to do.

Dropping my bag from my shoulder, I tell her, "I'm going to take a quick shower and decontaminate, then I'll get dressed and we can start dinner."

"I can't wait," she says with a smile as I head for the hall.

"Neither can I."

I lose my smile as soon as I'm out of her sight. Giving my bedroom door a push, I haul my heavy-ass backpack inside, trying not to think how I'll find time to finish my homework. I started it at lunch like I have every day of this school year, but lunch isn't long enough to put a very big dent in my workload.

I guess I'm staying up late again.

It's what I have to do most nights in order to get everything done, but most nights I don't have to do as much cooking as I do tonight.

Oh well.

Complaining about it—even just in my own head—won't change anything, so I shove down the stirrings of fatigue I'm already feeling after a long day of school, and head to the bathroom for a nice, refreshing shower.

After my shower, I tie my hair up in a cute ponytail with an orange scarf, then I head to my room. I put on a white, airy peasant-style sundress—the kind I'd wear traversing the cobbled streets of Italy if we could afford such an expensive vacation. I grab my favorite sunglasses and put them on top of my head, also like I would if we were sightseeing today and the sun was still up for a few more hours.

As I make my way out to the living room, I pull up YouTube on my phone and start the first loop of Italian background music I picked to play while I cook dinner.

Mom grins as soon as the lovely music starts playing and turns to look up at me as I enter the room. "Mood music?"

"Feels like you're in Italy listening to it, doesn't it? Now, come to the kitchen, let's get the smells going." Pausing, I wait to see if she needs help, but it must be a good day today because she makes it to the center island without any trouble.

"You don't have to hover," she tells me as she takes a seat. "If I need help, I'll ask."

"All right." I know she's a little sensitive about it, so I don't want to make a fuss. Instead, I dust that comment right under the rug and start collecting ingredients. "I'm going to start with the gelato since it takes the longest in the freezer."

It wouldn't take as long if we had an ice cream maker, but we do not, and buying one just for this was definitely not in the budget. I pull out the gelato tubs I ordered on Amazon, a pair of them for $15. That was more within my budget, so the long way it is.

Mom sits at the island and we talk and listen to music while I get the gelato started. Once that's done, I dump it in the container and put it in the freezer, then I set the first alarm.

Next, we make a mess on the counter making pasta from scratch. It's a laborious task, but at least the pasta this recipe calls for can be made without a pasta machine. I only needed a cheap pack of bamboo skewers, and Mom enjoys helping me shape it until we have enough for dinner.

I'm trying to do everything as traditionally as possible, so instead of a food processor, I grab a mortar and pestle for the assembly of the sauce. Mom laughs, thinking I'm joking.

"Nope, we're doing it old school," I tell her as I drop garlic in and get to crushing.

Turns out, that process sucks. My arm is not happy, but I keep at it until I need a break, then I grab the pecorino cheese and grate some in the bowl.

My alarm goes off, so I have to pause to mix the gelato. Then I'm back at it, adding basil and a pinch of salt. Before long, we have two plates of authentic Italian *pesto alla Trapanese*.

"This looks incredible," Mom says, reaching for her plate,

but I tell her to go sit down and I'll bring it to her. She starts to object, but I cut her off with a firm raise of my eyebrow.

"If we were in Italy, a hunky Italian waiter would be serving you. Under no circumstances would you be serving yourself. I don't want to hear it."

Reluctantly, she goes in and sits down. While the pasta was cooking, I made quick work of setting a table for two with a white linen tablecloth and a candle in the center.

I bring in our dinner and a plate of sliced Italian bread. I grab us goblets of water and the wine that paired best with this pasta, then I start the next music playlist and we enjoy a nice dinner.

After dinner is over, I clear the table, move it out of the way, and turn on our first movie of the night, *Oceans 12*.

We watch *The Talented Mr. Ripley* next, and as the credits roll, Mom says, "That's what I never did. I should have pulled off a heist."

I crack a smile and look over at her. "Hey, there's still time. I go to school with plenty of rich assholes we could rob if you need help finding a target," I joke.

Mom cracks a smile, but it doesn't reach her eyes. "I know you don't want to," she says, looking down at her lap, "but there are some practical things we need to talk about, Aubrey."

I pluck the sunglasses off my head and put them on the end table between the couch and Mom's trusty recliner. "Not while we're on vacation. Where should we go next weekend? We could stick with Italy but get more specific—maybe Rome on Saturday, Venice on Sunday? I'd like to see Rome and stop by the Trevi Fountain. Or we could hop the train to Paris. There's this restaurant inside the train station in Paris that Janie was telling me is really good. I looked around a bit and found a recipe for their mashed potatoes. I can look at the menu and find something else I can cook. We can binge *Emily in Paris*, and I can order one of those Amazon experiences, maybe a walking tour of the city, or I think we can tour the Eiffel Tower. Personally, I think I can kick ass at French cuisine, so I'm down if you are."

"That sounds nice," she says, her tone a bit subdued by my dedication to changing the subject.

"It's decided, then." Pushing up off the couch, I add, "I'm going to check on the gelato."

Mom sighs but makes no further attempts to ruin our night with ugly reality.

CHAPTER 2
AUBREY

WE'RE on night two of Italy—more delicious pasta, but tiramisu for dessert. Tonight, we watch *Under the Tuscan Sun* and *Letters to Juliet*.

I am mentally and physically exhausted, but I still have to clean up after dinner. Mom offers to help, but of course, I tell her no and take care of everything myself.

She's tired, too, so we call it a night.

Mom goes to sleep, while I unpack my book bag and set my textbooks and notebooks in stacks across my queen-sized mattress. Lunch was especially noisy today and I couldn't concentrate, so I didn't get the head start I usually get.

My phone lights up on the bed beside me. My gaze flickers to it, my brow creasing as I see a new text message and who it's from.

Jane Sebold, an old friend of mine from school.

Before my entire life tore apart at the seams and it fell on me to single-handedly hold the pieces together, I used to hang out with Janie all the time. We were best friends, and I know she was hurt when I had to take a step back, but I could only spread myself so thin before I couldn't even hold *myself* together anymore. Something had to give, and unfortunately, it was Janie that needed me the least.

I think about her often, especially when I see her at school, but we don't talk much anymore. I can't even remember the last time she sent me a text message.

Grabbing the phone, I touch the screen to brighten it so I can read her message without sliding it open. It's just one line: What are you doing?

In general, or right this moment?

I slide the message open so I can type back. "Homework. You?"

"Still?" she texts back. "God, you must have got a late start."

"Yeah, I was doing stuff with my mom," I type back.

"Oh, sure. How is she doing?"

"Pretty much the same. Just taking things one day at a time. How have you been?"

"I'm good," she texts back. "Really good tonight. I'm actually at this really cool party and I was wondering if you'd want to meet me here. We haven't hung out in a while, and I'm sure you could use a break for some fun."

I'm torn. It would be nice to see Janie again and hang out like old times, but I'm *so* tired. Plus, if I go over there I'll be around other people. That means I have to shower again as soon as I get home, and just thinking about doing all of that when I'm already exhausted…

I text back, "I wish I could, but it's late and I still have a ton of homework to do."

"It is Friday," she points out. "The homework isn't due until Monday. You can always do it over the weekend."

She knows I like to get my homework out of the way on Friday night so I don't have to think about school again until Monday, but it's not just that. Since most of my weekend time is already set aside to work and hang out with my mom, I also need to get some sleep over the weekend. That's when I catch up so I can function throughout the week. I'm always worn down by Friday night.

If I go to this party to see her, that means no homework gets done tonight. That means I have to do all of it tomorrow, so I'll have to stay up late again, which means I get zero hours of extra sleep this weekend.

This is why I let the friendship go in the first place. I do *not* have time for it.

But, despite all my good reasons, I feel guilty about telling her no. Even though I tried explaining to Janie that it wasn't personal, I know she took it that way. Why wouldn't I hang out with her if I truly wanted to?

She doesn't understand that I'm stretched so thin I feel see-through, and I literally *can't* juggle one more ball, no matter how much I might want to.

I don't expect her to understand what life is like for me now, though. Why would she? She's never had to shoulder so much responsibility. Grown men have turned away from the weight I have to carry every day.

For a moment, I feel sad for myself, but as soon as I realize what I'm doing, I stop. There is *definitely* no time for that bullshit.

Out of time.

That perfectly sums up my entire life right now, actually. I need more time, and there's no way to get it.

It's a frustrating realization. I really *want* to have time for Janie, I just… don't.

Right?

It feels impossible to add one more ball to the ones I already have in the air, but every bit of this has felt impossible, and here I am, doing it.

So I don't get enough sleep this weekend—that's why coffee is a thing.

Surely I can rearrange my plate to fit just one more thing.

I check the time. It's a little after 11—way too late to go to a party, but showing up now could work in my favor. I don't have to stay as long as if I had gone when the party started, but I'm still putting in an appearance, so at least Janie will know I'm making an effort.

I'm already dressed in my "vacation clothes," so I'm pretty much ready. I grab my purse and smear some lip balm on my lips, then I clear off my bed since I expect to be dead on my feet when I get back home.

Am I forgetting anything?

Oh, right.

Usually, I would tell Mom I'm leaving. Actually, in the past when I actually did normal teenage things, I guess I would have *asked*.

It doesn't feel like I need to anymore.

Thinking things like that can only possibly make me sad, so I shove it down, slide my purse strap on my shoulder, and quietly make my way out of the house.

Chase Darington's mansion is something straight off the pages of a glossy magazine. It's in an elite, hillside neighborhood where a lot of the rich kids from my school live. They have the beach in their backyard, but homes designed with lavish pools and so many expensive playthings, they're hardly impressed by what nature has to offer.

A wave of foreboding creeps down my spine as I park in one of the empty spots along the long, winding driveway that curves around the house. The place is already packed full of cars. There must be a ton of people here.

I hope I left enough room in case the people in front of me need to leave.

Not that I'm likely to stay longer than anybody else. I literally just want to pop in, talk to Janie for a bit, and then go home. I don't enjoy hanging out with these people at school, and I feel like I don't belong here already.

I don't even know where to go. I make my way to the front door, but when I knock, nobody answers.

I can hear music blasting from inside the house, so they probably can't hear me.

There's more ruckus around back. A girl shrieks, some guys laugh, and I hear a huge splash from the pool.

More music plays in the backyard. I guess since people are obviously back there and no one is coming to the door, I can just walk around back.

I feel awkward about it, and the feeling intensifies when I round the corner and find a couple making out with half of their clothes off in a private cabana.

"Whoa," I murmur, quickly turning my head to look away. I almost apologize, but I don't think they even noticed me.

Not far from there is another piece of furniture with two guys sprawled on it, one glancing over at the couple in the cabana with a smirk on his face.

"Hey, beautiful, where are you going?" asks a guy from the swim team as I walk past him. "Not feeling chatty, huh?"

Ew.

There are too many people here. I'm not fond of crowds, and I don't see Janie back here.

I've never actually been to one, but this isn't what I expected of a high school party. I pass another couple making out by the pool, then move out of the way as I'm nearly splashed by a guy and girl flirting and playing grab-ass in the sloshing water.

"Hey, you made it!"

I turn in the direction of the voice and see Mallory coming

toward me wearing a smile and a peach-colored bikini, but curiously lacking her entourage again. I think I can count on one hand how many times I've seen Mallory without Anae and Shawna in a social setting, and now she's approached me alone twice.

I offer back a smile. "Yeah, here I am."

"Great." Her smile widens. She turns and gestures to a wet bar area. "You can grab a drink over there. We've got everything. Here, I'll take your purse and put it in the coatroom."

My grip on my purse tightens. "Oh, that's all right. I'll keep it on me."

Her eyebrows rise in surprise. "It'll be kinda hard to swim and keep track of it. Not like any of the poor people are here tonight, but—" She freezes, realizing what she said.

I offer a thin smile. "It's fine. I'm not going in the pool. I have to keep my phone close in case my mom needs me, so… thanks, anyway."

"Are you sure?"

Déjà vu hits as she adopts the look of a lost robot. "Yeah, I'm sure."

"All right," Mallory says, walking toward the bar and clearly expecting me to follow.

I do because I expect she won't go away until I satisfy her, and I want to go find Janie. Maybe she's inside.

Mallory lingers until I grab a drink—two, actually. There's bottled water, which is what I grab, but she insists I have a real drink. She grabs bottles of liquor from behind the bar and makes me something herself.

I thank her and take the red Solo cup, then I make my way inside the house to look for my friend.

I find a lot of people inside—including one pair of definitely naked teenagers snuggled up beneath a fur blanket in the downstairs guest bedroom—but I don't find Janie.

I suppose as many people as there are here, we may keep missing each other while we're circulating. I find a corner off to myself where no one will bump into me, then I shift my drinks so I can reach into my purse and grab my phone.

I text Janie to ask where she is, but there's no immediate response.

"Is that for me?"

I turn, startled, as a guy I vaguely recognize but don't know the name of gets a little too close and takes the drink right out of my hand. "Um…" He takes a sip, watching me over the rim. "I guess it is now."

He smiles, lowering the cup and moving closer. "I'm Kevin."

"Hi, Kevin."

"Aren't you gonna tell me your name?"

"No."

Inexplicably, he smiles like I've just said something sexy. "Hard to get, huh? I like it."

I couldn't be more turned off. "Not playing hard to get. Now, if you'll excuse me, I need to go look for my friend."

I move around him and start heading back the way I came, but the guy follows me.

"I can be your friend."

He says it like I'll be enticed. I roll my eyes, hard. "No thanks."

As aggressively as he began, I think he might keep coming, but fortunately, he seems to get the hint because when I look back, he isn't there.

At least he took that drink I didn't want off my hands. What a pal, that Kevin.

I check my phone once I get back out near the pool. There's still nothing from Janie.

What the hell?

Someone shouts "hey!" behind me, but it doesn't occur to

me they could *possibly* be addressing me until someone grabs my shoulder and yanks me around.

I have to look up, my eyes widening as I look into the angry red face of Kalea Danson. I was in a group project with her once, and back when I used to sit with people at lunch, we sat at the same table a couple of times, but we don't really know each other.

She's definitely looking at *me*, though.

Angrily. Very angrily.

"Um… me?" I question.

Her eyes narrow. "Who else?"

I'm so confused. "I don't know. Can I help you with something?"

"Yeah." She shoves me and I fall back a couple of steps— not only because I'm taken completely off-guard, but because Kalea Danson is the only girl on the school wrestling team.

She's huge.

I'm not.

I would never intentionally anger her.

"What the hell was that for?" I ask, not even angry, just confused.

She turns her phone around and shows me a picture of me and Kevin talking upstairs. It must have been when he first approached and took my drink. He's definitely giving me a sexy look, but my back is turned, so you can't see that I'm definitely not reciprocating.

"You think you can talk to *my* man? I will break you in half," she says, giving me a once-over that lets me know she is not impressed with my scrawny ass.

"You have the wrong idea. I was not flirting with your boyfriend. At all."

She points to the phone. "I have proof, bitch."

"No. You can't see my expression from this angle. If you could, you'd see it looks like when you take a big whiff of soured milk. No offense. I'm sure he has his charms, but I don't see them. I'm guessing a well-meaning friend of yours snapped that and not you because trust me, if you'd have been there yourself, you would not think I was flirting with him. If anything, he was—" I stop myself a little too late, realizing I've said too much. Telling her he came onto me won't make her feel any better.

She takes an intimidating step toward me. "You wanna finish that sentence?"

"Not particularly," I murmur.

"You think I'm not enough for my own boyfriend?"

"Definitely not." I shake my head vehemently, not just because I don't want her to beat me up, but because I hate to think *she* thinks that. "And I think if *he* makes you feel that way, maybe he's not the one."

She gives me another shove backward. "You need to stay out of my business and away from my boyfriend. If I catch you talking to him again, you're dead."

There's literally no chance of that.

I might say that if she didn't keep pushing me, but she's starting to piss me off. "Look, it's not *my* fault your boyfriend started talking to me out of nowhere. I have no interest in him. Whatever your friend thought they saw, they were mistaken."

Kalea smiles, and I can feel trouble brewing. Before I can say another word, she picks me up and hurls me into the pool.

Bodies move swiftly out of the way as I land gracelessly in the water. My arms shoot out, terror seizing me as I plummet beneath the surface, sucking water into my lungs before I can think to close my mouth.

I can't swim.

I can't drown, either, so I claw desperately at the water, trying to doggy paddle like I did when I was a kid.

Calm down, calm down, calm down.

It's a frantic chant in my mind as I get my feet under me at the bottom of the pool. I use them to launch myself upward, then I try to use momentum to get to the surface. I don't know why it's not working, if my movements are too choppy, if I'm too panicked. All I know is there's water in my lungs and I can't breathe even though my body is begging me to.

I can't breathe.

My lungs burn and I start to feel sick from the lack of oxygen. I kick and move my arms, but they're getting heavy. So is the water. Everything feels so heavy, and the panic gets more desperate as my body pleads with me for just one gulp of air.

I'm going to die.

I read once that when your brain is cut off from its oxygen supply, you hallucinate. I guess that's the only explanation for the dark angel I see piercing the water's surface, shooting toward me like a bullet. His big, beautiful black wings unfurl and I feel a sense of peace that he's coming for me.

I shouldn't feel peace in the moment I lose control of my limbs because even though my thrashing wasn't making much impact, I know if I don't fight my way to the surface, I'll drown.

The surface is too far to reach, and my body isn't under my control anymore. My lungs are the last to give up. I can't hold my breath anymore. The impulse to breathe is too all-consuming. I *need* it.

When I can't hold my breath anymore, I suck in more water that feels like liquid lead as it fills my lungs.

I know I'm lost.

I feel myself sinking, falling back toward the pool floor as consciousness dips in and out of focus.

I almost hit the pool floor, but then my angel is there. He

grabs me and pulls me toward him, then his strong wings wrap around both of us and I'm not afraid anymore.

I could cry, I'm so happy.

She won't feel afraid.

There's peace in the last moments before you leave.

It brings me more solace than I thought possible to know this is what she'll feel when the clock runs out. I was so afraid it would be all sadness and fear to be ripped from the Earth before you're ready to go, but it's not.

I wish I could be there with her for all the rest of her moments, but I know she'll join me soon, and nothing will ever part us again.

If I weren't in a pool full of water, I think tears would be falling down my face. I curl close to my angel, feel the comfort of his powerful wings embracing me.

I close my eyes as we fly out of the pool and above the house, as we soar up through the darkness toward the heavens.

I feel the stars around us, but I don't look. I nuzzle my face into the neck of my angel and hold him tight, hoping he never lets me go.

CHAPTER 3
DARE

"ARE YOU GUYS FUCKING SERIOUS?"

I can't believe I'm the one to say something.

Me.

I hardly spend my time looking out for anyone else's well-being, but there is literally a girl drowning at the bottom of my damn pool, and no one is making a move to help her.

An average swimmer might not be able to do much more than toss something for her to grab onto without endangering themselves, but half the seniors on the swim team are here tonight, and we are certainly above-average swimmers.

I look at everyone crowded around, watching the girl thrash wildly at the bottom of the pool. One girl pulls out her phone to record it, but her friend grabs her arm and asks her if she's fucking crazy.

Scofield from the swim team finally starts to pull off his shirt and move toward the water, but Anae stops him with a sharp, "Don't."

I look over at my girlfriend, hiking an eyebrow in disbelief.

She must feel my gaze on her because she looks back

innocently. "What? She knows how to swim, she's just trying to get attention."

Anae's fucking crazy, so I don't take her word for it. I also don't take her orders like the rest of these assholes, so I peel off my shirt, toss it behind me, and dive into the pool.

The girl is near the bottom when I finally get to her. She's exhausted her body fighting to get back to the surface. She's sinking, but I pull her up.

She hasn't been down here too long, so she hasn't lost consciousness yet. I'm prepared for her to panic again, to grab at me and try to pull me down with her.

When someone's drowning and clinging to life, it's not unheard of for them to drag their rescuer down in their desperation to get back to the surface. It's animal instinct, a fight to survive. If pulling me down helps you get back up, you'll pull me down 10 out of 10 times. Anyone who says otherwise is lying to themselves.

I'm not worried, though. I'm the strongest swimmer on the team. If she starts fighting again, I'll immobilize her and tow her back to the surface, but there's not a shot in hell she's drowning me to save herself.

She doesn't try to pull me down or climb over me, though.

As soon as I bring her in, she hugs me. I'm already caught off-guard, then she nuzzles closer, resting her head on my shoulder.

Before I break the surface, her limbs have fallen away from me and her body has gone limp. Her eyes are closed when I get her head above water, her long dark hair floating like squid ink in the water behind her body.

"Get the fuck over here and help me," I bark at Scofield and Clemmons.

My orders trump Anae's, so they hustle their asses over and help me haul the girl out of the water so I can climb out myself.

The girl lies motionless on the tile surrounding the pool.

I'm dripping water all over the fucking place, but I push what I can out of my hair so it doesn't drip in her face when I lean over her, then I drop to my knees and see if she's breathing.

She isn't.

Fuck.

"Should we call someone?" Scofield says, glancing at me uncertainly.

"Oh my god, she's fine," Anae says, but this time there's an edge of nervousness, like it might be occurring to her she's taken it too far.

Not because the girl isn't breathing, but because people are starting to question her.

I don't answer. All my focus zeroes in on the girl and the noise around me dies away.

As a competitive swimmer, I know what to do in a situation like this. I tilt her head back and lift her chin to open her airway. I listen one more time to make sure she really isn't breathing, and when I confirm she's not, I position my hands in the middle of her chest and do compressions. After the first round, I pinch her nose, lower my mouth to hers, and breathe my air into her lungs.

I sense the nervousness of the people gathered around increase when I do a few rounds and the girl is still unconscious.

"Come on," I murmur, pressing her chest, and then leaning down to press my mouth against hers again.

Relief hits hard when her body jerks and she starts coughing up pool water.

I sit back on my legs and breathe a quiet sigh of relief.

That was fucking close.

Even though it's a hot night, the girl shivers as she tries to regain her bearings.

Glancing at the nearest of Anae's bimbos, I tell Mallory, "Go get her a towel."

Mallory's gaze flits to Anae but doesn't linger long enough to see whether or not she supports my order. She comes back a moment later with a fluffy turquoise beach towel and hands it to the girl with a meek, "Here you go."

The girl looks at Mallory for a moment, then snatches the towel and mutters a thank you as she drapes it over her back and pulls the ends around her shoulders.

Finally, the girl's gaze flickers to me.

She studies my face, a frown creasing her brow. "You're not an angel."

A smirk tugs at the corners of my lips. "No, I am not."

Her gaze flickers to the tattoo covering my right shoulder, a crow with spread wings. She looks down and breathes in, placing a hand on her chest.

Addressing the crowd, I say, "Someone call her an ambulance."

"No," she says quickly, shaking her head but not looking at me. "Thank you, but I'm okay now."

"You still need medical attention. There was water in your lungs. You need to be looked at by a doctor. You could still die."

"I won't die," she says almost dismissively. "I have too much to do."

"I don't think being busy is enough to keep you alive."

She shakes her head, pulling the towel off and trying to stand.

Her legs go out from under her instantly. I'm right there, catching her around the waist so she doesn't fall.

I pull her into my lap since her little ass doesn't want to listen. Looking directly at Scofield, I say, "Call her an ambulance."

"No," she objects again, struggling to move off my lap.

My cock stirs as she struggles to get away from me, but I ignore the heat kindling low in my gut and lock my arm around her even tighter.

Scowling, she turns her head and looks me dead in the eye. It feels intimate since she's on my lap, but she ruins it by being mad as hell and looking like a drowned rat.

A cute drowned rat, but a drowned rat all the same.

"You're wasting your energy," I tell her. "You're going to the hospital."

"I am *not*. I appreciate you saving me, but you're not in charge here, and I am *not* going to the hospital."

"You are on my property; you nearly drowned in *my* pool. You are going to the hospital so they can check you out, make sure your poor little family can't sue my father for your wrongful death, and then we can all get on with our lives."

Her jaw drops open. "You... you're just worried about me suing you?"

"My father would be pissed," I tell her simply. "I'm also of the opinion that dying out of sheer stubbornness is idiotic. Are you an idiot? I'd hate to think I ruined my shoes saving an idiot."

Fire ignites in her blue eyes. I guess she's feeling better.

"Let go of me," she says, clawing at my hands.

"Joke's on you, mermaid; I like to be clawed at."

Her wide eyes fill with open horror but her hands still. "What is wrong with you?" Since she's not getting any help from me, her attention shifts to my girlfriend. "You want to do something about your boyfriend?"

It's cute that she thinks Anae holds my reins.

Anae doesn't like admitting she doesn't, so I'm sure she's relieved when I take the focus off her by telling the almost drowned girl, "This isn't that kind of relationship. What's your name?"

"You don't know my name?"

"No."

"I know yours."

"Of course you do. I'm somebody. You're clearly not, so… your name?"

"Fuck you," she says, dismissing me with her gaze and turning on my lap to get her feet on the ground.

I let her go this time, mostly out of curiosity to see if she'll be able to stand on her own two feet. She wobbles, but regains her footing. She looks frustrated at the reality of not being able to trust her own body just because she nearly died, insulted at the notion that she has such practical vulnerabilities.

She has extremely high standards for herself.

Seems to be stubborn, too. If I let her, she'll wobble her ass to the car and get behind the wheel, and then if she *isn't* as well as she wants to be, she'll drive off the cliff and into the ocean. I won't be able to save her, then.

That would be idiotic, and it's not happening on my watch.

I'm not letting her leave unless it's in the back of an ambulance.

Of course, since I already commanded it, an ambulance is on the way. I just have to keep her from leaving.

I stand, grabbing her hip to pull her close, then I drag her with me on the way to retrieve my shirt.

"What are you doing?" she demands, looking down at my hand on her hip, her body close to mine.

She misses a step, confused that I'm hauling her with me. She looks back over her shoulder at Anae as if for help. It's kind of entertaining. Why would she look to Anae to save her when Anae is the one who threw her to the wolves, to begin with?

Not that she knows that, I suppose.

She's also likely much more normal than Anae, and

running things through her normal girl filter, she has to imagine Anae's not too happy to see her boyfriend with his hands on another girl.

"You never told me your name," I remind her.

"I've decided not to." She scowls up at me, then peels my hand off her hip.

I let go to grab my shirt, but I grab her wrist before she can get far. She tugs on it trying to get free, but her body has just been through a stressful ordeal. Even in full health, I could easily overpower her, so it doesn't net her the results she's hoping for.

"Chase, what are you doing?"

That name on her lips raises my hackles. I give her a sideways look as we walk. "My friends call me Dare."

"We're not friends."

"*Everyone* calls me Dare," I amend since that's more accurate.

"I don't want to call you anything, I just want to go home. I never should have come to this party in the first place. Let me go," she says more forcefully as she realizes I'm about to drag her into my house.

"Aubrey!"

I hear someone call out behind me, but it doesn't attract my attention because I don't realize that's her name. She looks back and relief transforms her features, then someone runs up in front of me.

"Hey, Dare, what are you doing?"

Rather than plow through the brown-eyed brunette with the mousy hair, I stop. "Making sure she doesn't leave before the ambulance comes."

Janie something-or-other's gaze flickers to my hand locked around Aubrey's wrist. It makes her uneasy, but she doesn't come out and say so. Her tentative gaze shifts to mine and she makes a pitiful attempt at a peace-keeping smile. "I can take over from here. I won't let her go anywhere. I agree with you, she needs to see a doctor."

"Janie, no," Aubrey says, sounding astounded that presumably her friend is betraying her. "I can't go to the hospital—"

Janie vibrates with, "Shut up and let me save you," energy. It causes me to crack a smile as she reaches toward my hand, obviously wanting to pry it off her friend's wrist, but then thinks better of it and meets my gaze, silently begging me to let go so this doesn't get weird.

I do.

Relief transforms her features as she grabs her friend's arm and gently pulls her closer. "Oh my god, are you okay? I was inside, I didn't even know you were here…"

Her friend begins to ramble, but I stop listening. I'm not interested in what she has to say. I'm interested in observing the girl in the striped dress.

If she were wearing literally anything else, the material might cling to her wet body, giving me a good glimpse of her tits and perhaps the rest of her curves, too. Instead, the stiffer fabric retains much of its shape and continues to do its job of keeping her covered up, much to my annoyance.

I don't get to look for long, anyway. Anae struts over in her Prada sandals and the black, slinky dress that is designed to capture and hold my attention. Unlike Aubrey's dress that hides her body even when she's soaked, Anae's dress drapes and clings strategically so there's little left to imagine—you know she'll look as good out of it as she does in it.

And she does.

Anae has a nice body, but a black heart.

I have friends who find that more interesting than I do. People are always fascinated by what isn't familiar to them. I suppose that's why it holds no particular interest to me. I already know what it's like to be heartless and calculating.

It's boring as fuck. Give me something I *haven't* experienced if you want to hold my attention.

Not that Aubrey does. She seems eager to be *rid* of my attention. She leans close to her friend and turns to leave without so much as a goodbye as soon as Anae approaches. I'm not sure which one of us she's more eager to be away from.

"I see you met Aubrey," Anae says, her tone snide as she utters her name. "I fucking hate that girl."

"I gleaned that when you tried to kill her."

She feigns innocence but doesn't put much effort into the performance. "It's not *my* fault Kalea threw her into the pool."

"Mm-hmm. And I'm sure it wasn't your fault that picture was snapped and sent to her, or that Kevin cornered her upstairs to begin with."

Plucking the toothpick out of her martini glass, she brings it to her lips and smiles at me playfully. "I'm entirely innocent." She catches the olive between her teeth and slides it off the toothpick, sultry suggestions dancing in her eyes.

I smile faintly. She wants me to be impressed by her maneuvering, so I give her nothing to keep her hungry. My tone verging on bored, I ask, "What did she do to incur your wrath?"

She rolls her eyes. "It's a long story." Her blue eyes meet mine curiously. "You seemed to like touching her."

With most girls, this would be a trap. Even the average queen bee would be vigilant enough to keep an eye out for anyone who might pose a threat to her coveted position.

Anae is a different breed, though. It's a blind spot and not one of her better qualities in my opinion, but Anae is so full of herself, she genuinely doesn't believe anyone is a threat to her. "And?"

Anae shrugs one shoulder as she takes a sip of her martini. "Would you like to touch her more?"

Now, she has my attention.

She knows it, too. She can't bite back a tiny smile, but she tries as she looks over at me.

"I'm listening," I tell her.

"I have an idea. I want to destroy that girl, and I'm having a hard time getting to her on my own. I don't know why, it should be easy, but it's like… she doesn't even *care* about high school."

She says it like the idea is unfathomable, which I guess it is to her. High school is Anae's entire world, the one place she can reign over at this point in her life.

"Anyway," she says, looking over at me. "I know you could crush her. I've asked around and she hasn't dated anybody in a long time, but she's not asexual or anything. She's had crushes before."

"Why does this matter?"

"Well, on top of everything you already have going for you, you just saved her life," Anae says. "Imagine how easy it would be for her to develop a crush on *you*."

I crack a smile. "I may have saved her life, but I don't believe I left her with an impression that I'm Prince Charming."

"Who cares," she says dismissively. "You weren't aiming to fuck her then. You can change your approach now. Don't tell me you're not confident in your abilities to seduce some poor little nobody."

"You want me to fuck her."

"Yes, and then once she's fallen for you, I want you to make her life hell. Break her heart into a million pieces, and make it hurt as much as possible. I'll help, of course. We'll do it together. Not the fucking her part, that's all you." She reaches over and rubs my bicep. "You deserve to have a little fun for your part in her downfall."

"Has she fucked anyone before?"

"I don't think so. I can do a more thorough check, but it didn't sound like it. So maybe she won't be good in bed, but I'm sure you can find a way to have some fun with her."

I think back to how my cock reacted to Aubrey squirming on my lap when she was trying to get away from me. "Yes, I'm sure I could find a way," I say dryly.

"I hope she's a virgin. It'll be sweeter if she is. Virgins like her always attach to their first fuck. Amateurs." She grins over at me. "God, it'll be so brutal. I can see it now, her sobbing and leaving you dozens of voicemails, desperate to understand what's happening when she's oh-so in love with you and you've gone completely cold. We'll fuck with her head so much. We'll grind her heart into dust. We'll ruin her and leave her alone and adrift in the cruel, cold world." She lets her hot gaze roam over my body. "Are you getting seriously turned on right now, or is it just me?"

I shake my head, cracking a smile. "You're sick."

"You love it."

I could take it or leave it, actually, but I don't say that. I'm not bored and looking for a fight; I'm intrigued by the idea of seducing and toying with the girl in the striped dress. I'm curious if she *is* a virgin or if she has some experience. I wonder what she's like to fuck, and since my girlfriend is asking me to, I have no reason not to find out.

Ordinarily, if Anae brought her petty bullshit to me looking for my help, I would remind her I'm not one of her fucking lapdogs and send her on her way, but this... this appeals to me. Even if it only cures my boredom for a week or so, it's something to do.

Anae has her own vision for how this will go down, but I'm not interested in collaborating. If she wants me to fuck the girl over, I'll do it my own way. If the cat and mouse game is fun, maybe I'll let it run a little longer and do something like Anae wants. If not, I'll fast forward and get to the part where I put my dick in her a lot faster.

Maybe she'll struggle like she did on my lap.

Maybe I can play rough with her since she doesn't belong to me.

Or maybe I'll discover something new when I push my way into her life. Different types of women fuck differently, after all. Sex with Anae has grown boring, but Aubrey is far from my ordinary type. Maybe sex with her will be different enough to be fun.

Whatever the outcome, it sounds like a good time.

"I'm in," I tell her.

Anae's eyes light up. "Really? Yay!" Sighing dramatically, she leans her head on my shoulder so the scent of her expensive French perfume wafts my way. "You're the best boyfriend ever."

That's not true at all, but I could do worse than having a hot girlfriend who wants me to fuck another girl, so I throw her a bone and give her a sideways squeeze.

"You want to go upstairs?" she asks.

I know she means to fuck, so I shake my head. "Not right now. I need to make sure my mark gets in the ambulance. I was serious about that. If she sues, my father will shut down these parties so fast...."

"Oh my god, she's not going to sue you. She's going to suck your dick. Stop worrying. We've got this under control."

"All of that hinges on her surviving this weekend. I can't fuck her if she's dead. I'm not into that."

"As far as you know," Anae jokes. "I watched a movie last weekend that made it seem surprisingly hot. You should watch it with me."

"Maybe after everyone else leaves."

I head inside the house alone while she wanders back toward the crowd of people—still buzzing about what happened—and presumably does damage control. With me, Anae is more open about her depravity because she knows I'm no better. With her subjects, she has to show a slightly edited image of herself since being a mean girl is one thing, but presenting as a total sociopath would probably be off-putting to them.

By now, she should be better at controlling herself. She isn't as observant as I am. I don't know if it's because she's so self-obsessed or what, but it interferes with her ability to be as diligently aware as she needs to be.

Me, I notice everything. I take notes without even thinking about it, categorizing the traits and weaknesses of everyone I come into contact with just in case I need to take advantage of them later.

Anae thinks we're two sides of the same coin, but she's wrong. She's not on my level.

Like a fucking creep, I go upstairs and find a dark corner with a view of the driveway. I lean against the wall and linger there until I see the ambulance pull up the drive, then I search for Janie and the girl I saved.

Aubrey, that was her name.

I find her and watch as she fights with her friend about getting into the ambulance. It's irritating and illogical unless she has a death wish. I don't like unreasonable, hard-headed people who insist on doing dumb shit just to be difficult. If she's that sort of person, I'll fuck her and be done with it, but I don't want to spend any time with her.

Should be easy enough. Those types tend to be severely vulnerable in ways they don't realize. I'll bombard her bloated ego with compliments and mirror her own self-image right back at her. She'll like me for seeing what a super special badass she is, and I'll have her on my dick so fast...

Standing in my driveway, she turns around and looks directly at me.

My heart drops.

I know she can't see me, but it feels like she can. She's too far away to make out her expression, but I can feel her anger burning so hot, it singes the path of my thoughts and I forget what I was even thinking before.

I watch her friend hover as the paramedics put Aubrey in the back of the vehicle.

Still, her angry gaze is fixed on this window like she knows I'm on the other side watching.

A faint smile tugs at the corners of my mouth. I lift my hand and use my pointer finger to draw a circle around her on the glass. I draw another circle inside, and then another. Finally, I complete the crude, imaginary target with a solid circle right over her face.

Bullseye.

The ambulance doors close and I can't see her anymore.

But I'll see her again soon.

Watch out, mermaid. I'm coming for you.

CHAPTER 4

AUBREY

AFTER ONE OF the worst weekends of my life (it wasn't the worst, but definitely top three material), the only logical solution I can come up with is to skip school on Monday.

I spent most of the weekend in the hospital.

I knew Chase Darington didn't know I had my mom at home to care for and I couldn't just dip out on her to laze around the hospital all weekend, that I wasn't willing to part with my time with her just to "be safe" when I knew I was perfectly fine.

I did expect Janie to understand that.

If circumstances were different and things were how they used to be, I wouldn't have fought going to the hospital after nearly drowning, but they're not. Nothing is how it used to be, and I could *not* afford to waste this weekend.

They didn't give me a choice, though.

I glared at the cliffside mansion and the asshole who lives in it—even though I knew he couldn't see me—as they loaded me into the back of the ambulance and drove me away.

I missed a shift at work I couldn't afford to miss.

Josie from next door had to bring Mom to the hospital

when I finally called her the next morning. I didn't even want Mom to know what had happened, I hoped I could be in and out of the hospital in a few hours and just sneak in before she woke up.

That didn't happen. I told her not to come to the hospital, but she insisted. At least they brought my backpack so I could get my homework out of the way, but Mom couldn't stay. Her immune system is severely compromised at this point. Catching a cold would hospitalize her, anything more severe than that would kill her.

I told her to go home and not to come back even though it killed me not to spend the time with her as we had planned. Josie checked in on her, but *I* should have been there.

The time is gone and can't be brought back, and all because I went to a stupid party I didn't want to go to in the first place.

The whole experience cemented my decision to be done with Janie, at least for the time being. After high school, we'll probably go down different paths, anyway, so I doubt we'll reconnect, but some relationships aren't meant to last. I don't have time to be friends with Janie right now, and I'm not going to take risks like the one I took the other night. It just isn't worth it.

My Monday is better spent with Mom than at school, anyway.

The day goes pretty well. We sleep in, then have brunch on the back patio. Josie gives me a ride over to the Daringtons' mansion to pick up my car. I go during school hours so I know I won't have to see Dare while I'm there.

Originally, I was going to try to pick up a shift tonight to make up for the one I missed over the weekend, but as much as I need the money, I decided not to. We already lost the weekend together. Yeah, I'm on the fast track to maxing out all our credit cards since Mom has no income, and mine is just part-time, but I have the rest of my life to work on paying that back. At the end of the day, will going to work tonight make enough of a difference to justify losing that night with Mom?

The answer's no. Of course it is.

The doorbell rings around 4 o'clock. It's a little earlier than I expect. I made a grocery order to be delivered around 5 since grocery shopping is another thing I don't have time for. I paid for everything—including the tip—on the app, so I don't grab my phone or anything, I just head for the door. The delivery people are supposed to leave our bags on the porch and go, so I don't expect to find anyone on the other side.

But when the door swings open, there *is* a person standing on the other side.

A tall, troublingly handsome person with dark hair and a jaw that could cut glass. His cool, deep brown eyes meet mine and my stomach drops, memories of the other night flashing back to me.

Me underwater, struggling to get back to the surface.

Him diving in after me, grabbing me, and dragging me to safety.

Saving my life.

He's an ass, but he *did* save my life. Of course, I'm grateful to him for that.

That's the only reason I don't shut the door in his smug face immediately.

Without even trying to hide it, his gaze rakes over my body. Mom and I were staying in today, so I'm wearing a pair of activewear Capri leggings and a plain purple T-shirt. His gaze lingers on my legs, then drifts to my boobs.

A shiver runs down my spine. Maybe he notices because a smile teases the corner of his mouth when our eyes finally meet.

"What are you doing here?" I ask without a hello.

"Making sure you're alive." His tone is light and playful despite his words echoing the assholey sentiments he expressed the other night.

I prop a hand on my hip and cock an eyebrow. "How gallant."

"Isn't it? I rode my steed over and everything." He glances past me into the house.

On instinct, I move closer to the doorframe and pull the door closed a bit to block his gaze. "As you can see, I'm alive and well."

"You weren't at school today," he remarks, seemingly untroubled by my shutting him out of my house.

"Yeah, well, if almost dying doesn't get me a sick day, I don't know what will."

He cracks a smile. "True enough. You're all right, though?"

I nod even though I know he doesn't actually care.

He finally drops my gaze, dropping his shoulder so the backpack I didn't notice him carrying falls. He puts it down on the porch, then opens the flap and reaches inside.

I scowl, full of distrust.

What is he doing?

I almost expect him to pull out some kind of release form his lawyer whipped up to assure I don't sue his family, so I'm guarded when a moment later, he holds out several sheets of notes, all written in different colored ink. "Here," he says, seeming to expect me to take them.

Still scowling, I ask, "What is this?"

"Notes from all the classes you missed today."

My eyes widen and shoot to his face. "You... took notes for me?"

"No. I don't even take notes for myself, I have nerds do

that for me. Today, I had them copy down notes for the classes you were in, too, that way you didn't miss anything."

Slowly, I reach to take the papers from his hands. "That… is both really awful and really thoughtful at the same time." My gaze flickers back to his, still uncertain. "Thank you."

He shrugs, then closes his bag and slings it over his shoulder. "It's nothing. You'll be at school tomorrow, right?"

The corners of my lips tug up. "Why? Want to give your note-taking nerd army a little heads-up this time if I'm not?"

He shrugs again, his brown eyes glinting with mischief. "Maybe I'm just hoping I'll see you in the halls. Make my day a little better."

He's full of shit, but it still drags a smile out of me as I roll my eyes. "Yeah, right. You literally didn't know my name at the party, now I'm the bright spot in your day."

I say it mockingly, but he grins, not taking offense. "Hey, maybe you are, you don't know. I did save your life. I feel like we have a bond now."

I try to bite back my grin, but fail miserably. "You're the biggest liar I've ever met."

So why is his obvious bullshit charming me so much?

God, I need to get out more.

I'm in a better mood than I have been all weekend. I can't deny, even if he's lying his ass off, this lighthearted break has rejuvenated me a bit.

"I need to get back inside, but… thank you for the notes."

"You're welcome." His reply seems almost sincere. His offensively perfect lips tug up into a little smirk I desperately don't want to find cute and he catches my gaze as he starts to turn. "I'll see you tomorrow?"

I nod, my tummy fluttering strangely as he starts down the front steps. "Yeah, you'll see me tomorrow."

When he gets to the bottom, he turns around so he can

look at me, and walks backward toward the driveway. "Good."

I watch him get into his car—a matte black Audi. I know his family is loaded, so even if it didn't look disgustingly expensive, I would expect it to be. It does, though. It looks ridiculously cool with tinted windows and sexy curves. I'm not even a car person and I notice how cool it is.

I don't want him to catch me watching him drive away, so I hurry back inside the house and close the door behind me.

When I enter the living room, Mom turns to look at me. "Was that a friend of yours from school?"

I know she worries about the toll her illness is taking on my social life, so I force a little smile and nod, holding up the pages of notes to show her. "Yeah. He was just dropping off notes for the classes I missed today."

"How nice," she says with far too much interest. "What's his name?"

"Uh… Dare. Chase. I don't know."

Mom frowns. "You don't know?"

"I mean, I do know. Everyone calls him Dare, but his name is Chase Darington."

Her eyebrows rise. "Chase Darington? As in, Darington Enterprises?"

I nod. Dare's father—also Chase Darington—started out as a residential developer, then moved into commercial. Now, he dominates both markets, and virtually anything anyone builds in this town goes through him. "Yeah. That's his dad's company."

"I didn't realize you were friends."

Since we're not and I don't want this blending of the truth to get out of hand, I drop her gaze, nod, and head for my bedroom. "I better go put these away."

"Do you need time to study them? I can entertain myself for a while if you do."

"No, it's fine. I can look them over tomorrow."

"Are you sure?"

No.

"Yes."

She flashes me a smile and I flash one back, then I run to my room to stash the notes I know I won't even have time to study.

CHAPTER 5

AUBREY

THE NEXT DAY, it's back to business as usual.

My boss texts me and asks if I can cover the closing shift after school. Despite my decision not to prioritize work right now, I say yes. Another medical bill came in the mail today, and I'm running out of credit limit. I've been paying the minimum payments and hoping like hell the credit limits would last as long as I need them to, but I live in constant dread of the possibility that they won't.

Much to my own annoyance, I find my thoughts drifting to Dare more than once while I'm at school.

I hate that I'm letting him get in my head when I know he was only joking around—Chase Darington would never *actually* flirt with me. Why would he? He's dating the queen bee, and while she may be rotten to the core, she's definitely prettier than me.

Still, I find myself watching for him in the halls.

I know it's ridiculous. I *tell myself* it's ridiculous. I even get a little meaner with myself, rationalizing that yeah, it's all fine and great to imagine Dare actually gives a damn about seeing me because *I'm* the one who needs a bright spot in her life.

It'll never be him, though. Logically, I know that.

Chase Darington isn't a nice person. I've never had a run-in with him—obviously, since he didn't even know my name before this weekend—but I've witnessed enough of his bullshit over the years, heard stories of even worse things than I've seen. He's the kind of guy who messes with people's lives just because he's bored. He's every bit as evil as Anae, and I wouldn't be fooled by *her* flashing a smile and pretending to flirt with me, so I shouldn't let him do it, either.

It doesn't matter, anyway. I don't have time for their bullshit games.

There's no reason to feel disappointed as I make my way out of the building without once encountering him today. We have English class together, but he sits over with a couple of his and Anae's friends while I sit in the back of the class near the door. I don't even think he knows we have that class together because he doesn't look my way.

I used to sit in the front row of every class. Getting good grades mattered to me, and I liked the lack of distractions in the front row.

It's not so much that good grades stopped mattering to me, it's just they've become less attainable lately. I'm spreading myself so thin this year, I don't have time to waste on shit that ultimately won't even matter. I don't know what I want to do with my life at this point, but I'm sure I won't use at least half the stuff I'm expected to memorize and recite back in some stupid standardized test.

I even considered dropping out, but Mom freaked when I suggested it. I know I don't have much of my high school career left, but it's the time commitment I'm struggling with.

Baymont High is a competitive school. It's difficult to coast here. If I dropped out now, so much of my time would free up. I could work and still have plenty of time to spend with Mom. Next year, I could get my GED, and then I could get back to college or whatever I end up doing next.

Mom won't hear it, though. I don't know if it would be the right call, either, I just need some relief, and I can't get any with my current schedule.

I'm nearly to my car, so I pull out my keys and tap the unlock button.

To avoid getting hit, I stay close to the parked cars, so I don't pay much attention to the one slowing down beside me until I catch a glimpse and realize it's matte black.

My tummy does a somersault and I look over, my gaze colliding directly with Dare's.

I don't know why, but I feel like I've swallowed my heart.

His lips tug up and his eyes glint with pleasure at the sight of me. "Hey, mermaid."

My gaze flickers to the jock in his passenger side seat but jumps right back to him. "Hey," I return a touch shyly.

"We're having a bonfire on the beach behind my house later," he says like it's normal to loop me in on his plans. "A bunch of people will be there. You should come."

"I can't, but thanks for the invite."

"Why not? Got plans with the boyfriend?"

"No boyfriend, just no time. I have to work, and after work, I have stuff to do at home, so I won't be able to stop by." I glance at him and offer a tepid smile. "Thanks, anyway."

Since we're only having a conversation in passing, I don't feel rude dipping out of it without a goodbye and walking to my car once I reach it.

Dare must not agree because when I get in the car, unload my bag, and start it up, I look in the rearview mirror to prepare to back up and he's still sitting there, blocking me in.

I meet his gaze in the mirror and offer a little wave goodbye, but still, he doesn't move.

I glance behind his car and see three more waiting to pass, but his car is unique enough that one look at it lets you know it's him, so no one dares honk at him even though he deserves it.

What the hell?

I wait another minute for him to move, and still, he fucking sits there blocking me in.

Sighing with irritation, I throw my door open and storm up to his open window. He's sitting there looking like an absolute asshole, one tanned arm resting on the car door like he doesn't have a care in the world as he holds everyone else up.

"Can you move? Literally no one else can leave until you do."

"Not my problem." He looks up at me. "I want to see you tonight. Until you make that happen, I'm afraid I can't move my car."

"That's insane."

"And yet, that's where we are." He shrugs. "Only you can move me."

He knows the way he says it causes my stomach to plummet. I can see it in his smugness, and I want to hate him—I actually *do* hate him a little—but I'm still weirdly charmed by his obnoxious bullshit.

What is wrong with me?

"I told you, I can't tonight. I'm busy."

"Find a way to make it work, otherwise we're all sitting here all night."

Someone in the car behind him finally leans out the driver's side window. "Hey, Dare, are we leaving anytime soon?"

He glances back at the guy and says, "Ask Aubrey. It's up to her."

The guy's gaze flickers to me with annoyance. "Can you just give him what he wants? I have a fucking dentist appointment."

My jaw drops open. How is it on *me* to cede to this lunatic's demands instead of on *him* to stop being a lunatic in the first place?

I look back at Dare.

He smirks.

"I hate you," I tell him flatly.

His smirk morphs into a grin. "Just give me what I want and we can all get on with our day."

The guy in the car *behind* the guy behind Dare calls, "Come on, Aubrey, we've got places to be."

"You've got to be kidding me," I mutter to Dare.

"Sorry," he lies, still smiling. "What do you say? You wanna come to my bonfire after work?"

"No."

Unfazed, he says, "But you're gonna do it anyway, right?"

I think about thwarting him. I should be able to if I'm determined. He can't literally blackmail me into coming to his stupid bonfire. Surely if I called the non-emergency police line and told them some asshole is blocking traffic and I can't leave the school, someone would come and help.

Maybe I could even walk into the school to tell the principal. I probably wouldn't even have to. Surely if I disappeared from his sight for a while, Dare would get bored with sitting here and give up.

Right?

I can't bank on any of it, though. Filthy rich kids like him get special treatment by the cops in this town all the time, and he's a liar, so if I go to the principal, he's likely to pop his hood and rip out a belt or something so he's "stranded." The other cars may eventually be able to get out of here, but I'm parked next to a curb, and the way he has me boxed in, if he decides to be a dick, *I* will be stuck here until his car is towed.

The answer hits me, and when it does, it's so simple, I can't believe I didn't think of it first. It's not my natural impulse. In fact, I really dislike doing it, but it's probably what he would do if the tables were turned.

I lie.

"Fine."

He looks victorious. I feel a twinge of guilt even though I know I shouldn't. He's a spoiled jerk using totally unfair methods to try to get me to comply, so he deserves to be disappointed.

I still feel a little bad.

I don't like disappointing people, even if they suck.

I'm surprised I'm even capable of disappointing him, but I remind myself it's not about me. Dare just likes things to go his way. He's only so adamant that I give in because I said no in the first place. If I fell all over myself just because he invited me somewhere, he'd be bored in three seconds.

I hope he finds some new shiny object to distract him soon because I do *not* have energy to dump into fighting off the attention of Chase Darington right now. I just don't.

I go back to my car and look in my rearview mirror.

He watches me for a few more seconds, but since he thinks I've ceded to his ridiculous demands of my time, this time, he drives away.

"Thanks for covering tonight."

"No problem," I tell the manager as she heads to the office to retrieve her things. She asked me to come to the office with her, so I figure she has some paperwork to show me since I'm closing on a night I normally don't.

"I need you to sign this," she says, grabbing a white sheet of paper and handing it to me along with a pen.

I take the pen and scan the page before I sign it. My heart

sinks into my stomach when I see it's an employee write-up form. "What is this?"

"It's just a formality," she assures me. "You've never been in trouble before so it's literally nothing to worry about."

My heart races faster and faster as I skim the "employee warning" form. There's a box for me to write a statement and give my side of things, but I've literally never been in trouble for *anything* before, so that doesn't make me feel any better. I've never had a detention or a speeding ticket. I've damn sure never gotten in trouble at work.

Scanning what she wrote on the report, I see this is about the day Anae came in and tried to return a shirt we didn't sell here. She called to complain, which I knew she would, but that's why I gave her a heads-up.

"I didn't do anything wrong, Stacey," I state.

"I know," she says, her tone appeasing. "Don't be upset about it, honestly. But I had to do something on paper, just to make it look like you were scolded. Her mom spends a fortune here. I can't afford to lose her as a customer. It's rich people problems, but we have to dance when they pull the strings, don't we?"

She's trying to joke around with me, but I'm pissed.

"I'm not signing this," I say, putting the paper down and dropping the pen on top. "If I sign this, I'm acknowledging wrongdoing. I did my job. What? You wanted me to make up an amount and give her store credit just so she didn't throw a fit? That's crazy."

"Welcome to life as a small business owner," she says, throwing her lip balm into her bag and grabbing her iced coffee. "I'm not excited about it, either, but I didn't have a choice. The customer is always right, you know?"

"No, they're not," I state. "Sometimes, the customer is batshit crazy."

She cracks a smile. "That's so true. Just sign the paper so I can file it away, okay? Then we never have to think about this again. If you don't sign it, I'll still file the paperwork, it just won't have your side of the story."

This is complete and utter bullshit, but I'm not going to pass up the chance to defend myself. I angrily jot down my explanation for not doing the return on the shirt that *was not purchased here* and note that I was perfectly nice and even the customer behind her was shooting me sympathetic looks because of the unwarranted fit Anae was throwing.

Stacey thanks me, but I'm so annoyed, I don't even want to talk to her. I can't believe she's chucking me beneath the wheels of the bus just because Anae's mom made a call.

I don't know why shit like this still surprises me. It's how things work around here. A rich kid wants something, so the world bends and bows to see that they get it.

I don't usually go on my phone while I'm at work, but being disciplined for not doing a damn thing wrong has drained me of the desire to go above and beyond tonight. Typically, I would straighten things and do what I could to put tomorrow's opening crew ahead. Tonight, I stay behind the register, lean against the counter, and scroll through social media while the store is empty.

On impulse, I pull up Anae's account. I don't follow her, of course, but her stuff is public so anyone can see it. I don't know why I'm surprised to see a picture posted from just a few minutes ago—the beach at dusk with a roaring fire and a bunch of their friends gathered around it—but I guess since Dare asked *me* to come to that bonfire tonight, I took that to mean she wouldn't be there.

I have no interest in being anyone's side piece anyway, but it seems like you shouldn't invite some girl you've decided to start paying weird attention to, to the same bonfire your girl-friend will be at.

Maybe it should be reassuring. Whatever has compelled

him to start paying attention to me, maybe it's innocent. I can't picture that word and Chase Darington in the same sentence, but the shady thing to do would be to keep us apart.

Anae's at the bonfire.

I wasn't going to go, anyway, but now I'm definitely not. After getting that bullshit write-up, I wouldn't be able to keep my mouth shut, and I don't need to confront her and make things even worse.

My gaze flickers to the clock. Closing time approaches, thank God.

I close the app so I don't accidentally like anything, then I slide my phone into the back pocket of my jeans and start doing all my closing work so I can get the hell out of here and go home.

CHAPTER 6

DARE

I WATCH the fire flicker against the midnight sky as I empty another beer bottle and toss it at some drunk girl lying on the beach a few feet away.

Her startled gaze jumps to me.

"Grab me another one."

She tries to sit up to go do my bidding, but before she can get to her knees, Anae walks over. "I got it."

The girl sinks back into the sand.

Anae drops onto the beach beside me, passing me a cold beer. "Are you sulking?"

"I am not sulking," I say shortly, grabbing the bottle and popping the cap off with my teeth.

"I wish you wouldn't do that. You're going to break a tooth."

"Fuck off," I say, but flatly and without malice.

"Aw, baby." She adjusts the strap of her Versace swimsuit so her tits look better, then she gets on her hands and knees and crawls over to me.

Her intention is to entice me with the view of her cleavage, but I don't even look.

Undeterred, she climbs to her knees behind me and

pushes her tits against my back, looping her arms around my neck. "Don't be too annoyed your new toy didn't show up. I told you, she's slippery. I would've been stunned if even you succeeded on the first attempt. You'll get her next time."

"I did not *fail*," I say, barely biting back how much she's fucking annoying me.

"Of course not."

Her tone pisses me off. I shrug my shoulders to get her off me.

Anae sighs, but moves off me and sits down on the beach beside me. Glancing over, she says, "Want to work out some of that frustration?"

I take a sip of my beer and meet her gaze coolly. "Not with you."

It stings, but she tries to hide it. Anae considers it an amateur move to get hurt by anything. "I didn't say with me." She fans out her fingers and admires her nails. "I just got a new manicure today and you play too rough. Some other bitch can do the hard work, I'll just coordinate." Her gaze flickers to the nearly unconscious girl I told to get me a beer. "What about her?"

I shake my head. "I don't need a blowjob. I need your phone."

"My phone?" She doesn't know why I want it, but she grabs her clutch and pulls it out, anyway.

I take it once she's put in her pass code, then I open her messages and start a new one. She has Aubrey's number saved even though I'm sure she has never used it. I figured she would. When it comes to a vendetta, Anae always does her homework.

I haven't had time to do mine, so I didn't have her number yet. Luckily, I'm good at memorizing shit, so I repeat it a few times in my head so I can transfer it to my own phone in a minute.

"What are you doing?" Anae asks curiously, lying on her side on the beach and peering over my arm to see what I'm up to on her phone.

I don't answer her.

I know Anae's text patterns, so I emulate them as best I can. "Good call staying home tonight," I type out with a kissy emoji after the text. "And here I thought you were a dumb bitch," I type, then press send.

It only takes a few seconds for Aubrey to text back, "Who is this?"

I glance at Anae. What would she say? Something that makes her feel superior and puts Aubrey down.

"The main attraction," I type back. "No side bitches need-ed." I press send, then without giving Aubrey a chance to respond, I add, "Stay the FUCK away from my boyfriend if you know what's good for you."

I fucked up ending with a period at the end of that sentence—*Anae doesn't use them*—but I don't think Aubrey knows her well enough to know that.

"Anae?" she guesses.

My lips tug up. At least she knows I'm coming for her if she knows it's my girlfriend who should feel threatened.

"Someone get this bitch a trophy," I type back, since that's the sort of thing Anae would say.

"Look, I'm not interested in your boyfriend," Aubrey texts back.

Ouch.

She's probably lying, though. She thinks she's talking to Anae.

She continues typing, "I have no desire to go to war with you. I don't have the time or the interest. Dare invited me out tonight. I said no. Then he literally trapped me until I changed my answer. I lied so he'd leave me alone, but I had no intention of following through. I'm not interested in being anyone's side anything. I am not your problem. If you have a problem with anyone, it's him."

She's rational and respects herself—possibly even others, even when they royally piss her off, which takes decidedly more integrity and self-mastery.

She's still human, though, with all the weaknesses that entails. I just need to get her pissed off enough at Anae that she *wants* to fuck her over. She's salivating for the chance. I'm not the incentive, she just wants to sink a blade into Anae's heart and twist it, and she'll happily use my cock to do it.

I delete the text chain and block Aubrey's number so she can't text Anae again without my knowing it. I clear the apps and start to hand Anae her phone back, but on second thought, I keep the phone, grab her wrist, and yank her on top of me as I lie back on the beach.

"Oh," she murmurs, surprised, but not unpleasantly as she splays her hands over my muscled chest.

I guide her hand up to cover the spot where my heart should be, then I hand back her phone. "Take a picture."

She smiles, inexplicably thinking I'm flirting instead of plotting. She runs her hand over my body and repositions herself so she's straddling my pelvis. Once she's satisfied with our positioning, she snaps a photo of me smirking up at her, her hand splayed across my chest.

She turns the phone to show me. It's a good picture, so I nod my approval. "Now, post it. Caption it, 'I fucking love him so much.'"

She's surprised, but catches on quickly enough and does as I tell her. "Done," she says, dropping the phone on the sand and shifting positions on top of me. "Now, can we stop focusing on your pet project for tonight? I'm horny."

I take a swig of beer, too distracted to stop now. I *should* drag Anae to my room and take my frustrations out on her pussy, but there's more work to be done, and there's no time like the present.

I'm not discouraged that my *pet project* hasn't panned out yet. I've hardly exerted any effort. But I *am* unable to focus on anything else because she just admitted to blatantly lying to me earlier today, and I didn't pick up on that. I believed her when she said she'd come to my bonfire tonight. I expected her to show up. I didn't expect her to be thrilled Anae was here, but I thought she'd come. Even when it became clear she wasn't coming, I imagined her agonizing over the decision for a bit first, but she didn't.

She never had a single fucking thought about coming.

That means I thought about her more than she thought about me today, and that's unacceptable.

While Anae is kissing her way up my flat stomach and letting her hands roam over my cut muscles like she was when she was posing us for the picture, I look at that new manicure she's so proud of and feel a wave of malice pass over me.

I reach down and grab one of her hands, dragging it off me. I bring her palm to my lips and kiss it to lower her guard. When she smiles at me, my grip turns steely so she can't yank her hand away as I grab her thumb and break her new nail right off.

"Dare!" Pain flashes across her face. She cries out—the first thing she's done all night to make my cock stir.

She doesn't like the pain, though. She scoots off me and curls her legs up on the sand behind her, cradling her hand against her tits like it's an ailing baby bird—if she actually *cared* about ailing baby birds.

"What the fuck?" she demands, shooting me a wounded look.

I tip back my beer bottle and drain the rest before tossing it on the sand by her legs. "I've gotta go."

"What? Where?" Confusion plastered across her face, she looks up at me as I stand. "You can't leave. We're at *your* house. What if your dad gets here and you're gone?"

"He won't. He's out fucking his girlfriend tonight, won't be home until early morning. Just make sure everyone goes home before you leave."

"Are you serious? Dare!" she calls as I walk away. "Where are you going?"

I don't answer her.

I just tuck her acrylic nail into my pocket and head to the house for a knife.

CHAPTER 7

AUBREY

I'M ALREADY RUNNING LATE as I rush out the front door.

I couldn't sleep last night. Too much on my mind. I kept hearing things, imagining an ominousness in the air that made no sense.

Or, I guess it did, and that's the problem.

I ended up giving up on sleeping in my own bed altogether. In case that feeling of dread was because something was going to happen to Mom in the middle of the night, I made Dad's old side of the bed my own and curled up beside her.

I didn't sleep much. I just watched her, made sure she kept breathing.

When the sun came up, my eyes were burning. I knew I would regret staying up all night, but I knew I wouldn't, too.

I made coffee and consumed the whole pot by myself. I no longer feel the exhaustion as I tap the button on my key fob to unlock my car.

The car looks strange, though. I can't put my finger on it. Does it look lower to the ground? Did I drink too much coffee and now I'm losing my mind?

I stop beside the car and drop my backpack. Dread fills

my belly as I realize the car looks lower to the ground because it is.

My tires have been slashed.

"Fuck," I whisper, bending down to look for the damage, but I don't know what I'll do if I even find it. I know there's canned stuff that fixes flats if they're not too bad. Maybe Dad left some in the garage.

There's not just one clean cut, though. There was rage behind this stabbing. A blade was plunged into each tire multiple times. This was definitely intentional, and definitely malicious.

Something maroon and glittery catches my eye. It's on the ground by the tire.

I pick it up and inspect it.

An acrylic nail?

It looks strangely familiar. I try to think of anyone whose nails I might have looked at lately. I'm not into fake nails, personally. I had them done once for a wedding and I was really excited because they were so pretty, but then I couldn't *do* anything with them on my fingertips. I ended up taking them off after just a few days.

I straighten up as something flashes across my mind.

Is that where I saw them?

To make sure, I pull out my phone and pull up Anae's social media account that I scrolled through last night. Sure enough, there's the picture she posted right after she texted me, her with her manicured fingers splayed across Dare's tanned skin.

Motherfucker.

Anae slashed my fucking tires. She must have broken a nail stabbing through the tough rubber.

I don't know how I'll get to school now—or, more importantly, work—but when I get there, I'm going to kill her.

I'll press charges. This is fucked up, and I have proof it was her.

I can't afford to replace the tires, and I don't know what to do about it. That's probably hundreds of dollars. My God, my credit cards are crying keeping up with my monthly expenses as it is, but adding this on top of it?

I'm so fucking overwhelmed, it's hard to breathe for a moment. I force myself to stop, to breathe, to think.

I don't have another car. I used to have my own, but I had to sell it over the summer because we needed the money to pay a medical bill before it got sent to collection.

I refuse to cry. I want to, but I don't.

I would just go back inside and stay home, but I have a biology test today. Making it up would be a pain in the ass. I *need* to go to school today.

There's no one to call for help, though. I don't have a support system anymore. My neighbor Josie helps out with Mom and even cooks us food sometimes, but I feel guilty about asking for so much of her help when I have nothing to give back.

I could call Janie, but I don't want to. I'd feel like I'm using her asking for a ride when, again, I have nothing to offer of myself.

Who am I fine with using, knowing I have nothing to give back?

Nobody.

Well… maybe somebody.

Somebody who wouldn't hesitate to do the same to me.

It's batshit crazy, but I click on Anae's picture and scroll down, looking for his screen name. No comment on that photo, so I go to the next one, then the next one. It takes about 12 pictures before I finally find engagement on one of her posts—*damn, what a shitty boyfriend*—then I click on Chase Darington's profile.

This is a long shot. I don't even know if he checks DMs, but I shoot him one asking if he's at school yet.

He must have had his phone in his hand because he answers promptly. "Nope, about to leave now. Why?"

I sigh, hating to ask him for anything—*it seems dangerous*—but I need to get to school, and *his* stupid girlfriend is the reason I can't. "Could you possibly pick me up on your way?"

"Oh, now you want to spend time with me," he shoots back playfully.

I'm tempted to smile, but my day is off to too tragic a start for any of that. "I told you I was busy last night," I remind him.

"You also told me you would come. When should I believe what you say?"

"When the answer is my own and you're not forcing me to give you the answer you want," I type back.

"I suppose that's fair."

I wait for more, but he doesn't give it to me, so I have to type back, "So… can you pick me up or not?"

"Sure. I'll be there in a few minutes. But… you will owe me one."

"Ugh," I say out loud, rolling my eyes. "I'm gonna have to disagree. You triggered your girlfriend's psycho tendencies inviting me to that stupid bonfire last night. She slashed my fucking tires, otherwise I would drive myself to school today."

"Sounds like something she'd do," he says, not even surprised.

They're so fucking crazy.

I shake my head and type, "Anyway, I'll deal with her later, but I really need to get to school right now, so…"

"I'll be there soon," he answers.

"Thank you," I message back.

He doesn't answer, but I don't expect him to.

I'd like to go back in the house until he gets here, but I have to make phone calls and I don't want Mom to ask questions.

I'm not sure who you're supposed to call when you need your tires changed. It's the kind of thing I would have had to ask Mom when I moved out on my own. I'd ask her now, but she'll know we don't have the money for that, and I'd have to explain why this happened since it's not like I got a flat driving over a nail. A deranged psycho from my school stabbed my tires because I made them mad.

Ugh, I hate my school sometimes.

Back when I was able to focus my attention on academics, Baymont High was a dream come true. Yes, it's full of spoiled assholes, but that's because it's one of the top schools in the state—and it's a public school. It's so expensive to live in this town, you pretty much have to be rich to go there, but since it *is* such a great school, some families with less money have made the sacrifice of moving to the area even if they had to rent out a room in someone's attic, or live in a house so small a Barbie doll would be hard-pressed to live there.

We were lucky enough to find a house.

See, I used to have big dreams. I thought it would be amazing to get into an Ivy League school. It wasn't just about the status, but the quality of the education I would get there.

My old middle school was a disaster area—literally. There was a lot of crime in the area. We had metal detectors, and kids still ended up getting stabbed every month or so.

Mom knew how miserable I was there and that the high school would be even worse, so she and my dad talked about how they could tweak their finances to move to Baymont, where the property values were a lot higher, but I could go to one of the best schools in California. It would be easier to get into Harvard or Yale—*I wanted to go to the East Coast after spending my whole life on the west one*—if I went to a school like Baymont High. There was no way they could afford to send me to private school, but maybe they could justify the higher mortgage if I would be able to go to a school just as good as private school because we lived there.

We all made the move, and I was ecstatic. I was so happy at Baymont. I didn't care that I couldn't afford the designer things like most of the other kids.

There were some kids like me there—ones without money, ones who didn't really belong. I found friends there. Some were kids of the help. Their parents cleaned the rich kids' houses or watched their younger siblings. Some ended up here incidentally due to advantageous marriages, others had parents who prioritized their kids' education like mine did and wanted them at Baymont, even if it meant finances were tight.

It was easy to tell the difference between the super rich and the *employees* of the super rich, so even though we all go to the same school, the socioeconomic lines are drawn in the sand, and there's not a lot of intermingling.

That was fine by me. I didn't come here to hang out with rich kids.

Besides, maybe that's what those Ivy League schools would be like, too. Maybe there would be a distinct line separating the haves and the have-nots, the kids whose educations were everything they had to rely on, and those whose parents' connections had more to do with where they would end up than anything else. Maybe Baymont was preparing me for it.

But then sophomore year happened. Mom got sick. We all went through the wringer with her, and it never let up. Junior year came and went. I kept up last year. It was easier when Dad was here.

But then he left.

Senior year... it's just impossible.

I hate that we made those sacrifices to move here *for me* and now I'm throwing it all away, but my world today is nothing like it was three years ago. My priorities aren't the same, and I don't know what life will look like when all of this is over, but I'm pretty sure I won't give a single fuck about the things that used to mean the most to me. I'm just not the same person who valued those things anymore.

I don't know who I am anymore.

I don't have time to figure it out, either.

This year, I'll be a mess.

When the clock runs out, that's when I'll start cleaning it all up.

CHAPTER 8

AUBREY

I'M SITTING on the curb when Dare's Audi comes down the road. I stand, watching the all-black car slow to a stop so I can get in.

This feels weird.

Wrong.

I walk around to the passenger side, anyway.

Every instinct I have screams at me not to get in that car, but I know they're just being dramatic. Poor, sleep-deprived instincts. Someday we'll get some rest.

I pull the handle and open the car door. Dare leans forward and watches as I slide in and close the door without looking at him.

I know I'm not doing a great job at trying to appear unaffected, but it's so weird being in the car with him. My stomach is in knots, and I know looking at him will make it worse.

I can feel his eyes on me. My skin burns beneath his gaze as I slide my backpack between my legs and settle it on the floorboard.

God, it's hot in here.

I glance at the temperature controls. "Can you turn the air up a little?"

He does, and the blast of cool air feels so nice on my flushed skin.

"Thanks," I murmur, lifting my gaze to look out the front windshield. I feel like I'm being a little rude, so I finally shift my gaze and look over at him. "Thank you for picking me up, too."

I knew looking at him would be a mistake. Chase Darington is obscenely handsome from a distance, but up close, here in his car that feels and smells like him, it's actually pretty overwhelming. It's not just his hard, clean-shaven jaw or those gorgeous brown eyes. His attractiveness isn't about the right classical features arranged in perfect order. It's something else. Something I can't quite put my finger on.

My stomach starts to ache. My head does, too. Probably from consuming so much caffeine on an empty stomach. Definitely not because I'm in the car with Dare.

"Glad I could help," he says. "I have to admit, I was surprised you called *me*."

The answer is simple, so I give it to him. "I didn't have anyone else."

He nods, then looks ahead and starts down the road toward the high school.

I have one more phone call to make, so I ask him if he minds, then I call the auto repair shop in our old town. It's a drive and it will cost more to tow it there, but I want to see if it would be worth it for cheaper labor because I cannot swing the last quote.

When I hang up and rest the phone on my lap, Dare glances over at me. "What'd they say?"

I just feel fucking sad. Utterly defeated. I open the Chase app on my phone so I can double check Mom's credit card balance.

I have about $1,200 left on that credit limit, so if I have to spend $600 on tires, another $100 for labor, and then another $90 for a tow…

Fuck.

It's too soon for the money to run out.

Maybe I can apply for another credit card.

I feel sick.

"Aubrey."

His voice calls my attention back to him, but I don't have it in me to hide my distress. "That I'm fucked."

"How much?"

"Like $800."

"That's not so bad."

"Maybe not to you." I shake my head, turning to look out the window so he doesn't see tears gathering in my eyes.

If I blow all this money on tires, how the hell am I going to pay the mortgage next month? Even if I pick up a ton of extra shifts I can't make enough, and that's not even factoring in bills, groceries, gas, credit card payments.

Fuck.

"She's paying for those tires," I say suddenly, shaking my head. "I found her fingernail. I know it was Anae. If she doesn't pay for it, I'm going to the police."

"Why don't you let me take care of it?" he suggests.

I look over at him. "What?"

"I'll buy you new tires."

My stomach hollows out. "Why?"

He shrugs, looking ahead with one hand on the wheel as he drives. "Money is obviously an issue for you. For me, it isn't. Leave your keys with me, I'll have it taken care of today."

I can't believe he's being so nice. I can't take him up on it, though… right? "Are you doing this for me, or for her?"

"Does it matter?" he asks, meeting my gaze.

It shouldn't even be a question. I mean, he's her boyfriend, so he should be doing it for her.

But I don't trust him. He doesn't strike me as a great boyfriend, and he's not known for doing nice things without at least having ulterior motives.

"Just answer the question."

He takes his time answering. Dare doesn't like when people demand things of him, I know that much. I almost bite my tongue thinking maybe I should just shut up and let him do it. I can't afford to pay the bill myself, so who cares why he's doing it?

But I can't help it. I care. I want to know.

"For you," he finally says.

My spine stiffens. That's the right answer, but the wrong one, too. "Why? We're not even friends. Why do you keep doing things for me?"

I feel his eyes on me. "Maybe I want to be your friend."

My lips curve up faintly. "I don't believe you."

"Why?"

I look over at him. "Because everyone knows you're a liar."

"Yeah?" There's an edge to his tone, despite how casually he says it.

Maybe it's because he didn't laugh it off and his tone caught me off-guard, but it begins to feel like that was a really mean thing to say.

Sure, I've heard that, but it doesn't entirely match up with what I'm seeing for myself. He was an ass the night he saved me, but since then... I don't know. He's being kind of nice to me.

What if he was just posturing that night? What if his reputation isn't entirely accurate?

What if he's truly trying to be nice to me, and *I'm* being the asshole?

Since I feel like one, I swallow and say, "I'm sorry, I shouldn't have… that wasn't nice."

I feel his gaze on me. I meet it, and see curiosity reflected there. "Are you a nice girl, Aubrey?"

I smile a bit sadly. "I used to be. Now, I'm just tired."

"What's making you so tired?"

I don't even want to answer that question, but it bubbles up inside me, desperate to get out. "My whole life. The weight of so much responsibility resting solely on my shoulders. The possibility that I'm doing my absolute best and it's not even close to being good enough, that it won't change anything."

"What would make your life easier?"

Money.

Help.

A freaking miracle.

I don't say any of that.

We're at the school now, pulling into Dare's reserved parking space right up front.

Looking over at him, I say, "I don't need anyone to make my life easier, I just need people not to make it any harder."

"Am I making your life harder?"

"Probably. You are the reason Anae slashed my tires in the first place."

"Yeah?" He holds my gaze, a challenge glinting in his. "How's that?"

"Because you invited me to your bonfire on the beach."

"I invited a lot of people to that bonfire," he states. "Only your tires were slashed."

I guess I can't really argue that. Anything I can say feels arrogant and presumptive. "Well, I need it to stop. I don't have the resources to battle Anae or the desire to deal with her drama, and there's honestly no good reason for her to have a problem with me."

"What if there is?" he asks idly.

"There isn't," I answer, surprised by my own forcefulness.

His question reminds me of the things Anae said when she texted me last night. I was dumbfounded when those texts rolled in accusing me of basically going after her boyfriend.

He's the one who keeps popping up in *my* world, not the other way around.

She's probably running things through her own filter, though. Anae is obviously so petty she'd go to any length to get under an opponent's skin. She would absolutely seduce a guy just to hurt his girlfriend, so she thinks I'd do the same.

She's wrong, though.

I may not like Anae, but I'm not about to stoop to her level.

It would be too uncomfortable to say any of this to him, though. I don't even know if he thinks he's being inappropriate. Maybe he thinks he's just being nice.

Probably not, though.

In my experience, guys know when they're stepping over a line, some are just too cowardly to admit it.

I don't want to know if he's that kind of guy. I don't want to know anything else about him. He's the boyfriend of Anae Richards, so his involvement in my life can only possibly complicate it.

Add that to the list of shit I can't afford.

Maybe I'm better off if he doesn't help me.

I'll go straight to the source. I can prove Anae did it, so if she refuses to pay for the damage she caused, I really will go to the police. It's not something I have time for, but I'll do it, anyway. I can't let her keep getting away with shit—that will only embolden her. She needs to face the consequences of her actions.

I reach for my bag in the floorboard and yank it up on my

lap. "Anyway, I don't want to be late to my first class. You don't have to pay for my tires to be replaced. It was kind of you to offer, and I appreciate the ride, but I'd rather deal directly with Anae."

"I don't think that's a good idea."

"I appreciate your input," I say, opening the car door and climbing out.

I hear his car door open. "That sure sounds a lot like, 'thanks, but I didn't fucking ask you,'" he remarks.

I can't help smiling as I grab my backpack and hoist it on my right shoulder. "Wow, you really excel at reading between the lines, don't you?"

He smirks, joining me on the curb and falling into step beside me. I can't help but read into his mildly suggestive tone as he says, "If you got to know me, I think you'd find I really excel at a lot of things."

"Just not taking notes," I say solemnly.

With exaggerated cockiness, he says, "That's grunt work. Below my pay grade."

I'm still amused, but that feeling ebbs as we near the entrance doors and *everybody* seems to be watching us. I've walked through these doors plenty of times over the course of my high school career, but I've never experienced it this way, like I'm walking the red carpet with an A-lister on my arm.

I guess because I've never *had* an A-lister on my arm, but Dare is definitely an A-lister at Baymont High. Maybe *the* A-lister. Sure, he might be mentally unstable, but his dad is richer than God, and his mom is a former Miss Bolivia who was in the Miss Universe pageant and everything. Between his looks, money, and general coolness, there's no one more popular at this school.

I'm uncomfortable with all the attention, but when I glance over at Dare, it doesn't seem to faze him. Maybe because this is what it's like for him every day. On the way in, a dozen people call out greetings. I feel hotter and hotter with each returned wave, each set of eyes seeing us together.

I'm already feeling claustrophobic, then the air is sucked from my lungs as Dare casually drapes his arm around my neck and over my shoulders, keeping me close as we enter the main hall. "While I can understand your desire to skip the middleman and go straight to Anae, it is true what you said: it's ultimately my fault your tires were slashed."

Oh my god, there are people everywhere and I feel all of their eyes trained on us. I try to shrug off his arm, but he just pulls me closer.

"Are you crazy?" I demand, trying—and failing—to pull out of his grasp. I look over at him, wide-eyed. "People are staring. Let me go."

He smiles like the wolf cornering Little Red Riding Hood in the woods. "No problem. I'll let you go as soon as you give me your keys."

I gape at him, disbelieving. "Are you… blackmailing me into letting you pay for my car repairs?"

"That seems like dramatic terminology, but yeah, I guess if you want to word it that way, you can."

I gape for another few seconds, but then I look around and see people staring at us and speaking in hushed tones. A girl with black pigtails grabs her phone and angles it like she's about to take our picture.

To report back to the evil queen, no doubt.

Dare notices the girl about to take our picture. Rather than let go and move away like a normal guy about to get caught in a compromising position, he leans closer. "Tick tock, mermaid. We have an audience."

"You are an actual mental patient," I say, my face on fire. "But fine. If you're that adamant about it, you can have the stupid car fixed. Now, please let me go before your girlfriend literally murders me."

Dare lets go, smirking as he steps away. "There. Now, was that so hard?"

"Yes, actually. You made it extremely difficult."

He holds out his empty palm expectantly. "Keys."

I hesitate, glancing at the girl with the phone. I guess she already took her picture because now she's looking at her phone screen.

It still feels like a bad idea, but I unzip the side pocket and dig out my keys.

He grabs them. "You need your house key?"

"Oh." I grab them back, singling out my house key so I can keep it.

Before I can take it off the ring, he says, "On second thought, you can leave it. I'll make sure you have your keys back before school's over."

I look up at him uncertainly. "Are you sure?"

He looks back, not a single flicker of uncertainty in his gaze. If he told me right now he's never felt uncertainty in his life, I'd believe him—and I'd be really jealous. "I'm sure."

"Okay." I let go of the keys and absently mess with the straps hanging from the bottom of my backpack. "Um... do you need my phone number or anything?"

He shakes his head. "I have it."

I frown. "You do?"

He nods, but doesn't explain how or why he has my number.

I guess it doesn't matter, so I don't bother asking.

"I guess I'll see you after school then?"

He nods, watching me as he backs away. "I guess you will."

DARE ISN'T in English class when I get there.

He usually gets there and takes his seat first, so I think today may be the day he realizes we have this class together, but it's not.

He doesn't show up at all.

That's really weird since we showed up to school together today, so he has to be here.

Right?

I hope he's not missing class because he's dealing with my car problems.

It leaves me a little uncertain as the school day approaches its end and I have no idea what's going on with my car. Dare hasn't texted me, so I don't know where it will be. Parked in the parking lot somewhere? Will we have to go pick it up?

Once I'm done at my locker, I head out front and find Dare's parking space. His car is parked there, so I know he hasn't left. I don't think he has practice after school today, but I don't know. I know he's on the swim team, but I have no idea what their practice schedule looks like, or if it's even the season for that. I imagine if he had something going on, he would have told me.

I feel awkward standing by his car as everyone files out of the school, so I dig my phone out and DM him to let him know I'm here.

He doesn't answer, but he comes out with a group of his friends a few minutes later. I watch them all say their good-byes and wander off, a couple of them glancing at me by his car and smirking before they go.

I sigh, knowing today is probably going to make waves.

I shouldn't care. It's Anae's own fault, plus she got me in trouble at work, so screw her, but… well, it's unlikely to make my life easier if she hates me.

"I have good news and bad news," Dare says as he approaches the car and opens his door.

I tentatively open the passenger door, too. "What's the bad news?"

He drops in, so I slide in as well. Looking over at me with a grim expression on his face, he says, "The auto repair shop didn't have your tires in stock. Since they had to order them, we should be able to pick it up tomorrow after school, but you won't have your car tonight."

I sigh heavily, sinking back against the seat. "And the good news?"

He smiles over at me as he fires up the engine. "That means you get to spend more time with me."

I cock an eyebrow. "Are you volunteering to be my personal chauffeur until I get my car back?"

"At your service. I'll pick you up in the morning and drop you off after school to get your car."

"That's really nice of you, but I feel bad."

"No need." He checks the rearview mirror, then starts to back out.

"I hate to ask, but I was planning to stop at the store for chicken and a few other things for dinner. Would you mind? You can drop me off at the door if you want and I'll be as quick as I can, I just hate to pay for delivery when I only need a few things."

"No problem. Damn, I can't remember the last time I went grocery shopping. I'll come with you. It'll be fun."

"To… grocery shop?"

"We have staff that handles stuff like that at my house. I can probably count on one hand how many times I have personally stepped foot into a grocery store."

I gape at him. "Are you serious?"

He nods. "My mom has stopped at the grocery store to grab cheap wine a couple of times after fighting with my dad and took me with her, and a couple of times we went out late at night to get ice cream for an impulsive treat, but yeah, we don't do our own grocery shopping. Never have."

I can't fathom what he's saying. "Do you know how to cook?"

He laughs. "No. God, no. I can make hot chocolate. Does that count?"

I laugh, not meaning to make fun of him, but my God, who can only make hot chocolate? "No, that doesn't count."

He shrugs. "I've never had to."

"You should still know how. What will you do when you go off to college? Bring a maid with you?"

"Maybe, if she's hot. You're not in the market for a new job, are you?"

I can tell by his too-charming smirk he's only teasing me, but he still turns my cheeks pink. "I might be. What's it pay?" I joke right back.

He slides me a sideways glance. "Depends on your skill set."

I can't ignore the suggestion in *that* statement, but I try. "Well, I'm a very good cook," I tell him. "I'm just okay at cleaning. Can't say it's a passion of mine, but I can get the job done."

"I'd have to sample the goods and see you in the uniform before I could make a firm decision."

I nod. "And I'd have to scoop out all of my dreams and aspirations, so it sounds like we both need time."

Dare cracks a smile. "Not into the domestic gig, huh?"

"Part-time, sure, but I need something of my own, too. Men leave, so I'm not about to tie my entire well-being to one. Maid, wife—if my status depends on a man's whim, it's not going to be the basket I drop all my eggs in."

"Ouch. Someone had a bad break-up," he jokes.

My lips curve up faintly, but I'm not amused. "Something like that."

"Who was the guy?" he asks.

"No one you know."

"I know everyone," he states.

I miss a beat, take a breath, then decide, what the hell? "My father."

"Oh. You got me there, I don't know him."

"Don't feel bad. Turns out I didn't, either," I murmur.

He's quiet for a moment, then asks, "What happened?"

I didn't plan to get into all this with him. I don't have time for my old friends, so I certainly don't have time to make new ones. I also doubt he has any real interest in being my friend, but I remind myself I shouldn't be so skeptical. Aside from that first night, he has been pretty good to me.

"My mom has cancer. She was diagnosed during my sophomore year. We've been fighting it ever since, did all the treatments, the diets, the prayers, the dumb shit you find on the internet when you're desperate for some last-resort method peddled by some grief-predator who swears they have the answers all the doctors don't. We tried everything. And, of course, it was *hard*. Constant soaring hopes and crushing disappointments, working our lives around Mom's cancer treatments, going into debt paying for what insurance wouldn't cover… It's been awful, I won't pretend otherwise. But that's what he signed up for. He was clearly a bit fuzzy on the vows he made—'forsaking all others', 'in sickness and in health', he seemed to think those were just for dramatic effect. He started a part-time job—that's what he told us, anyway—to make extra money. We were cash-strapped just living here so I could go to stupid fucking Baymont High, but then with all Mom's cancer stuff, she ended up having to quit her job, so we went down to one income. Anyway, he said he was working a second job stocking Nestlé products in stores in the area, but what had actually happened was he had met somebody. When he pretended to be working, he was actually going out with her while I stayed home and took care of Mom. He made fools of both of us, and then he left us for her."

"Fuck. That's heavy. I'm sorry."

I shrug, looking down at my lap. "It sucked. Mom said I was being too hard on him, that her illness had been a lot for him, and he was never a very strong man, so he couldn't handle it."

"And what do you say?"

"Me?" I look over at him. "I say fuck him. I'm 18-years-old. If I can stick it out, he could have, too. He's selfish. He shouldn't have married anyone in the first place if his 'commitment' was so conditional. I don't know what kind of person leaves someone they supposedly love at the end of their life just because the experience isn't pleasant, but it's not the kind of person I have any use for in my life." Anger heats my face and climbs up my ears as I think about the bullshit he said, telling me he hoped someday I wouldn't be so angry at him. Wanting me to meet the bimbo he left Mom for.

Yeah, no fucking thanks.

"He told me how nice she is." I look over at him. "Can you believe that shit? So nice she was fine with stealing the husband of a woman dying from cancer. Yeah, she sounds great." I shake my head. "I don't talk to him anymore. He still calls every now and then, but I stopped answering."

The car is quiet for a moment. Self-consciousness creeps up on me.

"Sorry for ranting at you. Bet you're regretting this chauffeur gig now, huh?" I remark lightly.

Dare looks over at me with a frown. "Why? Because you're being real? It's nice. I'm not used to it."

"Anae doesn't have deep, personal conversations with you?"

"Not that kind," he says dryly. "Anae's shallow. Even her depth is shallow as hell. She parades her darkness out and tries to impress me with it, but as far as real feelings... it's all skin deep. Everything is with her. Nothing hurts her, not really. Maybe she wasn't always that way, I don't know her reasons, I just know it's fucking boring."

"What's boring?"

"The whole act, the 'above it all, nothing can touch me' bullshit." He rolls his eyes. "Pain makes people interesting. Being unaffected isn't half as great as people seem to think it is."

"I don't know. She seemed pretty upset last night. I mean, it came out as anger, but it was fear. That's what jealousy is— fear of losing someone."

A frown flickers across his face so briefly I almost think I'm imagining it. I can't read his expression after that, and he falls silent.

I didn't mean to make him stop talking. The topics weren't fun, but I don't have anyone to open up to anymore, and I was enjoying talking to him.

It's probably better that it stopped, though. He's someone else's boyfriend. There's no reason for us to share our deep, dark secrets with one another.

I look out the window until we get to the grocery store, but when he pulls in, I realize he brought me to the wrong one.

"Um… I hate to be a complainer when you're doing me the favor, but this isn't the grocery store I meant."

Confusion flickers across his face. "Does it make a difference? This is the one we usually get stuff from."

"Yeah. Everything costs more here."

"Oh. Well, it's probably better quality."

"Probably. Unfortunately, I can't afford better quality. Bargain basement groceries fit my budget better."

Apparently unconvinced by my argument, he pulls into a parking space and turns off the engine.

Okay, then.

I guess I'm paying a million dollars for groceries today.

At least I only have to grab a few things.

Actually, since I won't have my car until tomorrow after school, maybe I should grab a few extra things—just in case there's some other delay, so I don't have to ask him to bring me again.

He grabs a basket when we walk in, then slows down and looks over at me. "All right, where do we go first?"

I gesture ahead. "We'll stop at produce. I need to get a couple of bananas."

He cocks an eyebrow. "For dinner?"

"For breakfast. I'm making chicken parmesan for dinner. Banana-free."

"Sounds good. Am I invited?"

I crack a smile. "No."

"Aw, come on. I need to sample the goods, remember?" he says, playfully nudging me. "You'll never land your dream job as my maid at this rate."

"How will I go on?" I stop and eye up the price written in

cheerful blue chalk—twice what they cost at my grocery store. I hope everything here doesn't cost double.

I grab two bananas and place them in the basket. Next, I grab some grape tomatoes for tomorrow night's dinner. We make our way to the cheese, then grab some boxed pasta. I'm trying to calculate all of it in my head on the way to the register just so I'm prepared when Dare grabs a bag of chips and tosses them on top by the register.

"You want any?" he asks.

I shake my head. "I'm okay."

He nods, then steps forward as the person in front of us moves. "What a novel experience. I like grocery shopping."

I snort. "This was hardly a shopping trip."

"You'll have to take me on a proper grocery shopping trip sometime. You can make me dinner afterward."

"Wow. How could I possibly pass up an offer like that?" I ask sarcastically.

"Maybe you can teach me," he suggests.

That surprises me and wipes the smile off my face since it's a real suggestion. "You want me to teach you to cook?"

He nods, glancing back at me. "And I'll teach you to swim. Just in case I'm not around to save your ass next time."

I crack a smile as the cashier starts ringing up our stuff. "If I didn't know any better, I'd think you're trying to spend more time with me."

"Do you?"

I glance up at him. "Do I what?"

There's something unsettling in his gaze, something... almost accessible. Despite how popular he is and how many friends he claims to have, I don't get the feeling Dare truly opens up to many people.

Maybe that's why my tummy flutters with nerves when I peer into those mysterious brown eyes of his and it feels like he's letting *me* in.

His voice is low, intimate. "Know better?"

My heart flutters.

I do my best to ignore it, breaking his gaze and opening my purse to dig out my wallet. The cashier isn't finished ringing things up, I just need a distraction.

Finally, she tells me the total, but before I can take out my credit card, Dare hands her his.

I look up at him, surprised. "You didn't have to do that."

He shrugs. "I wanted to."

"Thank you," I say softly.

He nods wordlessly, then takes his credit card. I wait for him to move forward so I can grab my grocery bags, but he grabs those, too.

As we head for the entry and exit doors, I can't bite back a faint smile. "You better be careful, Dare."

He looks down at me, his brow furrowing.

I let my smile widen and tell him mischievously, "If you keep this up, I might think that deep down, you're actually… kind."

His confusion clears and he smirks at me. "You better not go around telling people shit like that."

I laugh, looking both ways before we cross the parking lot. "Don't worry. I promise not to ruin your big, bad reputation."

"You better not."

His words are playful, but they unlock a few memories of things I've heard about him, things it's a lot easier not to think about when we're together.

He's not a nice guy.

I don't ignore that voice of caution in the back of my head, but it's hard to entirely heed it when I look over and see him carrying groceries he bought for me to his car, the car he's giving me a ride home in because he's paying for the repairs on mine.

These are all really nice things to do, and what ulterior motive could he possibly have?

Maybe he really just *likes* me.

I guess it's not so hard to believe. It's not like I'm some ogre, and maybe he's right—*even if he was joking*—about saving my life forging some kind of bond between us. I certainly didn't feel it that night—he was too busy being an asshole—but when it's just the two of us, he's like a different person.

A person I like?

I shove the thought away because it doesn't matter.

Dare is with Anae—even if it doesn't seem like he even likes her very much. I don't like her, but maybe that doesn't mean he and I can't be friends.

Friends?

I guess maybe we are becoming friends.

I don't have *time* for friends, but with my stupid car being in the shop, it does give us an opportunity to get to know each other we wouldn't have otherwise had. I don't get the feeling friendship with Dare would be as much of a time commitment, either. He has tons of friends; he won't wilt without my attention.

It could be kind of perfect.

CHAPTER 10
AUBREY

I STAND on the curb in front of my house waiting for Dare to pick me up for school.

It feels strange waiting for him. Self-consciousness creeps up on me and I'm not sure why.

It's a nice, warm day, so I decided to wear a skirt. I don't have many skirts. I rarely wear them, so I'm not sure why I wanted to today, but I can't stop tugging at it. The soft white fabric only extends to the edge of my fingertips if I lift my shoulders, so hopefully, no one bothers to check and see if I'm obeying the dress code. Faculty members never bother the rich kids, but sometimes if the less privileged students wear something that breaks the rules, they get sent home to change.

After what feels like a long time, Dare's car finally pulls up in front of my house.

My heart jumps. I offer a little smile and pull my backpack strap tighter over my shoulder as I walk around to the other side. I check to make sure no cars are coming, then I open the door and quickly slide in.

"Hey," I say in greeting, moving my heavy backpack to my lap.

Dare looks pleasantly surprised as his gaze rakes over what I'm wearing. My face heats. I've felt so stupid since the moment I put it on—the white skirt, the butter yellow cami top underneath, and then a white cardigan over it. I feel like a daisy, but he really seems to like it.

"You should wear more skirts," he states.

My skin heats even more. "Oh. Thank you. I mean, that wasn't a compliment, it was a…" I stop talking, mortified, and clear my throat. "I don't have many skirts."

Dare smirks, shifting out of park. "I'll buy you some."

I don't take it as a real offer so I don't bother telling him no thanks.

I didn't think through the skirt. My backpack is heavy so I have to spread my legs like I did yesterday to get it on the floor, but when I do, Dare's gaze gets caught on my bare legs.

I flush but pretend not to notice as I shove my bag to the floor and pull my seatbelt across my lap to secure it. "Thanks for the ride."

His gaze still lingers on my legs. I fight the urge to tug at the material and pull it lower. That'll just make it obvious I'm noticing.

Finally, his gaze lifts to meet mine. "No problem. Thanks for dolling up for me."

My blood freezes in my veins. So does my face. I can't believe he said that. "I… I didn't."

He smirks, shifting his attention back to the road. "Sure you didn't." He doesn't give me long enough to muster a response before he goes on. "How's your mom feeling today?"

I'm even more stunned he's asking after my mom's well-being than I am that he called me out on wearing a skirt for him. "She's… tired."

He nods like that's understandable. "I meant to ask, but

what stage is her cancer? Is she undergoing any current treatment?"

I stare at him.

Since I don't answer, he glances over at me. "I'm only asking because my family knows a specialist. I know you said you've tried everything, and I believe you, but this guy's been called a miracle worker. He's always up on cutting edge research and trials. A friend of my mom's went to him a few years ago when she was almost to stage four and about out of hope. Whatever experimental treatment he got her into, it worked. She made a full recovery and has been cancer-free since. I don't want to get your hopes up or anything, but if you wanted me to give him a call, maybe he could meet with your mom and see if there's anything he can do for her."

My chest feels tight. The number of times I've found hope only to have it snatched away after a long, soul-deadening fight that ended in defeat…

I'm afraid to hope again, but it's impossible not to. It's a cruel game, but when you want something so badly, you have to grab at it every time it's dangled.

"Are you serious? She isn't doing treatments anymore, we've pretty much exhausted all our resources and nothing has worked, so she decided to stop putting her body through all of it and just enjoy the time she has left. We still do what we can, of course. The stuff the nutritionist told us to do, like I still make her a cup of matcha tea every morning and stuff like that, but as far as chemo and other treatments… She has pretty much done everything. None of it worked."

"Well, it's your call, of course, but if you want me to reach out, I can."

"She's immunocompromised at this point, so we try not to go out in public when we don't have to. Is there any way you could set up a phone or video call first, just to make sure going there wouldn't be a total waste?"

"Sure, I can ask him."

Hope wraps around my heart. "That would be amazing, Dare. Thank you so much."

He looks over at me and smiles faintly. "No problem."

My heart hammers in my chest as I consider opening all this up again, talking to my mom about it. I know she's exhausted, but if there's a chance I could keep her, I have to try. It's all I want in the world.

I look over at him. "Um... can you also find out how much the treatment would cost? Since the divorce, Mom doesn't have insurance anymore, and mine is the only income. I'm guessing your family friend probably wasn't as worried about money. If he thinks there's a chance it might work, I'll pay whatever, I just have to figure out how. Maybe I can get another credit card. Most of ours are nearly maxed out. I have a few months left if I'm extremely careful, but... our financial situation isn't great."

"You only work part-time, right?"

I nod. "It's all I can swing while I'm in school and taking care of Mom. I talked to her about dropping out so I can get a second job or go full-time, but she won't hear it, and honestly... I'd rather spend the time with her now and work after she's—" My throat closes, not wanting to let the awful words out. "After she's gone. I already know I'll have to spend next year working non-stop to put even a small dent in my debt instead of going to college, but that's fine. I can make more money, but I can't get more time with Mom."

"Understandable. Have you considered a side hustle?"

I glance over at him. "Sure. Know of any that pay like $600 for an hour of work?" I joke.

He smirks. "Maybe. Depends on what kind of work you're willing to do."

"If there's a pole involved, it'll have to wait until next year," I joke. "Too many germs."

He cocks an eyebrow like he's surprised I'd even joke about stripping, but he's never needed money as desperately as I do, so he can't understand I'm hardly joking.

When we pull into his parking spot at school today, it seems like there are even more people standing around talking out front.

I didn't hear from Anae after I showed up with him yesterday, even after that girl probably snapped our picture, but showing up with him a second time is bound to draw even more attention.

"I'll have my car back after school today, right?" I ask as I pull the latch and shove my car door open.

"I'll update you at lunch. I should hear back by then."

"Perfect. Thank you again. I wanted to knee you in the crotch that first night, but you've really been a godsend ever since."

Dare laughs, caught off guard by my honesty. "Hey, you said I *wasn't* an angel," he teases.

"I spoke too soon," I tell him, smiling. "I'm reconsidering my opinion."

"What was that angel thing about, anyway?" he asks as he falls into step beside me.

"Oh. I hallucinated. It's common in near-death situations like that when your brain loses its oxygen supply. People hallucinate. It's angels and heaven stuff a lot of the time, that's why there are all these books about people seeing stuff like that when they have near-death experiences. I realize now I probably saw you diving into the pool to save me, but my oxygen-deprived brain saw an angel with massive black wings."

"Sounds terrifying."

I smile faintly. "It was comforting. Then we flew up above your house with me still in your arms. We were in the stars," I say, tilting my head back and looking up at the sky.

His gaze lingers on me. "Sounds nice."

I look over and smile back at him. "It was."

"Hey, Dare," someone calls, interrupting the moment.

It's probably for the best. I subtly move away from him to create some distance between us as the guy comes over to talk to him.

Dare's friend glances at me, his gaze lingering as he checks me out, but he doesn't address me or even vocally acknowledge my existence. I know he's a friend of Anae's, too, but if Dare wants to show up to school with some random girl who isn't her, he's not gonna say anything.

While Dare's distracted, I decide to make my exit. I touch his arm and tell him I'll see him at lunch, then I head inside the school before he has a chance to stop me.

After lunch I have government and AP psychology, and I'll admit, I did not do my government homework last night. I ran out of time, and it's not a favorite class of mine to begin with, so when my eyes started growing heavy, I gave in and listened to my body, prioritizing sleep over researching the DPC.

Now, I'm sitting on the quiet, empty side of a bustling table in the cafeteria trying to research the White House's Domestic Policy Council on my phone, but the wi-fi is being an absolute asshole.

"Stop being terrible," I tell it, tapping again on the link to the executive order that established the council in the first place.

Finally, it loads. I set the phone down and dig my little blue leatherbound copy of the US Constitution out my purse so I can refer to it.

"Did you just pull a copy of the United States Constitution out of your purse?"

I glance up as Dare drops onto the bench beside me, eyeing the thin blue booklet. "Of course. Don't *you* keep a copy of the Constitution in *your* purse?"

He smirks. "You're a nerd."

I crack a smile, opening the booklet. "No, I'm just a slacker. I ran out of time to do my homework last night and need to prepare for my next class."

"Should've told me. I could've alerted my nerd army and had a briefing ready for you this morning."

"You have so many connections," I say, shaking my head as my eyes scan a page before I flip to the next.

"Yep." His tone is teasing. "Do you find that sexy?"

"Yes, actually." Before he can make a fuss about my admission, I look over at him and ask, "Any news about my car?"

His expression playfully somber, he says, "Another good news, bad news situation."

"Why is it taking so long to replace tires? The guy I called said it could be done the same day. I could have literally waited in their waiting room and driven the car home."

"It will definitely be done tomorrow," he promises. "You have my word."

I sigh. "All right. Well, do you mind giving me another ride home?"

"Nope." He stands, startling me by grabbing the lunch bag I didn't even get a chance to open yet.

"What are you doing?"

"I'm hungry. Let's go out to eat."

"Like, leave the premises?"

"That's the idea."

I look around uncertainly, but close my book and shove it and my phone back into my purse before standing. "I don't usually leave school for lunch. Are you sure we'll make it back in time for our next classes?"

"Live a little, mermaid."

I'm startled as he reaches down and takes my hand. My heart flutters as he leads me out of the cafeteria, with fear that someone noticed and… something else.

I tell myself it'll be fine as he hauls me out to his car. I've never paid attention since I'm usually doing homework at lunch, but maybe he and his friends go out for lunch all the time.

The car is an oven when we get in, so I expect him to turn on the air conditioning. He rolls down the windows instead. My hair blows like crazy when he picks up speed. I laugh as it whips my face, and he looks over at me with a smile.

We head toward the beach, but there are a lot of restaurants and hotels that way, so I figure that's why.

We pull into the driveway of a place called Underworld. The owner must be a mythology buff because the sign has three dogs guarding the blue neon letters, like the three heads of a Cerberus guarding the gates of the underworld.

"You been here before?" Dare asks as he climbs out of the car.

I climb out too and close the car door. Smoothing down the short skirt, I say, "Nope."

He nods, then leads me inside. He tells the hostess we want a table on the beach. She grabs two menus and leads us through the restaurant and back outside.

"Can I get you started with something to drink?" she asks once we've taken our seats.

"Yeah, can we both get a Malibu mango sunrise and glasses of water?" Dare says, causing me to blink at him a few times.

"Sure." Her eyes narrow good-naturedly. "Can I see ID?"

His eyebrows rise like he's surprised she's even asking,

but he says, "Sure," and leans forward to pull his wallet out of his back pocket. I watch as he hands her what must be a fake ID because she looks at it, thanks him, and hands it back. Her gaze shifts to me, but before she can ask, he says, "You know what? Can you also put in an appetizer order? We'd love some spinach and artichoke dip, but we're meeting with the interior decorator at our new place in about an hour. I'd hate to keep her waiting."

Uncertainty flickers across her face, but he sounds so sure of himself as he casually utters that absolute bullshit, she decides he's probably telling the truth and nods, turning away to go put in our order.

Dare leans back in his seat and smirks over at me.

I cock an eyebrow. "We're moving in together now, huh?"

He nods. "It's a big step, but I think we're ready for it."

I crack a smile. "It's scary how comfortable you are lying. When I lie, I look like I'm holding back a murder confession with a hot face and guilty eyes. When you lie, it's like… you're telling the truth."

"Lying is easy, you just have to do it with confidence."

"No, thanks. I don't need to be a better liar. It's not a skill I find particularly useful."

"Nah," he says, like he's not surprised. "You're a good girl, aren't you? All the way, through and through."

I shrug. "I guess. I try to be a good person. When you lie, your word means less and less. I don't see the advantage of making it difficult for people to trust you."

"Maybe people shouldn't trust me," he says casually.

I shrug. "Maybe. In that case, go ahead and lie all you want, just don't be surprised by the consequences."

"The consequences today are that we're going to have delicious drinks with our lunch."

"Those are the immediate consequences, yes. The longer term consequences are that I will always be a little skeptical of anything you say because there's literally no way to tell if you're lying or telling the truth. Maybe you don't care if I believe you, but it's true either way. If there ever comes a day when you need me to believe you and I don't, it's no one's fault but yours."

"Why wouldn't I care?"

I shrug. "I don't know. A week ago, you didn't even know my name. Maybe my ability to trust you isn't something that matters to you."

Dare watches me, his gaze narrowed. The waitress brings over a tray with our glasses of water and two brightly colored orange and red drinks with curled orange rinds on top.

She asks if we're ready to order and since we are in a bit of a hurry, I quickly consult the menu while Dare orders, then order a chopped salad for myself.

Once the waitress walks away and leaves us to our drinks, Dare returns to the topic. "What if I didn't lie to you?"

I smile, lifting the icy alcoholic beverage and taking a sip. "Because I'm special?" I tease.

"Because I can see your point about it being hard to trust someone who lies to you all the time. I might omit things if I think you're better off not knowing them, but if you ask me anything directly, even something I'd rather keep from you, I promise not to lie. Not to you."

I cock an eyebrow. On the face of it, it's not a lot, but I have a feeling it's more than he usually offers people. "Why?"

"Because I want you to be able to trust me. How I behave with others doesn't necessarily have to be how I behave toward you. You trust me, and I'll never give you a reason not to."

That feels like a big promise coming from him. If he were anyone else, I might not consider it much of an offer, but I can tell it challenges him to make it, and that makes it a big deal. "I appreciate that," I say seriously.

He nods wordlessly like it's not a big deal, but I still think it is.

"Have you lied to me before?" I ask tentatively, wanting to test out this new arrangement, but cognizant that too far too fast might unravel the whole thing.

My doubts are bolstered when his gaze takes on a guarded look. Arms crossed, he nods. "I suppose you could say that."

What did you lie about?

That's too much. I don't want to obliterate his comfort all at once. He needs to get comfortable being honest with me, then if there are relevant lies that need to come out, they can.

"Did you..." I hesitate, my question sounding so monstrous in my head, I'm afraid to ask.

He sees my hesitation and gives me a push. "Go ahead, ask."

"Um..." I look up at him, feeling a bit guilty for even asking. It would be horrible to lie about something like that, but before I get my mom's hopes up, I have to know. "Were you telling the truth about the oncologist your family knows? Can he really help my mom?"

The guardedness in his gaze clears. "Yes, of course I was telling the truth about that. I don't know for certain he can help your mom, but I'll reach out to him today after school. I hope he can."

I breathe a sigh of relief. I didn't want to believe he would lie about something like that. It would've undercut all the nice feelings I've been having toward him. Anyone who lied to someone in my position about something like that would have to be too malicious to even try to understand.

A little voice whispers at the back of my mind that he could still be lying. Giving me truths he's comfortable parting with to support his claim and effectively lower my guard. Just because he said it doesn't mean that he means it.

I want to give him the benefit of the doubt, though.

I have heard a lot bad about him, but I can see something good in him, too.

It's the good I like most, but if I'm being honest with myself, there are aspects of the badness I don't hate. It's infuriating and somehow amusing at the same time how he manipulates the world around him. I haven't seen him be actually malicious; he's just a spoiled ass who likes getting his way. Who doesn't like getting their way? Most people just don't do the shit he does to get it.

"Can I ask one more?"

He nods.

"It's personal."

His expression doesn't change.

"It's about Anae."

He cracks a smile. "Just ask."

"Do you—?" I hesitate. It's too personal, too invasive. I don't even know why it really matters, but I can't stop myself from asking, even if I might not like the answer. "Do you love her?"

"No."

His answer comes easy. That feels like a relief until I remember how easily he lies, but I have a strong sense that he's not lying about this.

"Does she know that?" I ask.

He lifts his broad shoulder and shrugs. "How should I know what Anae knows?"

"Have you ever told her you did?"

"No."

My eyebrows rise in surprise. "Never?"

He shakes his head. "Why should I lie about that?"

"I don't know. Guys do."

He rolls his eyes. "Some guys, maybe. Personally, I don't need to tell a girl I love her to get what I want from her."

"Because you're just so irresistible?" I tease, grabbing my drink and taking a sip.

Dare's gaze lingers on my lips as I lick them. I put the glass down softly. His gaze darkens, then shoots purposefully to meet mine.

Thankfully, before either of us has to say anything, the waitress interrupts the moment to drop our spinach and artichoke dip off at the table.

"Thank you," I say a little more vehemently than is reasonable for just serving an appetizer.

"Of course," she says brightly. "Can I get you anything else?"

"Nope. We're good," Dare says, his tone wryly amused.

THE WINDOWS ARE DOWN as we head back toward the school. I'm feeling light and breezy like I haven't in… I can't even recall the last time I felt so free.

Maybe before Dad left.

Probably before Mom's diagnosis.

I know it's been a long time.

I want to stick my head out the window like a dog and let the wind blow my hair all to hell. I want to spread my arms and fly.

I probably shouldn't have had that cocktail at lunch.

I never drink, so I'm a total lightweight.

I'm sad when we drive away from the beach, but I know it's time to get back to the real world. We stayed way late at the restaurant. I missed my government class, but we'll make it back so I can finish up with psych before Dare has to take me home.

That's the plan, but then Dare misses the turn back toward the school. I think maybe he was distracted and he'll take the next road and circle back, but he keeps driving.

As we get farther and farther away from Baymont High, I stop catching the wind between my fingers and settle back in my seat. I'm a little tipsy and my head isn't right, but I try to focus as I look over at him.

"Hey, what are you doing?" I ask him.

"Driving," he answers without looking away from the road.

"I know *that*, but you're going the wrong way." I gesture vaguely behind us. "The school is back there."

"You don't say?" he says lightly.

"I don't want to be late for my last class."

"Which one is it again?"

"AP psych."

"Ah." He waves me off. "You don't need to go to psych class. You want to know about abnormal psychology? Just spend the day with me."

I smile. "Very funny, but I'm serious."

Finally, he looks over at me. "We're not going back to school, Aubrey."

"But I have class. And my stuff's there. How will I do my homework if I don't have my books?"

"I'll have someone collect your stuff for you and drop it at my place after school. We'll grab it before I take you home."

"I don't…" I don't really know what to say to that. I'm not used to having help with anything anymore, and he has help with *everything*. "Don't you ever do anything yourself?"

"Sure," he says easily. "Right now, I'm kidnapping a girl I know from school with no help at all."

"My apologies. That's terribly impressive."

"See?"

I grin and shake my head, but I don't fight him. I never get days off anymore, so a stolen hour with him… there are worse things in the world.

To my surprise, he drives me to his house. I follow him around back, tagging along as we move past the pool I nearly died in a week ago.

I shoot it a dirty look and maintain my distance, staying behind him since I feel safer there. He stops to raid the bar, looking at different bottles before deciding to grab rum.

"This'll do. You want anything else?"

"Bottled water?"

He rolls his eyes, but grabs me a cold bottle of water out of the mini fridge.

Once he has the alcohol shoved in my purse, he grabs my hand and takes me through his backyard. He keeps going until we get to the edge of the cliff, then he hauls me to the steep stairs that lead down to the beach.

Uncertain, I fall back a step. "Wait, we're going down these?"

"That is the way to the beach," he says dryly.

"Is there another way?"

"Sure. I can push you. You'll get there a hell of a lot faster, but I make no promises about the condition you'll be in."

I roll my eyes, muttering as I walk closer to the steps, "Some spoiled rich boy you are. You don't even have an *elevator* down to the beach?"

"I am an endless disappointment," he says solemnly.

I crack a smile, but it fades quickly as I place my hand on the railing.

Thankfully, there is at least a railing to hold onto, but I'm not comfortable walking down this staircase. I wouldn't love it completely sober, but with a little alcohol in my veins, it's a big fat no.

I go anyway.

We make it down safely, but as soon as my sandals sink into the sand, I begin to question my footwear choices. I grab onto Dare's shoulder to keep myself upright as I wobble on one leg, reaching down to pull off my sandal.

He glances at my hand on his shoulder, then back at me as I gracelessly tip over. I laugh, my nails biting into his shoulder, but I still lose my balance and fall on my ass in the sand.

"My god, have you never imbibed alcohol in your whole life?" he asks, amused, as he turns to look at me sprawled on the beach.

It doesn't occur to me until his gaze travels up my legs that they're spread and he can probably see my panties.

I shift my weight and move my legs to block his view, then climb to my knees. He offers a hand, I expect to help me up, but rather than help me stand, he plants that hand on his hip, then grabs my other hand and plants it on his other hip.

I look up at him, on my knees in the sand at his feet. I don't know how he looks even more handsome from down here, but all the amusement in my body dissipates, replaced with a strangely sensual heat.

A faint smirk tugs at his lips, hinting at the thoughts playing through his mind. "You look good down there," he murmurs. "Maybe you should stay for a while."

Heat travels through my belly as I think about what he means.

I drop my hands and break his gaze, pushing myself up off the beach without help.

Strangely, I feel a little more sober as I stand up.

I don't look at him. I look at the ocean, at the powerful waves folding in on themselves and riding in to crash against the shore.

"I love the beach," I say softly as I slide my purse strap back over my shoulder.

Dare places a hand on my hip and pulls me in closer to him. "Me too."

We walk down the beach until we come to a cluster of rocks. There's beach in front of it, but the water keeps crashing against the rocks and flooding the small area of sand.

Dare lets go of my hip and grabs my hand. He leads the way, but we don't make it all the way across before the water comes rushing back at the shore. I let out a shriek as the cold water hits my legs, startling me as I'm now standing knee-deep in the ocean.

He looks back, a smile that feels genuine on his handsome face. "You okay?"

I don't realize until he asks that I'm squeezing his hand in a death grip. I make a point to ease up, but I can't deny being in the water again sparks a bit of panic that tightens in my chest and raises the hair on my arms.

I want to get out of the water, so I nod quickly. He must see the discomfort on my face because he hauls me forward and we make it past before another wave comes.

Once we're in the clear, he hauls me up beside him again. "You freak out a little back there?"

"Just a bit."

His grip on my waist tightens. "I wouldn't let anything happen to you."

Maybe it's crazy, but I believe him.

He's so warm and solid, I have to fight the temptation to rest my head on his shoulder.

Once we're across the little stretch of beach beyond the rocks, there's another cluster of rocks, but this one has a cave nestled behind it. I'm not sure which way we're going, but he stops when we get to the rocks.

"Here, put these in your purse," he says, taking the sandals out of my hand and shoving them in my handbag with the liquor. He zips it as much as he can, probably so I don't dump anything, then he starts climbing the rocks.

"Careful," he calls back. "These are slippery, and they hurt like hell when you step on them."

He's right, they do hurt like hell to walk on, but my sandals are too loose and floppy. I consider putting them on to protect my feet, but I'm too afraid I would slip and die, and that would be infinitely worse.

"Why does hanging out with you always have to be so dangerous?" I complain as I brace my hand on the next rock.

Dare sits down, dangling his feet over the edge, and looks back to make sure I'm coming. "Don't worry, you'll get used to it."

I finally sit down on the relatively smooth surface of the rock he's perched on. Once I'm seated there and no longer concerned about slipping and falling to a painful death, I look out at the view, and all my complaints wash away.

Wow.

The ocean in front of us is an absolute sight to behold. The ocean stretches on right up to the fluffy white clouds and the beautiful blue sky. The water ripples and sunlight dances across the surface.

"Wow," I breathe.

He nods, reaching over and unzipping my purse so he can draw out the rum. "Nice, isn't it?"

"This is gorgeous." I look down, feeling the light spray of ocean water on my bare toes as the waves crash against the rocks. I look over at him with a smile. "Thanks for bringing me here."

He meets my gaze as he unscrews the bottle. "Thanks for coming with me."

"I didn't have a choice, remember? You kidnapped me."

"Right. Then, thanks for not calling the cops."

I laugh and he hands me the bottle. I've certainly never had rum straight from the bottle before, but I suppose there's a first time for everything.

It's actually pretty good. I take a small sip, then a second slightly bigger one before I pass it back. I expect him to use his shirt to wipe off the top since I just had my mouth on it, but he just takes a swig, apparently unbothered.

"We'll have to come out here one night and watch the sunset," he tells me.

"Oh, I bet it's gorgeous."

"It is." He looks over, bringing the rum bottle to my lips and tipping it back, making me take a bigger drink than I did before.

I pull back as the alcohol comes out too fast. I start to wipe my lips, but he pushes my hand away, using his thumb to rub away the little bit of alcohol that got on my lips.

Holding my gaze, he brings that thumb to his mouth. I watch as it disappears between his perfectly shaped lips, taking a breath that feels suddenly weighted. Not in a reassuring way like a blanket, but like I can scarcely draw a breath.

I shift my attention back to the water and try to change the subject. "Do you come out here a lot?"

"Yeah." He tips the bottle back and takes a swig. "I usually like to come here alone, though. It's peaceful."

"I hope I'm not ruining your peace," I say lightly.

"Of course not." He glances at me. "I like hanging out with you."

"I like hanging out with you, too."

He passes me the bottle. "Has the ocean always spooked you?"

The abrupt subject change startles me. I take a sip before answering. "Um… no. I was never afraid of water before. I guess it's probably just too fresh, you know? That was scary last week. I honestly thought I was going to die, and that feeling, the water filling my lungs…"

I don't even want to think about it.

I accept the bottle as he hands it back, but I didn't even notice him take a drink this time. "Can't be afraid of it. How'm I ever going to teach you how to swim if you're afraid of the water?"

I take a sip and crack a smile. "I don't know. It might not be a good idea."

"It's a better idea than you drowning," he returns.

I offer the bottle back. My head feels heavy. I don't mean to, but I lean my head against his shoulder to support the weight of it. "I think I should stop drinking."

"Nah, have a little more."

I'm too wobbly, so he wraps an arm around my shoulders and tips it back, making me drink more than I want to.

It feels good. I've only had alcohol on a few occasions, and never enough to get drunk. I don't recognize the feeling of fogginess, but the more it hits me, the less I resist when Dare keeps plying me with liquor.

I don't know how long we sit there, but it feels like forever. It feels nice, too. I feel so light and happy, so untethered to the heavy reality I've known lately. He makes me feel free, and I adore him for it.

"Come on," he says after a while, putting his rum bottle back in my bag and climbing off the rock.

"Dare, I don't know if I can…"

"This side's easier to get over," he assures me, continuing across the rocks instead of going back the way we came.

I'm uncertain, but he seems totally sure, so I move slowly, following him across the rocks to get to the other side.

He's right, it's a lot easier to get across over here.

Dare waits on the beach below while I try to figure out how to slide down the rock to the beach without scraping the backs of my thighs.

Reaching his hands up and grabbing my waist, he says, "I got you."

He lifts me off the rock. I slide down the front of his hard body as he lowers me until my bare feet touch the sand.

I'm so tipsy, I nearly trip over his shoe, but his strong grip keeps me upright. He leans in, making my heart pound hard in my chest, but he only leans his forehead against mine for a moment.

God, that's so sweet.

My heart fills up. He pulls back.

I follow him across the beach, but I couldn't walk a straight line if my whole life depended on it.

"Where are we going?" I ask him.

"There's a little lagoon over here," he tells me.

Sure enough, there's a cove with rock formations that block so much of the ocean's movement, it has created a dreamy little lagoon much calmer than the ocean. White caps still move in and hit the sandy shore, but the waves are small and not intimidating at all.

"This is so peaceful," I tell him.

He bends to pull his shoes off and leave them on the dry part of the beach. "Come on," he says, taking my hand and pulling me toward the water.

Since it doesn't look deep here, I follow him. My toes sink into the wet sand. I'm okay when we're ankle deep, but then the water gets deeper. It sloshes around my kneecaps, and he's still pulling me.

"Dare."

He must hear the nervousness in my tone because he stops and looks back at me.

"This is far enough," I tell him uncertainly. "I don't want to get my skirt wet."

He lets go of my hand and turns around. I gasp as he suddenly bends, catches water in his hands, and throws it at me.

"Dare!"

He laughs and the sound is so lovely, it's as if everything inside me lifts. "Too late. You're wet now."

There's a devious bend to his eyebrow when he says that. It turns my cheeks pink as I grab a handful of water and throw it right back at him. I aim for his face but he dodges. Droplets of ocean water still hit him, clinging to his thick dark hair.

Without meaning to, I move a little closer, then I'm chasing him and we're throwing water at one another until we're completely soaked.

My drenched clothes are clinging to my body at this point, so when he grabs me and makes me go farther out, I let him. Water sloshes past my hips, and my white skirt looks cool floating in the ocean around me.

I'm not sure how deep the water is over here, but he knows I can't swim, so I know he won't take me too far. He's taller than I am, though, so he may not realize how deep the water is getting.

"Dare," I say, pulling on his hand once the water is waist deep.

He stops and turns back to look at me. My bright yellow cami top is more of a marigold now that it's wet. The thin fabric is plastered against my skin, showing the outline of my breasts, the hardness of my nipples.

Dare's gaze darkens as he looks at me. He grabs me, pulling me over to him. He takes my hips to pull me closer, then his hands slide down and cup my ass. I'm startled at the way he squeezes until I realize he's lifting me. He tells me to wrap my legs around him.

My heart thuds dully, an ache between my thighs I've never felt in the presence of any other guy. He lifts me easily since we're in the water, and then my pussy is pressed against him, only the thin, wet barrier of my panties protecting me.

I don't feel like I need any protection from him, though. A week ago, I would have said that's a crazy fucking thing to even think, but right now as I bob in the water with his strong hands under my ass, I feel safe.

It's the same feeling I had that night in the pool when he

wrapped his arms around me and saved me from a watery grave.

Our positions are almost the same, too. I hadn't noticed because my head is above water, and since we were playing in the ocean, I'm not scared.

I realize that's why he brought me out here.

I freaked out when the water hit my ankles. Now, I'm submerged in the ocean, my feet not even touching the ground, and I feel completely safe.

It's him.

I feel safe with him.

Yearning I've never felt before hits me. It hits like a truck —I *want* him. I like him. I want to feel the way I feel when I'm with him all the time.

Maybe that's why I lean my heavy head forward and bury it in the crook of his neck.

Maybe that's why, when he pushes his fingers through my hair and tugs my head back to make me look at him…

Maybe that's why I let him kiss me.

My belly fills with butterflies as his lips touch mine. It's electric, euphoric. I wrap my arms around his neck and close my eyes, tightening my legs around his body to pull him closer. My heart pounds and my pussy throbs with need that twists in my gut when his fist tightens in my hair like he's as hungry for it as I am.

Anae.

Fuck.

No, I hate her. Fuck her. She tried to get me fired.

She's still his girlfriend. A guy with a girlfriend shouldn't be kissing you.

I can't argue that.

Damn my conscience.

Damn, damn, damn.

It happened so fast, I didn't have time to realize what was

coming. Now, I pull back, unwrapping my legs from his waist and lowering myself back to the ocean floor.

I don't meet his gaze.

It's not necessarily that I'm ashamed. I would never go after some other girl's boyfriend, but Anae is terrible. If I were dating her, I wouldn't want to be, either.

But he is.

No one's making him.

I don't get the impression anyone can *make* Dare do anything, so if he's with her, it must be because there's something he likes about her, and if he likes her…

Fuck.

I shouldn't have come out here with him.

"Hey," he says when I turn and start making my way back toward the beach.

"I need to get home," I say without looking back. "I'm sure school is over by now. My mom will wonder what's taking me so long."

He's still for a moment before I hear the water sloshing as he moves to join me on the beach.

I'm awkward, fidgeting with the things in my purse so I don't have to look at him. I almost put my sandals back on, but I still think that will make it harder to climb the rocks.

My head feels slightly less foggy than it did before he kissed me, but I'm still cautious as I make my way across the rocks to the other side of the beach.

Dare falls into step beside me. I feel him looking at me as we approach the steps leading up to his back yard, but I don't look back.

"Are we good?" he asks, finally breaking the silence.

I look over at him briefly to flash him a tiny smile. "Yeah, of course."

"You seemed a little freaked out back there."

I meet his gaze more steadily, even though it makes my

stomach hurt to utter my next words. "I don't kiss guys who have girlfriends."

"Even girlfriends you don't like?"

"Even girlfriends I absolutely hate," I verify.

He nods, looking more like he's been handed new information about me to file away than offended. "Got it."

We head back up to his house to get my school bag, no doubt dropped off by one of his nerd soldiers.

I'm horrified to learn it's past four o'clock.

Mom hasn't texted me to see where I am, so I'm also a little worried.

Dare takes me home, but the ride is much quieter.

I already miss the beach. The sunset I'll never get to watch with him.

I know I can't go back there. I never should have been there in the first place. Logically, I know I don't belong in Dare's world, and I certainly don't belong in his arms.

I thank him for the ride as I open the door to climb out, but I feel a little uncertain about things since I did sort of reject him.

"You're still picking me up tomorrow, right?"

"Of course."

Relief floods me. Because he doesn't seem to hate me, or because I have a ride to school? I don't know, maybe both.

Whatever the case, I'm glad I'll see him tomorrow once this awkwardness has passed and my brain isn't swimming in rum.

CHAPTER 12

AUBREY

I'M WEARING black jeans and a long-sleeved, mauve top when Dare pulls up in front of my house this morning.

My stupid heart is so happy to see him.

I ignore it as I climb into his matte black Audi, not struggling to get my bag in the floor today while maintaining my modesty since I wore jeans.

Dare's gaze still lingers on my legs as if they're bare, then slides to my face in that deliberate way of his. "Good morning."

"Hey," I say back, grabbing the seat belt and pulling it across my body.

He waits for me to secure it, then he shifts the car into drive and we're off.

It's a little chilly this morning, so the windows are rolled up. Not like yesterday.

Once I sobered up, the whole of yesterday started to seem batshit crazy. Kissing someone else's boyfriend in the ocean? I couldn't describe a scene less characteristic of something I would do if I actively tried.

I'm hesitant to blame it on the alcohol, but I did drink a lot of it.

Thankfully, it's a short ride to school, but it feels longer today with an invisible third passenger.

Awkwardness.

Oh, how I hate it.

When he pulls into his spot and turns off the engine, part of me regrets wasting our last car ride together not talking.

A small, shameful part of me also hoped things would go much differently. I know it's insane because we're just getting to know each other, but since he seems not to even like Anae... I don't know, some part of me hoped maybe he would be playful and comfortable when I got in the car this morning, and when I wondered why he didn't feel as awkward about it as I did, he would tell me he broke up with her. Not *for me*, necessarily, but because after some soul-searching, he realized he wouldn't even be kissing some other girl on his private beach if he actually liked the one he was with.

None of that happens.

The discomfort doesn't seem to bother him.

Before we get out, he finally says, "Since I imagine I won't be seeing you at lunch today, the shop said your car would be done by two. I told them to deliver it to my parking spot so you'd know where to find it."

"Oh. But we're *in* your parking spot."

"Just dropping you off," he tells me. "I'll park somewhere else today."

"That's really nice of you. Thanks."

"You're welcome," he says. "If my car gets scratched, I'm blaming you, though."

I crack a smile at the return of playfulness to his tone. "That's fair."

I finally allow myself to look over at him, and that thought echoes through my mind again.

I miss you.

It's absurd to miss someone who is sitting right beside me, even more absurd to miss someone I barely know, and yet...

"Maybe..." I shut my mouth, wishing I hadn't opened it. "No, never mind."

"What?"

"Nothing."

My stupid ass wants to have lunch with him again. Not even necessarily leaving the school like we did yesterday, but just spending time with him wherever. I could bring my bagged lunch, he could grab something from the lunch line.

And what? Sit together in the cafeteria and have a grand old time while Anae watches and doesn't mind *at all*?

He presses again, but I tell him nothing and pull the latch to let myself out of the car before I say something really stupid.

Thankfully, my brain seems to recover with some time away from him.

I get back to my usual routine of getting a head start on my homework during lunch. A bespectacled kid comes over to my table, blushing beneath his freckles as he hands me my car keys.

I expect he's one of Dare's nerd soldiers.

My suspicions are confirmed when I look at Dare's table and see him watching to make sure his delivery arrives.

My lips tug up. I can't help it. He's so shameless.

Shifting my gaze back to the messenger, I say, "Thank you."

The kid blushes even harder. He swallows, looking like he'd rather die than repeat what he's about to say, but he mumbles, "He also wanted me to give you this."

He holds out a scrap of torn notebook paper. I am

delighted and a little stunned to see Dare has written his phone number on it.

Who does that?

I know he *has* my phone number, so I'm surprised he would give his to me in such an archaic way.

Then again, Dare employs an army of nerds to do his menial labor instead of picking on them, so I guess he really just does things his own way.

I love that he doesn't fit the mold he occupies. I like to think he's a benevolent king who is nice to his laboring serfs, too.

"Thank you," I say again.

"There's a present for you in the car. It's from Dare." He utters that last part like he'll explode if he doesn't deliver the message fast enough, then he hustles away without another word.

A bit wryly, I wonder if Dare put the present there himself or had his messenger do it, but I probably already know the answer.

Since his attention is divided between watching me and his friends at his table, I have to wait a few seconds for Dare's gaze to shift back to me. I do a mock bow and mouth "thank you." He smirks, and I miss his energy sitting all the way over here.

No.

I cut that line of thinking off straight away and put my head down, burying it in my books. I've been so distracted by Dare, so caught up in my whirlwind appearance in his world. But it's over now, and it's time to get back to reality.

When the school day is finally over, I head out to the parking lot.

I have to remind myself I'm parked in Dare's spot right up front. Even though it's his spot to do with as he pleases, it feels conspicuous walking to my car parked there as a bunch of kids are flooding out of the school behind me.

I don't know what it says about him, but he's not *remotely* sneaky about the shady things he does.

I forgot all about the present he left for me over the course of my last two classes, but I'm reminded when I slide in and go to drop my heavy-ass backpack in the passenger seat. I nearly crush a pink striped gift bag. I catch its weight just as the top of the gift bag dents.

Shifting my target, I drop my school bag farther over on the seat and grab the gift bag, pulling it on my lap so I can see what's inside.

Layers of white tissue paper obscure the item. I push them aside and see two things—an envelope with my name on it, and a bit of white folded fabric.

I pull the note out first.

The envelope is sealed, so I tear it open. When I go to pull it out, I'm startled to find money stuffed inside along with the note. My stomach twists, a mix of confusion and… I'm not sure what. I count out the fifties in mild disbelief.

He gave me $300?

More perplexed than I was before, I open the note card. The inside is blank but for his writing.

> *Let's see how serious you were about that side hustle. ;)*
> *This is the first half.*
> *You'll get the other 300 after I get a picture of you*
>   *wearing what's inside the bag. Nothing else.*

What?

Oh, my god.

My cheeks burn as I set aside the card and the money and pull the folded fabric out of the bag.

It's a pair of white panties. They're the epitome of purity with soft fabric over the crotch, but lace everywhere else. They even have a little white bow in the center.

He has got to be kidding.

I'm floored. He is out of his mind if he thinks I'm sending him a picture of me in just my panties.

Before I head home, I grab my phone and carefully type in his number from the slip of paper he sent over at lunch.

"You have lost your whole mind if you think I'm doing that," I text him.

I wait a few seconds to see if he has his phone out, but he's probably heading to his car or driving home. I put my phone in the cup holder and head to my house, too, but I can't stop thinking about the panties he bought me and his insane request.

Once I'm in my driveway, I check my phone again and see I have a text from him. It's the first one I've ever received, and my tummy flutters a little.

"Why?" he asks. "It's exactly what you asked for. Less than an hour of work, and you'll make $600. What's the issue?"

There are too many issues! I don't even know where to begin.

I type back, "I was JOKING about stripping. I might be in dire straits, but sex work wasn't in my five year plan."

"Guess you don't need the money that badly then," he shoots back.

Yes, I do.

My energy dips a little when I realize it. It's depraved asking me to send him a picture like that for a lot of reasons, but the reality is, I do need money, and as shady as his terms are, he is offering some.

As reluctant as I am to do what he asked, I know I shouldn't turn down a chance to make an extra $600. It wouldn't buy me a whole month with all our expenses, but it would still be a relief to have an unexpected infusion of cash. And while I *was* joking about stripping, I can't say I'd never consider it. There are more important things than my modesty, and Mom's cancer treatment is definitely one of them. Keeping a roof over our heads is another. I know how she would feel if we lost the house, and as bad as her health is, she can't take stress like that.

I guess at least if I sent him a picture, he would be the only one seeing it.

Rather than acknowledge why this makes a bit of sense, I text back, "What would your girlfriend think about all this?"

His response is immediate. "I doubt she'd be as into it as I am, but they're not for her."

I roll my eyes. "You know that is not what I meant."

"Guys watch porn all the time. How is this any different?"

"It's totally different," I type back, wide-eyed. "You KNOW me. You don't know Scarlet O' Big Boobs."

"Brb, saving your number in my phone as Scarlet O' Big Boobs."

"Don't you dare," I send back, unable to bite back a horrified laugh.

"Too late." He sends back a screenshot to prove he did it.

"Why are you the worst?" I ask him.

"What are you talking about? I'm your fairy godmother. Now, get your little ass inside the house and take a picture if you want the rest of your money."

"I am not sending you a picture of me… like that."

"In panties?" he questions. "What do you have against panties? I guess you can leave them off if you really want to…"

The. Worst.

I shake my head, typing back, "It's not happening."

"I disagree," he texts back. "I don't have an exact ratio of how often I get what I want, but I should tell you, it happens more often than it doesn't."

I'm tempted to sit here and keep talking to him, but I'm sitting in the driveway with the car off, and it's starting to get hot.

I gather my things, shoving the gift bag and its contents into my backpack so Mom doesn't see them when I go inside. My phone vibrates just as I get through the door. It's another message from Dare.

"What are we having for dinner tonight?"

"My mom and I are having lasagna," I type back. "I have no idea what you're having."

He texts back, "I know what I want for dessert…"

I don't know if he *means* it as an innuendo, but that's how I take it.

It feels like a knot sinks from my chest cavity into my upper abdomen. Ignoring it, I type back, "I recommend some nice cold ice cream."

"Lol, you would," he answers.

"I have to go," I tell him. "I just got home and I need to take a shower before I start dinner."

"Sounds like the perfect opportunity for a photo op."

"Don't hold your breath."

"I've been holding my breath since we met, mermaid."

Ugh, he's so full of shit, and yet my stupid heart pitter patters like it believes him.

Doesn't matter, I tell myself.

Do the right thing.

Put the phone away and stop thinking about him.

I'm on Mom's time now, anyway.

"Hey sweetie," she calls out, looking back at me as if she senses I need a reminder.

I flash a weak smile back. "Hey."

"How was school?"

"Good." I start to drop my bags, but reconsider given what's inside. "I'm just going to drop this stuff off in my room and take a shower, then I'll come out and start dinner, okay?"

"Okay, honey."

I need to bring up that doctor Dare told me about, but maybe I should wait until I hear back from him. I know Mom is tired of fighting, I know she thinks she has tried everything at this point and it's all failed, but what if…?

Remembering what Dare's doing for me just puts him in my head again, and I had only cleared him out for a couple of seconds.

I try to ignore the sinking feeling that I like him far more than I should because I know what I should do if that's the case.

I should delete his number.

Block it, even.

I should stay far, far away from him.

Even if he didn't belong to the worst girl in the world. I don't even have time to like a normal guy; I certainly do *not* have time to like Chase Darington.

I'M EXHAUSTED by the time I fall into bed, and I haven't even touched my homework yet. I tell myself I'm just going to rest my eyes, but when I jerk awake to a pitch black bedroom, I grab my phone on the bed beside me and see it's 3 am.

Shit.

I also see I missed a text from Dare just after twelve.

"It's midnight, Cinderella. Where's my picture?"

Smiling faintly, I text back, "You are the most depraved fairy godmother ever."

The brain fog is too thick for me to realize he's probably asleep by now.

I'm still so tired, but unfortunately, I have to wake up.

By the time I'm finished with my homework, the sun is up and I have to be at school in a half hour.

"Perfect," I mutter to myself.

My phone vibrates. I look down, expecting it to be Dare, but it's just Mom asking me to add something to the grocery list.

Ugh, that's right. I need to make a grocery order again.

All the light, happy feelings I got talking to Dare evaporate. I don't even have time to shower. I'm so mad at myself for falling asleep, but it is what it is, I guess.

I run to the bathroom and splash my face with cool water to wake me up. I make quick work of getting ready, then I rush back to my bedroom and start cramming books into my bag.

I'm going to be late to school.

I pop into Mom's room to tell her goodbye and to remind her Josie will pop over and bring her dinner because I have to work tonight.

I wish I could just come home after school, maybe take a nap. I wish I could curl up on the couch with Mom and watch a movie, have no worries for at least a few hours.

I'm overwhelmed and feel like crying when I head out to my car, but I have to shake it off.

Since I'm not riding to school with Dare anymore and I don't have my own reserved parking up front, I end up parked at the back of the lot, hustling my ass off to get to homeroom.

The teacher shoots me a dirty look when I run in late, making apologies as I head to my desk. My tummy rumbles as I fall into my seat and drop my things so loudly, everyone in the quiet room stares.

Behind me, I hear someone whisper, "How tragic."

I look back at one of the rich girls Anae is friends with, her perfectly blended and glossed lips pouty as she feigns sympathy—whether at my raggedy appearance this morning, or my audible hunger, I'm not sure.

I shoot her a dirty look right back. Ordinarily, I would just ignore something like that, but I'm caught off guard by it. I don't know why this random girl is being mean to me. Sure, she's Anae's friend, but she wasn't there that day at the shop, and last I heard, Anae hadn't put any kind of social hit out on me.

Whatever. I don't care.

I turn back to face the front and try to get my things unpacked as quietly as I can. There was no time to stop at my locker, so my backpack is so freaking heavy.

It feels like people are staring when I walk out of class. I keep my head down, confused, as I hurry to my next class.

People *keep* staring.

Since that's highly unusual, it freaks me out a little.

Then, on my way to English class, I hear someone laugh and say, "Isn't that the girl from the video?"

The girl she's talking to chuckles and says, "Yeah. That sound was perfect."

"I love when they're top notch," the girl says, tossing her blonde hair and smirking at me as she walks past.

Video? Sound?

I stop outside English class when I feel my phone vibrate.

My heart practically stops when I see a link and a screenshot from Anae's phone number.

The screenshot shows a story someone posted on social media. It's an old, dorky picture of me from environment club —back when I had time to be in school clubs—added to a background with text that reads, "Doing her part for the environment by giving up showering apparently."

My stomach pitches as I swipe it away and click the link.

Clearly, it's the video those girls were talking about. It was shot by the girl in class who called me tragic. She must have taken the video after I turned around. I'm hunched over, digging through my backpack, face flushed and hair a little frizzy. She added stench lines and animated flies buzzing around to indicate I stink, and then turned the camera around to show her face "prettily" cringing and lip syncing "ew" to the tone of a late night show host's bit on SNL.

Generally, I am not a person who cares what people think about me, but I came into today already feeling raw as hell, and now to see someone purposely humiliating me for no apparent reason...

My eyes burn with tears that threaten to fall, but I don't let them.

I tell myself it doesn't matter, that they don't matter, and the enjoyment Anae clearly got out of sharing those with me certainly doesn't matter, but deep down, all I can think about is that Dare has probably seen them, and I wonder if he laughed at me too, even if just because his friends were.

Tears blur my vision. On impulse, I turn away from the door and head back to my locker.

Fuck it. I'm blowing off English class today.

Since English is the only class I have before lunch, and I'm certainly not going to show my face in the cafeteria, I head out to the quad and find a comfy spot beneath a shade tree.

I tell myself this is a good plan because now I can get a head start on my weekend homework. Given my lack of sleep last night, I doubt I would have been able to stay up late and do it tonight. That means I would have had to do it sometime this weekend, which I hate doing. Doing it this way frees up more time to spend with Mom.

It also means I'm so hungry my stomach feels like it's caving in on itself. I have a couple of sticks of gum in my backpack, so I chew those while I work just to get a little sugar in my system, but it's hard to concentrate when I'm so hungry.

Ignoring the hunger, I try to push through.

I'm doing an okay job until I hear soft footsteps on the grass behind me. I turn, half-expecting to see a teacher who just noticed I'm outside telling me I'm not allowed to be out here, but it's not a teacher.

A petite blonde girl with her hair pulled back into a pony tail approaches, her full pink lips pulled up in a smile. She's carrying a lunch bag with her.

I don't know who she is, so I'm extremely confused when she suddenly kneels on the ground beside me.

"Hello," she says.

She has a lovely voice.

Still frowning, I offer a guarded, "Hello," back.

She sets the lunch bag down and unzips it, her gaze focused on unpacking it, apparently. "I thought you might be hungry. This is my lunch, but you can have it. I'll just go through the lunch line and get something."

Embarrassment creeps up on me. "I don't need your lunch. I can afford my own."

"I know," she says, her tone light since she can probably tell I'm defensive. "But I thought maybe you didn't want to go in the cafeteria because of…" She trails off, not wanting to explicitly refer to the social media posts.

Oh.

She has seen them.

Of course she has.

It seems like everyone has.

Still a little untrusting, I look at her. "Who are you? I don't think we have any classes together. You're just offering your lunch to a complete stranger?"

"My name's Hannah. We don't have any classes together. I'm actually a junior. This isn't my lunch period, it's my study hall, but I've been seeing the things Anae and her friends have posted about you all day, and I think it sucks. I don't know if you saw, but they posted another story through the window of you sitting out here." She points back at the window into the cafeteria. "They were pretty proud to have chased you out of the building. When I saw it, I fibbed and told the teacher I needed to pee so I could go to my locker and grab my lunch." She looks down. "I just thought people were being really mean to you, and I didn't want you to be hungry just because you didn't feel like being around them."

My walls come down, my gaze shifting to the dish of fruit she's opening for me. "That's really kind of you, but you don't have to do that."

"I want to," she insists. "It's not a big deal at all. Like I said, I can just buy lunch today." She opens a little container and looks inside. "You're not allergic to nuts, are you? This is a banana nut muffin."

My mouth waters. "That sounds amazing. No, I'm not allergic."

She flashes me a smile and hands over the container. "I hope you like it. I made them myself."

Since she seems to be waiting to see if I do, I sink my teeth into the moist, fluffy muffin, and my tastebuds explode with happiness. It's probably only because I'm so hungry anything would taste good, but my God, this is the best muffin I've ever tasted.

"Oh my god," I say, covering my mouth.

Her big blue eyes widen. "Is it bad? I just made them this morning, they should be really fresh."

I shake my head, chewing and swallowing the mouthful of deliciousness. "Will you marry me?"

Startled, she bursts into laughter.

I grin back, meeting her gaze. "No, I'm not kidding. If it means you will make these muffins for me all the time, I wanna lock you down."

Delighted, she laughs again. "I'm glad you like them. I've never had them trigger a spontaneous proposal before."

"Then you're giving them to the wrong people," I tell her. "I'm more of a cook than a baker myself, but I'm tempted to beg for your recipe so I can try to make these at home."

"You can have it," she says easily. "It was my mom's recipe. I'll type it up over the weekend. I can give it to you Monday morning when I get my lunch bag back."

"You're an angel on earth," I tell her, looking over at the

delicious assortment of fruit she's given me, too. "What did you say your name was again?"

"Hannah." Her kind blue eyes flash with something that resembles guilt and she looks down. "I'm actually Anae's stepsister."

My levity dissipates, distrust pouring back in.

Anae's *sister* is giving me food?

I've already swallowed the first bite. I look down at the muffin, searching for what's wrong with it. I don't see anything obvious, like bugs or hair. "Did you put laxatives in it or something?"

"No," she says quickly, shaking her head. "No, I would never do that."

I meet her gaze levelly. "You're Anae's sister."

"*Stepsister*," she corrects, but still looks a little unhappy about it. "And as someone who lives with her, I can assure you, I know what a nightmare she can be."

My guards are still up, but Hannah really does seem guileless.

I look down at the muffin. I'm still a little wary that she could have messed with it. Anae is Dare's girlfriend and has been for a while. Maybe they do the same sorts of things. Dare has an army at his command and he deploys them to do errands for him. Perhaps Anae does, too, only her army is meaner.

I search the girl's face, but I can't find a single trace of malice. She seems really sweet, more concerned that I'll think she must be bad and refuse to eat her lunch because she sincerely doesn't want me to be hungry than because her older sister—*or stepsister, whatever*—sent her to torment me even more today.

It's a hard call after all the aggravation, but I believe her.

Nodding to let her know, I say, "Well, I'm very sorry you have to live with her."

Hannah cracks a smile. "It's not the best."

"I would still very much appreciate the muffin recipe."

Her smile widens. "Of course." Seeing I believe her, she opens her purse and pulls out a little bottle of spritzer and a small brush. "It's the most ridiculous thing ever that they're picking on you over some frizz, but do you want me to brush your hair out and braid it for you while you eat?"

I blink at her. "Seriously?"

She shrugs. "I can if you want. I promise I don't have lice."

"Um…"

Seeing my hesitation, she gestures for me to turn and climbs on her knees behind me. "I'm gonna do it. I've been wanting to practice this half-back waterfall style, anyway, and it's really hard to practice on my own head."

At first, it feels a little odd letting some girl I barely know do my hair, but as soon as her gentle fingers start working their way through my locks, my scalp tingles with pleasure and I realize how nice it feels to be pampered.

Hannah is literally an angel, gentle and friendly. My guards pop up a couple times to warn me she could just be an incredible actress, that maybe Anae sent her with Nair in her purse or something, and when she's finished working on me and I'm done with this muffin, I'll be bald and have a horrible case of diarrhea.

Like with Dare, though, I give her the benefit of the doubt.

It's much easier with her.

She doesn't have the feel of danger like he does. It's incredibly easy to lower my guards and trust her, whereas with Dare, I can feel how risky it is even as I'm doing it.

I wonder if she's ever met him.

I kind of hope not.

I can see him liking her, but I can also see him chewing her up and spitting out the bones.

Or falling madly in love with her great energy and never letting her go.

Not sure which one horrifies me more, but I find myself hoping she has evaded his notice.

Clearing my throat as she does my hair, I focus intently on the grape between my fingers and ask, "Do you know Dare?"

"Anae's boyfriend?" she questions. "I've met him, but I keep my distance when he comes around."

Smart girl.

I'm also thankful. I wish I only felt that way for pure, self-less reasons, but I'm not as lovely as Hannah. Yes, I think he would be horrible for her well-being, but I'm also afraid he would *like* her if he ever spent any time with her—*how could anyone not?*—and the idea of him liking someone else is somehow painful.

Which is *ridiculous* since he *has a girlfriend.*

My god, what is wrong with me?

"Do they seem… happy to you?" I ask, even knowing I'm crossing a line.

"As happy as a couple of spiders sharing a particularly juicy fly," she answers after a moment. "I don't know him well, but I know Anae. Mean people are mean for a lot of different reasons, but with Anae… I hate to say this because I don't like to believe something like that about anyone, but… I'm really not sure she's even capable of love. If she is, I sure haven't seen it."

Any lingering thoughts I had that Hannah might be a double agent are swept away with that statement. I definitely don't know Anae as well as she does. I think she's awful, but if even someone so close to her agrees, that must mean it's real and not because of some bias I have.

Hannah finishes braiding a ring around the back of my head, then she says, "There," with a trace of happy accomplishment in her tone.

I can't see, of course, but she gives me a little compact mirror from her purse and uses her phone as well to show me how freaking pretty she made my hair look.

I love this girl. I want to take her home with me.

"That is so cute," I tell her. "I love it."

She beams. "Isn't it? I love waterfall hair. I just think it's so pretty. And you have really nice hair to begin with. That style really works for you. You look so good."

"Thank you," I say, not for the compliment which I can tell she really means, but for being so nice to me. I've felt like utter crap since I got to school today, and just hanging out with her for a little while, it all melted away.

She smiles back like she understands what I'm thanking her for. "You're welcome."

Since Hannah has to get back to her study hall, she doesn't stay once she has finished my hair.

Even once she's gone, though, I feel better. After a while, I even feel silly for letting Anae and her friends get to me.

I can't help thinking that if I had time for friends, I would definitely want to be Hannah's.

And then, realizing she is the *second* person in Anae's orbit I have taken to lately, I can't help wondering what the hell is up with that?

CHAPTER 14
AUBREY

THIS FRIDAY HASN'T BEEN MUCH BETTER than the one where I nearly died, but at long last, it ends, and I am free to climb in my bed and go to sleep.

My bed feels incredible. I haven't even pulled back the bedding and climbed underneath yet, I just crashed on top and don't want to move.

I didn't bother turning on my bedroom light after I took a shower. I knew I didn't have any energy left to do homework tonight. All I want to do is go to sleep.

My phone lights up on the bed next to me.

I grab it, trying to ignore the niggling hope that it's Dare.

It isn't. It's just a social media notification.

I'm disappointed as I swipe the notification and open the app, but my disappointment ebbs when I see it's a follow request from Hannah Dupont.

I accept it, then tap home and look at my feed. Stories are displayed at the top. Hannah's profile picture is her lying in a field of flowers which is honestly the most appropriate thing I can possibly imagine. I smile looking at her in her powder blue dress, gazing up at the sky.

God, she's so pretty.

I wish I had time to be your friend.

Her story is the first one displayed at the top of the screen, so out of curiosity, I click it.

To my surprise, it's an extremely flattering picture of me under the shade tree at school today, my beautiful waterfall braid in peak condition since she had just styled it. The caption reads, "She's so pretty omg" with the hashtag #hairgoals.

The whole hair goals thing is obviously bullshit because Hannah has long, gorgeous curls women would literally kill for, but I know what she's doing. Putting this positive post and picture of me out there to combat all the mean ones Anae and her squad shared today.

My chest feels all funny. Kinda tight and… heartburny.

I'm caught completely off guard when I see a text from Dare flash across the top of my screen.

I tap it before it has time to disappear.

His text reads, "Should I be jealous?"

My brow furrows faintly. "Jealous?" I type back, unsure what he means.

"I've heard some ranting tonight about Anae's sister being in love with you. I figured it was just Anae being dramatic, but I want to make sure I don't need to get involved."

Involved?

"Why would that necessitate your involvement anyway?"

"I'm a territorial man," he states.

My tummy sinks. I don't even know what to say to that, so it takes a moment before I get up the courage to ask, "And what territory are you policing, exactly?"

"You know what territory I'm policing," he answers.

My palms feel sticky. I hold my phone, my heart beating a little too hard as I consider what to say to that.

"Hannah's just a friend," I text back, feeling ridiculous even having to say it.

"You sure?"

"Pretty sure. She also seems super sweet, so you stay away from her," I add with a winky face so he doesn't take my demand too seriously—while also taking it to heart because he doesn't need to go anywhere near Hannah Dupont.

"Are you saying I'm not super sweet?" he teases.

"I mean, I think you are, but opinions seem to vary."

"What does Hannah think?"

That question makes me uneasy.

It's almost like he knows I asked her about him, but… he couldn't possibly know that.

"How should I know?" I ask evasively, ignoring the uncomfortable feeling that I'm not being entirely honest with him.

"You know what I realized?" he asks.

"What?" I ask, an aching pit in my gut that I don't understand.

"Miss Hannah Dupont has one more picture of you in her phone than I have in mine."

He's not actually jealous of Hannah, right?

That would be crazy.

I'm sure he's only joking, but I can't shake the unease that he might not be, too. I don't actually know him that well, after all. I've never heard he's a jealous lunatic, but...

"Yeah, I guess she does," I answer. It's not cute or clever, but I'm too worried to be charming right now.

"So, I'm thinking, maybe if you don't want to send me one, I should go upstairs to her room and see if I can convince her to send me the one she has."

I feel sick—utterly sick—at the thought.

It doesn't make sense, but it feels…

It feels like a threat.

I push up from my laying position, folding my legs in

front of me on the bed and looking down at the phone, trying to think what to say.

He's not threatening me. I'm being ridiculous. He's teasing me, that's all. He just wants the picture of me in my underwear, and I know he's not above using unorthodox methods of getting what he wants. He doesn't even mean it. What kind of psycho would actually go up to his girlfriend's sister's bedroom and hassle her to send him a picture of another girl? Literally nobody would do that.

Then again…

Am I sure?

No.

He hasn't exactly seemed concerned with covering his tracks up to this point.

I look across the room at the pink striped bag on top of my dresser. The panties are inside. I suppose I could just put them on…

My fingers fly across the screen as I text back, "You wouldn't show anybody, right?"

"Of course not," he answers. "It's for my eyes only."

I try to feel reassured by that, but I don't.

It does get me off the bed, though. I strip off my pajama pants and the panties I put on after my post-work shower. I slip on the ones he bought me. They're snug, but I think they're supposed to be. These are not panties one wears for comfort while lounging around the house alone.

I turn this way and that, sucking in my tummy and looking at myself from every angle.

My God, am I really going to do this?

I think I am.

I try not to think about how fucked up this is as I hurry to the bathroom to fix my hair and make sure I look okay, but that's impossible. Piecing together all the information he's offered in his texts, it sounds like he is at Anae's house right now. He's just sitting there with her, texting me and asking for pictures of me in my panties?

Something unsettling moves through my tummy. Maybe it's just nerves, but a voice whispers, *don't do it*.

Maybe it's my conscience.

Poor conscience, we're usually much better than this.

I need the money, I remind myself.

I also don't want it to be my fault Dare notices Hannah.

I'm not proud that, in this moment, it's the second motivation that feels most prominent.

I'm also aware that neither of those should be the reason I send my first sexy picture to a guy, but I swat that rational thought aside and try to figure out where to take this picture.

I snap a couple in the bathroom mirror, but I cringe because they're both terrible. I need a different setting and some coverage. He said I couldn't wear anything but the panties, but he said nothing about props or positioning. Maybe it's a loophole, but I'm using it.

Carefully, I pull the full-length mirror off the back of the bathroom door and haul it to my bedroom. My room is small, so one side of my bed is pushed against the wall. I prop the mirror up there, then I grab a pillow and lie tummy-down on the mattress.

I move around and snap pictures in a few different positions, but my boobs either look nonexistent pressed against the pillow, or he would be able to see too much of them.

I feel out of my depths here. He probably won't care, but I don't have anyone else to tell, so I grab my phone and type out a text. "I don't know how to do this."

"You're nervous," he answers. "It's new to you. That's natural. Let's ease those nerves and get you in the mood. Are you in your bedroom?"

"Yes," I answer. "On my bed."

"Okay. Lie down on your back. Spread your legs like I'm

on the bed between them, kissing my way along your inner thighs."

His words stun me. I suck a deep breath in and let my thighs fall apart like he told me to.

Another text comes through. "Now I'm touching you just to feel how soft your skin is. Close your eyes and lightly run your fingertips along your collar bone."

I should not be doing this. Not with him.

But I do.

"Lower," he directs. "Squeeze your tits. Graze your nipples. Rub them until they're hard and you can feel the tension in your pussy."

Oh my god.

I do as he says, my eyes closed and my breathing more and more shallow as my body responds.

My heart nearly stops when my phone starts ringing. Dare's number flashes across the screen.

Should I answer it?

I want to, but I might die of embarrassment.

Deciding to risk it, I release my nipple and grab the phone.

"Hello," I answer, my voice a little hoarse.

His voice is warm with approval that goes straight to my pussy. "Just wanted to make sure you were listening. What a good girl you are."

I sigh, my eyes drifting closed.

"Are you still touching yourself?" he asks.

"Yes," I answer softly.

"Where?"

"My... my fingers are grazing my nipples like you told me."

"Good. Are they hard?"

"Yes."

"Grab one and squeeze."

I suck in a breath as I do.

"Harder."

The steel in his voice makes me gasp. My fingers obey before I even tell them to.

His tone gentles slightly. "I bet your tits feel amazing in your hands, don't they, mermaid?"

"Mm, yeah," I murmur breathlessly.

"Yeah. Now, imagine I'm lying there on the bed beside you. Watching you. Hard as fucking steel with how much I want you."

Oh my god.

"I can't wait to kiss and taste and *bite* every inch of those perfect tits."

He sounds so hungry. His words rob me of my breath. I squeeze my soft flesh harder and feel the tension intensify between my thighs.

His voice is like gravel. The roughness alone turns me on, and then his words... my God. "You're so fucking beautiful writhing on the bed, making yourself feel good. I want to touch every inch of you. I want to ravage you. Do you feel shy, baby?"

"No." It comes out as more of a whine. I should be embarrassed, but I'm not because I can tell he likes it.

"No, of course you're not. You have no reason to feel shy. You're perfect. You're all I want."

My heart contracts as I rub my nipples, imagining him watching me. *Wanting* me.

"Now, stop touching yourself."

Disappointment grabs hold of me, but I do as he says.

My heart pounds, my chest rising and falling rapidly, my body tense and aching for release.

"Fuck, I want to see you. Take a picture. Send it to me."

I wait a moment for my breathing to return to normal.

Finally, I roll back on my tummy, pulling the pillow

beneath me. My breasts are so sensitive from being touched and teased, I feel a thrill as my nipples graze the material and let out a faint moan.

"Fuck, Aubrey," Dare says. His tone is rough, but still a little teasing. "You think it's a good idea to tease me with those sexy little moans?"

"I'm not trying to tease you," I say, my tone soft and a little sleepy. "My body's sensitive. You turned me on."

"Yeah?"

He knows he did, so I don't bother confirming.

I have to open up the camera app on my phone, but my bedroom is quiet, so I know I'm not missing anything with the phone away from my ear. I bend my legs so my feet are in the air, then I snap a photo.

The picture is a little dark, but I'm happy with this one, so I open up our text thread and send it to him.

I put the phone against my ear and wait.

"Christ," he murmurs.

I smile softly. "You like?"

"I love."

"Good."

My pussy still feels needy, so I'm relieved when he says, "Now, for your reward. Put your hand down the front of your panties."

I swallow, sliding my hand down between my thighs.

"Play with your pussy. Get yourself off," he commands. "I want to hear you come."

I should be horrified at the prospect of doing something like that with a guy that's not even my boyfriend, but my body needs it, and I want to please him.

I don't even feel self-conscious as my finger finds my clit and strums that thrilling, sensitive little nub. I thought I would, but I can hear how much he enjoys every noise I make as I touch myself.

I feel sexy.

He made me feel sexy.

When I come, I cry out, but the walls are thin so I try to muffle the sound in my pillow.

My heart pounds, but my body feels so relaxed as I lie twisted in the sheets, hugging my soft pillow.

Dare's voice on the phone is the perfect salve to top off the experience.

"That was perfect, Aubrey. You're perfect."

For once in my life, I *feel* perfect.

And so relaxed. I can't remember the last time I felt so relaxed.

"Now, curl up and get some sleep," he tells me.

I smile softly. "I will. Thank you."

"Sweet dreams."

"You, too," I murmur.

I'm so spent, I can scarcely be bothered to reach for my charge cord to plug in my phone. I do, but it feels like a Herculean effort. My eyes are heavy and near-impossible to keep open, but the room brightens with a new notification on my phone.

Just in case it's him, I check it.

A new follow request.

I swipe the notification open to see that Chase Darington is requesting to follow me.

My teeth sink into my bottom lip and I smile.

Confirm.

Yes, Chase Darington, you can follow me.

I don't click his profile to check it out. I'm too afraid of what I might see, and too tired, anyway.

In the blissful but vulnerable state I find myself in, all I should be doing is going to sleep, so I close my apps, put my phone on do not disturb, and curl up for a restful night's sleep.

CHAPTER 15

DARE

I WATCH DISPASSIONATELY from the chaise end of my leather couch as Anae loops her arm around Scofield's neck, rubbing her ass on him as he holds onto her hips from behind.

They're "dancing."

Really, she's trying to get my attention, but it doesn't work. The harder she tries, the more I ignore her.

She doesn't like when anyone else ignores her, but when I do it, it gets under her skin in the best way. Makes her desperate, makes her feel how little control she has over me.

Seeing she's caught my gaze, she breaks away from Scofield and comes over to climb on my lap.

"What are you doing over here all by yourself?" she asks, wiggling her ass on me as she gets comfy.

Flicking a glance at the shrinking ice cubes in my drink, I say, "Getting thirsty." I tip back the glass and drain it, leaving only the half-melted cubes. I hand it to her. "Go get me more."

Her eyes narrow, but I can see the heat and anticipation dancing there. She doesn't like to be bossed around by anyone but me. "Whatever you say," she says playfully to disguise how much she means it.

I watch her head out to the bar to refill my drink.

Mallory comes over, a big smile on her face. She's past tipsy. I can tell because she drops onto the couch beside me, then falls over giggling and leans her head on my bicep.

I don't think much of it until her hand softly closes around it and she peers up at me, looking a little nervous, but a little hopeful, too. "Sorry, Dare. I'm, like, so drunk right now."

I resist the urge to drag her hand off me like it's a dirty net washed up on the shore. Mallory's pretty and all, but I don't fuck Anae's friends, and I'm getting strong come-on vibes.

She goes to sit up and *accidentally* puts her hand on my thigh.

What is this?

Her hand slides in until it's dangerously close to my dick. I grab her wrist, startling her. She looks up at me, unsure if my steely grip is part of the game, or…

It's or.

"What the fuck are you doing?" I ask her.

Her mouth opens and closes like she never dreamed I would *ask*. "I…"

I hear the clacking of Anae's heels on the hardwood, so I push her friend's hand off me and lean away.

Taking the hint, Mallory sits up and looks straight ahead, clearly embarrassed.

Anae leans over the back of the couch so her long hair falls on my shoulder. Rubbing my chest, she offers my drink. "Here you go, baby."

Fuck this.

I don't know what she's up to, but I'd bet my left nut she's fully aware Mallory just came onto me, and I'm not in the mood for her shit tonight.

I push her hand off me too and stand. Anae straightens, appearing startled. Mallory avoids looking at me altogether.

I nod at Scofield. "Come on, asshole. Let's go for a swim."

He blinks in surprise, following, but tentatively. "You're not gonna drown me, are you?" he asks, only half joking since he *was* just rubbing his dick against my girlfriend's ass.

"Dare, wait," Anae says. Her tone drips desperation she's not even careful to conceal, so she must really be worried I'm mad. I can tell by the fast clicking of her heels she's hurrying to catch up with me. "What's wrong?"

"I'm not in the mood to play games with you tonight."

"Who's playing games?" she asks, brilliantly feigning confusion—that, or it's real and I'm just being cynical.

I shoot her a look. "You're always playing games."

Her gaze flits to our friends standing nearby. She doesn't mind handling me when we're alone, but she hates doing it with an audience. Gently grabbing my arm, she says, "Come on, let's go talk."

She tells everyone else we'll catch up like she's in charge, and once they've wandered off, she pulls me back in the house.

"Why are you mad at me?" she asks, looking genuinely confused.

"You're testing me, and I don't fucking like it."

She stares, wide-eyed. "What are you talking about? Why would I test you?"

"Mallory."

It's all I say.

Her gaze breaks away from mine, only for a split second, but it's long enough for me to detect her guilt. She opens her mouth, fleetingly considers lying to me, then says in a conciliatory tone, "It wasn't a *test*."

"It was a fucking test."

"You've been distant this week," she whines, literally stomping her foot. Just once, but Jesus Christ.

"I've been busy," I say carefully. "You gave me a fucking project, in case you forgot."

"I definitely haven't forgotten," she mutters, looking down briefly before her gaze returns to mine. "If it's taking up too much of your time…" She stops, looking uncharacteristically unsure of herself.

I can feel her wanting to call me off. I doubt it has anything to do with filling my schedule like she wants to claim, but she'd die before admitting it was anything else.

She also knows she risks looking like a human being with actual feelings if she tells me she wants me to stop talking to Aubrey. Vulnerability is unacceptable to Anae. I wait to see if she waivers, but when she meets my gaze again, her shield has slipped into place.

"I could get someone else on it," she finally says.

I shake my head, looking off in the distance. "No."

"No?"

"It won't work. I haven't made much progress. There's no way someone else will make more."

Anae frowns.

This isn't how I wanted to do this, but the opening is here, so I dive in. "You left a lot out when you told me about this girl."

"Like what?"

"Like her mom's dying of cancer," I say, raising my eyebrows.

"Oh. Well, I didn't know that."

"Yeah, well… She's pretty preoccupied right now. You said she doesn't seem to care about high school. I don't think she has time to. Between single-handedly caring for her sick mom, working, and all this other shit, she doesn't have time for some guy."

"Even you?" she says, faintly amused by the idea that I've been outmaneuvered by some little nobody.

My pride doesn't love it so my jaw tightens, but that's the story I have to go with, so I nod tersely. "Even me."

Anae nods like she's considering, but maybe something doesn't add up. "You haven't made *any* progress?"

That might be too big a claim, so I walk it back. "I didn't say *none*, but not as much as I expected to. You probably won't want to hear this because you're intent on hating her, but she also doesn't want to get with your boyfriend. She doesn't like you, but she doesn't want to hurt you. She's not like us, she's an actual good person."

Anae rolls her eyes. "Please."

"She is."

"Good people don't exist. Some are just better at covering up their shittiness."

"All right, well, whatever you want to believe. The point is, she's not going to fuck me as long as we're together, so unless you'd like to break up, I don't really see me getting anywhere with her. It's a waste of time and a much bigger waste of energy. You've done enough to her. Can't you just call it a win at this point and back off?"

Anae regards me carefully. "I'm confused. Is the problem that she has a dying mom to focus on, or that you're my boyfriend?"

"What?"

"Well, you said no one would be able to get anywhere with her because of some sob story situation with her mom. That's why you didn't want me to get another guy on her, right?"

Fuck.

"But now you're saying she won't sleep with you unless we break up. So, either the problem is that it's you, and it makes sense to put someone else on it, or the mom is the issue and she's too distracted to focus on anybody."

I shrug. "I'm not her fucking shrink, Anae. I don't know which obstacle is the biggest. I'm just saying both issues have presented a problem."

She doesn't hide her skepticism.

She waits for me to say something else since this is as close to getting me on the ropes as she's been before.

I don't.

"All right," she says after a minute of hard-eyed mutual silence. "Well, why don't we give it another week? Obviously, I don't want to ask you to devote all your time to this, but if you can't get your dick in her by this time next weekend, we'll regroup and make a different plan."

I see letting it go isn't even on the table, so I shrug and turn toward the pool. "Whatever. Another week is fine with me."

I tug off my shirt and empty my pockets before diving into the pool with Scofield.

We do a few laps so I can show him up, and when he admits I'm faster, I smirk and look around for Anae. I don't see her over by her friends or by the side of the pool with her legs in the water where she usually is.

"Hey," I call out to Mallory.

She looks up from her phone. "Yeah?"

"Where'd Anae go?"

"She had to pee."

"Hey, I want a rematch," Scofield says, swimming up beside me and grabbing onto the edge of the pool. "Best two out of three?"

"You're on."

AFTER A GREAT NIGHT'S SLEEP, Mom and I have breakfast and go for a walk. When we get home, I spot a vase full of flowers on the doorstep that must have been delivered while we were out.

Mom's not feeling well enough today to walk the whole way, so she's in her wheelchair by the time we return home. We don't have a wheelchair ramp, so I roll her into the garage and see if she needs help up the steps.

Once she's safely inside with a nice cold glass of water, I come back out to grab the bouquet of white roses.

There's a card that says, "Sorry for your loss," but no other message, and it isn't signed.

"Who are they from?" Mom asks as I bring them inside the house.

I pocket the card and take the flowers over to the counter. "I'm not sure. Doesn't say."

If not for that weird card, I might have thought they were from Dare. I'm not sure he's a guy who sends flowers, but I don't really know what the alternative could be, either.

Dare.

I haven't talked to him since last night.

It's hard to believe last night even happened. I got so caught up, but I can't believe I sent him that picture.

Or took that call.

God, in the light of day, it's so embarrassing.

But last night… last night, it was so hot.

It's probably a flimsy excuse because I'm sure the flowers aren't from him, but when Mom goes in to take a nap, I plop down on my bed—the scene of the crime—and open the text chain between me and Dare.

Since we finished on the phone, the last text between us is the picture I sent him.

I feel flushed looking at it, so I delete it from the text chain before I type a message. "You didn't by chance send flowers to my house today, did you?"

"Flowers?"

"White roses," I specify just in case this is a playful bit.

"Did they say they were from me?"

"No, they didn't say who they were from. Obviously it wasn't you because you don't know what I'm talking about, so never mind, lol. Maybe one of the nurses sent flowers to Mom and they put the wrong card in or something. I just thought I would ask."

"I bet. Any excuse to text me," he sends back with a wink.

Despite myself, I smile like an idiot, sinking back into the pillows. "No."

"Yes."

"You're too perceptive, has anyone ever told you that?" I ask, not bothering to deny it any further.

I can sense him smirking on the other end. "Actually, yes."

"What are you up to today?" I text back.

"Not much. You?"

"Just hanging out with my mom."

"What time does she go to bed?" he asks.

"The time varies. Why?"

"Because I want to see you tonight, and I figure you'll probably want me to wait until she's in bed."

My heart speeds up. "You want to see me?"

"At your place. In your room."

In my room?

I chew on my bottom lip, debating. I would really like to see him, but I don't usually let people in the house since Mom is sick and we can't risk germs being brought in.

It would probably be safe to keep him in my room, though. I could bring him straight here and close the door. Mom never comes in here anymore.

What will we do?

My mind wanders to bad places, but we can't do anything like that. Last night shouldn't have even happened, but at least it was spontaneous. Tonight would be premeditated. He's asking me to let him come over, I'll have all night to think about it...

"What if I say no?" I ask.

"Why would you say no?" he returns.

"Remember that talk we had about how I don't kiss guys who have girlfriends?"

"Then I won't kiss you," he answers. "On the mouth, anyway."

Oh my god.

That's a more tempting offer than I want it to be, but I can't shake knowing it would be wrong.

"I can't do that, Dare," I text back. "I know last night crossed a line, but I didn't MEAN to cross it, I just... I got caught up. I can't make plans to knowingly do something like that."

"Why not?" he asks.

"Because it's wrong. You're not mine. You're not even single with the possibility of maybe someday being mine. You're in a relationship with someone else, and I don't want to be with someone who will cheat on me anyway."

I type all that, but I don't push send.

I stare at the message, a knot forming in my stomach as I reread it.

I can't send that.

It's the truth, though. A truth I don't want to even think about.

If he'll do it to her, he would do it to me.

Not that him being mine is even an option. He's clearly interested in something on the side with me, but it doesn't seem like he has any plans to actually leave her.

I'm not going to be that person.

Erasing that text, I try again. "You know what went down with my dad, and how much I don't respect him and the woman he left us for. I can't do that to somebody, even Anae."

"This is not remotely that situation," he sends back. "I am not married, and the only illness Anae has is narcissism. It's not fatal."

"I just… I can't. I'm sorry."

"Let me come over. We don't have to do anything sexual, I just want to talk. You told me about your parents' divorce, but I never got to tell you about mine. Besides, I owe you $300. I'll bring it with me tonight."

My brain tells me it's a bad idea, but my damned fool heart is on his side. I *want* him to come over, I just don't want to be a bad person.

He says it won't be sexual, though, so maybe it could be okay.

Just because I don't want to be his mistress doesn't mean I don't want to be his friend. Talking about family stuff is hardly romantic, and he *does* owe me that $300…

"Okay," I type back. "Mom should be in bed around 10:30. Is that too late?"

"Nope. That's perfect. I'll see you then."

———

It's 10:35. I'm standing outside my house, waiting for Dare to get here.

I guess I'm panicking a little, too. I've never snuck a boy over in the middle of the night before. I put Mom to bed about 20 minutes ago, but she might not be asleep yet.

What if she hears him come in?

I feel guilty, and I know that means he shouldn't be here.

Just as I'm thinking about texting him and chickening out, his matte black car comes creeping up the road and turns into my driveway.

He's here.

My heart fills up at the mere sight of his car. I can't see him through the tinted windows, but as soon as he climbs out in a comfy hoodie and jeans, I want to hug him.

Friends hug, right?

It's too murky. I tamp down the instinct and offer a friendly smile instead. "Hey."

He closes the car door and engages the locks before sauntering over to me, a smirk on his handsome face. "Hey back."

I stop short of hugging him, but I do take his hand. "Keep quiet," I say softly, easing the door open so we can slip inside.

"Is your mom a light sleeper?" he asks.

"Not really. I just have a guilty conscience and I don't want to explain you being here."

He chuckles at my honesty. "Got it."

"Do you want a drink or anything?" I whisper.

He shakes his head. "I'm good."

I nod and haul him down the hall toward my bedroom.

The light is off, so I switch it on and back up against the door so he can squeeze past. He does, pausing when he gets in front of me to look me in the eye. My heart drops as he lingers way too close to me.

I wasn't sure how long he would be here, so I decided to go ahead and change into my pajamas so I'd be ready for bed when he leaves. I'm wearing sleep shorts and a tank top with no bra underneath. His gaze rakes over me slowly, letting me know he's noticing.

I'm embarrassed when my nipples harden just because he's looking at them.

Mercifully, he moves into the room without mentioning it.

I close the door quickly, then linger there as he walks around my bedroom, wordlessly surveying the space. He looks at the pictures and bottles of nail polish on my dresser. Glances at the small, square table crammed in the corner and the bookshelf hanging over it.

It's not a big room, so there's not a ton of stuff to look at.

Finally, he walks over and sits on my bed.

His attention returns to me and he pats the mattress beside him. "Come sit."

"I'm okay," I say, my voice a little more high-pitched than I'd like it to be.

Dare smirks. "Are you afraid I'll bite?"

I smile faintly. "Won't you?"

"Possibly. You can try asking me nicely not to, maybe that'll work."

"I like how I have to ask you *nicely* not to do something you shouldn't do to begin with."

He shrugs, leaning back on my bed and gazing at me. "Hey, I don't make the rules."

I cock an eyebrow. "No? Then who does?"

He pretends to consider for a moment, then he says, "Actually, I guess I do."

"What if I ask, but not nicely?" I ask, taking a step closer, but still keeping my distance.

"Then your chances of success drop dramatically."

"I see how it is. You don't play fair."

"That is correct."

I'm still cautious about joining him on the bed, but I guess I can't stand here all night. When I sit down, I make sure there's a little space between us. "I haven't had a boy in my room since I was 14," I tell him. "I might be a little rusty."

His eyebrows rise. "Really? Damn, that's a while."

I shrug, criss-crossing my legs on the bed. "Mom's illness kind of swallowed up all our lives. It was really scary when she was diagnosed. Before that, it never occurred to me I might lose her anytime soon. She's so young, you know? There's so much of my life she should still be here for, and now…" I look down, shaking my head. "I don't know if she will be. Spending all the time I can with her has to take priority. I haven't really had the time to adequately nurture other relationships."

"That must be rough."

This time when I shrug, it's a little more pronounced. I feel myself getting defensive and try to curb it. "It's not ideal for anyone, but it's what you do when bad shit happens, you know? Life can't always be fun and games, sometimes it's hard and people have to make sacrifices."

He nods. "I get it. If my mom got sick, I'd probably drop everything, too."

"Are you and your mom close? I heard about the split, and I know a little about your dad from just… lore, I guess." He cracks a smile. "Other than her being a Bolivian beauty queen, I haven't heard much about your mom."

Dare lies back on the mattress, his legs still hanging over the edge of the bed. "We've always had a pretty good relationship. She moved to Miami after the split. There were some job opportunities for her there, and to be honest, I think she just wanted to get as far away from my father as she could. She wanted me to go with her, but it made the most sense to me to finish out high school here in Baymont."

"What happened, if you don't mind me asking?"

"Same shit that always happens. They'd been together for a long time, but they didn't actually spend much quality time together, so the spark went out. I guess my dad didn't feel special enough, so he found a younger model who wasn't sick of his shit yet and decided to be with her instead."

"Oh. Wow, I… wasn't expecting that."

He smiles faintly. "Yeah, neither were we. Apparently, it wasn't the first time it happened, just the first time he left. Mom told me when I was about 7, he had an affair, but they got past it. Guess she shouldn't have."

"I don't think I could ever get past something like that."

"No?"

I shake my head, then meet his gaze. "Could you?"

"I don't know. I've never been with anyone I liked enough to marry, so it's hard to imagine. Getting married isn't something that's important to me, so if I ever took that step, she'd have to be pretty damn special. If she's so special, it's hard to imagine she's someone who would fuck around on me. But, I guess, assuming I somehow utterly misjudged her character…" He turns his head and looks over at me. "Do I still love her?"

"Yes," I say, since that makes the decision harder.

He nods, considering his next move. "Well, if I still love her, then I have to keep her. I'm disappointed in her choices, but I'm not going to throw away a toy I'm not done playing with just because some other asshole wants it."

I grin, lying back against the pillows. "If you liken your hypothetical wife to a *toy*, I think you're probably right that you're never going to get married."

He smirks. "Hey, she cheated on me. She's gonna be treated like a toy for a while, whether she likes it or not."

I bite down on my bottom lip, trying not to smile at such an awful statement. Part of me finds it kinda sexy, and I don't understand why. "All right, so what do you do then?"

"Well, first, I have to kill the guy."

My eyebrows rise. "Oh."

"Yeah."

"That escalated quickly."

He shrugs. "Has to be done. He knew she was married to me, so he should have known better. No sympathy for dumbasses."

"All right, so first step, murder."

He nods. "Then, once I've bludgeoned her lover to death, I figure she's probably pretty mad at me."

"Seems likely."

"I don't care, though. She made this bed, now we have to lie in it."

"Sure."

"If we're going to move on, we'll need a change of scenery. Life wherever we are clearly isn't going the way it should, so I take her somewhere more remote."

"With no new men for her to cheat with."

He smirks. "Sure, but I'm not really worried about that. If she's such a fucking nympho that I literally can't let her go out in the world, I have concerns about my judgment."

"Maybe you love a really beautiful idiot with no self-control. I'm sure she has other lovely qualities."

"Maybe," he allows. "In that case, I guess I have to build her a tower or something and keep her locked up away from the rest of the world."

"Murder. Imprisonment. Your solutions to marital distress are illegal."

"This is why I shouldn't get married," he tells me.

I crack a smile. "At least not to someone who's going to cheat on you."

"I'll have this talk with her before the wedding so she knows it's not something she should ever do."

"Unless she *wants* her own princess tower, of course."

"Then she should just tell me that, she doesn't need to put us through all this bullshit to get it."

"What an accommodating husband."

"I try."

"All right, so you built her a tower."

"On an island," he adds. "Make sure her little ass can't go anywhere."

"What if she's a mermaid?"

His eyes sparkle with mischief. "Maybe she is. Are you my wife in this scenario?"

I know he's only joking, but my heart sinks. "I... I would never cheat on you, so if I'm the wife, this has all been a big misunderstanding."

"Yeah?" He rolls on his side to look at me, then pushes up to his knees and moves across the bed toward me. "You'd never cheat on me?"

My heart hammers. It feels like it's lodged in my throat as he crawls closer, only stopping when he's straddling me. I try to swallow past the lump, not breaking his gaze as I shake my head to confirm.

"Why?" he asks.

Arousal stirs between my thighs feeling his weight on top of me like this. My words feel thick as they spill out of my mouth. "Because... because that would hurt you, and I wouldn't do that."

He smiles, reaching his hand toward me and stroking my cheek. "You wouldn't hurt me?"

My heart contracts. He's making me feel profoundly vulnerable with his words and his actions. "Not on purpose."

"Because you care about me?"

Needing out of this situation before he does something I don't want him to, I try to drag us back to the playful scenario we were talking about before. "I mean, if I'm your wife, of course I care about you."

He remains on top of me, but allows me to steer us back into safer waters. "Maybe you don't," he suggests, his lips curving up. "Maybe you married me for my money or my connections and it was never about love."

I shake my head, not smiling. "That's not something I would do."

"No?" His hand leaves my face, but it doesn't go far. He drags his fingertips across my collar bone just like he talked about last night on the phone. "Maybe I made you marry me."

My heart stalls and I feel short of breath. "Why would you do something like that?"

He shrugs casually, but it feels misleading. "Maybe you wouldn't stop saying no to me, made me obsessed with you."

Somehow, my heart drops even lower, but arousal stirs between my thighs. "I don't think that's how that works."

His fingers glide lower, tracing the curve of my neckline. "I don't know. I find myself thinking about you an awful lot."

I swallow as he hooks a finger in the thin material of my shirt, caressing my skin just underneath. "You do?"

He nods. "Ever since the night I saved you."

I can't think of anything to say. I'm too focused on how much I want him to keep touching me like this. And how much he shouldn't.

"So, maybe enough got to be enough."

Logically, I know what he's saying is really bad, but it feels so good as his finger dips lower, tracing the curve of my breast. Tingles start between my thighs.

"Maybe I decided to claim you, whether you wanted me

to or not." His finger moves over and under the gentle curve. "Keep you forever. My pretty little plaything." His fingertip grazes my nipple. I gasp, shifting my body in an attempt to move him since he's taking it too far.

"Dare, stop," I say, reaching down to gently remove his hand.

His lips curve up. "Yeah, that's what you said." Rather than stop, his palm closes around my breast and he squeezes. Leaning close, he whispers in my ear, "I didn't listen, though."

That is so fucked up.

I should be repulsed, horrified.

"Dare…"

"Sh," he says, fingering my nipple and making me gasp against his shoulder. He stays on top of me, but shifts his position so he can use his knee to nudge my legs apart.

"Dare," I repeat, more breathless, more conflicted.

He hears me, but ignores me.

"You have to stop," I tell him, meaning it. "I told you I didn't want to do anything like this—"

Before I can finish, his hand covers my mouth. I gasp, startled, but he keeps it there as he teases my nipple and presses his lips against my neck.

Oh, God.

Pleasure dances down my spine as his lips explore the sensitive column. His thumb moves back and forth over my nipple, stoking my fear and arousal in near equal measures. I feel so helpless pinned beneath him, his hand over my mouth so I can't even ask him to stop.

He moves lower, his mouth hungrily claiming my throat. His grip on my mouth is so tight, I'm getting scared. I turn my head to try to break his grip, but it only tightens more.

I don't know if he can feel my panic, but if he can, he doesn't seem to care. He kisses my neck harder, then he bites me as he pinches my nipple. I cry out, but the sound is muffled against his palm.

Is this what it's like to be with him?

It's a little terrifying. Maybe only because of our circumstances, but he isn't listening to me, and I'm not sure what to do.

Tears sting my eyes and I try again to break free. But he doesn't let me. He kisses me harder, his tongue lapping at my skin and soothing the spot he just bit. He's paying my breasts more attention now, squeezing and groping them like he owns me.

"Dare," I cry against his hand. It's muffled, but he knows I'm trying to say his name—or at least say something.

"Sh," he murmurs, roughly kissing his way up my neck and along my jaw. He kisses my face right at the edge of where his hand is sealed over my mouth. It feels like an acknowledgment of my distress, and a deliberate way of letting me know he's not going to move his hand.

I blink rapidly, spreading the moisture gathered at the corners of my eyes.

A tear squeezes out and he sees it.

He cocks his head, lets go of my boob, and catches the tear on the pad of his thumb. He examines it, then looks into my eyes as he puts his thumb into his mouth and licks it off.

My eyes widen, my tummy dropping in mild horror.

Did he just taste my tears?

His lips tug up, a glint of amusement in his deep brown eyes. "Are you scared, mermaid?"

I swallow. I hate admitting it, but I nod my head.

I don't know what he's going to do to me. This is all so fucked up and confusing.

"Good," he says, his eyes darkening with satisfaction. He brushes his thumb across my cheek and my breath hitches. "You should be scared. Next time you think about opening your legs for someone else, remember that you married a madman, and cheating on him is ill-advised."

My eyes widen, my tummy pitching.

He finally moves his hand, his eyes gleaming with dark amusement as he moves off me and falls back onto the pillows beside me.

I can scarcely breathe. My tummy flutters with nerves. It takes me a second to process that I guess he was... playing?

Was he?

It sure didn't feel like he was playing. It felt real. I thought he might actually...

I feel a little shaky, but I also feel dumb if he was just playing the scenario *I* dreamed up in the first place. He was much more committed to the role than I was.

"You okay?" he asks, looking over at me.

I nod, but my stomach feels sick. "Yeah." I force a smile and look over at him. I can still feel his bruising kisses on my neck. "I'm fine."

I tell him I'm fine, but my heart and my body feel so confused.

"Come here," he says.

His tone is almost gentle, more reassuring than I expect from him.

Part of me wants to get off the bed and get away from him, but the overwhelming majority nudges me to do as he says.

I turn until I'm cuddled up against him, his strong arm wrapped around me. I try to relax, closing my eyes and breathing in his scent.

He holds me and strokes my hair.

He's the one who mildly traumatized me in the first place, but he's also my only source of comfort, so I let him pet me and calm me down. Now that I'm not afraid he's going to make me do something I'm not ready for, it's easier to relax.

As I relax, my body grows heavier.

My eyes do, too.

Sleep starts to pull me under.

I tell myself to stay awake, that no matter how comfy I am, I can't fall asleep on him. If I'm that tired, I should tell him to leave, but...

I don't want him to leave, not yet.

I close my eyes, just for a minute.

I only need to rest them. Once I get my second wind, then we can start talking again.

CHAPTER 17
DARE

DARE, *stop.*

Her cry whispers across my memory, making my cock feel like a rod of steel trapped inside my pants.

I scared the living shit out of her, but she's still lying here snuggled up with me, letting me stroke her hair and caress her arm.

I love that she admitted it, too. She didn't pretend to be unbothered. Fear danced in her pretty blue eyes as I touched her, kissed her, held my hand over her mouth and left my mark on her soft skin.

Fuck, I liked that.

It was a lot for her. Whether or not she's a virgin like Anae thought, she definitely hasn't gone a single round with a guy like me.

Her response tells me a lot, though. She didn't launch off the bed the moment she could have, cussing me out and telling me to get the hell out of her house. If she had the stubborn personality I thought she might have that first night, she probably would have.

But no, my mermaid is soft beneath her scales. Life hasn't been easy on her, and she doesn't have a soul to support her as she shoulders burdens no one our age should have to shoulder alone.

That would be enough to toughen anyone up. I'm glad I found her before it got much worse.

Now, she needs to be trained to suit *my* needs.

I won't be as hard on her as life has been.

Or maybe I will, just in different ways.

She has been still and quiet for so long, I wonder if she's still awake. I stop stroking her hair and shift her weight to look at her face. Sure enough, she's asleep.

She's so vulnerable in her sleep.

I watch her face for a moment to make sure she stays asleep, then I slide my hand up under her tank top. Her tits are so fucking soft, I can't get enough of touching them. I watch her face as I gently squeeze and caress her flesh.

She must be tired or a heavy sleeper because she doesn't wake up.

Even though she's asleep, her body knows it's being played with. Her nipple beads, pressing against my palm in a bid for attention.

My cock strains against the fabric of my jeans. I let go of her tit just long enough to reach down and unzip it. Once I've relieved some of the discomfort, I put my hand back, careful not to wake her.

There's something intensely arousing about playing with her vulnerable body when she doesn't know I'm doing it.

She fits perfectly curled against me, her knee over my thigh. I palm her tit and replay the sounds of her moaning on the phone last night in my head, knowing if she were awake —and not being such a pain in the ass about Anae—that's what I'd hear right now.

I think about undressing her, kissing my way down her stomach, licking that pussy I know is already wet for me. I think about plunging my cock into her—she'd wake up, but then what? It would be too late to stop me. Would she just let me keep going, or would she fight me?

I replay that first night by my pool, the way she squirmed and struggled to get away from me. The way my cock reacted.

I eye the little swatch of skin exposed between the hem of her tank top and the top of her sleep shorts. I move my hand down her belly, pushing my fingers past the band of her shorts, but stopping to trace the waistband of her panties across her soft skin.

I glance at her face.

Still asleep.

I'm curious just how heavily she sleeps, how much I could get away with, but I don't know if I should take it that far tonight. Actually, I know I shouldn't, but…

I slide my fingers beneath her panties, my cock aching as my fingertips graze her warm skin. I keep my gaze trained on her face as I touch her. With her knee thrown over mine the way it is, her legs are spread enough to cover her pussy with my whole palm. She's still asleep, but as I lightly drag my fingertip across her hot little slit, she stirs.

I stop moving until I'm sure she's not fully awake. I give her a moment to fall back into a deeper sleep, then I rub at her opening until I can slip my finger inside her.

Fuck, her pussy is hot.

Hot and tight.

I want a taste but I can't risk moving her that much, so I carefully draw my finger out of her panties and suck it into my mouth.

She tastes delicious.

I want more. I want to roll her on her back and eat her pussy while she sleeps, but I'd probably have to drug her to get away with that.

I could wake her up. Even if she doesn't entirely want to, I think I could make her give me a taste. I could fold her body into a position where I could restrain her, hold her hands behind her back with one of mine. Sure, she could call out to her mom for help if she really wanted to, but she wouldn't. With all her mom's health stuff, she wouldn't risk upsetting her.

It shouldn't turn me on to think of making Aubrey helpless and using her against her will when I actually like her, but apparently, that's where we are.

She should just get over not wanting to be an asshole back to Anae, then she could fuck me without reservations and we'd both get what we want.

Because I want to experience that, too. I want her arms wrapped around my neck, her straddling my lap with her bare tits pressed against my chest. I want her leaning against me and breathing me in as she takes my cock into her body.

I want all of it.

I suppose raping her right now might get in the way of ever getting to enjoy that little scenario.

How unfortunate.

If I stay here much longer, I might talk myself out of keeping my eye on the bigger prize, so I do the most sensible thing I can in the moment. I roll Aubrey onto her back, straddling her for just a moment and letting my cock press into her softness.

Her eyes drift open. She's bleary and foggy, maybe a little confused.

I smile reassuringly and lean down to gently kiss her lips. "Go back to sleep," I murmur.

"Hm?" she questions, too sleepy to even kiss me back.

"I'm gonna go home. I'll see you tomorrow at school."

I know she won't even remember talking to me, she's so out of it.

When I'm off the bed, she curls up on her side on top of

the blankets. There's an extra one on the bottom of her bed, so I grab that and drape it over her body, just in case it gets chilly overnight.

Belatedly, I remember to zip my pants back up, then I draw out my wallet. I told her I'd give her the cash I owed her for the picture, so I count out $300 and place it on her nightstand. I look over at her again, considering, then on impulse, I grab another hundred.

She deserves a tip.

I turn off her light on my way out of the bedroom. The house is dark and quiet. I move carefully on my way to the kitchen. The house is old, so the floor creaks.

A stack of bills are tipped over on the counter, spilling onto a grocery store sale ad. I move the ad and see quite a few things circled. Probably her grocery list. On impulse, I grab my phone and take a picture of it.

Next, I examine the flowers in the vase on the counter. No card.

These must be the ones she asked me about.

I don't like the idea that some mystery person sent her flowers, but she said they must be from her mom's nurse or something along those lines. Her mom's sick, so I suppose that could be true.

I step away from the flowers and walk to the fridge, looking for any little hint I might find about her. I expect to find family photos, perhaps a drawing or craft from when she was a little girl. There's one picture of Aubrey and a woman with a scarf on her head, presumably her mother. The older woman resembles Aubrey, but with added stress lines etched into her skin.

Other than that one picture, the refrigerator is covered with old appointment cards, each one with a different specialist's name on it.

EVEN IF IT HURTS   165

No sign of her father. If there ever was, Aubrey erased him.

She holds a grudge.

Then again, I was a complete asshole to her that first night at my house, and she gave me a second chance.

She also said she didn't *think* she could get past her husband cheating on her. With her mother's experience so fresh, she could have said she never would outright and I would have understood.

She doesn't forgive those who abandon her.

I think that's more accurate.

The floor creaks and my gaze darts to the hall. A moment passes and no one emerges from either of the bedrooms, but I had better get out of here so Aubrey doesn't wake up and find me snooping through the remnants of her life.

Before I go, I leave a new appointment card on the counter for her.

I let myself out the front door, but halfway to my car, I can't remember if I locked it. The crime rate is low in Baymont, but even if there's little chance of someone breaking in the one night her door is unlocked, I won't leave her unprotected like that.

I go back to the door and turn the knob. Sure enough, the door opens.

I think about locking it from the inside, but quickly change my mind.

I haven't had an opportunity to test my copy of her house key to make sure it works. I wasn't sure I ever would unless I ended up needing to use it, but now I'm here when they're both asleep, so I might as well try it out.

I draw out my wallet, using a finger to spread the tightest pocket. I tilt the wallet, and the copy I made of Aubrey's house key falls into my palm.

It's shiny and new, a tight fit when I slide it into the lock, but once I've turned it, I try the knob again and the door is locked.

Satisfied, I nod and tuck the key back in my wallet.

I'm a realist, so I can foresee a scenario or two in which I might want into Aubrey's house, but she might not want to *let me* in.

Good to know my key works just in case I ever need to use it.

CHAPTER 18
AUBREY

WHEN MY ALARM goes off the next morning, I wait for the usual dread to sweep over me. Exhaustion, my constant companion, to beg me to stay in bed.

But I actually feel surprisingly well-rested.

I reach for my phone on the nightstand, and when I lift up to grab it, I notice something else.

Money.

That wakes me up the rest of the way. I frown, turning off the alarm and sitting up on the edge of the bed. A bunch of twenties are spread out underneath my charge cord. I grab them and count them out on my lap.

It's $400.

Dare must have put it here before he left.

I feel bad that I fell asleep on him. I didn't even get to say goodbye.

I think about texting him, but I know there's little point. It feels recent to me, but it was last night. Besides, I'll see him at school.

Since I was cuddling with him in the clothes he likely wore out in the world all day, I take a shower and get dressed for the day before I make breakfast.

Mom is awake in her chair in the living room when I come in. The house is quiet, and she has a book open on her lap.

"Good morning, honey," she says.

"Hey." I lean in and kiss her temple before heading to the kitchen. "You want a spinach omelet this morning?"

"Sounds good," she says, closing her book. "Did you leave that appointment card for me on the counter?"

I frown, grabbing a carton of eggs out of the refrigerator. "Appointment card?"

She grabs a little white card off the end table and holds it up. "What is this? Why do you have an appointment card for a doctor in New York?"

"New York?"

I have no idea what she's talking about, so I walk over and grab the card.

I'm well versed in appointment cards at this point, but this one is confusing. It says we have an appointment next Saturday at 2:15—at a cancer center in West Harrison, New York.

"Um... hang on. I need to text someone."

"Aubrey."

Mom's tone is firm, like it used to be on the rare occasion I got in trouble.

I look up at her. "What?"

She's giving me a look. "Why do you have that?"

"I'm not completely sure. It *may* be the doctor a friend was telling me about, but I have to double check."

"Aubrey," Mom says on a sigh.

"I know, Mom. I know you're tired of the doctors and the appointments," I say, walking in to sit on the arm on her chair. "But Dare was telling me this guy helped his mom's friend who they thought was a lost cause. They're up on all the newest research, and they have access to trials maybe we didn't know about. It can't hurt to just *talk* to the guy and see if there's something he can do for you. What if there is?"

"Honey, we can't afford to fly to New York for a consultation. Even if we could, you know how leery I am about flying. All those people crammed in a metal tube in the air, all their germs floating around. I get sick every time I travel on a plane. When I'm in perfect health, that's mildly annoying, but now?"

"Well, yeah, I didn't realize the guy was in New York. He didn't tell me that part. It's possible he just didn't think about it because his family has money, so they could probably fly out for something like this. I'll ask if they have a location we could drive to."

Mom shakes her head. "Honey, I know you meant well, and I'm sure your friend did, too. This is very sweet, and I truly appreciate the effort, but we've already tried *everything*. We've been through all this, and I made the decision to stop for a reason. It wasn't working, and I don't want to spend the rest of my life at doctor's appointments."

"I know, Mom, but what if—?"

"Honey." She places her hand over mine, her eyes sad but resigned.

A lump forms in my throat. "I just don't see how you can pass up—" I stop and try again. "We might not even have to go anywhere. I did ask Dare if he might be able to do a video call. The appointment could be for that and the card only says New York so we know it's New York time."

"Well, if it's a call, I suppose it can't hurt, but I'm not going to let you blow the money we need to live on sending me to some hopeless out-of-state meeting."

I don't argue with her because there's not much time before school, and I don't want to rile her up right before I leave, but I don't want to believe it would be hopeless, either.

I guess that's how I've felt every step of the way, though.

Every time we heard about some new treatment we could try, I thought that would be the one.

And every time, it wasn't.

It's too depressing to think about, so I put it out of my mind. I don't text Dare about it. I'll just ask him about it at school.

It feels like a shitty day as I head down the halls of Baymont High, the books for my first couple of periods held snugly against my chest. I got here early so I could give Hannah her lunch bag back. I forgot all about the recipe, but even if I would've remembered, I'm sure I would still stare at her in open confusion as she held out a basket full of baking supplies.

"What is this?" I ask.

"Everything you need to make the muffins," she says. Her smile dims a bit. "Well, not everything. I couldn't put eggs or butter in the basket or it would have to be refrigerated, but everything else is there."

"That is unbelievably generous. You didn't have to do that."

She shrugs. "No biggie. I have to get to my locker, but if you have any questions about the recipe, just shoot me a DM. I gave you overripe bananas on purpose, by the way. Those work better for things like banana bread or banana muffins."

"Noted. Thanks again, Hannah."

She flashes me a smile and then she's off.

I don't have enough time to go back to my locker and stash the basket before class, so I guess I'm just going to be toting this basket around with me for a while.

If I'd have known, I would have worn my hair in braided

pigtails with a blue checkered dress and ruby red slippers, really gone for the Dorothy look.

I smile faintly, amused by how random I must look walking through the halls with a basket full of baking supplies. I'm just passing the bathrooms on my way to home-room when Mallory steps in front of me.

A frown flickers across her face as she glances at my basket. "What is happening here?"

"On my way to Oz. I'm hoping to find Anae a heart. Might be beyond even the wizard's capabilities, but I'll report back," I tell her.

Shooting me a dry, narrow-eyed look, she says, "That's ironic coming from you."

"Is it?" I frown. "I don't think it's ironic. Maybe you're thinking of a different word."

Taking a step back and gesturing dramatically to the entrance of the girl's bathroom, she says, "Anae would like to speak with you."

My eyebrows rise and I shoot Mallory a doubtful look. "In the bathroom?"

"For privacy," she says primly.

"No thanks."

I take a step forward, but she moves in front of me again. "Believe me, you'll want to see this."

There's a smug confidence in her tone that gives me pause. I glance down the hall, tempted to brush it off and head to class, but it sounds like Anae is up to something. I guess I can spare a minute to pop in and see what she wants.

The queen bee is waiting in front of the sinks wearing a white silk button-down with a tweed skirt and pointy-toed mules. Her secondary minion flanks her while Mallory escorts me. Anae smirks when I walk in, tapping something on her phone screen and then gazing at me like the cat that got the cream.

"What do you want?" I ask her.

"To ruin your day," she says with feigned sweetness. Her brow furrows a bit when she sees the basket I'm carrying, then she seems to recognize it, and she gasps softly. "That little tart. She was making that for you?"

I don't want to get Hannah in trouble. It's clear it was for me if she saw Hannah assembling it this morning and me carrying it now, but I don't bother verifying. "Can you get on with ruining my day? I've got class."

Her eyes are still narrowed with dislike, but she makes a visible effort to shake it off and get back to whatever had her excited. "I guess low-class whores have to stick together." As she says this, her gaze lingers on my neck.

I don't know why until I glance in the mirror and realize, to my utter horror, Dare left bruises on my neck from his bites and rough kisses last night.

I lose a shade of color, but Anae doesn't miss a step. Her heels click as she walks over to stand beside me—odd, in and of itself—then she tilts her phone screen so I can see it.

My heart drops into my stomach when the video she posted on her social media account a minute ago starts playing. It's her and Dare in bed together. He's shirtless. She's wearing a skimpy white top that looks striking against her sunkissed skin. They look gorgeous in what appears to be her bedroom, lying together under the covers. They're both sitting up in bed. It looks like they woke up together and are casually messing around on their phones as they while away the morning. His hair is mussed from sleep and he looks so handsome. He's on his phone, but looks over to find her posing at the camera.

Text pops up on the screen that reads, "When you're in bed with your boyfriend and he tells you about the fugly skank who sent him nudes."

My heart bottoms out of my body completely. She smirks

in the video and he reaches over, his big hand covering the camera. The video then transitions to the photo I sent Dare the other night of me in the panties he bought me with a caption above it reading, "Pathetic."

My heart—and every other organ in my body—seems to halt. My soul rips free and flies away. I can't breathe, and only dimly register the white text she added below reading, "Nice try, Aubrey. The boy is mine."

She added the hashtags #weshareeverything and #couplegoals.

All I can hear is the beating of my heart thrumming in my ears.

She didn't *really* share that picture of me on her social media... right? She's not that evil.

How did she even get it?

Did he give it to her?

The video definitely makes it look like...

I can't breathe.

I reach out blindly and grip the edge of the sink to keep myself standing up. My brain is frozen with horror. Somehow, I get out, "Take that down. Right now."

I know it's too late, that some people will still have seen it, but most people should be on their way to class...

Yeah, walking the halls, playing on their phones.

Oh my god. Everyone is going to see this.

"Anae, I'm serious. Take it down."

"Nope," she says cheerfully, pointing at her phone screen without touching it. "Would you look at that? Already 37 likes."

Oh my god.

Oh my god, oh my god, oh my god.

I feel like throwing up. I'm on the verge of hyperventilating. My heart pounds so hard I can't hear anything else, and I can't think clearly.

She looks over at me, smiling as she drops her phone into her Chanel handbag. "Hey, maybe it'll go viral."

I want to kill her.

I want to grab a fistful of her glossy blonde hair and bang her head against the edge of the sink until she is lying in a bloody heap on the fucking floor.

"Take the video *down*," I tell her, "or I will go to the police."

"No, you won't," she says easily. "Even if you do, I don't care. What's the fine, like a thousand dollars? That's a pair of shoes for me, and a price I would *happily* pay to see this look on your face." She folds her hands together like it's just too darling and looks over at Mallory. "Isn't this a lovely moment? I'm going to treasure it."

I let go of the sink and turn around, making a beeline for the exit.

"Oh, and Aubrey?"

I glance back at her.

She loses her smile, her eyes cool and threatening. "In case you didn't get the message: stay the fuck away from my boyfriend."

Tears blur my vision as I leave the school without going back to my locker for my books. I don't even think to look both ways before crossing the parking lot, but fortunately it's pretty dead since the first class of the day is starting.

My hands tremble as I fish my keys out of my purse and jam the car key into the ignition. I feel too shaky to really trust myself to drive, but I also *have* to get out of here.

While I'm driving home, the horror and humiliation wash over me again and again. I get a couple of messages. One from Hannah that just says, "Oh my god, are you okay??" Another from Janie that says, "Did you really send that picture to Chase Darington?"

I don't answer since I'm driving, but when I finally pull in, I don't answer, either. I don't want to talk to anyone.

Well, no, that's not true.

I sniffle, angrily swiping a tear away from my puffy eyes and grab my phone out of the cup holder. Finding the message chain between me and Dare, I type, "WHAT THE FUCK?"

I push send, sniffle again, then debate what else to say. There's so much, I don't even know where to begin.

I have no clue where he stands on all this.

It's hard to imagine I wouldn't have heard from him right away if he saw the post and was somehow surprised by it. It's hard to imagine how that could even be. How would she have gotten the picture if he didn't give it to her?

And when did she shoot that video? I only sent him the picture Friday night.

Then again, it was late, and he was at her house.

Did he spend the night?

That sick feeling intensifies. I'm almost afraid of him texting me back. I don't know what he'll say, if it will be something that cripples me. I don't know if we'll ever talk again after this.

I don't know if we *should*.

He was a complete asshole that first night. What if that was the real him all along? What if he only started being nice to me to get something incriminating for his girlfriend to humiliate me with?

That's too horrifying to imagine.

Especially because it worked.

I want to block his number and never talk to him again. Maybe I wouldn't get my answers, but at least I wouldn't have to risk finding out the guy I was starting to like was a mirage and I've been alone all along.

I can't do that, though.

I have no clue what's going on with Mom's appointment with that specialist, and if somehow this isn't as bad as it seems to be, I still need to ask him about it.

"How could you show her that picture?" I type. "I trusted you."

Whether he's been playing me or not, that's the truth.

I sit there for a few minutes staring at the screen, hoping I'll see the three little bubbles that mean he's texting me back while dreading it at the same time.

Dare doesn't have read receipts on, so I can't tell if he has seen my messages or not.

Ugh, I hate that.

I don't really want to go in the house because Mom will want to know what's wrong and why I left school, but I can't sit out here in the car all day, either.

While I'm waiting to see if he responds, my gaze catches on something blue in the yard. It looks like a stray piece of litter. I open the door and go over to clean it up, but when I do, I find three more just like it scattered across the lawn.

What the hell?

I look around to see if there are any others, and my gaze catches on the porch. It's littered with messy stacks of pamphlets, like someone took a huge bucket of them and dumped them all over my porch.

I look down at the ones in my hand, identical to the ones on the porch, and that's when it hits me what the pamphlet is for.

A funeral home.

My hand curls into a fist, crumpling the pamphlet. I look toward the door and the flower delivery from yesterday flashes to mind.

My first thought is who would be malicious enough to send me shit like this, but it doesn't take a Rhodes Scholar to connect those dots.

Furious, I gather up as many pamphlets as I can carry and haul them to the trash. They're so scattered I have to make three trips before I get all of them.

Once the yard is clean, I look around to make sure there are no stragglers. The last thing I need is for Mom to find one of these next time she's outside.

That fucking bitch.

I hate Anae Richards so much, I could explode.

I go back to the car to retrieve the books I had on me and the basket from Hannah. I grab my phone, and when it lights up, I see Dare finally texted me back.

Twice.

The first message just says, "What are you talking about?"

The second says. "Fuck. I didn't give her that picture."

"Then how did she get it?" I demand.

"I don't know. She had to have gone through my phone."

"You don't have a pass code?"

"She knows it."

That settles in my gut like a rock. It's the most Anae has ever felt like his girlfriend, and her actually *feeling* like his girlfriend makes what he's been doing with me feel a lot ickier.

My desire to talk this over with him evaporates into thin air. It doesn't matter anymore. The picture is out there now. Even if it gets taken down, people have screenshots.

How will I ever show my face at that school again?

Defeat settles over me and brings numbness with it. It's a relief in a way. After the lows, all the fear and the dread, to feel nothing is better.

"You can cancel the appointment with the specialist in New York," I type back. "My mom won't go. She can't risk getting sick on a plane, and we can't afford the airfare anyway."

"Aubrey, I'm so fucking sorry she got her hands on that

picture. It's my fault she did, but that video is bullshit. She shot it weeks ago, she keeps a bunch of drafts on hand in case she's low on content—or, apparently, she needs to fucking frame me and pretend I did something I didn't."

"It doesn't matter. I never should have sent it. I don't think we should hang out anymore."

"Look, just hang in there, all right? Don't give up on me. This isn't as black and white as it looks right now."

"How?" I ask, hating how sad it makes me feel. "It doesn't matter," I add before he can answer. "I need to focus on my own stuff right now. All of this is a distraction I don't need. I don't even know how I'll show my face at school again knowing how many people have probably seen that video."

"I'll get the video taken down ASAP," he assures me.

"It won't matter. They've all seen it. The ones who haven't will see screenshots. I'm just over it."

"I'll fix this," he tells me.

"You can't fix it. Nobody can. My whole life is a mess no one can fix and I'm sick of it."

Tears burn behind my eyes because I'm not just talking about the picture.

"Thanks for trying," I add. "I'm turning my phone off for a while, so…. Bye."

CHAPTER 19

DARE

ANAE IS on her way to lunch, Mindy and Mallory flanking her, when I come up behind her and grab her by the arm.

Mallory backs away, wide-eyed, and Mindy gasps at the violence with which I grab her.

Anae is not all that surprised, so she turns to face me with a pleasant smile on her face. "Hey, baby. How's your day going?"

"I think you know exactly how my day's going." My grip tightens and I drag her out of the hallway so I can talk to her without an audience.

"Anae," Mallory calls, her concern evident as I haul her friend away.

"Go ahead. I'll catch up," Anae calls back before being yanked into an empty classroom.

I slam the door shut, grab Anae by the throat, and throw her up against it so no one can come in and catch me by surprise.

Startled, she makes a little noise as she struggles to breathe. She grabs at my wrist, silently and instinctively seeking mercy.

"You went through my fucking phone," I state, my voice dangerously low.

Her delicate throat works as she tries to swallow despite the tightness of my grip. Her face is already flushing from the strain, so I ease up just enough for her to explain herself.

"We always go through each other's phones," she manages.

"Not like that. You were looking for something. You went behind my back."

Her eyes rise to meet mine. "You lied to me."

Her expression doesn't change. There's no hurt that I can see, only anger and maybe a little confusion.

I know how vengeful Anae can be over even a small slight, but she knows better than to play those games with me.

I keep my hand around her throat, but I ease up a little more, cognizant of potential bruising. "About what?"

She swallows. "You said you hadn't made much progress with her. I saw your marks all over her neck."

"I put those there when I went to her house last night," I say, hoping it stings to picture me in Aubrey's bed. "You stole that picture out of my phone before then."

"You should be thanking me," she says, trying to take control of the situation.

I release her and take a step back. "Thanking you?"

Anae inches away from the wall, rubbing her neck. "I made your job easier," she goes on. "She hates me even more now. Wait until tomorrow, she'll be begging for your dick just to piss me off."

"What do you have planned tomorrow?"

"It doesn't matter," she says, straightening her shirt collar and meeting my gaze coolly.

"It does fucking matter. Now you're trying to keep things from me. That's not how this works. This was not the plan, and you don't go changing the plan without even consulting me. I'm not one of your fucking minions, Anae. You don't lead, and I follow you around without question. Try to weave your web around me again, and I'm out. And I'll tell you something else, you're taking that goddamn video down before we leave this fucking room or I'll take your phone and do it myself."

Her eyes narrow. "The whole point of all this was to torment her and make her life hell, so I don't know why you're so mad about this stupid video."

"You made me look like a fucking idiot."

"Only to her," Anae states. "No one else thinks your girl-friend went through your phone and put your balls in her purse. The *only* person who could possibly see it that way is Aubrey, and who cares what she thinks?"

She's fucking got me there. The way she did this, she didn't make me look bad. She only made Aubrey look bad.

"She's not going to fuck me now," I state, shaking my head. "She thinks I gave you the picture. She doesn't want anything to do with me."

"She's mad right now. She'll calm down," she says dismis-sively, reaching out and running her hand down my chest. "You'll reassure her that I stole the photo—*which I did*—and you're so sorry, and she's so special to you," she says, rolling her eyes. "Trust me, this won't get in the way of you fucking her."

"You put doubt in her head about me," I state.

"Did I?" She feigns innocence. "Oops."

I push her hand off me. "I don't fucking like that."

"I don't see why it matters," she says, watching me care-fully. "You don't really like her. This is just a game. Right?"

"It matters because you undermined me. You went behind my back, and you kept me in the dark about what you were doing. I didn't even know about the video until *she* texted me about it. What makes you think I want to keep playing games with someone who plays like that, hm? Why shouldn't I say fuck your game and walk away right now?"

"Simple. You want to fuck her. This way, you get to."

Her cockiness pisses me off, and I really want to knock her down a peg. "I don't need to play with you to fuck her, Anae. I can dump you right now, and then I can go fuck her later tonight without any problems. Maybe it'd be nice to be with a girl who doesn't play fucked up games with me for a change."

Anae stiffens. "I wouldn't advise it."

I bet she wouldn't. After the video she posted, getting her ass dumped and me going to Aubrey would make *her* look dumb as fuck.

I smirk. "Doesn't feel so good to be on that side, does it?"

"Look, I'm sorry I went through your phone," she says. "I should have asked, but… you lied to me, and it threw me. I wasn't trying to one-up you or make you feel stupid."

"Bullshit."

"I wasn't," she insists.

"Yes, you were. Don't fucking lie to me. I know how you work. You got it in your head that I might actually like Aubrey and you had to get ahead of it, even if it meant blowing us up in the process."

That actually gets through to her because deep down, she knows that's exactly what happened.

Now that I've landed a hit, I don't let her have a chance to recover.

"You went through my phone like some insecure, basic-ass girlfriend. What the fuck is that, Anae? If I wanted to date a normal girl, I would. I thought you were different."

Because I took a swing at her own idea of herself—*Anae thinks she is supremely different*—I make contact.

She swallows and looks down guiltily. "You're right. I shouldn't have done that."

"I told you I was working on this girl, and I thought we had an understanding that how I went about that was up to me. If I don't do this my own way, I don't do it at all."

"I just… You've been leaving me out," she says. "I thought we were going to do this together. I thought you would tell me things. I don't care if you fuck her, you know I don't care about that, but the secrecy concerned me. It's just not what I expected."

I shake my head, looking off in the distance.

"I'm sorry," she says softly because she knows she stands a better chance at forgiveness if she pouts. Wrapping her arms around me and leaning her head on my shoulder, she asks, "Forgive me?"

I sigh like I have to think about it. "You've gotta delete that fucking video," I tell her, but I'm calm this time. "I told her I'd get it done, and right now, I need to buy some good-will just to get her to talk to me again."

"Fine," she says, easing back and taking her phone out of her handbag. I watch as she opens the app, then I watch her delete the video.

Some of the tension in my shoulders eases. The damage has been done, but at least it won't keep circulating. "Thank you."

She nods and slips her phone back into her bag. "I'll have to make a post and pretend it got taken down for going against community standards or something. What are you doing later? Maybe I can come over, we can shoot something on the beach around sunset."

"Sure. I'll let you know if it changes, but I don't think I have anything pressing tonight."

"Good." She leans in to give me a kiss. "I've gotta catch up with the girls. Let me know if you need anything, though, all right? Even if it's just to bounce ideas. Don't be afraid to talk to me about her. I'm not one of those clingy, jealous girl-friends; I'm happy to brainstorm with you. I'll help you corner her if you need me to, or I guess back off a little if that helps. Just let me know what's going on. If you don't tell me what's happening, I think nothing is, and you know me, I'm a woman of action."

I crack a smile. "Noted. I'll do better at keeping you in the loop from here on out."

"Thank you." She smiles. "That's all I wanted."

I watch her leave and my smile drops.

I'm glad that's handled, but I've still got major fucking damage control to do.

CHAPTER 20
AUBREY

I DON'T TURN my phone on again until late Tuesday morning.

I already told Mom I'm exhausted and need to take a day off from school to get some rest, so I don't have to set an alarm or go to work.

After a while, disconnected from the little rectangle of technology that keeps me constantly threaded into other people's lives, I find peace. It doesn't matter that out there in the world around me is a revealing picture I never wanted anyone to see. Here, in the sanctuary of my house, all is as well as it can be.

That's the reality I need to live in for a while. The one I was living in *before* Anae Richards slithered into my life.

Unfortunately, the moment I turn the phone back on, my peace bubble pops. I never have much action on my social media accounts since I rarely post anything, but today, I have quite a few notifications. Every new comment is some form of insult—body-shaming, name-calling, creative insinuations that I'm an ugly whore. It's a great time.

Once I've deleted all the comments on my various socials, I go to my text messages. I'm already feeling icky from all the social media hate, and then I see I have a text from Dare, and that makes me kinda sad.

"She took the video down."

The text gives me a small measure of relief, but considering all the hate I've deleted this morning, I know a lot of people already saw it—or maybe heard about it after it was taken down. Either way, the information (and the screenshots) are out there, and there's nothing that can be done about it.

"Thanks," I text back even though he sent it yesterday.

He texts right back. "How are you doing?"

"I'm great. Never been better. Someone wrote me a haiku! Want to read it?"

Without giving him time to answer, I paste in the creative insult someone anonymous internet person left on one of my photos last night.

Aubrey
By: Anonymous

A busy morning,
a nasty whorebag who sucks,
Her ass is ugly.

"Wow," he texts back.

"Right? That's an impressive amount of effort to put into an insult."

"That's what happens when you go to the smart school."

Reluctantly, I crack a smile—the first one since all this crap happened.

He texts again before I can respond. "Want me to find 'em and beat 'em up for you?"

"Maybe. You can dunk their head in a toilet and give them a swirly."

"Hang them up on the flagpole outside the school," he adds. "Someone's gotta punish them for telling lies like that about your ass."

"But will you write them a clapback haiku for me? I feel that's the true test."

"I'm not much of a poet, but I'll get my team of nerds on it, have them make a whole slew of haikus."

I laugh. "You and your nerd army."

"At your command, my queen," he shoots back.

My smile fades a bit, but my tummy feels fluttery. "I'm not your queen," I type back, surprised by how sad it makes me feel.

"You wanna be my princess? I can build you a tower to get you away from all these haiku-writing fiends."

"On your prison island?"

"Naturally."

"Maybe. Are you coming with me? Can we bring my mom? Are there restaurants? I have a lot of questions."

Mom's voice startles me and I nearly drop my phone. "What are you smiling at?"

"Nothing," I say guiltily, fumbling to text back a quick, "gotta go," to Dare. Returning my attention to Mom, I flash a smile and hope she doesn't ask more questions. "You ready for brunch?"

She nods, but her gaze lingers on my phone. "Who were you talking to?"

"No one."

Her lips tug up. "So, Chase Darington."

"No? What? I mean, yeah, but why—"

Shit.

I abandon this sinking ship of a denial and stand. "I'm going to make French toast."

It's evening before I get a chance to get on my phone again. Usually, I'm on it off and on, but since I know the phone brings only misery today, it's easy to leave it alone.

I have some new notifications, two comments calling me a whore and a slut which I promptly delete, and two new text messages.

I open the one from Dare first. It reads, "What are you doing tonight?"

"Just hanging out at home with Mom," I answer, even though it has been a couple of hours since he sent it. "You?"

He doesn't respond right away this time, so I close that message and go to the other one. It's from a number I don't have saved in my phone.

There are actually three texts. The first is a link, the second is a message, and the third appears to be a video.

I read the message first. "Hope this doesn't happen to your mom."

I frown, then I click the link.

My frown deepens as I read the headline and first few lines of the article to realize it's a news story about a morgue employee who was discovered having sex with one of the corpses in his care.

Nausea grips me, but I ignore it and the warning not to and click the video.

It shows a man in a white uniform running his hand up the motionless leg of a woman on a metal table, then touching her bare belly. It cuts to a new scene and the sounds of metallic creaking blare out of my phone. Startled and sickened at the same time, I silence my phone, but I can't look away from the horrifying video of a morgue-worker raping a corpse with my mother's face photoshopped onto it.

I throw the phone across the counter without thought, just wanting to get it away from me. The video is still playing, so once I'm sure I won't throw up, I grab my phone and turn it off.

What the actual fuck?

Furious and sick to my stomach, I try to think what to do. I don't know. My hands are shaking. I don't want the video in my phone, but I save it and send it to Dare with the message, "Did Anae send this to me?"

I can't believe *anyone* would send that to *anybody*, but I don't know who else dislikes me enough to do something not only so cruel, but so fucking disgusting.

I was in the middle of preparing dinner, but I'm no longer hungry. I brace myself on the edge of the counter, closing my eyes and trying to keep down the bile.

I go back to the message and take a screenshot of the number before I block it. It's not Anae's number, but when I open the browser on my phone and try to look it up, it registers as a mobile number in Baymont, CA. Not exactly helpful.

On second thought, I unblock the number and call it.

No one answers, and the automated voicemail gives me no clue as to who it is. I leave a voice mail anyway because I'm angry. "You are a sick fuck and you deserve to die alone."

I end the call and put down the phone, my heart hammering in my chest.

CHAPTER 21

DARE

"WHAT THE FUCK IS THIS?"

Anae is lounging by the pool at her house, her long blonde hair pulled up in a ponytail, and a pair of Chanel sunglasses on her face as she reads a book for school.

She glances over at me, then down at the fucked up video I'm watching on my phone. "Cinematic genius," she offers.

"Was this you?"

She shrugs daintily. "Maybe."

"Are you insane?"

"I made sure it couldn't be traced back to me," she assures me. "I told you before, the school stuff didn't seem to be penetrating her skin, but when you told me about her mom, I realized I just needed to attack from a different angle."

I shake my head, not even knowing what to type back. "Don't do shit like this anymore. You delegated her to me. I'll handle her. You calm the fuck down."

Anae pouts. "But it's fun."

"Did you write that fucking haiku, too?"

Her frown is legit. "Haiku?"

I shake my head, looking down at the phone. "Never mind."

I have a few of my most trusted nerd soldiers investigating who's behind the haiku, but I haven't heard anything yet. I'm kind of glad it wasn't Anae.

Deleting the video off the chain of messages, I tell her, "Don't taunt her about her dying mom anymore. That's low, even for you."

"Oh, come *on*," she says as if I'm being unreasonable. "She deserves it."

"Does she?" I look over at her. "You never even told me what provoked all this?"

It must be something stupid because she shifts in the seat, adjusts her tits to try and distract me, and looks out at the shimmering pool water. "I told you, she crossed me. It doesn't matter what it was, she was snotty to me and she needs to learn her place."

"Seems a lot of energy to expend on someone who seems perfectly nice to me. Are you sure you're not overreacting?"

"It doesn't matter," she states. "She's on my shit list, and that's that."

I shake my head and text back Aubrey to let her know Anae is definitely capable of something like that. She may not seem like a techie, but over the years of airbrushing imperfections out of her photos and her life, she's become pretty technologically adept. The Photoshop job in the video was crude as hell, but it was supposed to be.

"There you are. I need another drink," Anae says, grabbing her empty glass off the end table and holding it out as if a maid just appeared on the scene.

I look up and see Hannah Dupont in a blue one-piece swimsuit with a towel draped over her arm. She averts her gaze when we inadvertently make eye contact.

"I didn't know you guys were out here. I was just going to go for a swim."

Anae shakes the glass. "Swim all you want, just get me a drink first."

Hannah is awkward with the towel, starting to drape it around her shoulders, then clearly considering her waist. I smirk because it seems like my presence is making her uncomfortable. She turns around and disappears inside the house without a word.

Anae scoffs. "She's so fucking useless, I swear to God."

Annoyed, she puts her empty glass back down and resentfully resumes reading her book. Hannah comes back out a couple of minutes later to get it. She's wearing a bathing suit cover that does what the towel didn't—hides her from me.

She takes Anae's glass and glances at my bare chest in passing, but doesn't look me in the eye. "Do you need anything?"

I shake my head slowly. "I'm good."

She nods and heads in the house to get Anae a refill.

Curious, I wait a moment so it's not obvious I'm going after her, then I tell Anae I have to piss, and I head inside the house.

This is the girl my mermaid didn't want me to notice. I suppose I can see why. Hannah Dupont is a pretty nice package. She's short, probably only about 5'2", but her body is top tier, she's got this soft blonde hair you want to reach out and touch, and most puzzling of all, she's kind. I'm not talking the type of kind where she makes inspirational social media posts to cast a certain image—she's truly, deeply kind-hearted and just seems to have a gentle soul.

Seems to me, a soul as gentle as hers would be too easy to tear apart. She doesn't interest me, personally, but I can see why Aubrey likes her.

"Hey."

Hannah jumps, startled, and looks back at me over her shoulder.

I stop behind her at the kitchen counter.

I can feel how nervous that makes her.

"Hey," she says, her tone light, but tension lying just beneath the surface. "Did you change your mind about that drink?"

"No. I'm not thirsty."

"Okay." Since I've told her I don't want what she offered, she sets about ignoring my presence and walks over to the refrigerator.

I lean a hip against the kitchen counter and watch her. "You're friends with Aubrey, aren't you?"

She looks vaguely annoyed at me for asking. "Yes. New friends, we haven't known each other for very long."

I cross my arms. "What do you think about that video Anae posted?"

Hannah sighs, reaching for a pink straw from a tube of them on the back of the counter. "I think you're very cruel to drag Aubrey into Anae's path when you know what she's capable of."

That's fair. I smile faintly. "You don't like me much, do you?"

"If I'm making a list of my favorite humans, you're not on it," she answers.

My smile widens. "Even your 'fuck yous' are nice. I like that. You can keep being her friend."

"Ugh." Hannah rolls her eyes. "Thank you *so* much for your permission, King Dare."

"Has she talked to you about me?"

"If she did, I wouldn't tell you."

I smirk. "All right, then." I push off the counter. "Well, it sure was nice talking to you, Hannah."

She shoots me a look before I walk away, but doesn't bother returning the polite nicety.

CHAPTER 22

AUBREY

I'M CURLED up in bed, unable to sleep because I'm dreading the alarm going off so much, when I hear a tapping noise on my window.

It's a soft tapping, but there's nothing close to my window that should blow against it. Fear creeps up on me as I look over at the glass. It's dark out there, but it's dark in here, too, so I can see the shadowy silhouette of a man standing there.

My heart leaps, but then he moves and I realize it's only Dare.

Relief floods my system. I throw back my blankets and climb out of bed.

I can't remember the last time I opened this window. Maybe never. I turn the lock and lift it up, gazing at him with an expectant look on my face. "May I help you?"

"You sure can. You can move so I can climb inside."

I smile faintly, taking a step back. "Didn't I tell you I didn't think we should hang out anymore?"

"Yeah," he says, climbing in the window. "But I decided that wasn't going to work for me. Why should we let a few haters stop us from enjoying each other's company?"

"It's not the haters I'm worried about," I say dryly. "Your

girlfriend is a total psycho who may or may not have sent me necrophilia porn."

"That is pretty weird when you put it that way," he says. "It wasn't porn, though, if it makes you feel any better."

I stare at him.

He closes my window, locks it, then turns around to face me. "I nosed around on her laptop while I was over there earlier. It was a clip from some fucked up Spanish film called *The Corpse of Anna Fritz*. We should watch it. Looked fucking nuts."

I blink at him. "No thanks."

He shrugs. "All right. We'll do something else, then."

"I was just about to go to bed."

He smirks. "I like that plan."

"Alone," I specify.

"I like that much less." He walks over to my dresser, casually running a hand along the surface. "I saw your friend Hannah earlier."

I tense. "Oh?"

He nods, flicking a glance at me. "She's Anae's stepsister, so they live in the same house."

"Right." I lick my lips. "Um… Did you guys talk, or…?"

He nods again, looking at an old picture of me and Janie propped up against the mirror. "I asked her what she thought of that video."

"Oh." My heart thuds in my chest. I never messaged Hannah back when she asked if I was okay. I was too mortified, and some part of me wasn't sure if she would be on my side once she knew I sent a picture like that to her stepsister's boyfriend—even if they don't get along. "What did she say?"

"That I'm an asshole for dragging you into Anae's path." He smiles faintly, turning to face me. "She didn't use that word. She used something nicer. Cruel, I think it was."

I crack a smile. "I'm not sure if cruel is any nicer than asshole."

He shrugs. "Not the first time I've heard it. Won't be the last."

His footsteps are slow and deliberate as he meets my gaze and closes the distance between us.

My heart speeds up. Butterflies scatter in my tummy as he moves so close, I have to look up to hold his gaze.

He smiles, and my heart drops free from its cage.

His hand moves toward me, and then he's stroking my jaw, causing gooseflesh to erupt all over my body. "Do you think I'm cruel, mermaid?"

Entranced, I shake my head.

"No?" His voice is low, intimate, but confident in a strange way.

He knows he's taken control of me.

He knows he's my body's conductor, orchestrating every flutter, every beat of my pounding heart.

It's impossible not to think about how we're in my bedroom alone, in the dark.

I lick my lips. They're suddenly so dry, I wish I had some water.

"You haven't been cruel to me," I say.

He shakes his head, his thumb stilling on my face. He slides it over and grazes my bottom lip, sending a thrill straight through me. "No," he says. "I don't want to be cruel to you."

He dips his head. My heart thunders. His lips meet mine, and it's like I'm not even breathing my own air anymore. I'm melded to him as he pulls me against him, holding my body close and backing me toward the bed.

I kiss him back, but I keep my hands to myself. It's the hardest thing in the world when I want to touch him. I want to slide my arms around his waist and hug him, or wind an arm around his neck to pull myself up to his height.

Because I don't, he breaks the kiss and looks down at me, his eyes slightly narrowed.

I don't want the trouble that comes with him, but I can't deny wanting *him*.

"Get on the bed."

My heart drops at his command.

I back up until the backs of my legs hit the soft material of my bedding, then I sit down and scoot back toward the middle.

Dare walks to the edge of the bed and looks at me, then he pulls off his hoodie.

I'm frozen as the T-shirt underneath rides up a little to show a swatch of his toned abdomen. The tease makes my body warm, but then he reaches back, grabs the T-shirt, and pulls it off, too.

Oh my god.

Tension gathers between my thighs. I shift awkwardly on the bed, unsure where to look. I want to look away because it feels somehow rude to stare, but he's *so* beautiful. His eyes are dark and hooded, his body a work of absolute perfection. His chest is smooth and muscled, his abs cut like he belongs on the cover of a fitness magazine. He's too beautiful to be real, and far too beautiful to be here, in my bedroom.

He looks at me as he reaches for the button on his black jeans.

I'm not sure if I should say something or wait and see what he does. I didn't even really say he could be here, let alone undress in my bedroom.

"Can I tell you a secret, Aubrey?"

I nod.

He pulls down his zipper. "The first time you turned me

on was the night you nearly drowned. When I was holding you in my lap and you were struggling to get away from me."

My heart beats in my throat.

"Is that fucked up?" he asks, letting go of the zipper.

I shake my head. "I don't think so. I was moving around on your lap, so your body probably got confused."

He shakes his head slowly, kicking off his white sneakers. "No, I wasn't confused."

"Oh. Okay," I say, unsure how to respond to that.

I suck in a breath as he pushes the jeans down past his hips, then steps out of them and stands there in just a pair of stark white boxer briefs.

Holy shit.

Finally, he climbs on the bed. He comes toward me and I don't know what to do, so I start to scoot away to make room for him.

Quick as lightning, he grabs my hips and drags me down, forcing me on my back on the bed. I gasp as he climbs on top of me, straddling me, then braces his hands on the mattress and looks down at me.

The dark look in his eyes makes it hard to breathe.

"It was the struggle I liked."

My eyes widen.

"I liked that you were trying to get away from me and I wouldn't let you."

I try to swallow, but my throat doesn't seem to be working.

"And when we were playing the other night? I liked when you were afraid."

He uses the side of his finger to trace the curve of my face. I stiffen at the contact. I don't mean to, it's just the stuff he's saying... I'm not sure how to take it.

He smiles, but there's a devious tilt to it. "You're afraid right now, and I like that, too."

I lick my lips, but it's pointless. My mouth is so dry. "I'm not afraid."

He leans down, putting his full weight on me and resting his forearms on either side of my head. "You're not?"

He looks so serious.

"I think you're messing with me," I say, my heart pounding in my throat.

He laughs softly, looking down. "Maybe I am." Then he looks back into my eyes, his smile dissipating. "But what if I'm not?"

I don't know.

Why would he like to scare me?

"Anae thinks I'm too dark for you," he says.

I hate that he's bringing her up right now, but I'm more confused by the *way* he's bringing her up—as if they've discussed the possibility of a relationship between us. That's insane. No one talks to their girlfriend about other girls they're interested in.

"What do you think?" he asks.

"I… I think Anae and I probably wouldn't agree on much."

He nods. "It's true. You're nothing alike."

"Do you like to scare her?"

He smirks and shakes his head. "Anae doesn't get scared. Not of things like this, anyway."

"Oh." I hesitate. "Do you like that?"

He shakes his head. "Not particularly."

"Do you like me?"

He smiles, shifting his weight to one hand so he can thread his fingers through my hair and cup the side of my head. "Very much." His thumb strokes my face, a devilish glint dancing in his eyes. "Do you like *me*?"

My heart fills to bursting at his teasing. My brain tells me to hold my tongue, that I'm being lulled into a false sense of comfort and he doesn't need verification of what he already knows, that I'm signing a contract I can't fulfill, but I can't look into those beautiful eyes of his and say anything but the truth. "More than I want to," I admit.

"Good."

He leans in and kisses me again, and this time, it's impossible to hold back. I wrap my legs around his waist, buzzing as the weight of him comes to rest between my legs. My hand slides along his hard jaw to his neck. He shifts, and I gasp against his lips as I feel his cock pressed between my thighs.

"Do you feel what you do to me?" he asks roughly before biting at my bottom lip. His hand covers my boob and he squeezes, triggering a whole new wave of arousal between my thighs.

"Dare," I gasp.

He pulls his mouth from mine, and I feel bereft immediately. My fingers sink into his dark hair as he slides down my body, kissing and sucking my tender flesh as he works on getting my shirt off. I lift my arms, letting him pull it over my head. He tosses it on the floor, then he's back up and kissing me again.

I was wearing pajamas, so I don't have a bra on underneath. His hand covers the soft globe and he squeezes it again, kissing me harder, bruising my lips.

My hand slides down his chest to his flat stomach, then lower until I reach the top of his boxer briefs. I'm curious, but not brave enough to go past the fabric.

"You wanna feel me?" he murmurs against my lips.

I shouldn't, but I nod.

He reaches down to grab my hand. My chest feels thick and tight. I hate the feeling, but I like it, too. With his big hand around mine, he guides my palm down until I'm cupping his hard-on through the fabric.

I can't believe this is happening.

My fingers curl around him, and he groans. My gaze shoots to his face. It definitely seems like he liked it, so I caress him a little more.

It's addictive, not just the feel of him in my hand, but the sight of the taut muscles in his neck as I touch him.

I'm doing that to him.

I want to do it more.

This time as I stroke his dick through the fabric, I tilt my head and kiss his neck. I kiss right where the tension is, trying to absorb it from him. His fingers rake through my hair as I make love to his neck.

"That's good, baby. I like that," he says. "Now, reach inside. I want to feel your hand on my skin."

I want that, too. I'm still a little nervous, but emboldened by the response I've already gotten. I want to make him feel good.

My hand slides beneath the fabric, my palm caressing his warm skin. I curl my fingers around his cock and look up at him, watching his eyes close as I touch him.

I love this.

He kisses me hard on the mouth as I feel my way around his cock, then he drops his head and kisses lower, across my clavicle and my chest. He stops to squeeze and caress my boob, flattening his palm against it and catching the nipple between his fingers. A noise slips out of me as he squeezes the taut peak, then lets go and slides his hand down between my legs.

My sleep shorts fit loose and he pushes right past my panties. I gasp, arching off the bed, as his finger presses into me.

"Relax," he says, pushing his finger deeper.

He pushes so deep it starts to hurt. I squirm, trying to get him to stop without verbalizing it.

His gaze drifts back to mine. "You're a virgin, aren't you?"

I nod, my face flushed.

"Sh, it's okay," he murmurs, kissing my forehead, then my brow. His lips drift lower and he kisses my face all over, making me smile until I hear the words he murmurs. "I'm gonna hurt you."

My smile drops and so does my stomach. I look up at him, unable to keep a glint of fear out of my eyes. "What?"

"Because you're a virgin," he specifies. "Not on purpose."

"Oh." My heart flutters. He says it like it's a foregone conclusion that we're going to do this, and I guess... I mean, I do want him, but I haven't even had time to think about this. I didn't even invite him to come over tonight. I was trying to go to sleep.

He doesn't give me time to consider, either.

He withdraws his hand and sits back on his legs, dragging my sleep shorts and panties off me.

I'm shy about him seeing me completely naked, so as he's turning to toss them off the bed, I climb under the covers.

He's amused when he realizes what I've done. "Are you hiding from me?" he teases.

I bite down on my bottom lip, bunching up the soft blanket in my hand and covering myself with it.

He shakes his head, then drags off his own underwear and tosses them.

Chase Darington is completely naked in my bed.

His muscles flex, emphasizing his physical perfection as he moves the covers aside and climbs under them with me. Mercifully, he pulls them back over us once he's settled between my thighs.

"You okay?" he asks, watching me carefully.

I nod, my heart still hammering. "I just wasn't expecting this tonight."

"Is that why you're hiding from me?"

"I'm not hiding from you, I just..." The mean comments

about the picture resurface, creating doubt where he had wiped it away the night I took that picture.

Worse, the pictures I saw of Anae on her social media account play across my mind. Maybe I haven't seen her naked, but I've seen her in a bikini. I know she's completely perfect, and she's the one he's used to seeing naked.

Nobody would make mean comments about her butt.

He slides a stray strand of hair off my face and asks, "Seriously, what is it?"

I feel like such an idiot saying it, but… "That haiku."

He frowns.

"It's so stupid. I know it's stupid. Who cares what some random internet troll says about my butt."

His face freezes like he can't believe what he just heard. "Are you kidding me?" His hand slides up my thigh and cups my butt. "This ass? This *perfect* ass?"

I throw my head back into the pillows, smiling helplessly. "The poet hates it."

"The poet is a fucking moron and is probably jealous of you, let's be honest. He or she wishes I wanted *their* shitty nudes, and I don't. I only want yours."

I'm grinning helplessly, but his last words dig in deep and plant hooks in my heart. "Only mine?" I ask softly, pushing my fingers through his hair.

"Only yours," he promises.

"You're not just saying that to be nice?"

He smirks and gives me a kiss. "I'm not nice," he tells me.

Tenderness fills me as I caress the side of his face. "You're nice to me."

"Sh." He presses his finger to my lips, reminding me, "That was supposed to be our little secret."

If I do this, will *I* be *his* little secret?

The thought whispers across my mind, but I don't have time to entertain it.

Dare grabs something off the bed, something I didn't notice before.

A square, foil packet.

Chase Darington is naked in my bed, on top of me, holding a condom.

He doesn't ask if I'm ready or if I even want to.

Instead, he rips the packet open with his teeth, takes the little rubber ring out, and reaches down to slide it over his dick.

Ready or not, here we go.

CHAPTER 23
AUBREY

MY BODY TENSES as Dare positions himself between my thighs.

I loved kissing and touching, but this part I'm afraid of. It could hurt, physically and emotionally because the man between my thighs about to take what doesn't belong to him doesn't belong to *me*.

Only a fool would let him do this.

"Dare, wait," I say softly, pushing against his chest and looking down where our pelvises are pressed together. "I think maybe we're moving too fast. I mean, I know we are. This is—"

He covers my mouth before I can say another word.

Fear shoots through my veins, a reminder of the other night when he held his hand over my mouth and touched me even though I wasn't sure he should.

He wouldn't do that with my virginity… right?

I'm not sure, and I can't tell looking up into his face. It's intense, but strangely blank. Maybe shielded is a better word. I don't know, but I want to fix it, so I do the only thing that springs to mind.

I kiss his palm. He watches me. I watch him back. I kiss

the hand covering my mouth again, and then I turn my head and kiss his fingers, offering tenderness instead of resistance.

It works. His grip on my mouth eases. Figuring he must like what I'm doing, I keep kissing him. I kiss his wrist softly, then kiss his corded forearm. He has exceedingly sexy arms with prominent veins and sunkissed skin. He's so beautiful, it's easy to worship him. Natural, even.

I feel like I've narrowly escaped some kind of danger, but I don't know if it's true. Maybe there never was danger, or maybe there is and I'm not free of it. All I know is when he reaches out and grabs me by the throat, I don't fight him, and I don't resist.

He watches my face, waiting for a reaction.

His grip isn't painful, just controlling. It's not enough to demand entrance to my body—he needs to control my breathing, too.

I think it pleases him that I don't fight, but I've never been grabbed by the throat before, so I'm not sure how I'm supposed to react.

He keeps his hand where it is and leans down to taste my lips. That's the only way to put it. It's not a kiss, it's a tasting. I don't partake, I just sit here with my heart beating wildly in my chest as he samples me.

"Delicious," he murmurs against my skin when he's finished.

He's in control here. That's the way he wants it, and I let him have it, keeping my doubts to myself as he reaches down and guides his cock back to my entrance.

He slips just the head of his cock into my slick pussy. My tummy tenses with nerves, my brain still reeling a bit that this is actually happening.

He pushes deeper until his cock comes up against that same fragile barrier his finger hit when he was exploring me with his hand.

His grip on my throat shifts to a tender caress. "It's okay," he says, his sure tone a salve on my frazzled nerves. "You don't have to be scared. I won't make it hurt more than it has to."

It feels like that could apply to our whole relationship.

Deep down, I know this is a bad idea, but as his cock nudges the last barrier of resistance, I don't ask him to stop. I brace my hands on his muscular arm and his shoulder. I tell myself to relax because tensing can only increase my discomfort.

He pushes forward, and I feel a twinge as my body stretches to accommodate him. My grip on him tightening seems to alert him to the discomfort because he stops.

"I'm sorry," I say. "It just…"

"Shh." He leans down, softly pressing his lips against mine to reassure me—or to silence me. I guess I'm not sure.

Then, with one brutal plunge, he breaks through. I cry out in surprise and pain, but he muffles the sound, capturing my mouth and catching my cry in his.

"It's over now," he assures me, pulling back slightly, then easing forward much more quickly. "Oh, fuck," he groans, throwing his head back as he forces himself all the way into me.

At least I think he's all the way in. My body is tight and resisting the invasion, trying to squeeze him back out. It's no match for his will, though. He shoves deep every time it tries to expel him, filling me in a way I never knew was possible.

It still hurts as his thick cock moves through the tight channel, but as he moves inside me, it starts to hurt a little less.

He lets go of my throat to reposition, then leans over me and kisses my mouth, murmuring, "Do you know how fucking good your pussy is, Aubrey?"

My heart thrills at his words.

"Fuck, I could stay inside you all day." He pulls his hips back, then drives forward. "So fucking hot. So fucking tight. You're so fucking wet for me. Christ."

I can definitely feel how tight a fit he is. It continues to hurt a little every time he drives his cock in, impaling me so hard and so deep, I can feel the force of the impact in my guts.

I love the sound of his skin as it collides with mine, though. I even like the twinges of pain when he throws his head back and closes his eyes as his cock fills me to the hilt.

I love being full of him, even if it hurts.

His thrusts are so hard and so relentless I'm sure I'll be sore tomorrow. It's like he's trying to leave a mark on me, and remembering the way he bit and kissed my neck before, maybe he is.

I don't know. I don't know how sex is supposed to be.

He grabs my throat after a while, his beautiful body coated in perspiration. He looks down at me with a dark look in his eye that momentarily terrifies me, but then it's gone and his grip eases, and I try to shake the feeling of having been in danger.

He slides his hand down between our bodies, pressing a finger inside me while he continues to fuck me. I gasp as he curls his finger and it brushes my sensitive clit. A whole new wave of sensation rolls over me as he teases my clit and pounds his cock into me at the same time. I feel wild and desperate, grabbing his sides and arching off the bed.

"Dare," I say on a gasp as his finger on my clit works actual magic.

I don't know if it's the blood rushing through my body or what, but my vision fades out and I can feel pressure every-where—in my body, in my head, between my thighs. It's worst between my thighs. I can feel him working me up to a fever pitch, and when I come, it's hard not to scream. I start to, but Dare pushes me into his shoulder. It's an insane thing to do and I don't mean to, but I bite his shoulder as the pleasure shudders through my body in waves.

"Oh, Christ, Aubrey." He drives deep and groans as my pussy convulses around him, squeezing even tighter and triggering his own release.

I go limp, but he's still holding me off the bed, pulled tightly against his slick chest.

He lets me down gently, then drops his full weight on top of me, burying his face in the crook of my neck.

Happiness and affection float around me like bubbles in a warm, comforting bath. I wrap my arms around him and hold on tight while my racing heart slows to a more normal pace.

This is the best feeling in the world.

I love having him in my arms like this, both of us sated from our bodies being joined together. It's not until I realize I left a mark when I bit him on his shoulder that even a single bubble pops.

"Crap. I'm sorry, I didn't mean to do that," I say, stroking the mark with my fingers.

He shifts to look over at his shoulder and smirks before relaxing against me again. "That little nibble? Next time, bite me harder."

I'm startled, so I laugh. We're tangled together so I can feel him all over me, my laugh reverberating through him as well.

If this is physical intimacy, I love it.

A bit lazily, I turn my head so I can kiss him. I know he's tired. So am I, but I want kisses. He happily obliges, tangling a hand in my hair and pulling me close as he kisses me. It's tender and raw, and I don't know how I'm just finding out about this.

I feel too many lovey feelings I have to keep in, but I'm sure it's just the hit of oxytocin. I'm rational enough to know I need to keep my mouth shut and just enjoy the high.

When we're able to move again, Dare moves off me, but I almost don't want him to. I love the feeling of his weight pressed against me, and I want to keep cuddling.

Thankfully, he doesn't go far. He grabs a tissue off the end table and pulls the condom off his dick, then he curls right back up in bed with me. He rolls on his side, pulling me close and settling his arm around my waist.

"You're mine now," he says, tone thick and deep and gravelly enough to make my heart skip a beat. "No one's going to take you from me."

I don't know why his words make my heart sink. They're nice… aren't they?

They are, but at the same time, they're odd.

Maybe it's just our situation.

Maybe it's the things I don't want to think about, like the fact that he has a girlfriend who isn't me.

I definitely don't like that, and as much as I enjoyed having sex with him, my brain reminds me that's exactly why this was a bad idea.

Crushing on him and not wanting to admit it to myself when I knew he was with Anae was one thing.

How much worse will it be now?

There are things I haven't had to think about before, things I've deliberately not thought about when they popped up in my mind because I told myself there was no reason to. Yeah, he kissed me. Yes, he touched me in my bedroom. Yes, I sent him that picture, but all of those things… they weren't quite this.

Now I've slept with him, and that opens up a whole new world of worries.

I don't want the guy I'm sleeping with to sleep with anyone else.

I know I risk making big waves if I bring it up, especially right now. I know it's quick, and we haven't even made any concrete commitments to each other, but he *did* just say I'm his.

"Dare?"

"Yeah?"

I don't know if I'm relieved or not that he's still awake.

"Are you mine, too?" I whisper.

His arm around my waist tightens. "Of course."

He says it easily, like it's a given.

I don't think it is, so maybe he doesn't understand what I'm asking, or maybe he does, and there's stuff he hasn't told me yet.

He clearly came over tonight with the intent of sleeping with me, and now that he has, he's clearly claiming me as his, so maybe he made preparations for that he just hasn't told me about yet. He mentioned being at Anae's house and snooping on her laptop, but he didn't say anything else.

Surely he would have mentioned a breakup or something, right?

But he also said that thing about Anae thinking he's too dark for me. In the moment, it seemed crazy because how would that even come up? But maybe that's how it came up. Maybe they got in some fight or he told her he wanted to break up, and when she demanded to know why, it came out that he wanted to be with me instead. Maybe that's when she flung back that he was too dark for me, that I wouldn't be able to handle him.

Bite me harder next time.

I shake off the thought that there could be some weight to that argument. I'm just not used to him yet, that's all. All of this is new to me. The sex and the intensity. For all I know, that's how most people fuck and I just don't know it.

Whatever the case, it's clearly how *he* does it, and I didn't dislike it, I just have to get used to it. I know we like each other, but we still have to get to know each other more, too.

I'm looking forward to it even if all of this suddenly feels a little scary.

Before this, we weren't beholden to each other in ways that I feel we will be now, and deep down... I'm not even sure he's having the same thoughts I am.

Has anything changed for him at all? Or does he think we'll just keep going like we have been, but now he gets to fuck me when he feels like it?

I wasn't ready for this level, but now we're on it, so I guess we'll have to figure it out.

I hope this wasn't a mistake.

I swat the thought away.

I don't care if it's a rational concern. I don't want it to be.

It's too late now. There's no going back.

Either this was a good thing, and our relationship will evolve in a way that won't shatter my heart into a million pieces, or...

It won't, and it will.

CHAPTER 24
AUBREY

THE HATEFUL ALARM blares from my nightstand, disrupting my lovely dreams.

Blearily, I reach for it, but I'm startled to find a barrier keeping me from moving freely.

I look down and see Dare's arm still wrapped snugly around my waist.

My eyes widen as I look at the window and verify it is, in fact, morning.

Oh my god, he spent the whole night!

I hope Mom isn't awake. I don't know how I'll get him out of here if she is.

He grumbles in my ear, "Smash that fucking thing."

I crack a smile and reach for it. He loosens his grip so I can get my finger on the button to turn it off.

I can't believe it's morning. I can't believe he slept over. We must have just fallen asleep. I'm sure he didn't mean to.

I look back at him over my shoulder. My tummy sinks seeing how beautiful he looks, sleepy and disheveled in the morning. "I guess we fell asleep. You're not going to get in trouble, are you?"

He shakes his head dismissively, "Nah, my dad doesn't care if I'm home or not. Doubt he noticed."

My lips tug down sympathetically and I roll over, rearranging my covers so I can curl up beside him and rest my hand on his tummy. "You and your dad aren't close, huh?"

"Not really. He's a dick and so am I. We butt heads."

I crack a smile, absently caressing him. "You're not a dick."

He smirks over at me. "That's the post-orgasm high talking."

I roll my eyes. "No, it isn't. I slept that off."

"Mm-hmm," he murmurs, unconvinced as he rubs my arm. "How'd you sleep?"

"Very, very well. You?"

"Same."

I sigh, resting my head on his bicep. "I dreamed I got to take Mom to Italy. I think she was still sick, I could feel it hanging over us like a reality I couldn't shake, but it was still a nice dream."

"I take it you've never been?"

"No. She always wanted to. She planned a trip there with a guy she was seeing before my dad, but I guess they broke up before it happened. When my mom and dad got married, they planned to honeymoon in Rome, but then she found out she was pregnant with me. They didn't have the money for a vacation *and* a baby, so they skipped the honeymoon altogether, and they never found the money to go after that."

"You should go now," he says, like it's just that easy. Like we can just take a trip to Italy because we feel like it.

I crack a smile. We lead such different lives.

"We can't," I tell him. "Mom can't risk getting sick on the plane ride over. Planes creep her out ever since her diagnosis. So many people, so many germs. If she gets sick, it could kill her, and that's obviously a pretty high-stakes risk to take. As much as I'd love to take her on her dream vacation, even if I could afford to, I just can't, unfortunately. I'd never forgive myself if something happened to her because of it."

"Would you even be able to do anything once you were there?"

"If we could teleport?" I ask lightly. "Yeah, sure, there's stuff we could do. We're fine outdoors, as long as we can keep our distance a bit. We have to be more diligent if we go somewhere indoors. If I hear a cough or a sniffle, we're out of there. But in Italy I know they have a lot of sidewalk cafes, so I think there's a lot of stuff we could do that would be perfectly safe. Most of the stuff she wants to do. It's just a pipe dream because we can't get there. It's not like you can drive to Italy. I've been trying to recreate the experience here at home," I say, peeking up at him to see if he thinks I'm a total nerd. "I make her a lot of Italian food, and we'll watch movies with a lot of great shots of Italy. I've done that with other places, too, but Italy was her bucket list trip. That's the one she really wanted to do. I'm sad it's my fault she never got to. She should have just taken the vacation and I could have slept on the floor or something," I joke.

He smiles down at me. "I like that. Are you going to teach me an Italian dish?"

"If you want me to."

"What are you making for dinner tonight?"

"I don't know. I have to see what I have the groceries for. I've been a hermit the past couple of days. We need a lot of stuff."

"Send me a list," he says. "I'll take care of it. Include whatever you need for whatever you want to teach me to make. I'm coming over for dinner tonight. We can cook together and I'll meet your mom."

My heart stalls. "Oh. Um..." I clear my throat. "I don't really... I don't really have people over."

His eyebrows rise and he indicates us, right now, in my bed.

"You came in through the window and are only in my room. You'll probably think I'm crazy, but as soon as I get home from school or work, I go straight to the shower. I'm extremely careful. I don't even want to risk bringing germs in on the clothes I've worn out in the world all day."

"All right, so I'll bring a spare change of clothes. We can shower together," he teases.

I grin. "We are not showering together."

"Fine, I'll shower alone and think about you. It's not a big deal. I can do your little cleanliness routine, then I can help you make dinner."

"That would be really nice."

"It's settled, then."

I stay under the covers as he pushes his back and climbs off the bed. My gaze travels, pausing so I can admire his muscular back and perfectly rounded butt.

Just looking at him, I get another hit of yearning like I had last night, but there's no time for that now. As much as I'd love to stay in this bubble with him, I have to get ready for school, and he needs to get out of here.

While he gets dressed, I slip my pajamas back on and creep out of my bedroom to see if Mom is awake.

She's not in the living room, so when I see the coast is clear, I go to retrieve Dare, hauling him down the hall and practically pushing him out the door.

He laughs at my paranoia about getting caught, but clearly our parental situations are not the same. Maybe his dad wouldn't care if he got caught sneaking a girl out of the house early in the morning, but my mom definitely would.

He gives me a kiss before he goes, and I lean in the open doorway, watching him walk to his car.

I hate to see him go.

I wish last night would have lasted forever.

It may not have been deeply reassuring, but this morning was.

I'm afraid that going to school today could ruin all of it.

I tell myself only an illusion can be ruined by reality, so I shouldn't be afraid.

But I am.

Illusion or not, I like what I have with him. I like how he makes me feel, and I love how I made him feel last night.

I don't want to risk reality shining a light on us and blowing it all away.

I don't want to see him with her.

I swallow, giving him a little wave as he backs out of my driveway, then takes off down the road.

I tell myself he'll be back later this evening. We made plans. He'll help me cook and meet my mom. Everything will be fine.

I just wish it felt more like the truth.

CHAPTER 25

AUBREY

BECAUSE LAST NIGHT went the way it did, I think I underprepared for my first day back at school.

People smirking in the halls, knowing they saw that picture of me? Sucks.

Some openly calling me a skank and a whore as I walk past? Not great.

When I open my locker and a whole ream of paper with the screenshot of her video (including the "pathetic") showing my picture spill out into the hall and cause everyone in the vicinity to stare?

Zero out of ten, do not fucking recommend.

I tell myself to shake it off and pick the papers up as quickly as I can, but they've spilled everywhere. They're covering the ground in front of the lockers. People are stepping on them as they walk past. Some guy stops and grabs one, then keeps walking.

"Hey, give that back," I call after him as I hurry to pick up the others before anyone else grabs one.

"Suck a dick," he answers. Then, turning around and smirking, he says, "Oh, wait, you're already sucking Dare's, aren't you?"

His friend laughs, he smirks more maliciously, and they turn and disappear down the hall with my picture.

Assholes.

I'm late to homeroom by the time I get every last stray paper out of the hallway. Seats are assigned in this class, so we always sit at the same one.

When I hurry in, a couple minutes late, and get to mine, I find another copy of that screenshot picture taped down on top of my desk, and next it is a printout of the haiku I deleted from the comments on my post.

Face burning, I tear them off and sit down while the teacher gives me the evil eye for coming in late *and* being so distracting.

By the time I get to English class, I'm so tired of having that picture thrown in my face and insults hurled at me, I just want to leave.

Especially because this is the class I have with Dare.

He hasn't realized I'm in this class yet. He's already seated in his usual seat with his friends around him by the time I get there. The guy who stole my picture in the hall is one of them, and he's sitting right next to Dare.

Dread settles over me as I drop my bag. I have my whole bookbag with me today because I think I'll eat outside again. I need a break from the nonstop bullshit.

"Hey, there she is," he says with a shit-eating grin, nudging Dare. Then, loudly, he says, "Think she'll sign it for me?"

Dare turns slowly, clearly surprised to see me over here in the corner. He frowns, stands, and grabs the paper out of his friend's hand without looking.

He balls up the paper on his way over. I look up at him, a little relieved, but a bit nervous, too. He hasn't famously been fantastic to me in front of his friends, and I'm not sure what's coming.

"Have you been in this class all year?"

I nod. "Sure have."

"Huh. And here I thought I was observant."

I crack a smile. "I'm easy to miss. My class before this one is so far away, I barely get here on time, and I sit by the door so I can be the first one out."

"Good strategy."

I nod, glancing at his friends. They're watching, a bit confused. I guess I can see why. The way Anae's video framed it, I sent this picture of myself to him unsolicited. Even though people saw us arrive at school together last week, I guess they didn't think he actually liked me.

Which, again, makes sense if he still has a freaking evil girlfriend.

Haven't been able to get confirmation on that yet. Maybe I would have at lunch, but there's no way I'm putting myself through the cafeteria today. *Everybody* has an opinion about us even though literally none of them have any of the facts.

"What time should I come over tonight?" he asks.

The girl in front of me turns around to steal a not-so-subtle look at us.

I clear my throat and look up at him. "I don't know, like six?"

"All right."

The way he looks at me makes me feel melty. He's not trying to, I just really like him, and I feel like him coming over and talking to me in front of everyone like this is partially to get some of the heat off me.

The bell rings, so he glances at the teacher, then back at me. "Guess I better go." His lips tug up.

I smile faintly, but my face feels so hot because I can feel people watching and I hate it. "Okay. I'll see you later."

He touches my shoulder, then turns and heads back to his seat.

At least after that, none of his friends in this class smirk at me or say another word.

Knowing Dare is coming over later, I utilize my lunchtime outside to eat the food I packed myself and get started on my homework.

I'm relieved when I head back in to know I only have two classes left and then I can go home. Unfortunately, on the way to my next class, I get a text message.

It's from Anae. Not her fake number she sent the disgusting video from, but her own number.

My stomach sinks when I see it's another video from her social media—this one isn't intended to overtly humiliate me, though. Just to hurt my feelings.

It's a video of her and Dare in his car with the windows down on the way to school this morning. Her caption reads, "When you and the BF decide to carpool."

I hate myself for feeling so disappointed.

He never *said* they broke up.

But he did come to my house with the express intention of fucking me when he knew I didn't even want to *kiss him* when he had a girlfriend.

I had hoped that meant...

My heart cracks a little more when I see that Dare liked the video.

What?

When I went through her stuff before, it seemed like he never liked her shit, so for him to like this feels... deliberate.

Not deliberate in the sense that he expected me to see it, of course, but like maybe he has a guilty conscience and thought since he fucked someone else last night, he should give his actual girlfriend a little extra attention.

I close the message without responding and tuck my phone in my bag. I feel sick to my stomach.

People still stare and whisper on my way to class—kids at this school love their gossip, after all—but I don't even pay them any mind.

I want to go home and curl up alone in bed, but I've already missed so much school, I don't want to miss more for no reason. I'm useless in class, though, and when the bell rings and school is over, like an absolute masochist, I hurry outside because I know Dare tends to leave first since he parks up front, and I want to see if she gets in his car.

She said they carpooled and implied it was today. He *was* wearing the same shirt he was wearing in English so I'm probably grasping at straws, but he *did* say she banks footage. Maybe she posted that today, but the footage was old. That would be far preferable to him actually leaving my house after taking my virginity and sleeping in my bed all night and then deciding to drive over to his girlfriend's house and give her a ride to school an hour later.

I feel like a crazy stalker girl semi-hiding behind the little free library box so I can keep an eye on Dare's car. I'm worried he'll spot me. He and Anae are standing in a group of their friends chatting. I'm not encouraged by the fact that she is *also* wearing the same outfit from the video. It's starting to feel very much like I'm grasping at straws here.

Then they say their goodbyes. Anae has a big smile on her stupid face as she turns, her high pony bouncing, and follows Dare to his car.

Please don't get in.

She did send me that video. She's probably crazy enough to coordinate her hair and outfit to make sure she matched the video she was using.

The last straw slips through my fingers as she opens up the passenger side door, laughing at something he says, and gets in. My gaze drifts to him. He's smiling that same smile that melts me as he gets in the driver's side.

I want to die.

This hurts a lot more than it should.

I know it's my own fault. I read into what he said last night and interpreted it the way I *wanted* it to be. I wanted so badly for them to be over, I just… tricked myself into finding evidence to support it.

I sit down on the black slatted bench on the quad. I'm visible now, but I don't care.

He's backing out, so I doubt he'll see me, anyway.

I feel like a fool.

I feel like what people have been calling me all day—a pathetic skank.

I swallow past a lump in my throat and take a couple of breaths.

It doesn't matter.

I tell myself that, but I don't believe it.

This is exactly what I was afraid would happen today.

A familiar voice calls out, "Hey," and a moment later, Hannah sits down on the bench beside me, adjusting her purse strap and smiling until she sees my face. "Rough day?" she asks sympathetically

I nod woodenly. "Really rough."

She gives me a sympathetic look. "I'm sorry. I'd invite you over to vent about it, but considering Anae would probably be there, I don't think that would help."

"No, it sure wouldn't."

Probably be there.

Her words just trigger more questions. Is he taking Anae straight home, or are they hanging out? Will he take her to his house, or go to hers?

I feel sick.

"Are you sure you're okay?" Hannah asks.

"I think I made a really big mistake."

The words slip out and my eyes well up with tears.

Hannah puts her books down on the bench and leans over to hug me. "We can go somewhere else if you need to talk. We could go get ice cream," she offers, pulling back and smiling. "My treat."

I offer a watery smile because it's a nice offer. "Thanks, but I can't."

Some guy walking by calls out, "Hey, Aubrey, show us that ass."

Hannah shoots him a dirty look. "Keep it moving, perv."

I shake my head, looking down. "I hate everything."

"Chase Darington is very persuasive," she tells me. "When he sets his mind to something, it's pretty much a done deal. If he convinced you to do something stupid, you wouldn't be the first."

"Since I met him, I feel like I've torpedoed my whole life."

She nods sympathetically. "Sounds about right. He's not a good person, Aubrey. He and Anae are two peas in a pod, and she's definitely not a good person. She's sick."

As easily as all of this spills out of me, I'm at war with myself as far as believing it. I still don't want to. I want my illusion back. I want Dare telling me I'm his and he's mine, and I want it to be true.

"You're sure you can't hang out? We could go to your place if you want," she says. "I'm supposed to go over to my friend Parker's for dinner, but she'll understand if I can't make it."

I shake my head. "No, I can't. I wish I could. I really do want to be your friend, I think you're great, but I have family stuff right now that takes priority and pretty much swallows up all my time. Unfortunately, I just don't have time to be a good friend right now."

"So?" She shrugs. "My friendship doesn't come with a

minimum time requirement. Just because you're busy doesn't mean we can't be friends. Shoot me a text whenever you feel like it or need to talk. If you have time to hang out, cool. If not, no biggie."

I crack a smile. "If you're not a sapphire, this school has no business sorting students into houses."

She grins. "I am, actually."

"I figured." At our school, the sapphire house stands for kindness and friendship. "I'm an emerald," I tell her.

"How funny. I must be drawn to the courageous. My best friend Parker is an emerald, too. You know what?" she says, like a light bulb just went off. "Dare's onyx. Those onyx guys are always bad news."

"Wisdom and loyalty, my *ass*."

Hannah laughs. "I'm pretty sure they're the school's equivalent of Slytherin, they were just too afraid to say that."

Even though I felt—a bit dramatically—like I'd never smile again five minutes ago, I find myself smiling, too. "Fucking Slytherins."

"I'm a total Hufflepuff, I can't hang with Slytherins," Hannah says, shaking her head.

I shake my head, too, a little in awe. I've never had a friend with energy as pure as hers before, but it's addictive and oddly uplifting. "My head feels so much clearer when I'm around you. Every time I see you, you clear the Dare fog. Maybe you should move in with me so I can get back to making good decisions on a regular basis."

Hannah cracks a smile. "Don't tell him that. I ran into him at my house when he was over visiting Anae, and he followed me to the kitchen to grill me about you."

My heart stalls. "He did?"

She nods. "He wanted to know if we talked about him."

My eyes widen. "What did you say?"

"I didn't tell him anything. I'm not his spy. Anyway,

before he wandered off, he told me I'm *allowed* to be your friend. If he knew I helped clear your mind about him, he'd change his mind. And I know you probably think you'd never let him tell you who to be friends with anyway, but believe me, when Dare wants to get something done, it gets done. He probably, wouldn't go about it in a straightforward way where you'd see what he's doing, he would just find a way to turn you against me so it seemed like your decision. He did that with one of Anae's friends he didn't like. She lets him play, but not with her friends. So he fucked one of them. Anae went for her so hard, she had to leave school."

My eyes are stuck roughly the size of dinner plates. "What?"

She nods solemnly. "Be careful with him. He's tricky."

"When you say she lets him *play*...?"

"He's allowed to fuck other people as long as she knows about it and gives it her blessing."

My stomach sinks.

My chest cavity seems to shrink, making breathing nearly impossible.

"He... didn't tell you that," she realizes belatedly.

"No, he sure didn't."

And there have been a *lot* of times he probably should have.

What the hell has been the point of torturing me and letting me feel like a terrible person for liking him when, apparently, he's in some kind of open relationship?

And why would he leave a relationship like that?

He wouldn't.

That's the simple answer.

I'm a fucking idiot.

I don't want to be in a relationship like that, and he's not going to leave a situation where he has unlimited free passes to do whatever the hell he wants to be monogamous with me. Why would he?

"Sorry," she says, grimacing. "It's not common knowledge, but with the picture and everything, I thought you knew."

I shake my head. "Apparently, I don't know anything."

CHAPTER 26

AUBREY

AFTER COUNTLESS ROUNDS of back and forth with myself over whether I should cancel dinner with Dare tonight, the clock runs out.

A knock at the door tells me he's here, and my stomach twists with anxiety.

I know I should have canceled. Hannah was the breath of fresh air I needed to clear the fog Dare constantly leaves me shrouded in. If I'd have taken advantage of that clarity, maybe I could have put myself back on track, but I know the moment I let him back in, he'll fuck me all up.

I didn't even know what to tell Mom about him coming over for dinner. Earlier, when I was still in his bubble and I hadn't gone to school yet, I had fantastical notions of telling her he was my boyfriend.

My, how things change in the span of one day.

I'm miserable when I walk to the door. I don't want to open it. It feels like opening the door to a vampire I know will suck all the common sense out of me and inviting him in to do more damage.

The door opens and Dare stands there, a charming smile on his handsome face and bags full of groceries hanging off his arms. Nothing about his smile changes, exactly, but the moment he sees my face, he knows something is off. I can see it in his eyes.

"Hey."

"Hey," I say back, my tone subdued. I take a step back to let him inside.

He walks in, watching me carefully as he walks past, but my mom is here and he must want to make a good impression because he puts that winning smile right back on his face to greet her.

I introduce them, but not with stars in my eyes and a goofy grin on my face like I probably would have earlier. I thank Dare and take the grocery bags to the kitchen so I can unpack them while he talks to my mom. He has his gym bag with him and tells her he'll be back to talk to her after he showers.

Realizing he's a guest in this house and might not even know where the bathroom is, I abandon the groceries to show him the shower and get him a towel.

As soon as we're far enough away from my mom, he grabs my wrist and hauls me into the bathroom with him.

I glance at the door as he closes it and blocks it with his body, trapping me in here with him. "Um, my mom is literally right out there. I told you nothing could happen in here."

"What's wrong?" he asks.

"Nothing."

"Bullshit. Try again."

I sigh, avoiding his gaze. "Nothing is wrong, I just don't want my mom to think… I don't know, that we're doing something we shouldn't be in here."

"I don't think your mom has anything to do with it. I'll ask one more time. What is wrong?"

I open my mouth to say nothing, but he said he'd only ask once more, and I don't know what Dare's next move is when his first attempt doesn't work. "I heard some things today," I finally say, so hesitant I don't look him in the face.

He doesn't sound surprised. "What kind of things?"

"Discouraging things."

"Like?"

My heart aches, and on the surface, I don't want any more pain, but deep down, I know I should rip off the Band-aid. "Like you and Anae have an open relationship?"

He shakes his head. "No, we don't."

"You're not allowed to fuck other girls?"

He misses a beat. "I am," he says slowly. "But it's not an open relationship."

"How is that not an open relationship?"

He sighs, looking irritated. "You really want to talk about the mechanics of my relationship with Anae?"

"No. I don't want there to *be* a relationship with Anae. I'm such a fucking simple-minded idiot, apparently, it never occurred to me you guys had some kind of arrangement. I just thought you liked me, and—"

"I *do* like you," he interrupts.

"I feel so stupid," I say, raking my hands through my hair. "Why wouldn't you tell me that?"

His jaw locks. I don't expect this to go well. Honestly, I expect it will probably be the end. I have to play the crazy girl, and he has an ideal set-up with someone else. Why wouldn't it?

He closes the distance between us, grabbing my jaw and forcing me to look up at him. "You said you were going to trust me. Do you?"

"Yes, but—"

"No, not but," he says, not letting me finish. Slowly and deliberately, he says, "The deal was, if you trust me, I will not give you a reason not to. Wasn't that the deal?"

My heart thuds. "Yes."

He nods carefully, holding my gaze. "So why aren't you trusting me?"

"Because there is an awful lot you left out."

"Left out, yes. I didn't lie about it."

"That seems like a technicality. If I'm just one of many girls you feel like fucking aside from your girlfriend, I think I deserved to know that beforehand. I never would have..." I swallow, unable to get the awful words out.

His tone is calm, measured. "You never would have what?"

"Last night wouldn't have happened," I say softly.

The confession brings the sting of tears to my eyes. They're glistening on the surface before I can stop them.

"Why are you crying?" he asks.

"Because you're going to break my heart," I whisper.

His grip on my jaw tightens. He directs my gaze back to his and looks me dead in the eye. "No, I am not."

"You already are," I tell him, trying to pull away, but he doesn't let go. "I don't know how Anae does it, but I can't. I can't be emotionally invested in someone who's sleeping with other people. I didn't ask before because it wasn't my business and we weren't even supposed to be... anything, but after last night..." I blink away the tears.

"Tell me what you need to feel better," he says.

"I need you to break up with Anae," I blurt.

His lips thin like he expected that to be my response, but he really hoped it wouldn't be.

That fucking sucks.

"I can't do that right now," he says carefully.

I pry his fingers off my jaw and back away from him. "You mean you don't want to."

"No, I mean I *can't*. It's complicated. Getting out of a relationship with Anae isn't that simple. Her attachment to me isn't emotional, but I'm a significant part of her identity and the life she wants. She gives me the leeway she does because she thinks it will keep me around. She doesn't understand things like love, she understands transactions. I fit the image she wants to be associated with. Just because she doesn't love me does not mean she'll let me go."

I shake my head because that sounds like utter bullshit.

"I know how this sounds," he says, seeming to realize I'm not buying it. "You don't know her, Aubrey. You don't know what she's like. No one does."

"You do," I state.

He straightens and stares down at me. For a moment, he's wordless, then he says, "Yes, I do."

"Why? If she's such a fucking mystery to everyone, why do *you* get her?"

"Because we're similar."

I hate that.

"And because we're similar, she feels more comfortable being open with me about certain things. She knows I won't judge her."

I cross my arms, loathing this secret club they're in together.

"And because I know how she thinks," he says, pulling me out of my defensive stance and taking my hand, "I can tell you with absolute certainty that if I break up with her right now to be with you, I would be putting you in danger. I like to think I could outsmart her and keep you safe, but that's not a chance I'm willing to take when there are better options on the table."

My eyes widen.

What?

Like… danger, danger?

"What… do you mean?" I ask uncertainly. "I mean, she's horrible, but… she's not dangerous."

He doesn't appear to agree, but he doesn't explain why.

His hand tightens on mine. "I need to leave you out of this, Aubrey. There's stuff you don't know, stuff you don't *need* to know. This web was tangled long before you fell into it. It didn't bother me before, but now…" He drops his gaze for a moment, then looks back into my eyes. "I'm working on getting out, but it'll take some time. I know it isn't easy, but I need you to trust me."

Well, that's sobering.

I swallow, unsure what to say.

He knows he has me, but he closes the distance between us, cupping my face in his hand and stroking my cheek with his thumb. "Who told you these things and upset you?"

I hesitate, remembering what Hannah said about not letting on that she helps me see things clearly where he's concerned. The lie feels sticky in my mouth, but I know I have to utter it. "I ran into my friend Janie after school."

He nods, his gaze shuttered. "The one you were with the night you came to my party?"

I nod, but I can't hold his gaze. I'm not nearly as comfortable lying as he is. Still, I hope he bought it. I don't want him to get the idea that Hannah's a bad influence.

Or… a good influence?

He makes everything confusing.

"Well, you did tell her you didn't have time for her, and now it's clear you've been spending time with me. Maybe she's a bit jealous," he reasons. "Wanted to stir things up."

Right. Because someone giving me sound and reasonable information he held back is clearly trying to stir things up.

I should keep my mouth shut, but I look up at him, wanting some kind of reassurance beyond what he's given me. "She said you're tricky."

"Tricky," he repeats, like he's tasting the word and trying to ascertain where he's had it before. "That's a gentle word."

"It's not like I didn't already know that, but…" I shake my

head, looking up at him. He's still holding my face. "Please don't be fucking with me, Dare. Don't jerk me around and make a fucking fool of me."

"I am not jerking you around," he promises. "I am on your side, regardless of how it might feel sometimes. I do not want to fuck anyone else. You're the only person I want to be with."

I want to believe him, but I'm not sure I do. "You liked her video today."

"Yes, I did."

I blink, a little surprised he doesn't even act annoyed or guilty in any way about being called out on it. "So, you hardly ever engage with her content and now, after last night, you're liking her video of you guys hanging out together and her calling you her boyfriend? What am I supposed to think of that?"

"That if I'm doing something I ordinarily don't, I must have a reason."

That knocks a bit of the wind out of my sails. "Well, I did figure you had a reason," I mutter, dropping his gaze because I already know he won't be impressed with my crazy girl rationale. "I thought you had a guilty conscience and wanted to show her some attention after spending the night with me."

He shakes his head very slightly. "I don't get those, and I've never cared to protect her feelings. Anae posting that picture of you went off-script. I have her under control again, but now I'm aware that she has started perceiving you as a big enough threat that she's acting on it, so I have to move carefully. She's more impulsive than I am, so there's a very good possibility she will veer off course again if she feels provoked. I have to offer small reassurances right now to make her think I'm not going anywhere. Nothing overboard that would alarm her because it's out of character for me, but

I have to keep up appearances to keep you safe. I cannot dump her. I understand I could be lying about all this just to keep you on the side, but I'm not. That's why I've asked you to trust me implicitly. I know it's not the easiest thing to do, but it's the only way this works."

He's asking a lot and I'm not sure I'll be able to do it. There's a lot already on my plate, and what he wants me to do is effectively ignore the reality I'm seeing with my own two eyes and trust whatever he tells me instead.

That seems crazy.

"Aubrey." He flexes his hand on my jaw, forcing me to look back up at him. "Listen to me. Anae will try to get under your skin. She'll do whatever she has to do to accomplish that end. She'll make posts that hurt. She'll lie to you. She wants to scare you off without doing something to alienate me, and as long as that's where we have her, we're fine. If she begins to sense she's losing control, that's what will drive her to go off-script. Let her see a reaction if that's what she wants, but don't let it truly get to you. I'm asking you to effectively stop thinking for yourself when it comes to this, stop trying to make sense of it. You won't be able to. You're not like her. You don't think the way we do. Trust that I am looking out for your best interests, and let me handle this."

I smile faintly at the absurdity of it all. "'Ignore the reality in front of your eyeballs, don't question it *or* me, and let me do all the thinking for you.' Anything else, master?"

He smirks, backing me up against the wall. He keeps space between our bodies so our clothes don't touch, but he leans in to kiss me. Playfully, he says, "Exactly. Now, is that so hard?"

"Do you want a girlfriend or a robot?" I mutter against his intoxicating mouth.

"I want you," he states, making my tummy flutter. "If there's no imminent threat, you're free to notice all the reality you want, but in a scenario like this, I need you to stay out of the way. I need you to trust me and let me handle it. Let me protect you."

I sigh. "For a girl whose father dipped out amid the worst time of her life, you're asking for a lot."

"I know," he says gently, caressing my cheek and leaving a soft, tender kiss at the corner of my mouth. "I'm not him. I'll never abandon you the way he did."

He may be the least trustworthy human I've ever encountered, but that promise is like a salve over a wound I didn't even know I had. Gazing up at him, vulnerability in my eyes, I ask, "Promise?"

He nods and leans in to give me another kiss. "I promise."

CHAPTER 27
AUBREY

MY MOOD IMPROVES MARKEDLY after our encounter in the bathroom.

Firstly, because Dare said all the right things.

Secondly, because he followed it up by covering my mouth, sliding his hand down the front of my jeans, and fingering me until I could scarcely remember my own name.

The post-orgasm buzz gets me through his shower, and when he comes out in fresh, clean clothes, he comes into the kitchen where I'm getting our dinner ingredients together and wraps his arms around my waist from behind. He's so much taller he towers over me, but I've never felt safer than I do in his tight embrace.

I didn't intend on all the PDA in front of my mom since I didn't even know what to call him, but Dare isn't shy. He bends to kiss my cheek and the side of my face as I move the sourdough bread across the counter. He kisses the corner of my mouth and I giggle—actually giggle.

I'm smitten again, and maybe the forecast is foggy, but I like not being able to see the danger. If he's intent on killing it before it gets to me, do I really need to?

It's nice to be light and happy again.

It's nice to feel confident that he has my back.

"So, Chef Aubrey, what are we making for dinner tonight?"

"I'm going to teach you how to make a sandwich," I tease.

"Seriously? I know how to make a sandwich."

I smile and look up at him. "I thought we'd start with the basics. We're going to make homemade sweet potato fries and turkey melts for dinner tonight."

"Sounds delicious."

I nod, grabbing a sweet potato. "We're going to keep the skins on, so the first step is to scrub this clean." I hold it out. "Here you go. Get to scrubbing."

He pulls a face, not removing his arms from around my waist. "Really? I usually pay people to scrub things for me."

"Nope. We're doing everything ourselves. I believe in you," I say lightly as I hand him the sweet potato.

Reluctantly, he lets go and grabs it, but he looks lost standing at the sink. "What do I scrub it with?"

I laugh and walk over to show him.

While he's doing that, I get the cookie sheet ready and pop it into the oven so it's nice and hot when we put the fries in.

Mom comes in to sit at the island counter like she usually does when I cook. "Mind if I sit?" she asks.

"Of course not," I say. I was reluctant about this when he suggested it, and wasn't really sure if it would be awkward, but overall I just feel happy that I get to spend time with both of them.

"I'm the guest here, Mrs. Gale," Dare says lightly.

It's the kind of overly respectful bullshit that *seems* obviously out of place to me, but Mom doesn't know him, so she doesn't second guess his charming act. "Please, call me Emilie. I'm not even a Mrs. anymore."

"I heard," he says with a nod, grabbing a knife to start slicing fries. "Dropped the dead weight. Good for you."

She cracks a smile.

"Aubrey tells me you don't want to go to the consultation in New York this weekend."

"It's a long trip, and we can't really afford it."

"Yes," he says with a nod. "I understand that. Aubrey told me about your compromised immune system, too. I understand that makes things more difficult, but I think I have a solution."

My ears perk up because this is the first I'm hearing about this.

Dare goes on. "My father shares a private jet with a friend of his. I explained your situation, and we're having it professionally cleaned on Friday—of course, it's already very clean, but this way we can be sure no one left behind any germs for you to catch. The cabin crew will be kept as small as possible, and every person will have their temperature checked before they're allowed to board the plane. They've been informed an immunocompromised individual will be on board, and have also been informed that if Aubrey hears so much as a sniffle, she has full authority to throw them out of the plane."

Mom laughs and Dare smiles. Her gaze shifts to me uncertainly because this is obviously an overwhelming amount of effort to help her from someone she has never met before. "Oh, I couldn't ask you to do all that for me…"

"It's already done," he assures her, slicing through the sweet potato. He's much more comfortable cutting than cleaning. "I did ask about a video call since that's what Aubrey asked me to do, but he wanted to meet with you in person so he could make sure all your test results are up-to-date and give you an examination before he gets started. He'll need you to send over your medical records so he can look at them ahead of your visit. He's not there to waste your time. If there's nothing he can do, he'll tell you that. If there's some-

thing you haven't tried that he thinks stands a shot at working, he'll tell you that, too."

Mom looks at me. I see the same thing I felt when he first
mentioned this to me—a reluctant gleam of hope.

I walk over and place my hand over hers on the
counter. "I think it's worth trying, Mom. What's the
worst that can happen? He can't help? Then we come
home."

"I suppose 'ride on a private jet' is a good bucket list
item," she says, considering. "But this all sounds very
expensive."

"It's on me," Dare assures her. "The trip, anything you
need as a result of the trip. I'm covering all of it."

Mom looks over at me, wide-eyed. "Is he an angel?"

I grin. "I thought he was when I first met him, too."

Dare smirks at me because we both know he's the furthest
thing from an angel, but Mom has no clue.

I'm glad she doesn't because if she knew how complicated
things were with him, she might not accept his help. Since
he's here kissing me and cooking with me and meeting my
mom like a normal boyfriend, she has no reason to suspect
otherwise.

Although I don't think Dare will take up cooking as a
hobby anytime soon, he proves quite an adept pupil. We
finish up our light dinner and eat at the table while Mom and
Dare get better acquainted.

She embarrasses me telling him I hadn't told her I was
seeing anyone, but she could tell by the big grin on my face
every time I would get a text from him.

Dare grins at me across the table. "Aw, mermaid. Do I
make you smile?"

When you don't make me cry.

But I don't say that. My face heats and Mom laughs, and
honestly, it's a great time. I didn't really expect Dare to be

good with parents, but by the time he stands and clears the plates for us, I can tell Mom is fully charmed.

"You sure you don't need help?" I ask him.

"Nah," he says, grabbing my plate and stacking it on top of his and Mom's. "I've got it."

As soon as he's out of the room, Mom reaches across the table and puts her hand over mine. "I love him."

I crack a smile. "I'm pretty fond of him, myself."

We visit some more and enjoy dessert while Dare dazzles Mom with his life experiences and future plans.

I ask if they want to watch a movie before he leaves, but Mom decides she's going to head to bed a little early and give us time to ourselves.

"Are you sure?" I ask her.

I'm on the couch with Dare, his arms wrapped around me.

Mom smiles and waves me off. "You kids have fun. I'll see you in the morning."

Dare waits until Mom is down the hall, then he kisses my neck and teases, "Your mom likes me."

"Well, sure. Who wouldn't love the generous, all-American charmer I just had dinner with?" I tease. "Now, if the Dare I know would like to come back out, he's who I'd like to cuddle with while I watch this movie."

"Hey, Mom's approval is crucial to my Aubrey domination plan."

He says it like he's joking, but I don't even know if he is anymore. "There he is," I say dryly.

We cuddle up on the couch and pick a movie to watch. Dare behaves himself for the first half. I sit between his legs, his strong arms locked around me. He loves to have his arms around me, and I love it, too. Makes me feel safe and relaxed.

As we get nearer to the end of the movie, he starts distracting me. He pulls my hair away from my shoulder to expose my neck. I know as soon as he does it he's about to cause trouble. My skin prickles in anticipation with only his eyes skimming the curve of my neck.

His finger follows. He places his fingertip at the top of my neck, just below my jawline, then he lightly traces the curve all the way down. My eyes drift closed when he does it again, and my body sinks back against his when he does it a third time. My body is primed for his attention, so when he slides his hand down my shirt and grabs my boob, my nipple is already hard for him.

"Maybe we should save this for the bedroom," I say softly, shifting on his lap. "I don't want my mom to—"

He grabs my jaw, turning my face up, and silences my objections with a hard kiss. He squeezes and caresses my breast as he kisses me, and as much as I really don't want to do anything sexual on the couch in my living room, I can't deny my body is swiftly siding with him.

Stupid body.

"Dare," I murmur against his lips, but he doesn't listen. The solid wall of him behind me moves, and I sink a little.

I start to sit up on my own, but Dare lets go of me, climbs on top of me, and shoves me back on the couch.

My pussy throbs, liking his roughness and the fact that I know where it's leading.

He's on top of me looking down, a dark gleam in his eyes. The room is dark but for the light of the TV. He looks a bit sinister, but also familiar now, and oh, so beautiful.

I reach up to caress his face.

He tugs his T-shirt off and tosses it on the ground.

Then, he slides his hands up under my shirt and tugs the fabric up until it's off me.

I sigh at his utter disobedience as he tosses my shirt on the ground with his. I'm still in my bra and jeans, but when he starts to unbutton them, I grab his hands to try and stop him.

"Dare, we can't do this here," I whisper.

He doesn't like being told no.

Or maybe he does.

Whether he does or he doesn't, he grabs my wrists, pinning them above me on the couch, and leans in to murmur roughly, "I can do whatever I want to you, mermaid. *Wherever* I want to do it."

My heart pounds. I surely didn't agree to that.

I look up at him, his beautiful face shadowed in the dark room. "Please, let's just go to my room." When my words don't move him and I feel him reaching around my back with his free hand to unclasp my bra, I kiss his neck. "Dare, please."

My pussy throbs. I don't know if it's begging him or the helplessness I feel being pinned down while he completely fucking ignores my pleas to stop. Maybe it's just because it's him. Maybe he's being an ass, but he smells and tastes and feels like the same person who made love to me last night because he is.

The material goes slack. He drags it off me and tosses it, his hand covering my breast immediately. "I fucking love your tits," he rumbles, turning my tummy upside down and making it flutter at the same time. He dips his head and takes one in his mouth.

I want to stop him, but it feels so good. I gasp, pulling at my wrists overhead to try to free them, but his grip tightens.

"Dare, please…"

In response, he sucks my nipple into his mouth. I squirm, pulling at my pinned wrists and stealing a glance at the hallway. I'm trying to be as quiet as I can, but I'm still worried Mom will hear us.

He bites down and I cry out. He claps a hand over my

mouth, holding it there while he sucks and bites on my breasts. I try to fight him, and he gets more aggressive, shoving me deeper into the couch cushions.

When he pulls up from assaulting my breasts and gazes at me, there's a wildness in his eyes, like last night when he gripped my throat while he was fucking me.

It's like he's teetering on the brink of losing control.

Fear shoots through my body and maybe makes an appearance in my eyes because something shifts in his demeanor. He eases up on my wrists and moves his hand off my mouth.

I suck in a shuddering breath, looking up at him with uncertainty in my gaze.

He lets go of my wrists, and reaches for the button on my jeans. This time, I don't try to stop him. I'm too afraid of what will happen if I do.

I hear the zipper slide past the metallic teeth, feel the material around my hips go slack. I look away as he grabs the belt loops and tugs my jeans down and off, leaving me in just my panties.

I wore sexy ones tonight in anticipation of things maybe going this way, though I imagined we'd be in my room and I'd be more on board than I am currently. They're black with a bit of delicate lace detail.

Dare's hand slides over the crotch until he's cupping my pussy in his palm.

I close my eyes as he rubs me, teasing my slit through the fabric. My pussy pulses with need, but I still don't want this to happen here.

Dare drops down between my thighs. I feel him down there and open my eyes only a moment before he grabs my spread thighs and lowers his mouth to my pussy.

I'm still wearing underwear, but he kisses me through the fabric and it's the hottest thing I've ever experienced. I feel myself getting wetter as he kisses my pussy through the fabric like he's kissing my mouth—hungrily.

The will and decency melt out of me. I'm desperate for his touch, no matter where we are. When he slides my panties off and uses his thumbs to spread me open, I can barely stifle my own cry of pleasure. I wish I had his hand over my mouth again as his tongue darts inside me, licking my tender flesh.

I grab his hair, tugging him closer. He puts his hands under my ass and raises me off the couch, steadying me as he fucks me with his tongue. I move my hips in time with his lapping, riding his face and chasing the pleasure he offers. I've never been kissed so intimately before, but it's fucking incredible.

My thighs shake beneath his fingers as he moves his tender assault to my clit, strumming that magical bundle of nerves until I'm bucking against his mouth, writhing and clawing at the couch cushions.

When my orgasm hits, it hits so hard I can't stop myself crying out. I grab a pillow and pull it over my face to muffle the sound as I whine and cry, lifting off the couch as his mouth stays latched on my pussy.

I collapse, boneless. His tongue laps my pussy one more time, then he pulls out of me and rises up to look at me.

I'm sated and completely unable to move, dazed and happy and oh-so-sleepy from the orgasm.

Dare lies down on top of me, resting his face in the crook of my neck and kissing me.

My hand slides down between us. I can feel how hard he is and I want to help him out with it, but I can't move a muscle.

I rub his cock and he groans into my neck. I smile sleepily and turn my head slightly so I can murmur in his ear, "Just let me get my bones working again and we can go to my room."

Dare chuckles against my neck, but doesn't seem to be in a

rush. Which, honestly, is so great of him because I'm sure he's not comfortable.

I'm going to make him come so hard as soon as we get to my room, I just need a little rest first.

When my eyes open, it's because I'm unconscious and being lifted, and my body doesn't know what's happening. My heart thuds dully in my chest, but I look and see Dare close, his arms braced beneath my body.

He's carrying me.

I lock my arms around his neck. I'm unsure about being carried like this, but he's so strong, it doesn't seem to be a problem for him.

Once I realize he's not going to drop me, I smile softly and rest my head on his broad shoulder.

"You fell asleep," he tells me in case I'm not sure.

I'm so tired. We haven't had sex yet. I need to stay awake. I lick my lips and try to hold my eyes open, but they're so heavy.

Dare places me down gently on my bed. I rally enough to pull the bedding back so I can climb underneath. I'm completely naked, and his gaze rakes over my body as I do.

"Are you going to join me?" I ask, pulling back the covers and patting the mattress beside me.

He smiles, leaning in and kissing my forehead. "Not tonight."

I pout at him and he kisses my pouty lips. He tangles his hand in my hair, kissing me more hungrily and making my heart pound. He must like when I pout.

"Fuck, you're a tempting little thing," he tells me, adjusting his cock as he straightens.

I smile, lowering the blanket and rubbing my boobs since

I know how much he likes them. "You sure? There's room for one more…"

His eyes flash dark. "Believe me, I wish I could," he says.

I don't know why he can't, but I am exhausted.

I suppose if he doesn't mind not getting any satisfaction tonight, I can be okay with it, too.

AUBREY IS asleep before I even leave her bedroom.

My cock stirs, tempting me to go another round with her. Her tits beckon me. They're dying to be played with, and I'm only too happy to oblige, but I force myself to ignore the impulse and cover them up.

I'm glad the crushed up Ambien I sprinkled in the bottom of their dessert bowls was enough to do the trick. I wasn't sure, but I didn't want to risk giving either of them too much, either. Just enough to make Mom sleepy so she'd go to bed early, and Aubrey to sleep deeply enough that I could finish what I started the other night.

Fuck, she was beautiful passed out on the couch—her face peaceful, her tits jiggling as I thrust into her wet pussy again and again.

So. Fucking. Beautiful.

I ignore my aching cock and retrieve Aubrey's clothes off the living room floor. I take them back to her room and dump them on the floor so her mom doesn't find them in the morning, then I ease her bedroom door shut.

Goodnight, beautiful.

I turn off the television and lock up on my way out.

It's late. I dozed on top of Aubrey for a bit after I fucked her, my cock still buried inside her body. I don't know what it is about her that brings me peace and makes it impossible not to fall asleep with her. I've certainly never encountered it before.

I put those thoughts away and drive away from Aubrey's house, getting into more familiar territory as I draw closer to Anae's.

Where our mansion is pretty modern, Anae's house was designed to resemble a French *château*.

It wasn't hers back then, of course. She and her mother only moved into this house when her mom married Hannah's wealthy, widowed father. He had it built for his first wife who was, by all accounts, a lovely woman. Anae's mother detested the place because of that fact, but Anae loved the house immediately because it was the kind of place she imagined a princess would live.

She was younger then. She didn't know she had more in common with evil queens than sweet-tempered princesses.

I use the code to open the entry gates since everyone inside is fast asleep. They open and I drive past, cutting the wheel and rounding the circular driveway.

I park near the front door. I don't lock my car since I'd prefer not to flash the lights. I don't expect anyone to bother with it while I'm inside.

The house is dark since everyone is sleeping. I don't turn on any lights. I've been here enough to know my way around, even in the dark.

I keep my steps light as I make my way down the hall upstairs. When I find the bedroom I'm looking for and let myself inside, my steps fall more slowly and deliberately.

I've been to Anae's plenty of times, but I haven't been in this room before. It's massive, with a giant bed made up of soft blue silk and white fluffy pillows. I flick a glance at the girl sleeping there, but she doesn't move, so I look around a little more.

I touch ribbons from various awards, peruse the romantic books on her shelves, and the fluffy white chair in the corner with a cozy blanket draped over it. I see a rolled up yoga mat beside her dresser and some clutter on top, but it's the pictures that catch my attention.

Always the pictures.

She has more of them than Aubrey does. I grab one, a picture strip of her and a red-haired girl making silly faces, sticking their tongues out, and hugging in various shots taken in a photo booth.

I don't know the other girl, so I put that one back and continue looking.

I stop when I find one that appears more important. It's old, the edges yellowed over time. It's a photograph of a little blonde girl in a blue frilly dress with smiling parents behind her, each of them holding one of her hands. The picture was shot in the driveway in front of this house and appears to be the sort of thing there would only be one copy of.

I slide it into my jacket pocket.

Once I have what I need, I cross the large room and approach the bed.

My presence still hasn't woken her and I don't have all night, so I sit down on the edge nearest her. Her body shifts slightly as the bed sags, and her eyes flutter open.

Then widen with horror when she sees me sitting on her bed.

Gasping, Hannah grabs at the blanket draped over her, clutching it to her breasts and quickly sitting up.

"Hello, Hannah."

Her chest rises and falls rapidly, fear glinting in her big blue eyes. "Wh—what are you doing here?"

I reach over and run my hand across the blue silk covering

her body. I hear her fearful gasp, then look up to meet her gaze. "Letting you see how easily I can get to you."

She draws a shuddering breath but doesn't say anything. Her gaze breaks away from me and darts to her bedroom door. She looks around the room, probably to see if Anae is lurking, too. When she realizes I'm here alone, her gaze returns to me. "Why—why would you need to get to me?"

"I think you know why."

She shakes her head, still looking at me like I'm here to crush all her dreams.

And I can be, if she fucking tests me.

"I thought our last talk went well," I tell her. "Imagine my disappointment when I went over to Aubrey's tonight and discovered a little bird had been in her ear."

I knew Aubrey was lying when she told me it was Janie she'd run into as soon as she told me what was said, but I don't tell Hannah that because I don't want Aubrey to curry any more favor with her. Let her think Aubrey sold her out to me.

"You told her I was in an open relationship with Anae."

She swallows. "I told her the truth, nothing more. That Anae let you—"

I reach out and grab her by the throat. She gasps with horror, dropping the blanket as both of her hands go to my wrist.

And they'd better because I'm squeezing hard.

"Stay the fuck out of my relationships," I say slowly, clutching her delicate throat even tighter.

She struggles to breathe and her nails start digging into my hand as she frantically fights to free herself from my grasp. I don't want scratches that I can't explain to Aubrey, so I ease up a little, but don't release her.

"I thought you were going to be a good friend," I say. "Good friends support their friends' romantic relationships."

Even though I literally have her by the throat, she glares at me. "Not when those friends are in relationships with abusive assholes who jerk them around."

"That's a bit foolish when I have my hand around your throat, isn't it?"

"You're not going to kill me," she says.

"You're right. Tonight, I'm only here to scare you. See, tonight, I left Aubrey's house with my balls empty, so I'm in a pretty good mood. But if you have your way, I have a feeling Aubrey will stop opening her door to me. I can't have that."

"If she stops wanting to see you, it will be your fault, not mine."

"No. See, I have a pretty good hold on her when it's just the two of us. She doesn't have any other friends at this point, so there's no one to make waves but you. As Anae's stepsister, you're in a unique position to make even bigger waves than the average person. I need you not to."

She pulls on my arm, trying to get loose of my grip.

I let her go.

She rubs at her neck, shooting me a wounded look. I'm hoping she'll roll over nice and easy, but she dashes those hopes. "That poor girl has been through enough, Dare. I won't help you trap her."

"Well, then I'm afraid you won't be her friend any longer."

"It's up to Aubrey who she's friends with," she says, but I can see she knows better even as she says it. "She's not like Anae," she adds quickly. "If you lay a finger on me, she'll blame you, not me."

"That's true. But you should think about what will happen if your mission to save her from me works. If I lose Aubrey, and I can't get her back. If I think it's your fault."

Wisely, she swallows and eases away from me.

I smile. "If that happens, little orphan Hannah, I will be

back. I won't kill you, but I'll make you wish I had. Can you imagine if I fucked you? The abuse you would have to endure at your sister's hands."

Her voice is small because she knows she's entirely defenseless against such a threat. If I wanted to take her right now, I could, and even if her cries woke them up, no one in this house would lift a finger to help her. "I would never let you fuck me," she states.

I lean in to look her in the eye. "And I wouldn't care how much you screamed and begged for me to stop."

She braces her hands beside her on the bed and draws in a shaky breath. "Get out of my bedroom."

Her voice shakes. I debate scaring her a little more to really drive my point home, but I don't want to risk her saying something to Aubrey.

That'd be a bit fucking stupid unless she has brutal rape fantasies, but I don't know how bright Hannah Dupont is.

Better not risk it.

There is one more thing I can do, though.

"I'm surprised they let you keep this bedroom," I say, gesturing around the spacious room that has obviously been hers since childhood. "The way Anae and her mom feel about you, I'd have thought they would've stashed you somewhere less… comfortable." I meet her gaze. "Maybe I'll mention that to her."

Then, the cherry on top of her punishment. I draw the photograph of her with her parents out of my pocket. She frowns when I hold it up, her eyes widening when she realizes what it is. Her gaze darts to the dresser, but the sound of me tearing it in half jerks her focus back to me.

"No," she cries, reaching for it.

Too late.

I drop the torn pieces on her bed. "If I have to come back, it'll be much more than an old picture I tear through."

Gathering the torn pieces of the picture in her hands and looking at me like I've just broken her heart, she says softly, "You're a monster."

"And you're no longer Aubrey's friend. Next time you see her, walk the other way. If she messages you, be busy. The friendship is new, so it should be easy enough to unravel."

"You already have Anae, and she would do anything for you," Hannah says. "Why can't you just leave Aubrey alone?"

I pause on my way to the door and look back at her. "I think I might be in love with her."

Hannah's gaze softens a smidge, but I almost think she looks... pitying. "This isn't love," she says softly.

"How would you know?" I toss back. "Nobody loves you."

She gasps like I just struck her.

I smile because I did, with the ugliest weapon I have at my disposal—the truth.

I turn the doorknob and leave without waiting for a response, satisfied that now Hannah Dupont knows she had better mind her fucking business—or else.

I WAKE up to my alarm and the bed all to myself, but I also have a text from Dare that makes me smile.

"Should have taken you up on that offer. It was a long night without you."

I sigh happily and text back, "Don't worry, you can have a rain check." I add a heart emoji and press send, then I fall back in the bed with the phone hugged to my chest.

I hope he'll text back, but he must be still asleep or busy getting ready because a few minutes pass, and nothing.

I guess that means I should get up.

Strangely, when I sit up on the edge of the bed, I feel sore between my thighs like I did when we had sex. I know he went down on me pretty enthusiastically, but I didn't think that would make me sore.

I guess maybe it's leftover soreness from the night before, but I'm sore in places I wasn't yesterday. Weird.

I shower and brush my teeth, then I get dressed for the day and head to the kitchen to make Mom her tea and some breakfast for both of us.

"How'd you sleep?" I ask her as I grab the matcha tea.

"Very well," she says, looking back at me. "Did you and Dare have fun?"

"Yeah, we watched a movie and cuddled a bit before he went home."

"He seems very affectionate," she remarks.

I smile. "Yeah."

"He really seemed to like you, too."

My smile widens. "Yeah."

"I'm glad," Mom says seriously. "You deserve to have some sunshine in your life."

Sunshine makes me think of Hannah.

I grab my phone and shoot her a message telling her we're having the last of the muffins I made with her recipe this morning with a little crying face emoji. I expect her to message me back, but after a few minutes have passed and I've given Mom her tea, I check my phone and see she hasn't responded. Rereading the message and thinking maybe it came off weird, I add, "I can't wait to make them again, though! Thanks so much for the recipe."

I set my phone aside and make Mom some oatmeal to go with her muffin. Once she's set up, I head to school.

That feeling of dread moves over me as I approach the building.

The video with my picture is inching toward old news so there aren't as many clear instances of people judging me, but there are still a few nasty looks, a couple of people who call me names to their friends without even trying to keep me from hearing.

I don't let it get me down as much this time, though. I'm focused on this weekend.

Dare said he will give us a ride to the plane and pick us up when we get back home. It'll take a little under six hours each way and we're not spending the night, so we'll be spending a lot of time on the plane that day.

At lunch, I brave the cafeteria. I eat and keep my head down, not paying attention to anyone around me.

I'm working on homework when the freckled soldier Dare sent last time approaches.

"Dare wanted me to give you this," he says, passing me another handwritten note.

I smile. "Thank you."

He blushes, nods, then hurries away.

I unfold the sheet of paper and read the note.

Meet me on the beach behind my house tonight.
Come to the cave.
I want to watch the sunset with you.

It's cute that he sent a note instead of simply texting me like he could have. I fold the note up and tuck it in my book, then I watch his table until I catch his gaze and give him a little smile.

He gives me a small smile back, but then he gets pulled into conversation with one of his friends.

I wasn't planning to see him tonight, but watching the sunset together sounds romantic. I'm looking forward to it.

It's windier than I was prepared for when I get to the beach.

I wore a thin blue dress with flowers on it. It's feminine and soft, the same vibe as the skirt I wore that Dare really liked. Thankfully, there's no one else around because it keeps blowing up and I have to make a constant effort to keep my panties from showing.

I start looking for Dare as soon as I reach the bottom of the steps. I don't see him, but it's getting pretty close to sunset, so maybe he's already over on the rocks by the cave. I trek over there quickly so we don't miss it, but when I get to the rocks, he's not there.

I look past the rocks at the cave. The note did say to come to the cave, but that's not where he said we should watch the sunset last time we were here.

I consider crossing the dangerous rocks and going to look for him in the cave, but something feels off. Rather than go over there, I grab my phone out of my purse and send him a text. "Are you in the cave?"

Dare texts back immediately. "What are you talking about?"

"I'm at the beach, but I don't see you," I text back. "I'm by the rocks. I know the note said the cave, but this is where you mentioned watching the sunset before."

The message goes through and I wait for him to text back, but instead, my phone rings.

I swipe the screen and put it to my ear. "Hey."

"What the fuck are you talking about?"

My stomach drops at the coolness in his tone. "The note you sent over at lunch. You—you asked me to meet you at the beach so we could watch the sunset together."

"You're on my beach? Right now? Where are you, exactly?"

"By the rocks."

"Did the note say to meet me at the rocks?"

"No, it said the cave. I didn't want to cross the rocks if you weren't over there because I know last time—"

"Get the fuck away from the rocks, Aubrey. Come back toward the steps. Do it quickly. I'll be down in a minute."

My stomach sinks. I look around, a bit paranoid, but it sounds like he doesn't have the first clue what I'm talking about. I don't see anyone else on the beach, but I turn and hurry back toward the stairs, anyway.

I watch Dare hurry down the steps along the cliff down to the beach with a knot of concern in my tummy. The stairs are steep, and I know he's an athlete, but he should still take them carefully. I'm relieved when he hits the sand, but he runs to get to me quicker, then pulls me into his arms protectively and surveys the beach.

"Do you have the note on you?" he asks.

I nod, reaching into my purse and drawing it out.

He grabs it, looks at it, and shakes his head. "This isn't my handwriting." His gaze flickers to me. "Who gave this to you?"

"I don't know his name. A chubby kid with glasses and freckles. He's given me stuff from you before."

"Okay. Fuck." He looks out at the water, then around the beach one more time. Still seeing no one, he keeps his arm around me and takes me back to the steps. "Let's go. You walk ahead of me. If you get a message like this from me again, don't just automatically listen to it. Clear it with me first in person or on a call, but make sure you hear my voice. No texts, no notes."

"This isn't from you?"

He shakes his head, his expression grim.

That's so confusing. "But why would someone else send this to me?"

"It's from Anae," he says simply. "She copies handwriting pretty well."

"And she used your soldier?"

"Apparently," he says, his tone grim. "You'll get something from him again tomorrow. Don't let on that you know he's been compromised. Don't talk to him for long, but if he lingers near you with you ignoring him, that would be ideal. Keep the sheet of paper he gives you. I'll need it back."

My head is spinning, but I don't question him, I just hurry up the steps. Knowing Anae sent me here and not him is creepy.

Why did she want me here? What was the purpose of that?

Doesn't seem like it could have been good.

I hate to admit it, but I'm a little scared. "How unhinged is she?"

"Severely."

We make it to his yard. I take a cautious look around, but seeing no apparent danger, I turn back to look at him. "Do you think she wanted to hurt me?"

"Possibly." He drapes his arm around my waist and pulls me close. "Don't worry, I won't let anything happen to you. But you need to listen to everything I tell you and follow my directions exactly."

I lean on him, nodding my head as I rest my face on his hard chest.

"I like this dress," he murmurs.

It's hard to smile right now, but he draws a little one out of me. "I thought you would." I stay where I am in his arms, but I glance toward the beach. "Look, the sun is setting."

He turns slightly so he can watch the sunset while he holds me.

"It's beautiful," I say softly.

"It sure is." He pulls me back, his hand sliding around my neck, then leans down and gives me a soft kiss.

Sighing against his mouth, I wind my arms around his neck and kiss him back.

As much as I'd love to get swept up in him, I'm too shaken up by what just happened, so I pull back after only a moment. "I think I better get home," I tell him. "She has left stuff at my house before, so she clearly knows where I live. What if she lured me here just to get me out of my house?"

"Why don't I take you home," he suggests. "I'll give you a ride to and from school tomorrow, too. You can pick your car up when you get back from New York Saturday night."

"Are you sure that's a good idea?"

He nods. "I want to have your car checked out, make sure nothing was tampered with. Can you start keeping it in the garage?"

"We mostly use our garage for storage, there's not really room for the car."

He nods again, but I can see his wheels turning. "All right. Well, I'd still like to have it looked at. Either way, you'll be safer with me. Do you think we could convince your mom to let me spend the night tonight without letting her know why?"

"Um... not sure. But if you sneak in after she's asleep, we don't have to ask."

"All right. Text me when she's going to sleep and I'll come over."

Trying to find a bright spot in all this, I say, "At least you didn't have to wait long to cash in your rain check."

Dare smirks, sliding his hand down and grabbing my ass. "Make sure you keep this dress on, but ditch the panties."

When Dare takes me home, he checks around the house to make sure nothing seems suspicious. My neighbor Josie comes out and watches curiously as he comes around the side of the house. I tell her he's my boyfriend for simplicity's sake. He tells her there was something wrong with my car again, so it's being looked at and that's why he gave me a ride home.

He walks me to my porch and gives me a kiss, then he tells me he'll see me in a couple of hours.

I'm excited for him to come back, but still really nervous

about whatever Anae had planned. If that plan was thwarted, where is her head at now? Was she really going to hurt me?

I feel like I'm in a tense horror film as I walk in the house and find Mom not in the living room. Dread curls around me and I grip my phone as I walk down the hall.

"Mom?"

Thankfully, she's just in the bathroom.

I don't want to worry her over nothing, but I still find myself checking every room to make sure nothing is amiss.

I'm fully aware how crazy this is, and I feel crazy, but I don't know what else to do.

It occurs to me that Hannah might know where Anae is, so I shoot her a quick message even though she never responded earlier. That one wasn't urgent and this one is.

"Hey, sorry to bother you," I write, "but I was just wondering if you could do me a favor. No big deal if not, but do you know if Anae is home right now?"

I wait, chewing on my bottom lip. Her icon shows she's online and a moment later she messages back, "No, she left a while ago. Why?"

"This is going to sound crazy, but I think she tried to lure me to the beach behind Dare's house."

"WHAT? Did you go?"

"No. I mean, yes, but not where she told me to. The note told me to go to this cave, but Dare would have told me to go somewhere else if we were meeting to watch the sunset like she claimed in the note. Something felt off, so I texted him, and he said it wasn't from him at all."

"She's really good at forgery," Hannah sends back.

"Yeah, that's what Dare said."

"It wouldn't be the first time she did something like that either. When my dad first died a few years ago, she started leaving me notes in his handwriting to convince me he was still alive. It was seriously messed up, but the handwriting looked so much like his, I started to believe it."

My eyes widen. "Oh my god! What kind of psychopath would do a thing like that?"

"Sociopath," Hannah corrects. "Psychopaths tend to be more cool-headed. Anyway, yeah, it definitely sounds like she set you up."

"Well, that's freaking scary."

"Yeah, it is," Hannah agrees. "I'll keep my ears open. It's unlikely she would plot around me, but if I overhear anything, I'll let you know."

"Thanks," I send back. I hesitate to say what I'm thinking, but it feels so crazy in my head, I need another opinion. "Hey Hannah?"

"Yeah?" she writes back.

"I can't swim. Anae knows that."

I don't complete the path of my thought, but Hannah is able to piece it together. "Then whatever you do, don't end up alone with her anywhere there's water."

CHAPTER 30
DARE

"ARE YOU STAYING FOR DINNER, ANAE?"

We're on the couch watching TV. Anae's lying back on a tower of pillows, her bare legs stretched across my lap. She tilts her head to look back at my dad standing in the archway, her hands instinctively going to the plunging neckline of her dress to draw his attention there while she toys with it. "Oh, I don't think so, Mr. Darington," she says with feigned sweetness. "Cinderella's making my favorite tonight."

I give her leg a squeeze. "You sure? You should stay."

She looks at me, surprised. "Yeah?"

I shrug. "If you want to."

Her eyebrows rise and she tips her head back to look at my dad while giving him a strategic peek at her cleavage. "All right, I guess I'll stay."

I glance over my shoulder and watch my dad tear his gaze from my girlfriend's tits, nod gruffly, then disappear into the other room.

Anae smirks and leans up to whisper in my ear, "Your dad wants to fuck me."

I smirk, my gaze trained on the TV. "No kidding."

She settles back against the pillows again, her ego momentarily satisfied. "Does that make you mad?"

"He can *want to* all he wants. Only I *get to*."

She grins, turning her head and glancing at the television.

"Speaking of fucking," I say slowly, still absently trailing a finger along her smooth legs. "I finally fucked Aubrey."

Her gaze snaps back to me, instantly alert. "You did?"

I nod. "You were right, virgins are boring fucks."

She smirks a little, but she's too curious to be satisfied with that crumb. "I told you."

I nod, looking back at the TV. "Under the covers, lights out, clumsy hands."

"Ugh, I'm sorry, baby. Insecure people are so gross."

"The first time was so tiresome, I decided to drug her for the second round."

Her face registers surprise. "Really?"

I nod, tracing the curve of her kneecap. "That was a little more fun, but she was literally passed out, so I can't give her much credit for it."

Anae bites down on her bottom lip to contain her amused smile. "I didn't know you were into that."

"Yeah, neither did I," I say dryly. "Your little stepsister has been a surprising pain in my ass. I had to pay her a visit the other night."

I feel her stiffen, but she tries to play it cool. "You visited Hannah the other night?"

"Mm-hmm. While you were asleep."

Anae swallows. "What kind of visit was it?"

"Just a short one. Had to put a little scare in her to get her to back off. I was surprised to find she was still in her old bedroom," I remark. "All that expensive silk on her bed. So comfortable."

"You were on her bed," she repeats, trying not to sound alarmed.

"Yeah," I say smoothly, smiling as I look over at her. "She didn't like it much, either."

"Did you fuck her?"

I shake my head. "No. Like I said, just giving her a warning." My hand stills on her leg. "She told Aubrey you let me fuck other people. For obvious reasons, that wasn't something I wanted her to know."

Anae's eyes widen. "Are you fucking serious? That little cunt. Does Aubrey suspect anything?"

I shake my head. "It shook her confidence in me for a minute, but I was able to iron the wrinkles back out pretty easily. Since she hasn't had sex before, it's easy to control her with it."

"She sounds boring," Anae states.

"She's no you, that's for sure."

Anae meets my gaze and smiles.

"Anyway, while my little *gift* hasn't been the most entertaining, it still made me appreciate you for not being like that. You should have seen the insecure fit she threw when she thought I might want to fuck other people after we're married or wherever she thinks this is heading."

Anae laughs. "What a fucking child."

I smirk. "Yeah, I had to exercise a lot of restraint dealing with that."

"I bet. My poor baby," she croons, but I can tell how delighted she is. She can't stop smiling.

I resume stroking her leg. "Since you gave me a gift, I'd like to get one for you. Is there anything you've had your eye on lately? I plan to do a little shopping this weekend."

The possibility of presents catches her attention. "Actually, yes. There's this gorgeous Dior necklace I'm dying to get my hands on, but it's a few thousand dollars. Mom has been such a cheap-ass lately, she won't let me buy it. It's ridiculous."

"Done," I tell her. "Send me a link so I get the right thing, I'll pick it up this weekend."

Anae sighs contentedly, resting her hands on her abdomen. "You really are the best boyfriend ever."

I smirk and give her leg a squeeze. "That's why I'm yours."

CHAPTER 31
AUBREY

WHEN DARE PICKS us up to take us to the airport, it's so early that it's still dark outside. Even though I know where we're going, it doesn't really hit me until we literally drive up to a matte black private jet that I am going *on a private jet.*

Dare isn't fazed as we all get out of the car. Mom walks up ahead to give us a moment to say our goodbyes. Dare wraps his arms around my waist and pulls me close.

"I wish you could come with us," I tell him.

"Me too. We'll go somewhere another time. I've got a lot to deal with here this weekend, and you'll only be there long enough for the doctor's appointment, anyway. When I go with you, we'll go somewhere fun." He leans in and kisses my lips, murmuring teasingly, "Maybe Italy."

I bite down lightly on his bottom lip before I pull back. He cocks an eyebrow in surprise.

"What? I'll miss you."

He cradles my head in his palm and pulls me in to give me a slower, more lingering kiss. "I'll miss you, too." When he breaks the kiss, he says soberly, "But, to be honest, I feel more comfortable with you in New York today. At least I know you'll be safe there."

"Thank you again for doing all this for us. I can't tell you how much I appreciate it."

He smirks down at me. "You can show me when you get home."

I grin and steal a look over my shoulder at my mom to make sure she didn't hear that. Seeing she didn't, I look back up at him. "Oh, I will. Come over tonight after my mom's in bed and I'll let you do anything you want to me."

"Oh yeah?" he murmurs with interest.

I nod and lean up to kiss him one more time. "I better go. It seems like they're waiting for us. I don't want to be rude."

He chuckles, but lets me go. "Here," he says, reaching for his wallet.

I frown, watching him open it. "What's this for?" I ask as he holds out a credit card.

"Anything you might need. I told you the whole trip was on me. I don't want you paying for so much as a coffee."

"You are much too generous," I tell him, leaning in to give him one more kiss. "Thank you, Dare."

He smiles, caressing my face briefly before letting me go. "You're welcome, mermaid."

Dare falls back and I walk over to join Mom in looking up at the plane. It's lit from the inside, the staircase already open for us to climb aboard.

"This is crazy," Mom says.

"Right?"

"His plane matches his car," she adds.

I crack a smile. "He has an aesthetic, that's for sure."

"It's a bit ominous for such a nice boy," she remarks.

I bite my tongue rather than respond to that. "Well, I guess it's time to board."

A pretty brunette flight attendant smiles at us. "No luggage?" she asks since we just have our purses.

I shake my head, and she waves for us to come aboard.

Mom walks up ahead of me. I trail behind so I can wave at Dare one last time before I disappear inside the cabin.

The interior has a black, gray, and silver color scheme. The flight attendant shows me and Mom to our seats and says we'll have to buckle in for takeoff like we would on a regular flight, but once we're in the air, we'll be free to roam around. She asks if we'd like anything to drink and tells us we'll have brunch in a couple of hours.

It feels strange to have the whole plane to ourselves, but I'm so much more comfortable flying with Mom this way. I'm not sure if we have to on a private plane, but I put my phone on airplane mode to prepare for take-off just in case.

Once we're in the air, the flight attendant comes over to tell us we can unbuckle. Everything is so much more laidback and unofficial than a plane packed full of people with lights overhead that do most of the communicating.

"Since brunch won't be for a couple of hours, would you like a bowl of fresh fruit for breakfast?" the flight attendant asks.

I glance over at Mom. She nods eagerly and tells her, "Sure."

She invites us to come with her. We walk past a living room area with a long black leather couch in front of a television. There are cozy looking fur blankets draped over it.

We have some fruit and bottled water, and take a tour of the spacious cabin. There's a bedroom with its own private bathroom and a plane seat in the other corner. If Mom's feeling tired after the appointment, she could have a nap in here, and I could sit there and keep an eye on her.

"Would you like your hot stone massages now, or later?" the flight attendant asks.

"Our hot stone massages?"

She smiles and nods. "Mr. Darington thought they would help you both relax before your mom's appointment."

I look over at Mom. She looks back. "An *angel,*" she says emphatically.

I chuckle and tell the flight attendant, "I guess we'll have those now."

CHAPTER 32
DARE

THE NECKLACE ANAE wants is not exactly what I was expecting.

Typically, Anae likes statement pieces. She likes bold and expensive.

This isn't cheap, but it's surprisingly delicate and feminine for her tastes. If I were picking out a gift for her, I would never look twice at this.

Aubrey, however, I could see wearing this. I could see it on her when she wears one of her cute little dresses or short skirts. Something girly and flirty that I could shove up before I drive my cock into her.

I imagine how she'd look lying across my bed with the thin chain wrapped around her delicate throat, my cock jammed in her pussy. I picture grabbing her throat, tempting the delicate chain to break as I squeeze and she cries out.

"Can I help you with something, sir?"

"Yes," I tell the saleslady, pointing to the necklace with the diamond rose pendant in the jewelry case. "I want this."

While the saleslady grabs the necklace and walks over to the register, my phone starts to vibrate in my pocket.

"Hey, baby. I was just thinking about you," I say when I answer.

The saleslady flicks a curious glance my way. I ignore her and draw out my credit card.

"How'd your mom's appointment go?"

The saleslady quietly reads me the total and I pop my card in the reader.

On the other line, Aubrey talks a million miles a minute about the appointment. She tells me the guy I sent her to is amazing and seems so hooked up. She tells me he thinks her mom is a really good candidate for a clinical trial that's starting soon and they're really hopeful about it. There are only 20 spots available, but if her mom wants one—and they can afford it, of course—she's got it.

That's how it usually works with this guy, so I'm not surprised. In my world, the best kept secrets are often pay-to-play, and even then, you have to know the right people to open those doors.

"That's great news," I tell her.

"Can I tell him she's in? I know you said you'd pay for whatever, but she'll have to travel back and forth a few times, we may even have to stay here for some of it, and there's a 'referral fee' that doesn't feel super ethical, but…"

"Of course. Whatever she needs, tell him I'll take care of it. He knows my family, he knows we're good for it."

"Thank you, Dare. Thank you so, so much."

I smile faintly and mouth thank you to the saleslady as she hands me the little white Dior bag. "Of course, baby. I'm glad the appointment went the way you wanted."

Now that the last of my shopping is done, I make my way out of Dior and casually walk past the Fossil store where Rina Cahill is working today. Aubrey prattles on about her mom in my ear, and I listen like a dutiful boyfriend, but my attention is admittedly split.

Rina is a boring-looking girl with a forgettable face and an unremarkable presence. Admittedly, I'm a little biased since I came into my impression of her already knowing she's the hack poet who wrote that bullshit about Aubrey, but honestly, seeing how entirely unspecial she is, I'm not surprised she has nothing better to do than sit around writing mean shit about people she doesn't even know on the internet.

She should've kept her criticisms to celebrities who will never know or care who she is, and she should have left Aubrey's ass out of it.

Her shift isn't over, apparently, so I dip into a nearby store to buy Aubrey a new bikini for our date tonight. I find a skimpy one. It looks more like a bra and panty set with clear mesh above the crotch so I can see more of her skin while still covering up the best bits, solid black on top with a cute little bow in the center.

Rina's still working when I walk by again, so I stop into another store and grab a pair of heels with a black and white polka dot bow for Aubrey to wear with the bikini. She'll be fucking gorgeous dressed like this. She'd never dress herself this way, but she's more modest than she needs to be. She has a beautiful figure, she just needs a confidence boost.

She'll look like a Playboy bunny by my pool tonight, and I can't wait.

At long fucking last, I walk by and see Rina grabbing her purse. I followed her to work this morning, so I know right where she's parked and made sure to park nearby myself.

I put my shopping bags in the empty passenger seat and turn on my car. Rina mindlessly navigates out of her spot and starts down the row toward the stop sign.

My phone dings—not *my* phone, but the burner in my cupholder. I grab it to see a new message from Rina. "Almost there" she typed with a smiley.

"Can't wait to see you," I type back.

"Can't wait to see you more," she responds.

Ugh, she can't even come up with her own words. Some poet she is.

My actual phone buzzes again. When we hung up, I told Aubrey to text me when they were heading back to the plane. This is that text. I grab my phone, tapping talk to text and say, "Have a safe flight, beautiful. Can't wait for tonight."

I follow Rina to the park where we agreed to meet up. The sun is about to set, so it'll be dark soon.

"You're late," she teases via text. "I'm waiting for you on the bench by the water."

"You better not be wearing panties," I tell her.

"I'm a good listener," she says with another smiley face.

"Is there anyone around?" I ask her.

"No," she answers. "It'll just be us."

"Fantastic. Now, be a good girl and take off your bra, too. Put it on the bench next to you. I want it waiting for me when I get there."

"God you're hot," she tells me.

I snort, grabbing my regular phone and turning it off. I stash it in the glove compartment, grab a pair of black leather gloves, and pull up my hood.

"Are you wet for me, pretty girl?"

"God yes," she answers.

"Good. That's how I want you and I don't like to be disappointed."

"I would never disappoint you," she promises.

Before I put the gloves on, I text her one more time. "If there's still no one around, get on your hands and knees with your forehead pressed against the bench. I want your ass in the air, your pussy exposed when I come over so I can play with it. I want you to come for me before you even see my face. If you're not waiting for me in position like a good little slut, there will be consequences."

With that, I pull on the leather gloves, grab the nail gun from Dad's construction site out of the passenger side floorboard, and go to meet my date.

WHEN WE DISEMBARK from the plane, I'm grinning from ear to ear.

I haven't felt this happy in a long time.

Dare is waiting for me, leaning on the hood of his car. He smiles when he sees me, and I run into his arms, throwing mine around his neck and kissing him like we're in the end scene of a rom-com.

Smiling warmly and kissing my lips, he secures his arms around my waist. "I missed you, too."

"Today was the best day," I tell him, unable to keep the happiness from bursting out of me.

"It sure was." He pushes a chunk of hair behind my ear. "I'm looking forward to spending tonight with you."

He told me when we talked earlier he wanted to do our date at his house tonight instead of mine. I like to sneak him into my room instead of coming to his place so I don't have to leave Mom alone just in case she needs me, but as much as he has done for us today, I feel compelled to let him have his way.

Originally, he said we would go pick up my car from his house on the way home, but since I'm going to his house after, we drop Mom off at home first. I follow her inside and make sure she has everything she needs, but she tells me she's tired after such an eventful day and wants to go to bed, anyway.

Then I run back out to Dare's car and slide in the passenger seat.

He looks over at me out of the corner of his eye as he prepares to back out of the driveway. "You ready to learn to swim, mermaid?"

"No," I say good-naturedly. "I guess at least knowing I have the star of the swim team teaching me, you won't let me drown."

He smirks as he cuts the wheel and backs onto the road. "Nah. I didn't save your ass just to let you drown tonight."

It's still a warm night, but not super hot, so he rolls down the windows on the ride over to his place. My car is parked in the driveway, but he pulls up ahead of it, then stops.

He comes over and grabs my hand, and together we walk around back like I did alone that first night I showed up at his party.

To my surprise, when we get back there, he has presents waiting for me. I gasp at the completely unexpected show of romanticism—there are candles lit all around the pool, a bucket of champagne chilling with two flutes waiting on the table, and laid out on a pool lounger behind it is a brand new bikini and the prettiest pair of polka dot heels.

When we draw closer, I see that on the table with the champagne is also a round box of red roses and a little white bag from Dior.

"Dare," I say, turning to look at him with my jaw hanging open.

He smiles, walking up behind me and securing his arms around my waist. "I told you I missed you."

I laugh, leaning back into his embrace. "I wasn't even gone for a whole day."

"I wanted to surprise you."

"I am definitely surprised." I turn around in his embrace so I can give him a hug. "Thank you so much."

He slides his hand around my neck, pulling me even closer and kissing me. "Now, go change into that bikini so we can get started."

Swimming lessons are over, but we're still in the pool.

We've been in and out a few times, but I'm feeling downright languid as Dare pins me against the pool wall and devours my neck. He's being rough so I know he's leaving bruises, but the champagne is hitting me surprisingly hard so I don't even seem to care. I have my legs wrapped around his waist, and I'm so turned on, I rub my pussy against him.

Dare tangles his fingers in my hair, tugging my head back hard and biting my neck. I gasp at the bite of pain, but he soothes it with his lips as he reaches behind my neck and unties my bikini top.

The bikini top hardly covers my boobs as it is. I should feel shy when the material drops away, but when his hand covers my bare boob and he squeezes, all I feel is warmth.

"Maybe we should move this inside," I suggest.

"Too far," he murmurs, kissing his way along my neck.

I'm so tired, but I want to blow his mind, too. Ugh, traveling is hard.

"Dare, please, can we get out of the pool?"

He finally lets up, staying with me as my tipsy ass gets to the ladder to climb out. He climbs out behind me, watching with a smirk as I adjust the skimpy material covering my ass.

"Put your pretty heels back on," he tells me.

Those heels are *high* and I'm not convinced I won't die wearing them, but I sit down on the lounger and do as he says.

He shakes his head, pouring out the last of the champagne and handing me a glass. "Fucking gorgeous."

I flush under his praise, but I really like it, too.

I feel intensely sexy standing here in these beautiful heels and only my bikini bottoms. I sip the champagne he poured me and caress my boobs with the other hand.

"Take the bottoms off," he rumbles lowly.

My eyes widen. "Here?"

He nods.

I swallow the champagne and set the glass down, then I push down my bikini bottoms. They drop to the ground and pool around my heels. I step out of them carefully, then I grab the champagne flute and drain it because I need some liquid courage.

"Come here," he says, indicating the ground in front of him.

I walk over, the clicking of my heels against the tile sounding so loud in the quiet night. My eyes are feeling heavier and heavier. I hope he doesn't notice how sleepy I am.

He pulls me close until we're belly to belly, his hand at the small of my back. He looks down at my face, appraising. "Are you tired?"

"Mm-hmm."

He smirks, dipping his head and tasting my lips. "Remember, you promised I could do whatever I wanted to you tonight."

I smile against his mouth. "Oh, I haven't forgotten. Can we go to your room now?"

He nods and grabs the Dior bag off the table, but leaves the flowers. He takes my hand and hauls me inside.

I keep an eye out to make sure his dad isn't around since I'm completely naked, but we make it to his bedroom without being seen.

Dare drops the Dior bag on his nightstand and nods for me to get on the bed.

I leave the heels on because he hasn't told me otherwise and climb on his bed. I sink back into the soft, heavenly bedding and resist the urge to curl up and go to sleep.

"You haven't even opened your present yet," he says, untying the bow and opening the Dior bag himself.

God, his pillow is so soft. I tug it close, letting my eyes drift shut for just a moment.

Dare climbs on the bed with me, the Dior bag in hand. He puts it down on the bed between us, then draws out a jewelry box.

"Even the box is pretty," I murmur drowsily.

He smiles and opens it up. Inside is a beautiful rose gold necklace with a little rose pendant, a single diamond at the center.

"Oh, Dare, it's beautiful."

He takes the necklace out, reaches over, and secures it around my neck. Then he leans down, softly kissing my lips. "I'm glad you like it."

"I do. Thank you."

"Did you like the champagne?" he asks.

"Mm-hmm."

The soft material of his blanket feels so good against my skin.

Dare rolls me onto my belly and spreads my legs so he can climb between them. My pussy throbs as he grabs my ass, massaging the globes in his hands.

"You had quite a bit of it," he says.

Did I?

"I wouldn't be surprised if you passed out," he murmurs teasingly as he leans down over me and kisses my bare back.

"No, I won't pass out," I murmur thickly against the pillow. "I want you to fuck me."

"Oh, I will," he assures me, sliding a finger in my pussy without warning.

I gasp and push my butt up in the air instinctively. "Should I take off the heels?"

My head feels swimmy. Maybe he's right.

Maybe I did have too much champagne.

When I wake up, it's still dark outside.

I feel a little woozy and confused, not quite sure where I am. I'm tummy down on the bed, and fuck, I'm dehydrated.

Instinctively, I look to my nightstand to see if I brought a bottle of water to bed with me, but I'm startled when I see Dare lying next to me in a room I hardly recognize.

Oh, right.

I'm at Dare's house.

We came to his room after the pool.

I try to remember what happened. I know we got on the bed, and he gave me a necklace.

I touch my neck. It's still there.

I was naked except for my heels. I wiggle my toes. No heels.

When did I take them off?

The last thing I can remember, he had told me not to take them off. He was between my legs touching my ass and my pussy, but I can't remember anything after that.

Did I black out?

There's no way I had that much to drink.

My pussy feels a little tender, though. I guess we had sex?

I feel weird about not remembering it.

I see a bottle of water on the nightstand so I reach over Dare's sleeping form and grab it. I take a few big gulps, but as I'm leaning over to return it to the nightstand, his arms slide around me.

I smile, sinking against him.

"Good morning," he rumbles.

God, his voice is so sexy when he's waking up.

"Good morning," I whisper back, threading my fingers through his hair and snuggling up half on top of him, half beside him on the bed.

"How'd you sleep?"

"I don't know," I say with an uneasy smile. "I don't remember falling asleep. I don't even remember... Did we have sex?"

"Well, if you don't remember, maybe we should go another round," he teases, rolling me onto my back.

I smile as he climbs on top of me. He leans down to kiss me, and I wind my arms around his neck.

"You want me to eat your pussy?" he asks, kissing the side of my mouth.

"Mm, I wouldn't say no," I tell him.

He kisses his way along my jaw and down my neck. God, his mouth feels so good. He can't pass up my boobs, so he stops there, kissing and sucking on my nipples before he moves lower and kisses his way down my tummy.

My tummy muscles tense as he does. I sigh as he parts my legs, spreading them wide so my pussy is on display for him.

I feel a little shy held open this way, but seeing the raw hunger on his face as he looks at me makes it hard to feel that way for long.

He's on his knees now, his face between my thighs, his tongue licking its way along my entrance. I gasp at the thrilling sensation, my fingers digging into the bedding as I wait for it to delve into me.

"Your pussy was so fucking good last night," he says before licking me again. He uses his thumbs to spread me open, then covers me with his mouth.

I breathe hard, grabbing the edge of the mattress as his tongue swipes my clit.

He pulls back and looks up at me. "I want you just like that again when I'm finished tasting you."

He shoves a finger in me all the way to the knuckle as he resumes licking my clit. My pussy feels a little sore, but it's easy to ignore when he's eating me out.

I come with a cry I don't have to smother at his house. Dare rises up, grabbing me and practically throwing me onto my stomach on the bed.

He knocks me right out of my post-orgasm bubble with the violence. At first, I think maybe he dropped me, but then he parts my thighs and shoves his cock into me so aggressively, I cry out.

My heart pounds as he forces his way deeper into my body. I try to push myself up, but he places a hand on my back and shoves me face-down into the mattress.

"Oh, fuck," he says, driving into my pussy, not letting me move.

I'm so stunned for a moment, I can't react. I let him fuck me, but I don't know how to feel about not participating—and I *can't* the way he has me pinned here.

My whole body is flushed, but I can't tell why. I feel like I'm doing this wrong and I don't want to disappoint him, but he's not really giving me a chance to do anything. Surely this utter lack of participation isn't what he wants.

He thrusts into me again, and maybe it's just because my pussy is so sore, but it hurts. I try to grin and bear it, but he fucks me harder and harder, and it becomes difficult to hold in the cries.

How hard did he fuck me last night?

If he was this brutal, no wonder I'm sore.

"Dare, can we switch positions—"

"No."

He pauses to reposition himself over me, then resumes pounding into me. It feels like a deliberate violation, but surely he doesn't mean for it to.

Occasionally, a little cry slips out of me. If I didn't know any better, I'd think he really likes it because rather than ease up and see if I'm okay, he shoves into me harder.

I finally give up on trying to contribute and squeeze my eyes shut, holding onto the bed as he drives into me like he's trying to break me in half. My pussy stings and I'm upset. I just want it to be over.

Finally, I hear him groan with his release, and then it is.

He collapses on the bed beside me, looping an arm around my waist and pulling me back against him.

I don't know how to feel. I wanted to have sex, but… I don't know if I wanted it like that.

My heart is still pounding. I feel a little afraid, but also ridiculous to feel that way.

"Was that… okay for you?" I ask tentatively.

"Mm, yep. Just what I wanted."

"Okay," I say quietly.

He kisses my temple. "Are *you* okay?"

I'm a little relieved to know he's at least aware he should ask. "Yeah, I'm okay."

He starts playing with my hair, and the tenderness slowly melts away the last of my uncertainty. I'm so relaxed I'm nearly ready to fall back asleep when he murmurs, "You don't have to hold the cries back, you know."

My eyes pop open. "What?"

"You were whimpering when I fucked you. You don't have to hold back here. Be as noisy as you want."

I'm a little confused. "Did you *want* me to cry out?"

"I want you to if you feel like it."

I swallow. "Did you like fucking me like that?"

"Yes," he murmurs, petting my hair again, then leaning in to kiss my shoulder.

"It didn't feel... a little mean to you?"

He doesn't answer right away and my heart sinks. I don't want him to feel bad, I just... wasn't prepared for that, and I don't really know what to think about it. Finally, he leans in and kisses the shell of my ear before rumbling, "Sometimes, I like to be a little mean."

"Oh," I whisper.

He trails a finger lightly down my arm. "Sometimes, I want to fuck you like I want to destroy you."

I swallow. "But you don't want to destroy me?"

"But I don't want to destroy you," he verifies.

"Oh. Okay."

"It's just a game," he says, like that will reassure me.

I guess it does.

I don't think I *liked* what just happened, but if he did, I guess... I guess I'm open to it.

I like what's happening now, at least. I love when he's tender with me, when he pets me and relaxes me. I love when he leans in and kisses me like I'm something precious to him, even if he just fucked me like I'm definitely not.

IT'S light outside when my eyes open again.

I am lying in Chase Darington's bed with his arm draped over my waist. I can feel his hard, muscular length pressed against my side, see his handsome face looking peaceful as he sleeps. I am exactly where I want to be.

Memories of last night wash over me. They're violent and brutal and a little confusing, but in the light of day, it doesn't bother me so much. So he likes rougher sex than I do. He's more experienced than I am. Maybe I'll grow to like it, too.

Besides, it's not just bad memories. Before the confusing sex, we had the most romantic night. He bought me flowers and this beautiful necklace. We drank champagne, and he gave me my first swimming lesson because he wants to make sure I stay safe.

And that was *after* he went to such extreme lengths to make sure I could safely get my mom to a doctor's appointment on the other side of the country—an appointment that he paid for, and a treatment that might save her life.

Looking at the overall picture helps me with my perspective.

I think the sex only threw me so much because I was

unprepared for it. If I knew what he wanted going into it, it wouldn't have been so jarring and… scary.

I shake that thought off, turning in his arms so that my back is facing him. I'm thirsty, so I grab the bottle of water off the nightstand and take a drink.

"Pass that over here, would you?"

His voice rough with sleep makes me smile. I ease back in the bed, pulling his sheet around my breasts, and pass him the water.

He takes a few greedy sips, then hands it back to me. "Thanks, baby."

I put the water back, then snuggle up in the blankets. He grabs me around the waist, pulling me back until I'm spooned against his hard body.

"You sleep okay?" he murmurs.

"Yeah. Your bed is incredibly comfortable."

He smirks. "And the company wasn't so bad, either?"

"Oh, right, you," I tease. "Yeah, I like you, too."

He squeezes me and starts tickling me as an act of revenge. I laugh and squeal and cry for mercy, but end up curled right back up against him.

His arms tighten around my waist. "Do you have anything planned today?"

"I have to work tonight."

"Do you have to? You can't get out of it?"

I crack a smile, hugging his arms around me. "No, I can't get out of it. I need the money."

"I'll pay you not to go," he says. "I'll pay you double what you'd make working."

That is tempting. "I… I don't want to screw them over, though."

"They've never screwed you over?"

I think about Stacey writing me up for the Anae thing. "Yeah, I guess they have."

"So, call off. I'm sure you never do it. Live a little. I want to take you somewhere. Spend a little more time with you before we have school for another week."

"Where do you want to take me?"

He leans in and kisses his way along my jaw. "Just somewhere I always liked to go with my parents when I was a kid."

I expected him to say something totally different, but that feels like he wants to open up to me and show me a little piece of him I haven't seen yet. I don't know if I can pass that up. "I'll call and see if anyone can cover my shift. I'll have to go home first and get ready, anyway."

He moves my hair and kisses my neck. "All right."

Since his body is fitted right up against mine, I can feel him getting hard as he holds me close and kisses me.

Reluctance tugs at me as his hand finds my breast and he squeezes. My body isn't ready to go another round, and after the last one, I'm not positive my mind is, either, but when he grabs a condom and sits up in bed, I let him pull me on top of him.

I shift on his lap, instinctively trying to move away from the part of him that hurt me last night. He grabs my hips, taking control and guiding himself between my thighs.

I grab his shoulders, my teeth sinking into my bottom lip as I ease down on his cock. I go slowly, but it stings so bad.

"Can you please be a little gentler this round?" I ask, a bit self-consciously. "I'm sore from last night."

He cradles the side of my face and leans in to run his lips along my jaw, leaving little kisses there. "I'm sorry."

My heart thumps like a drum and sinks at the same time. There's something about the combination, his sweetness after his roughness, the apology I didn't expect… I don't know, but it pulls me in.

He continues to touch and caress my face tenderly, murmuring, "I didn't mean to hurt you."

I wrap my arms around his neck, pulling him closer as his lips find mine. "It's okay," I murmur against his mouth. "I know you didn't."

Since he was rough on my body last night, he goes easy on me this morning. He lets me stay on top and control the pace, lifting my hips and taking him into my body only as hard and as fast as I'm comfortable with.

It's fascinating to watch his face while we fuck. I can tell when he's holding himself back, see the strain in his neck, the tightening of his strong jaw. I run my fingers over his face, marveling at his beauty, that he can be mine.

Well, mostly.

Pressure builds up inside my body. I start to move faster, chasing the taste of pleasure. It hurts a little, but it feels good, too.

"That's it, baby." He tangles a hand in my hair and tugs as I ride him. "Take it deep in your pussy. Come down on me hard."

His words tighten the tension in my lower belly. I hold on tighter, closing my eyes as our bodies slam together.

"Fuck, yes," he says, kissing my chest, biting my nipple. "Harder, baby. You're perfect."

Pleasure breaks open inside me and I ride him harder. I don't care if it hurts, I want to be perfect for him.

My orgasm slams into me with more force than expected. My body convulses with incapacitating pleasure. I come apart in his arms, my limbs shaking as he buries his face between my breasts, groaning against my skin as his release hits hard.

I can feel his pleasure as his fingers bite into my skin. He's gripping me too hard, but I don't complain. His grip eases when it passes, and his whole body relaxes.

He wraps his arms around my body and hugs me, his face

casually pressed against my boobs. He kisses one, and then the other. It's like a little thank you for letting him use me, and maybe that's a fucked up thing to thank someone for, but it feels nice.

I run my fingers through the thick locks of his dark hair. I hold him close and kiss his face. I wait for our heartbeats to return to a normal pace.

I love when he hugs me like this. It feels so intimate. I feel so close to him, and not just physically.

After a while, he lets go.

He invites me to shower with him, but I tell him I have to go home and spend a little time with Mom if I'm going to be going out with him for the day.

He tells me not to forget my roses, then gives me a kiss and heads for the shower.

I sit up on the edge of the bed, my body trembling slightly as I adjust to my post-coital high. I'm still sore and keep trying to reposition myself in a way that doesn't hurt, but it seems sitting comfortably is completely off the table today.

I get dressed, gather my things, and head downstairs.

I'm startled when I get to the living room and find a man sitting on the couch.

A man who looks a lot like an older version of Dare. His hair isn't as dark as Dare's and they have different eyes, but their facial features are quite similar.

I shift uncomfortably, my grip on the gifts Dare bought me tightening. "You must be Mr. Darington."

"Mm-hmm. Who are you?"

"Aubrey Gale. Dare and I go to school together," I say, somehow unable to come up with a better reason for why I'm walking down the stairs with major bedhead, clothing bundled in my arms, and a Dior bag in my hand.

He sips his coffee and watches me over the brim. "Is that right?"

"Thank you," I say a bit belatedly. "Letting us use your jet to take my mom to her doctor's appointment was incredibly generous of you. It might've saved her life."

"Ah." He nods. "You're that one."

My spine stiffens, but I guess I can't fault him for speaking so dismissively. In all likelihood, he's aware that Dare is still technically with Anae and *not* aware of the circumstances.

"You should thank Dare," he says. "He paid for the trip out of his trust fund." Then, giving me a not-so-subtle onceover and a slow smirk, he says, "Actually, I guess you already did."

Wow.

I don't like him.

My spine is still stiff from his first swipe, so it can't get much straighter. I clear my throat and glance toward the glass doors that open out to the pool. "Well, I have to get home, but thanks again."

"Anytime," he says, his tone so condescending and assholey, I want to throw a shoe at him.

God, what an unbearable ass.

No wonder Dare doesn't like him.

Dare picks me up after Mom and I have lunch.

I wear a little white dress and the polka-dot bow heels he bought for me. Walking in them still feels dangerous, but I love the way he looks at me when I'm wearing them, like he can hardly keep from fucking me right then and there.

I'm a little confused when he pulls into a parking spot in front of a hair salon. He takes my hand and we walk up to the building. I'm still confused when he opens the door for me and follows me inside.

"This is where you came when you were a kid?"

"No." He lightly grabs my hip, ushering me inside. "This is our first stop. We'll go there after."

"Okay," I say, casting him an uncertain smile. "Are you getting a haircut or something?"

He smiles faintly. "You are."

My heart flips over. "What?"

He runs a hand through my hair a bit absently, his other still on my hip as we wait at the reception desk. "I know you can't afford to come to places like this, so I wanted to bring you."

"Do you not like my hair?" I ask uncertainly. As much as he plays with it, I figured he did.

"I love your hair. That's why I want to take care of it." He presses a kiss to the side of my head.

That's rational, and I guess I *haven't* been able to get it trimmed for a long time. It has probably been two years since my last haircut.

"I don't want to lose a lot of length, though," I say, looking up at him.

"I like your hair long, too," he assures me. Then, wrapping his hand around my throat and pulling me close, he kisses me. "Trust me," he murmurs.

The receptionist smiles as she comes over to assist us. I feel out of my element in the expensive salon, and cast a look back at Dare as she leads me away.

The lady doesn't ask what I want, she just puts me in the chair, ties the cloak around my body, and gets to work. I guess that means Dare already told her.

I wish someone would have told me.

I'm a bit nervous as she washes and conditions. My anxiety ramps up when she gets out her scissors.

In the end, Dare was right, though. She only gave me a trim, just making the cut neater and sleeker, and styling it so my hair feels like silk between my fingers when I touch it afterward.

"So, what do you think?" she asks, turning me to look in the mirror.

"I actually really love it," I tell her.

She grins. "Yay! Now, let's go show your boyfriend."

I was worried when I walked away from him, but I feel happier and significantly more confident when she leads me back out to the waiting room to show off my more polished look.

A slow smile spreads across Dare's face when he sees me. He stands, and I do a little spin to show him my pretty hair. "What do you think?"

"You look gorgeous, as always."

I smile, and Dare wraps an arm around me, leading me over to the counter so he can pay.

I may not have initially wanted the haircut, but my hair feels so amazing, I can't stop playing with it in the car.

He drives us to the next place, but I'm not immediately sure what it is. There's a strip of shops across the street from where he parks the car.

He takes my hand and we walk across the street. Before we go inside, he stops and glances at the decal on the storefront we're in front of.

"We should take a selfie together," he says.

I blink in surprise. I don't actually have any pictures of us together yet. I wasn't sure he would want to take any since things are still complicated with Anae.

He smiles like it's no big deal. "Gotta show off that new haircut, after all."

"That's true," I say, flipping my hair playfully. "Hair this good should be shown off."

He comes up behind me, wrapping his arms around me in a tight hug. My heart jumps and I hold out my camera, preparing to take a picture of us. Right before I do, he presses a kiss against my cheek.

My heart hammers with happiness when I look at the picture. We look so much like a couple. I look like a cherished girlfriend, not… whatever I technically am.

"Post it," he says.

My eyes widen and my smile falls. "What?"

He nods at my phone. "You can tag me if you want."

"Um… are you trying to get me killed?" I ask lightly, but also not, because what the fuck? "If Anae sees it…"

"She will." Almost casually, he reaches over and toys with the necklace he bought me. He gives me another small smile, but no explanation.

I frown down at the picture.

I don't think posting it is a good idea, but I guess if he really wants me to…

I don't tempt fate by tagging him, though.

I feel uneasy as we walk into the shop. I don't have a ton of followers, but it seems impossible that the picture won't get back to Anae. I don't understand why he wants her to see that.

"Dare, I think I should at least private the picture so no one else can see it," I say, unable to get it off my mind. "Of course it would be nice to be able to put pictures of us up on social media, but I don't think it's a good idea to provoke her."

"Stop worrying about her," he tells me, giving my hand a squeeze. "I've got all that under control."

How?

I want to ask, but I don't. Dare is looking around the shop, so I try to be in the moment and look around with him.

It's definitely not where I thought he would bring me.

"This is where my parents met," he tells me.

I look around the simple popcorn place. There's prepackaged stuff on the shelves, and a popcorn bar in the back where you can order individual paper cones of the different flavors. It's a cute little popcorn shop, not some extravagant place like I would have imagined. "Oh, yeah?"

He nods, looking around at the flavored packages of popcorn lining the shelves. "She was here on a date with someone else, some dorky guy who made her laugh. My dad took one look at her, saw how beautiful and happy she was, and knew he had to have her."

I don't know why, but hearing that makes me feel a little sad. Maybe it's knowing how it all turned out.

"She used to talk about him a lot." He glances back at me. "The guy she left to be with my dad. I think she regretted it as soon as the initial thrill wore off. The guy she was seeing was some broke fuck from New York. He had no real skills and could never give her the kind of life my dad could, but he did something my dad didn't know how to do. He made her smile."

That feeling of sadness deepens. I haven't met his mother, but I feel sad for the girl he's telling me about, the one who got swept up with the wrong guy and left the right one.

Dare turns to look at me. "I always want to make you smile."

His words take me off guard like a sock to the stomach. I soften, walking over to hug him around the waist. "You do make me smile," I assure him.

"It doesn't always occur to me to... express what someone means to me. I think I picked it up from my father. He's not great at that, either."

"You do, though."

He wraps his arms around me, too. "I try to remind myself to, but if I ever forget, I need you to remind me. My mind doesn't work the way yours does, so I'm sure over the course of our relationship I'll come up short from time to time." He looks down at me, one hand coming up to cradle my face. "I may hurt you accidentally, but I'll never do it on purpose."

I lean up and give him a little kiss. "I trust you."

He smiles, a glint of fondness in his eyes. "Good." Breaking the intensity, he lets me go and grabs my hand. "Now, let's get some popcorn."

CHAPTER 35
AUBREY

I RETURN HOME with the taste of cinnamon-sugar popcorn on my lips, the imprint of Dare's fingers on my thighs, and happiness in my heart.

It has been a rollercoaster of a weekend, but it feels nice to finally have a little calm.

Dare walks me to the door and kisses me. I ask if he'll be back after Mom goes to sleep, but he teases that he should probably give my pussy a break. He grabs my neck and pulls me close, giving me one more lingering kiss. Then he lets go, and walks down the steps. I sigh a little, hanging onto the railing as I watch him walk back to his car.

I shower and spend the rest of the night hanging out with Mom.

When I go to bed alone, even though I completely agree about my pussy needing a break, a small part of me still hopes he'll show up at my bedroom window. Even if we don't have sex, he could still cuddle with me. I enjoy sleeping with his strong arms around me.

I drift off to sleep still hopeful, but when I wake up, it's morning, and I'm in bed alone.

I grab my phone to see what time it is. Just a few more

minutes and my alarm would have gone off. I have a single social media notification. I swipe it open to see a few likes on my post of me and Dare at the popcorn shop, but none of them are Hannah.

I wonder if she's seen it.

I don't think she'd like it even if she did.

I go to my private messages and send her a quick one. "I had a dream you and I went to this cute little popcorn place Dare took me to yesterday. Do you like popcorn? We should go sometime."

I wait to see if she comes online, but maybe she's still asleep or busy because she doesn't.

My alarm goes off, but since I already have my phone in my hand, I shut it off quickly.

Oh well. Guess I had better get ready for yet another glorious day at Baymont High.

I'm worried about the picture Dare had me share. I made it so only my followers can see it, but it feels inevitable that someone will have taken a screenshot and sent it to Anae.

I use the new shampoo and conditioner Dare bought me at the salon. It smells fabulous and makes my hair feel so soft.

While I'm in the shower, my mind drifts to Hannah. I imagine getting out and finding a message from her that she loves popcorn. I imagine making plans to go there together because I think she'd really like the place.

When I get out of the shower, there's no message from Hannah.

I sigh, a little disappointed, and finish getting ready for the day.

When I get to school, there's a strange energy in the air. It's as if I've walked into the middle of a stage production without even having glanced at my lines.

Something's up and I'm out of the loop.

Dread moves over me. It wasn't long ago I never would have stepped foot into Baymont High and assumed whatever drama was circulating had a thing to do with me, but since Dare came into my life, it seems like I'm always involved.

I'm glad I got to school a little early this morning because although Hannah didn't message me back, I see her heading my way down the hall. Since she's in the grade below me, we don't have a lot of opportunities to actually see each other at school. I'm ready to ask if she got my message about the popcorn place and if she maybe wants to go this weekend, but my smile drops when I see she is definitely *not* smiling.

"Hey," I say.

She thrusts a sheet of paper at me. "Have you seen this?"

I frown, taking the paper. I scan it and see it's another damn haiku, but this one's not about me. "No? What is it?"

"These were printed off and left on the counters in restrooms all over the school."

I take a minute to actually read the haiku so I can see what she's so worked up about.

Rina
By: Anonymous

A hateful message
of seventeen syllables.
Good luck typing now.

"Okay," I drawl, glancing at her uncertainly. "I still don't know what this is?"

"Haven't you heard what happened?" she asks.

I shake my head.

"Rina Cahill was attacked over the weekend."

I have no idea who that is. "Attacked how?"

Hannah sighs. "Someone nailed her to a park bench, Aubrey."

My jaw drops. "Oh my god! How horrific."

She nods. "Yeah. Someone catfished her. She thought she was there for a hookup. This psycho lured her there, and then nailed her hands to the wooden park bench they were supposed to meet up at."

"Wow, that's insane. I can't believe something like that happened in Baymont. I don't know what that has to do with this, though," I say, holding up the paper.

Hannah swallows. "You know that crappy haiku someone wrote about you? Turns out it was her."

My heart stalls.

I look down at the paper again and read the poem more carefully.

"Was Dare with you over the weekend?" she asks.

Wide-eyed, I look up at her. "You think Dare did this?"

"I think a haiku has seventeen syllables, and Rina got seventeen nails pumped into her hands. The poem definitely implies the two things are related. I don't know who else is crazy enough to do something like this that would do it in your defense."

Her implication seems to be that Anae might be crazy enough to do it, she just wouldn't do it for me.

My stomach twists with fear. "Do other people think that?"

She shrugs almost apologetically and glances around. "I wouldn't worry about anyone ever calling you an unflattering name again, let's just say that."

If people think he did it, he could be in big trouble. I grab my phone and shoot off a text to Dare, asking where he's at.

"That's not all," she says.

"Oh, come on," I say off-handedly. "Isn't that enough?"

I feel bad as soon as the words are out because she looks seriously distraught.

"Look, I don't want to have to tell you any of this, but I think you should know. Dare came to my house last week and told me to stay out of your relationship. I wanted to listen because, honestly, he's giving off pretty strong serial killer vibes at this point, and the threat he made..." She trails off, shaking her head. "I know he's not bluffing. I know he'll hurt me if he thinks I have anything to do with you leaving him, but I'm *sick* at the thought of you being with him, Aubrey. I'm so afraid he's going to hurt you."

Tears well up in her eyes and the sight makes my heart hurt. I grab her and hug her, shaking my head. "I had no idea he threatened you. I'm so sorry. I wouldn't let him hurt you, Hannah. I'd never let him hurt you."

"But you know he hurts people."

I hesitate, pulling back. I don't know what to say to that. "I mean, I've heard things, but I've never actually seen him hurt anyone."

"He is not a good guy, Aubrey," she says, shaking her head. "He's dangerous. Usually I can see the good in *anyone*, but..." She drops her gaze, shaking her head like it makes her unspeakably sad to say this, then looks back up at me. "I don't know if there's any good in him. I know there must be some reason you like him, so maybe there's a side of him I just haven't seen. But maybe there isn't, Aubrey. Maybe he's faking it."

That makes me profoundly uncomfortable because it's not the first time the notion of illusions has floated across my mind where Dare is concerned.

"I don't know what's going on behind the curtain, but

something about him just... I don't feel any good coming from him."

I look at her, unsettled. It's just like the other times. She's blowing away his fog.

Before it can fully clear, he rounds the corner and comes down the hall toward us.

Seeing him coming, I put a little more space between me and Hannah. She notices the shift immediately and turns to look.

As soon as she sees him, I feel the spike of fear in her. I don't know what he said when he was at her house, but it must have really frightened her.

"I have to go," she says quickly.

"Hannah, wait." I try to catch her arm, but she hurries past me so she doesn't have to face him.

I'm frowning when Dare gets to me.

"Good morning to you, too," he says.

"Did you threaten Hannah?"

His gaze sharpens. It feels predatory and sends a shard of fear slicing through my nerves.

I shouldn't have asked like that. That was tactless. What was I thinking?

Actually, what I was thinking is I have an awful lot of violence to ask him about today, and it's hard to consistently say the right things when my mind is completely blown.

"Did she say I threatened her?" he asks levelly.

I swallow. I can't tell him what she said, but I guess I should communicate that she didn't completely tell on him. How do I do that?

"I don't understand what you have against her. She's like the sweetest person in the whole world. Maybe your read is off because you're so used to hanging out with the Wicked Witch of the West, but Hannah is a *nice* person who would never wish either of us harm."

He smirks, but there's no humor there. "Not you, at least."

"Not either of us. She's my friend, Dare. I need you to be nice to her."

"You need me to be nice to Hannah?" he says, grabbing me and lightly trailing his finger over one side of my jaw while leaning in and kissing the other. "I can be nice to her. How nice do you want me to be?"

Something in his tone makes my stomach rock. It feels vaguely like a threat, but I'm probably reading too much into it based on my prior assumption that he would be attracted to her, and knowing Anae let him sleep with other people. "Just… she's my friend. You two should get along."

"If she wants to get along with me, then she should stop putting whatever poison she's putting in your head to make you mad at me every time I see you after she does."

"She isn't poisoning me against you, Dare. She's just…"

Making sense?

Obviously, I can't say that. Without giving him more ammunition, I don't know how to refute the claim that she's trying to turn me against him.

"She just wants what's best for me," I finally say.

"And she doesn't think that's me," he states.

I'm so distracted arguing with him about Hannah, it doesn't even occur to me he's kissing me in plain sight until a girl stares as she walks past us in the hallway. I gasp and try to pull back, eyes wide. "Oh my god, what are you doing? People can see."

Rather than let go, his grip on my jaw tightens. His other hand goes to my waist so he can control me better as he rumbles, "Let them see."

I can feel a cold sweat about to break out. "Dare, let me go."

"No." His grip on my jaw tightens almost painfully. "I will kiss you wherever and whenever the fuck I want to," he says carefully. "And I don't care if Hannah or Anae or anyone else fucking likes it. You're mine, and I will do whatever the fuck I want to do with you. Do you understand?"

I swallow, my heart pounding unsteadily in my chest.

When I don't answer, he runs his fingers along my jawline. "I don't like being mean or threatening to you, Aubrey. I don't like that Hannah brings out this resistant side of you. Every time she's around, you pull away from me, and I don't know why. I know if she were a man, I would assume she's competition and I would treat her accordingly." He places a gentle kiss against my cheek, at odds with his words. "Should I expand my view a bit, hm? Should I consider her my competition?"

My heart nearly drops out of my body. "No, of course not."

"Anyone who tries to split us up will have a very bad fucking time if I find out about it," he informs me.

"She wasn't trying to split us up."

"But she told you I threatened her. Did she think you would like that?"

You did threaten her!

I know rationality isn't what he's looking for here, though. He's trying to intimidate me, and he's not doing a terrible job.

"She didn't tell me what you said," I point out. "She could have. If I knew what you threatened to do to her, I assume we would be having a different conversation."

He smiles, but it's not a nice smile. "We would. But I don't think it would be different in the way *you* think it would be. I told you I won't lie to you, Aubrey, and I won't. Yes, what I threatened to do to Hannah was bad. But if I tell you, it will make you want to leave me, and if you leave me, then I'll do it. So, would you like to know what I threatened Hannah with?"

I feel sick, but I shake my head no.

Not with terms like those.

"All I want is for us to be together and happy without other people trying to get in the way of that," he says in a way that makes it sound so sensible. "Is that so bad?"

I shake my head again.

"Is that what you want, too?"

My tummy roils, but I ignore it and nod my head. "Yes, of course."

"Good." He kisses the side of my face, then finally lets go of my jaw.

He held me so tight, I'm afraid there may be fingerprints. I rub the skin lightly, looking up at him.

His attention has shifted to the sheet of paper in my hand. "I see you've read the poem. Much better than hers, if I do say so myself."

"Did you have your nerd army write it?" I ask a bit stiffly, trying to get back into the frame of mind of a girlfriend whose boyfriend isn't openly threatening violence to one of her friends.

He smirks. "Nope. Penned that one myself, just like you asked."

Just like I asked?

My blood runs cold. "What are you talking about? I never asked for this."

"Not seriously," he allows. "You said something about me penning a clapback poem for you being the true test. Personally, I prefer my revenge to be a little more draconian, but I decided to cover all the bases."

I can only gape at him. "You really did this," I say softly. "All of it?"

"What? I was just supposed to let her humiliate you and get away with it?" He caresses my jaw, his gaze oddly tender for what he's saying. "I don't think so, mermaid. She needed to pay. So, she did." He kisses my forehead and takes a step back without letting go of my arm. "I've got class, but we'll talk more about this later, okay?"

I nod, my insides feeling entirely hollow. I try not to let it show, but I'm not sure I'm doing a good job. It's not until I meet his gaze and manufacture a small, reassuring smile that he finally releases my arm.

His gaze lingers for too long on my face. I can tell he's not satisfied with my reaction, and the way he's being today, that makes me nervous.

Hannah's words reverberate inside my head. The memory of her fear when she turned and saw him still makes my blood run cold.

I'm afraid of him thinking more about how she might be an obstacle in the way of our relationship. I visualize beautiful, lovely Hannah on that park bench with nails through her hands and the monster that is my boyfriend standing over her.

I want to throw up.

I don't want him to think he needs to punish anyone else.

"Dare?" I call before he gets too far.

He turns to look back at me.

"I love you."

The words come out in a desperate tumble. I have no idea if it's what he needs to hear or not, but relief trickles through me when he smiles.

"I love you, too."

SITTING on my bed all alone, I go over my options.

I could go to the cops.

Of course, the cops in this town are notoriously crooked, often paid off by wealthy families, and Dare's family is one of the wealthiest. So, following that path, he gets off with no more than a slap on the wrist somehow, and then what?

Then I'm fucked. Not only does that mean no more treatment for Mom, but likely no more warmth for me—which would render me completely incapable of shielding Hannah from him. I don't know if he would even care to go after her if he didn't want me anymore, but he might. Just to prove a point.

I look down at the empty notebook page where I would ordinarily make lists or notes for a difficult problem I'm working out, but the page is blank. Not because I don't have any ideas, but because I am terrified to commit them to paper and risk Dare seeing it.

I can't go to the cops. The only way that works out in my favor is if justice is actually served, and it usually isn't in this town. Also, there's no way I can pay the referral fee for

Mom's cancer treatment with the tens of dollars I have to my name.

Fuck.

I don't know what to do. I still have feelings for Dare, but he really scared me today. It wasn't just all the crazy shit he did, but how *casually* he talked about it—like it was no big deal. Like I would also think it was no big deal.

Maybe it's because he's used to talking to Anae about his misdeeds. She probably wouldn't care. Hell, she would probably laugh and find it funny, and together they would chuckle about the permanent damage he did to someone over a stupid haiku.

I didn't plan to be the girl's bestie anytime soon, but I think a horizontal crucifixion might have been an over-reaction.

Also, there are the details I've heard since. The sexual shit that her attacker—who is apparently my boyfriend—said to her via text. I don't know how to feel about it.

I mean, I do. Pissed. If I had the freedom to, I would feel pissed, but after our argument over Hannah got so scary, I'm not sure what I'm allowed to feel.

I don't like that, either. If he did something wrong, I should be able to be mad about it. I was pretty clear with him that I am *not* Anae and if he wants to be with me, there will be no *playing* with anyone else.

But it's also kind of hard to lay down rules for someone who literally does whatever the fuck he wants without seeming to worry about the consequences.

Maybe I won't even need to sort all this out myself. What he did was so insanely illegal. Even with his dad's connections, I'm not sure he'll be able to get out of this one.

There's a scratch at my window and I nearly jump out of my skin.

I have a guilty impulse to clear my notebook out of the way, but then I remember I haven't written anything down.

My limbs are heavy with dread as I climb off the bed and go over to open my window.

Dare climbs in, and I back up, crossing my arms in an unconscious gesture of self-protection.

He notices immediately. I watch him catalogue my stance and flick a glance at my face, but he doesn't focus on that right now. He closes the window, then looks around my bedroom. His gaze drifts to the notebook and he picks it up.

"What's this?" he asks.

"I was just working on some homework."

He cocks an eyebrow. "Doesn't look like you got very far."

My cheeks warm and I glance at the blank page. "No, I guess I didn't."

He nods knowingly, dropping the notebook and moving closer to me. "Had other things on your mind?"

I nod.

"Have you been talking to Hannah?" he asks casually.

My stomach drops just hearing him say her name. I shake my head quickly. "No. We haven't spoken since this morning."

He nods.

Since he brought her up, I try to think how to approach what I want to say. "Please don't go back to her house."

He cocks his head curiously.

"I mean, if you're there to see Anae or whatever, fine, but... please just leave Hannah alone. She doesn't deserve to be dragged into this. All she wanted to do was be nice to me when your girlfriend targeted me, and she doesn't deserve to be... mistreated." To my horror, tears well up in my eyes by the end of that statement.

Intrigued, Dare closes the distance between us, looking into my glistening eyes. "You care for her."

"She's my friend," I say to make sure that's clear. "I just like her, that's all. As a person." My heart thuds. "She's not your competition, it's nothing like that, I just... She doesn't deserve to be scared or hurt, and I feel like it's all my fault."

My eyes are still full of tears. I'm so angry at myself for getting more and more emotional about this. All that will do is give him more cause for concern.

"You want to protect her," he finally says.

Two tears slip over the rims of my eyelids and slide down my cheeks at the same time. I nod, unsure what to say that won't make things worse.

He catches my tears on his fingertips, looking at them like they fascinate him.

"It must be horrible to feel so afraid," he says calmly, rubbing his thumb over my tears until he's rubbed them into his skin. "To feel so powerless," he adds, taking a heavy step forward and meeting my gaze. "But you're not powerless, are you? I told you Hannah would only be in danger if you left me, and you weren't thinking about doing that, were you?"

It feels like a bucket of ice has been dumped into my veins. I shake my head. "No. Of course not."

"No," he says, though his tone is a bit mocking like he wants me to know he knows better. "Of course you weren't." He stops walking and looks me over. "Take off your clothes."

My heart sinks, but I do as he says, quickly removing my PJs and tossing them in the corner. I stand here in just my panties as he roams closer.

"Those, too."

My hands are unsteady as I push down my panties, step out of them, and then kick them aside.

"Get on the bed," he says.

I take a few breaths, trying to keep calm as I back up and climb on the bed.

The mattress sinks under his weight as he climbs on with me. "Are you afraid of me, mermaid?"

That question when he's using that nickname makes me feel emotional all over again. "I don't want to be," I say, since it's the closest thing to the truth I think won't offend him.

"You don't have to be," he says, gently laying his hand over my bare tummy. "It doesn't bode well that you are already. I don't like to think Anae was right, but maybe I am too dark for you." He circles my belly button with the tip of his finger. "Unfortunately, I've already decided you're mine, and you being afraid of me won't change that."

I don't like to think that Anae was right, either, and I definitely don't like to imagine being trapped in a relationship with someone I'm afraid of. "Are you like this with her?" I ask, hating that I even have to.

He lies on his side, sliding his hand up toward my rib cage. "No. To be honest, you trigger completely different instincts in me than she does. None of this would ever work on her, so why would I do it? That's a lot of effort for no result."

I frown. "What do you mean?"

Lightly, he drags his fingertips over my skin causing goosebumps to sweep over me. "There are two types of people in the world, Aubrey. Predators and prey. You're prey. Hannah's prey. Anae and I are both predators. We don't hunt each other. We hunt you."

My eyes widen.

"Tactics that work like a charm with you wouldn't move the needle at all if I tried them on her. I can't bully her by threatening violence against people she cares about because she doesn't care about anyone," he adds. "What's the point in threatening to burn the world if the person just shrugs and genuinely doesn't give a fuck? You, I can bully by threatening violence to Hannah. Hannah, I can injure just by ripping up a piece of fucking paper. In that sense, it's much different with you. I know it's not nice, but when I want to win, I know I can because I know exactly which buttons to push to completely disarm you."

"You didn't always win with her?"

"No, I did, but the games were different. For example, her trying to drown you at the beach the other day because I was making her mad. Not the kind of thing you would ever do, and see how the strike wasn't even at me, it was at the prey she knew I was hunting?"

Hunting.

He is saying a lot of things.

His hand stills on my belly and he meets my gaze. "She didn't try to take me down, she just tried to take my kill. It's almost sportsmanlike."

His words turn my blood to ice water. "So, I don't really mean anything to you, then? I'm just... prey?"

"No, I didn't say that," he murmurs, sliding his hand up to cover my breast. "I'm very fond of you. I told you I loved you just today, didn't I?"

Are you even capable of love?

I don't ask. I'm too afraid to.

Besides, would he even know?

"But you asked if it was different with Anae, so I'm telling you how it's different."

"Are you still sleeping with her?"

My fear grows the moment my words are out. I didn't want to ask. I'm terrified of the answer.

"No," he says, squeezing my tender flesh. "You told me you didn't want me to sleep with anyone else, so I haven't."

"And she doesn't find that odd?"

"Her sex drive was never as high as mine. That's why she started finding prey for me to play with from the get-go. She wanted me by her side, but she didn't want to spend all that time on her back. This way, everyone got what they wanted."

I guess that makes sense. I can't imagine it myself, but I know Anae and I don't think the same way. "What about..." I stop, trying to think how to ask. "Um, I heard how that girl at the park was found. People said she was naked."

"She wasn't naked. She was wearing a skirt with no panties that she had changed into in the car. She wore a shirt but no bra because I told her to take it off."

My stomach sinks. "Why did you tell her that?"

"Because I wanted her to be deeply humiliated when they found her," he says simply. "I would've penetrated her with something as well if I were single, but I had a strong hunch you wouldn't like that."

"Yes, that's correct," I say quickly. "Do you mean your dick?"

He makes a face. "No. A pinecone or a stick off the ground. I thought about it, but I didn't want to touch her. I don't know if you would consider it me breaking the rules even if it's not for pleasure."

"Let's say all forms of penetrating other people with anything? Off the table."

He smirks. "That's what I figured."

My god, what a twisted thing to smirk about.

I shake it off. I knew he was a little twisted. This is more than I was prepared for, but at least he's being open with me about it.

"So, you didn't do anything sexual with her."

"Of course not."

"But... people were talking about these messages." I look over at him. "They were very sexual."

"Yes," he says patiently. "They were a trap. I didn't mean them. She's attracted to sadistic Doms, so I played one to get her where I wanted her."

Played one…

He sounded pretty convincing from what I heard.

This is a lot to digest.

"I did all of it for you, Aubrey. Why would I do anything that hurt you in the process?"

That would be sweet if it weren't so psychotic.

I watch his hand on my breast as he palms and squeezes it. He catches my stiffening nipple between his fingers. I moan without meaning to at the wave of pleasure that rolls over me. "You're not worried about getting caught?" I ask a bit thickly.

"No. I have that all taken care of. I was able to take out someone who hurt you and someone who betrayed me in one fell swoop." His lips tug up and he squeezes my nipple harder.

I close my eyes, instinctively rolling my hips.

"Sometime this week, the police will want to interview you. They'll ask about Frank Tunstall, the kid I had delivering you notes until Anae intercepted him. There will be eyewitnesses who can corroborate how he bothered you at lunch sometimes, how he had a crush on you and wanted to impress you."

My eyes flutter open. I frown, but he squeezes my nipple hard and knocks the look right off my face.

"You will tell them that yes, he came over and talked to you sometimes. He passed you notes, one of which was the haiku he gave you Friday. The only one you kept."

He *did* give me a haiku Friday, but it wasn't the one I saw today. It had nothing to do with that girl, it was just a nice haiku about a beautiful girl in a white dress. I took it as a love note from Dare. It made me smile, but didn't mean much to me because I knew he had his nerd soldiers write it for him.

It clicks into place.

He had *Frank* write it for him. Probably so that there

would be verifiable record of him having written a haiku before to try to impress me.

"You're framing him," I murmur.

"Yes. He should have known better than to betray me. The last kid who did went through a plate glass door. Nearly lost an eye."

I had heard that story, but I didn't know it was real.

"This one will probably have to serve some time, but he's only 17, so it shouldn't ruin his life, only set him back a bit." His hand stills, cupping my breast, and he leans in to kiss the corner of my mouth. "I like talking to you about things."

I reach up and absently slide my fingers through his hair. I have no idea how to feel about all this, but I guess I'm glad he's talking to me about it, too.

His mouth claims mine, and I close my eyes as I kiss him back. He moves on top of me, still wearing all his clothes while I'm completely naked. I feel bare and breakable beneath his weight, completely incapable of keeping him from any part of me he wants access to.

I also feel like he is very well aware of the imbalance, and likes it this way.

He breaks the kiss and pulls back to unbutton and unzip his jeans.

"Dare."

"Yes, baby?"

"How do I know you won't hurt me?"

"Well, it helps not to give me a reason to." He takes his cock out, leaning over me and lining it up at my entrance. "But at the end of the day," he shoves his cock into me, "you just have to trust me."

CHAPTER 37
AUBREY

THE REST of the week goes just how Dare said it would.

The police come, and I tell them what he told me to.

Frank gets arrested, but no one at Baymont High really believes he did it. Dare was careful so all the evidence lines up against him, but there's one glaring impossibility: there's no way in hell Frank Tunstall had the confidence to say all that Dom shit Dare said in the text messages.

Getting away with it only makes him cooler, though. The kids at our school are idiots and don't realize actual danger lurks in their midst.

I suppose I shouldn't be so hard on them. I was one of them, once.

Now I know he's dangerous, but he's the danger that spends every night in my bed. My guard dog unless I give him a reason to bite me, too.

There's something comforting about it, but it's scary at the same time.

For the first few days after the run-in with Hannah, I have a hard time fully shaking the lucidity of our situation even though I don't talk to her again. The popcorn message is left on read, our date never to be.

Dare ups his efforts, giving me pretty pink flowers, and presents, and the kind of sex I prefer. He makes love to me rather than being so rough, making me come multiple times every night to try to fog my mind again.

By Wednesday, it starts to work.

He tells me we're hanging out on Thursday and takes me to his place. We have another swim lesson, then he takes me up to his bedroom.

At first, he's gentle with me like he has been. He lets me climb on top of him, smiling in a softer, unguarded way that lulls me. He wraps his hand around my neck as I straddle his hips and lean in to kiss him. My pretty new hair falls in his face and he grabs a lock, rubbing it between his fingers.

"Tell me you love me," he rumbles.

I feel a thrill in my tummy. "I love you," I say softly, bending to kiss my way along his hard jaw.

"No matter what."

My tummy drops. With anyone else, that would mean something entirely different. With him…

I swallow, knowing non-compliance isn't an option unless I want to set him off. "No matter what," I say, the words feeling like poison in my mouth.

He grabs me, switching our positions and throwing me back on the bed. I gasp at the impact, then he's on top of me, between my thighs, looking down at me.

My heart pounds in my throat. He watches me for a moment, then he grabs a condom.

I'm relieved.

The night he took me in my bedroom after all the Hannah stuff, he came in me. He knows I'm not on birth control, and I was afraid that was going to be a thing he started doing, but it was the only time.

I don't know if he wanted to mark me that night, or scare me a little. I do know it was risky, and as I'm in no way ready to be tied to him with a baby, not something I want to happen again anytime soon.

The crinkling of the foil packet reassures me that he hasn't completely lost his mind.

I think he just wanted to see if I would *let him* come inside me that night because he could feel me slipping away. I didn't *want* him to, but I knew if I told him no, he would do it anyway, and I would just lose a chance to reassure him.

Once the condom is rolled over his dick, he pushes it into me. He closes his eyes, leaning over me and bracing his weight on the bed. I gaze up at him, still grimly aware of his beauty as his muscles flex while he fucks me.

His eyes open, and he looks down at me with that dark look I usually see mid-fuck, the one that felt scary even *before* I knew all the violence he was capable of.

Now, it feels terrifying.

What is he thinking when he looks at me that way?

Maybe it's crazy that when he scares me like that I want to pull closer to him, but I think it's what he wants. I can't outrun him or outmaneuver him, so staying close to him feels like the only way to stay safe.

I reach up to caress his face. I bring him down to me, my touch gentle, and kiss his lips as he hammers into me.

I initiated the kiss, but when he kisses me back he dominates my mouth, tangling a hand in my hair and driving into my pussy harder. I cry out at the brutal impact, and he growls against my mouth, then kisses me even more ravenously.

His hungry kisses still make my heart flutter.

Knowing what he's capable of, I don't feel like they should.

He makes me come before he finishes, but in the aftermath as I lay curled in his arms, I feel sick to my stomach.

His low voice in my ear startles me. "You're staying here tonight."

"Okay," I say softly.

His arms tighten around me and, before long, he drifts off to sleep.

I'm nearly asleep myself when I feel his body jerk. It startles me awake, but my blood runs cold when it sounds like he's panicking. I pull his arms off me and roll over so I can look at him.

He rolls on his back, still tense, his eyes still closed.

"Hey," I say softly, grabbing his shoulder and shaking it a little to wake him up. His eyes open and dart to mine, and for just a moment, I see a mix of fear and vulnerability in his eyes that cuts straight through all the shit we've been through this week and sinks a blade into my heart.

"It's okay," I say, wanting to comfort him. "It was just a bad dream."

He closes his eyes again, seeming to realize it, but he's still… vulnerable.

I've never seen him like this before. It's strangely intoxicating. I caress his bare chest and lean down to kiss the side of his face, anything to calm him down.

His hand covers mine and he sighs. His other hand slides into my hair and he pulls me down so my face is against his firm chest.

"Fuck," he rumbles.

"It's okay," I say again, my voice gentle. I kiss his chest. "It's okay, baby."

I feel the tension slowly ease out of his body as I comfort him. My heart aches and I can't get close enough to him.

He pulls my head back with the hand he still has threaded through the silky locks of my hair. He tugs me back just enough so he can kiss me, then he pushes me against his chest and sighs.

"I love you," he murmurs.

My heart does a somersault. I hold him tight and murmur, "I love you, too."

"I'm sorry I've been so hard on you this week."

His apology startles me. It's not the first one he's given me, but the way he has been all week, it's totally unexpected. "It's okay," I say, even though I'm not sure it is.

"I just don't want to lose you," he says.

My heart contracts. His admission feels so raw and sincere. I know he's been kind of crazy, but it really does seem like a lot of his crazy has revolved around being afraid of losing me.

I tilt my head and look up at him. I slide my hand up to caress his neck as he looks back at me, so open I think I could wound him if I tried.

But I don't want to wound him.

"You're not going to lose me," I tell him.

He caresses my arm. "Promise?"

I nod even though my brain tries to caution me about making a promise I can't keep. I'm not ready to quit on him, I'm just a bit spooked by all that's happened.

His request brings me back to a time earlier in our relationship, too. It wasn't that long ago, but it feels like a lifetime since he promised to never abandon me. Now, he just needs the same reassurance from me.

"I promise," I whisper.

He pulls me close and kisses me, then he rolls me on my side and wraps his arms around me, pulling me against his body.

I wrap my arms around him right back.

For a while, it's so quiet I don't think he'll speak again, but then he asks, "Do you still trust me?"

I have to think about it for a few seconds. A little bit ago I might've said yes just to appease him, but now that he's being more like the version of him I'm not afraid of, I give myself a moment to search for the truth.

Do I still trust him?

I've found out new things about him, that's for sure. Things that aren't comfortable or easy, things I don't even like. In some ways, I feel like he completely tricked me into having feelings for him. If he had come out of the gates with brutalizing near-strangers and threatening my friends, would we be here right now? Of course we wouldn't. Even the way he has admitted to bullying me this week and pushing me around. I'm not comfortable that he knows he can do that. I'm not comfortable that there's really nothing I can do to stop him. Sure, I could call his bluff, but then what happens if he's not bluffing?

Because I believe Hannah was right. I don't believe for a minute that he's bluffing. I've seen him do damage now. Some stupid girl wrote mean shit about me online, I let him know it bothered me, and he nailed her to a fucking park bench.

Malicious and crazy, but at the same time, that's pretty impressive dedication.

He might be unhinged, but he certainly showed up for me.

And while it is scary knowing he can do shit like that without apparently feeling any guilt, I'm also aware he doesn't seem to do damage impulsively. I don't think I have to be afraid of him flying off the handle and doing something he doesn't mean to do.

He has pretty much laid out his entire play for me as far as setting Frank up. Every move he made was deliberate. There were even moves he made preemptively *before* he ever planned to set the kid up, just in case he needed to someday. Dare doesn't just make careful plans, he creates insurance policies for himself in case he ever *needs* to make a plan on the fly.

Sharing as much as he has with me when I didn't even ask…

He's given me all I need to lock him up if I really wanted to. I could take what I know to the police. He has trusted me with information they couldn't possibly refute. Hell, I know where the leather gloves he wore when he attacked her are.

But then there are all these other things. He says he's handling Anae, and I've pretty much stopped even worrying about that. She feels like a potential threat to my actual well-being, but she doesn't feel much like his girlfriend anymore.

I thought there would be some blowback after I posted that picture of us together and there wasn't. He hasn't told me anything changed, but he did also kiss me at school.

I don't know. The Anae stuff feels like a superficial issue at this point. He has made his intentions with me clear. He's not treating me like a side piece, he's treating me like his girlfriend.

"Was that a hard question?" he asks lightly.

I tip my head back and look up at him. He doesn't look truly bothered, so I kiss his chin. "*Can* I still trust you?" I ask him honestly. "A lot has happened since you told me I could. There was a lot you didn't tell me."

He absently caresses the small of my back. "I told you there would be," he says. "There are some moves I need to make without cluing you in beforehand. That's why I said I needed you to really trust me. If you only trust me until I do something you're not sure about, that's not trust. I need the kind of trust that, even when it looks like I've crossed lines, you don't believe it. You believe that I have your back."

"You want me to be a fool for you," I say, smiling faintly.

He doesn't smile back. "You're not a fool if you're right. I need you to trust that I would never *make* a fool of you, Aubrey."

I sigh. "Why can't things just be easier with you?"

He cracks a smile. "That's just not how I work. Sorry."

"Well, what if that's not how I work?" I ask honestly. "Maybe I'm just not a very trusting person."

He shrugs. "You've gotta trust me anyway."

"And if I don't?"

"You go to the tower," he states somberly.

I crack a smile. "That can't be your answer for everything."

"It's not my answer for everything. I have many other answers—flowers, gifts, fucking, outright emotional black-mail. Honestly, I think I've *hardly* used the tower."

I laugh, pushing against his chest, but his grip on me only tightens. "You're shameless," I tell him.

"And you're stuck with me," he states. "I can see myself being with you forever, Aubrey. I'm not bullshitting you. I can see us having kids and a family, birthday parties and fuck-ing… trips to the popcorn store. I'm not one foot in this thing. I want it all, and I want it with you."

My insides feel suddenly hollow hearing him say that. "Really?" I ask softly.

He nods. He certainly looks serious. Stroking my face, he says, "Yes, really. I can't promise I'll always be easy to deal with, but I can promise I will *always* be there for you, what-ever you need. I've tried showing you that even in the middle of all this fucking madness. I'm serious about you, Aubrey. Of course you can trust me. You've just gotta let yourself."

I like what he's saying, and I *want* to be able to trust him.

I did before, so maybe I can again.

Maybe it will be different this time, too. This time, I'll actually *know* who I'm giving my trust to.

The reality of him is clear now, and if I renew my commitment to trusting him... this time, my eyes are open.

It feels wrong, but it also feels right.

It's definitely the only way forward.

"Okay," I say. "I trust you."

He smiles and it makes my tummy feel funny. He leans down and kisses me, then settles his arms around me. I absently rub his back as our bodies relax again so we can go to sleep in each other's arms.

This feels nice. We feel close again.

I know all of our problems aren't magically wiped away, but for the first time since I walked into school Monday morning and found out what Dare was truly capable of... I feel hope.

CHAPTER 38
AUBREY

Hey baby, I'll be over later sometime after your mom's in bed. Make sure you're dolled up for me. ;)

I SMILE at the winky face as I reread the text Dare sent me earlier. I'm used to him coming over when Mom's in bed, so I've been wearing cute pajamas and no bra—often no panties, too.

Tonight, I tie my hair up in a ponytail and spritz myself with this yummy body spray he bought me. I gloss my lips with a moisturizing balm but no lipstick because he doesn't like to get it all over his face. For PJs, I change into a sexy little pink silk crop top and sleep shorts duo he bought for me. It's too sexy to wear in front of Mom, but Dare will undress me before he fucks me, anyway. I'll change into something more modest in the morning after he sneaks out.

I climb into bed and strategically drape my crop top so he can see the under curve of my tits and snap a picture of myself in bed.

"See you soon," I text back, attaching the picture.

"Christ," he sends back immediately. "Not soon enough."

I chuckle and reach over to put my phone on charge, then I curl up in bed to rest a bit before he gets here and inevitably wears me out.

When my eyes open again, I can feel Dare's hand sliding down the curve of my ass. Arousal sweeps over me instantaneously as I hug my pillow, parting my legs so he can slide his hand between my thighs and touch my pussy.

"Fuck," he grumbles, putting a knee on the bed.

I'm in the mood, big time, so I roll my hips. He grabs them and kneels on the bed behind me, bringing his hardening cock against my ass.

I sink back on him and grind a little.

"Fuck, baby."

I smile. "Get in bed. I rested up. I'm ready for you."

"I wish I could," he says.

I frown, tugging my hips out of his grasp and taking a seat on my butt. "You can't?"

My bedroom is dark and Dare is still fully dressed. He's wearing dark wash jeans, and a black jacket with a black hoodie underneath.

"Were you out burgling before you came over?" I tease.

He smirks, pushing me back on the bed and climbing on top of me. "Maybe."

I spread my thighs and wrap my legs around him, trying to pull him down on me, but he's too strong and I end up just hanging on him like a monkey. I don't care. I'm turned on and I've been waiting for him all night. I lift myself and rub my needy pussy against him.

He slides his hand up the leg hole of my shorts and groans when he finds I'm not wearing panties.

"Fuck me," I whisper, leaning up to kiss his neck.

"I bet you're already wet for me, huh?" he murmurs, pushing a finger into me.

It slides in, the passage eased by how wet my pussy already is.

"Fuck, Aubrey."

"Yes," I say, grinning mischievously. "Fuck Aubrey."

He pulls his finger out of me and lights up my phone, glancing at the display like he's debating whether or not he has time. He looks vaguely agitated, but he undoes his pants and whips his cock out, anyway.

"This has to be quick," he tells me.

He pulls my sleep shorts off and keeps them bunched up in his hand. He smacks my ass and tells me to get on my hands and knees with my ass in the air.

I do as he says, crouching down like he's shown me to before and leaning my forearms on the bed.

I groan as he sinks his cock into my pussy. He's so hard and thick. I sink down and close my eyes, so relieved to have him inside me.

He makes quick work of fucking me, reaching under my shirt and squeezing my tits without even taking it off. I don't know what his hurry is, but I figure this is just round one, anyway.

I grab my pillow and bury my face in it when I come, convulsing around his dick and bearing down, squeezing him and making him shoot his load inside me.

Thankfully, he grabbed a condom before he fucked me, so he grabs a tissue off the nightstand and yanks it off.

"Christ," he murmurs, rubbing my ass and letting me sink down on the bed.

I'm feeling sleepy and satisfied now. "Aren't you spending the night?" I ask him.

He tosses my sleep shorts on the bed beside my face. "Put these back on."

My heart hasn't even stopped pounding and he wants me

to get dressed? Still a puddle on the bed, I look back at him. He's zipping back up and adjusting his clothes.

"Come on, Aubrey. Get dressed, baby."

I feel distinctly like he's handling me and it makes me frown.

Curiosity piqued, I push myself up on the bed and tug my sleep shorts back on. "What's going on, Dare?"

"I want to take you somewhere," he tells me.

"It's the middle of the night."

"I know." His gaze drops to my neck. "Where's your necklace?"

I point to the dresser.

He walks over to get it and brings it back to me. "Put it on."

This is a weird request, but I take the necklace and fasten it around my neck. "Do I need to get dressed, dressed?"

He shakes his head. "No, what you're wearing is fine. Come with me."

I take his hand, but I don't like the way he's rushing me out of here. "Wait, I need my purse."

"You won't need it," he tells me.

"My phone," I say, trying to hang back, but his grip on my hand tightens and he practically drags me out of my room without it. "Dare, what the hell?" I whisper.

"Where are your car keys?" he asks softly.

"Um… in here," I say, pulling him toward the kitchen counter. "Where are we going? Are we taking my car?"

He takes my keys and leads me toward the door. "Come on."

This feels wrong. It's only when he opens the door and starts to push me outside without even letting me grab my shoes that I realize he shouldn't even be in my house. My window is locked. The front door was locked. I usually let him in when he comes to my window, but tonight I just woke up and he was in my room.

"Dare, how did you get in my house?"

His grip on my arm tightens. "Just be a good girl and get in the fucking car."

His words aren't the best, but his voice is cold. That's what scares me.

My heart sinks. I look over and search his face for some sign of what the hell is happening here, but he gives away nothing. "What's going on?" I ask him.

He escorts me around the car, still with that iron grip on my arm. He opens the door and pushes me inside.

I pull my legs in and look up at him, confused and a little scared by the way he's acting. "Dare…?"

He doesn't look me in the eye, just shuts the door and walks around to the driver's side.

Goosebumps cover my whole body. Maybe it's because it's a chilly night and I don't even have a sweater. Maybe it's because my occasionally psychotic boyfriend is acting like a psycho… and a cold one, which I'm not used to.

I tell myself everything is fine. He was the Dare I knew five minutes ago when his cock was inside me, so he can't just… shut it off like that.

But I don't have an explanation for what the hell is happening, and I don't know why he's scaring me like this when we just got past issues over him doing this shit.

When he gets in, he locks the car doors and rolls down his window. He holds the keys out the window, and my heart actually fucking stops when I see Anae grab them.

"Took you long enough," she says, glancing at me, then back at Dare.

"She couldn't find her keys," he explains.

I can't breathe. Anae flashes me a chilling smile, then takes my keys and starts walking toward my car.

I grip the car seat, trying like hell to breathe.

What the fuck is happening?

"Dare?" My voice shakes. "What the hell is going on? Why is she at my house?"

Rather than answer, he backs out of my driveway.

Bile rises as I look at my house while we're driving past it. The windows are all dark. All the neighbors are sleeping. And Anae is backing out of my driveway in my car.

"Dare, please talk to me," I say, my voice small. "What is going on? I'm so confused."

He doesn't say a word. Doesn't so much as look at me.

Oh my god.

I tell myself to remain calm, but I feel like throwing up.

I tell myself not to cry because it's ridiculous, but I'm too afraid not to.

This is Dare. He loves me. He won't hurt me. He won't let anyone else hurt me, either.

Right?

Memories start to flash before my eyes, but it's not a melodramatic end-of-my-life highlight reel. I'm replaying our relationship in my head, making sure everything checks out. That kiss in the ocean. The heat in his voice when he called the night I sent him the picture. The nights he held me in his arms. The way he touches me all the time, like he can never touch me enough. He's so loving, so affectionate.

So how the hell does he sit there right now like I'm not shaking with fear in the seat next to him?

I watch him, trying to get his attention or make him uncomfortable. I know he can *feel* me looking at him.

His lips tug up. It's the first trace of an expression since he hauled me out of my house. "That won't work on me, mermaid. I guarantee I can stare at you longer than you can stare at me without looking away."

Just hearing him call me mermaid is like a balm on my

frayed nerves. "Dare," I say cautiously, reaching a hand over and touching his thigh. I don't know what's going on, but I feel a desperate need to reach him. "What are you doing? Where are you taking me? Why is she here? Please, tell me what's happening."

I'm hopeful for an answer this time. A magical answer, I guess, because it would have to make sense of a whole lot.

Why is Anae here?

Why is Dare being so cold to me?

Where is he taking me?

Why is she following him in my car?

It would take a magical answer to explain all of that and not be something horrible.

I'm having a very strong and very real fear that Dare isn't on my side right now, and I have no fucking idea what to do with that.

He has backup, and I don't even have shoes.

CHAPTER 39
AUBREY

MY FIRST MISTAKE may have been getting into the car with him, but my second—and arguably worse—mistake was not opening the car door and jumping out back when we were on residential roads and I could have run to someone's front door screaming for help.

The road we're on now is curved and dark. A distracted driver could easily veer right off the road and plummet into the dark abyss of the ocean below, never to be seen again.

I'm crying again, but he doesn't seem to care.

My stomach churns violently as I try to figure out where I stand so I can figure out what to do.

I'm completely lost.

I don't know where we are in Baymont—*if* we're even still in Baymont—and I don't know why the man who claims to love me seems to be betraying me.

I tell myself it can't be that. It *can't*.

But what the hell do I do if it is?

He hasn't spoken to me again since he called me mermaid. I keep waiting for the Dare I know and love to make an appearance, but all I get is a fucking stone-faced, unfeeling monster.

That thought frees a different set of memories.

The ones I wasn't there for.

As much as it kills me to admit, there *is* still a side of Dare I've never seen.

I wasn't there the night he attacked Rina.

I wasn't there the night he threatened Hannah.

Even though Dare has vaguely threatened and hurt me before, maybe it wasn't the same when he did it to them. I tried not to think about it, not especially wanting to see him in that light, but when he threatened Hannah, he couldn't have been kissing her jaw and letting just enough malice creep into his tone to make her realize she had better toe the line or risk unleashing him. That's how he threatened me because we're in a relationship, but...

And then I hear myself, and what the *fuck* am I thinking? That's how he threatens me because we're in a relationship? Like it's fucking normal for the person you're with to threaten you?

Usually, when clarity smacks me in the face like this, Hannah is around. Some part of me wonders if that's where we're heading—to Anae's house. I don't know where it is.

I think about asking him again where he's taking me, but while a few minutes ago I was desperate for him to speak to me, right now, I don't want to talk to him at all.

It makes sense to feel that way, but I don't have time.

"You said you didn't love her," I say woodenly, my legs pulled up against my chest, my feet on the edge of my seat.

Dare glances over at me. "You wouldn't have fucked me if I loved her," he states.

He's never hit me before, but I feel like he just did.

Is he saying...?

My emotions are too raw to take a hit like that right now. I hug my knees closer and rest my face against my legs, trying not to cry.

He can't love her. That can't possibly be true. He's had a whole fucking *relationship* with me, and the things he said about her…

There's no way he loves her.

There's no way he lied to me, because if he was lying about that, he could have been lying about *everything*.

Trust me, he said.

He asked for the impossible, and I fucking gave it to him, and now here I am.

"Did you give her that picture?" I whisper.

"No."

I feel so fucking sad. At worst, I thought Dare might break my heart, but whatever this is, it's much worse.

"Where are you taking me?" I ask softly.

"One of my dad's developments," he finally answers. "The model home. We're almost there."

A development sounds potentially big and empty, with no one around to help me.

What are they going to do to me once I'm there?

I think of the nail gun he used on Rina. All of the other construction tools they have at a construction site.

Oh my god.

They're going to kill me.

Tears spring to my eyes as a fresh wave of terror rolls over me. My whole body shakes as the realization hits me.

The coldness. The fucking psycho bitch in my car.

She didn't try to take me down, she just tried to take my kill.

I'm just prey to them. He doesn't love me.

They're both monsters.

No, no, no. That can't be true.

But it makes the most sense. I don't understand how or why. I'm so fucking confused and heartbroken, and *nothing makes any fucking sense.*

Dare hits the turn signal, presumably to signal Anae that

this is where the turn is because there's no one else on the road.

My brain tells me this may be my last chance to plead with him for mercy, but my broken heart doesn't think he has any.

I think about how fucking stupid he must think I am. He comes to my house to kidnap me, and I think he's there to cuddle.

"Good thing you got that last fuck in, huh?" I mutter.

"You asked for that fuck," he reminds me. "Practically begged for it."

Talk about salt in the fucking wound.

He hasn't been exactly chatty during this horrendous drive, so I'm surprised when he says, "Don't mention that to her."

My eyes widen and I stare at him. "Are you *fucking* kidding me?"

If I could rip his face off his skull right now, I fucking would.

The sound of a car door opening outside gets our attention. Dare's gaze flickers to the rearview mirror, then he looks back at me. "I'm serious, Aubrey. I didn't plan to fuck you. Do not fucking tell her that."

Oh, I'll tell her, all right. In explicit detail.

"I'm going to tell her you came inside me," I state, smiling at him. "That you told me you wanted to have a family with me."

"Christ," he says, looking more aggravated than I have ever seen him before. "This is not the fucking time for that."

"If you don't want your *side piece* to tell your *stupid fucking psycho girlfriend*–"

Anae opens the passenger door.

I don't wait for her to grab me and pull me out.

I launch myself at her, digging my nails into her scalp and ripping at her hair.

"What the fuck!" she shrieks, falling back a couple of steps, unprepared for the attack.

"Jesus Christ." Dare slams the car door and a second later, he's grabbing me and pulling me off her, easily restraining me as I fight like hell to get away from him and attack her some more.

If they're going to kill me, I want to at least rip her fucking hair out first.

"You dumb whore," Anae yells.

"You're a fucking psycho," I scream back. "An *unhinged* fucking psycho who can't even keep her boyfriend satisfied when she lets him fuck around."

Anae literally seems to grow two sizes, that's how full of rage she is.

"This is really fucking great," Dare bitches.

"How *dare* you," Anae says like a dragon about to breathe fire.

"I didn't lose my keys!" I say, struggling to turn back to face her while Dare restrains me. "He fucked me while you were outside waiting—"

Dare's hand clamps down hard over my mouth. The shock of cool leather startles me out of my blind rage and I realize, *oh shit,* he's wearing his black leather gloves.

"Are you fucking serious, Dare?" Anae demands. "You really had to bang her one more time before you brought her outside? You are such an asshole."

I try to scream out more juicy details, but Dare keeps his hand firmly covering my mouth. "Open the goddamn door," he barks at Anae.

She glares at me as she storms past him to do as he ordered. I glare right back.

Dare has me pulled against his body as he drags me

inside. Leaning in, he murmurs in my ear, "You are not being a very good girl."

I would like to shove him off a cliff, so if he thinks I care at all what he thinks of my behavior, he's very confused.

Anae is muttering about how stupid we both are as she irritably kicks a can of paint across the floor.

"Can you not do that?" Dare says. "I need you to stop acting like a child for a minute and help me get control of her."

I try to bite him, but I can't reach with my teeth.

Anae is irritated, but she still comes over to help him. "What do you need me to do?"

"Get some rope out of the closet over here," he says. I feel his body shift as he indicates a coat closet behind us.

Anae walks past, glaring at me and muttering, "Stupid cunt."

Dare sighs, hauling me through the massive marble foyer into a large living area with vaulted ceilings. The place is staged, so there's top-of-the-line furniture and a big beige area rug spread out on the ground below it. I look around for things it would be easy to kill me with. The end table is glass with sharp corners. Don't want to fall by that or get my head bashed into it. There's a big ball sculpture on top of it that could potentially be heavy.

The room is overwhelmingly white which seems less than ideal for a murder scene, but the couch *is* covered in thick plastic.

Dare takes me over to it, forcing me down on the couch and coming down on top of me.

He has to let go of my mouth for a minute as he positions himself so he's straddling me, pinning my hips down to keep me from getting away from him.

"Get your hands off me," I tell him.

He does exactly the opposite, forcing my wrists together

over my head and pinning them with one gloved hand so he can put his other hand over my mouth.

I'm shocked Anae manages to enter the room quietly, but she isn't wearing her heels. She must have realized sneakers were more practical for committing felonies.

She sits down on the end of the couch by my feet and loops the rope around my ankles before tying it so tight, the rope cuts into my bare skin.

"All right, we need to regroup," Dare tells her.

"Can we just kill her now?" Anae asks. "I'm sick of this bitch."

My stomach drops. I knew that had to be the plan, but to actually hear it...

Anae stands, smirking when she sees my horror-stricken face. "What, you didn't think we brought you on a field trip just to let you leave alive, did you? I don't fucking think so, Aubrey. The funny thing is, this is all your fault. We weren't going to kill you from the get-go. Dare was supposed to seduce you, fuck away your stupid little virginity, and make you fall for him, sure, but I was going to leave you with a broken heart. Until you kept fucking pissing me off," she says, her eyes narrowing.

My stomach hasn't stopped dropping since she started speaking. I look up at Dare. He's looking down at me, a look in his eye that I'm too scattered to put a name to right now.

"Oh, yeah. You thought he just *noticed* you because he saved your life," Anae says, rolling her eyes. "I don't think so, bitch. He didn't notice you at all. *I* asked him to go after you, so he did. All of this was bullshit. A *fiction.* You're nothing to him. A *game.* Not even a game, just an insignificant little pawn on the board. I am the queen here, Aubrey. He is *my* king, and you? You are nothing."

"All right, we're getting a little close to a villain monologue here," Dare says, glancing back at her. "You want to wrap it up?"

"I want to see you with her," Anae says.

Dare looks over at her. "What?"

"You already went off plan if you fucked her tonight. You weren't supposed to leave your DNA on her."

"I used a condom," he states.

This is *mortifying.*

"I want to make sure you don't change your mind," she states, watching him. "Why don't you fuck her face, leave some cum in her belly?"

"I'm not going to change my mind," he says. "You think I'm going to take it this fucking far and then change my mind?"

"Rape her and leave it in her cunt if you'd prefer. I just want to see you hurt her," Anae says, her gaze locked on his.

Silence falls for just a few seconds, but it feels like longer.

Anae might let him get away with a lot, but I've clearly rubbed her the wrong way because she's adamant about this.

"I don't fuck at your command," Dare says dismissively, breaking her gaze.

"I do a lot for you, Dare," she says solemnly. "Do this for me. Please."

Dare licks his lips, turning his head to meet her gaze. If I can tell he's hesitant, so can she. "Okay, and suppose, no matter how well we bury her tonight, eventually, she's found with my cum in her fucking body. How are we supposed to explain that?"

Anae smiles thinly. "Shouldn't be too hard. You fuck her all the goddamn time. You fucked her before the car ride. Surely you're due to have another go at her." Then, looking at me, she says, "But don't worry. We can be abundantly cautious. I'll carve out whatever part of her you leave your cum in. We can get rid of that somewhere else."

Chills cover my body at the coldness in her eyes as she talks about carving me up.

Fear starts to work its way around all the hurt and adrenaline flooding my system. If I stand any chance of getting out of here…

I don't think I stand a chance of getting out of here.

Dare doesn't look at me. He climbs off me, hauling me in front of him like an oversized sack of potatoes, and tells Anae, "Go make sure there's plastic down on the bed in there."

"You should suffocate the bitch while you fuck her," Anae says.

"I'm getting a little worried about your dedication to seeing me commit necrophilia," he states. "I'm not into it. Move on."

"If she's the dead girl, I think you could handle it. I wish you could fuck her to death, but I don't know how that even works."

My stomach roils so violently, vomit nearly comes up.

"I guess you could strangle her while you fuck her," Anae suggests.

"Again, no. We already have a plan for how to kill her. We can't keep going off course. Getting sloppy is how you get caught. This is why I don't do crime with you, Anae. You're too goddamn impulsive."

Anae pouts as she enters the bedroom and smoothes out the massive sheet of plastic over the bed. "That's not true."

"Grab her feet," Dare says. "Help me get her up there. Fucking gently," he adds, sounding annoyed. "If you kill her before I fuck her, I'm not fucking doing it."

"What if I just break something?" she asks. "That way she's in pain the whole time."

"No," he says firmly. "If you keep letting your temper do the planning, you're going to piss me off."

"I don't see why I can't just give her ankle a little twist," Anae complains as she helps him lift my legs.

"You're not the one who has to fucking carry her everywhere," he states, easing me down on top of the mattress. "Now, shut the fuck up so I can get this over with."

"Oh, please. Like you aren't going to enjoy it," she says, rolling her eyes and taking a seat on a white chair with a view of the bed. "You like drugging her and raping her. I would think kidnapping her and raping her would be right up your alley. I'm practically giving you one last date night. You're welcome."

What the fuck did she just say?

Has Dare drugged and raped someone before?

The way she said it, it seemed like he did it to *me.*

Dare sighs, sitting up on his knees over my body and stopping just short of raking his gloved hands through his hair. He's annoyed, but I can practically feel him remembering not to leave more DNA on the scene than he needs to.

My god, he's really going to kill me with this psycho.

I could not have been more wrong about him.

And now, I'm going to pay the ultimate price.

CHAPTER 40
AUBREY

DARE LOOKS DOWN AT ME, but not to communicate anything. There's no expression on his face that's remotely for me, or about any of the shit I just heard. He's not worried about what I think, just how he wants to attack what he needs to do next.

"I need you to come over here and loosen the rope around her ankles a little."

Anae gets up and walks over, making her way around the bed and doing as he says. She's spiteful, scratching my skin with her long nails as she works the rope, but I'm still relieved when the rope isn't as tight.

"Good," Dare says, looking back at my ankles. "Now, go back to the closet and see if there's more rope for her hands."

"I don't think there was," she says. "Do you have some stashed somewhere else?"

"Yeah. There's green rope out in the garage if you want to go grab it."

Anae looks at me, then him on top of me almost like she's reluctant to leave. "Don't get started without me," she says. "I want to watch every second. That way, I can always relive this moment when I wear my trophy." Impulsively, she leans in to wrap her arms around his neck and give him a hug, kissing the side of his face. "That was a brilliant plan by the way, baby. God, I love your twisted mind."

I don't immediately know what she's talking about, but then Anae glances at the necklace I'm wearing and smirks. My stomach drops, the pendant suddenly burning like a hot coal branding my flushed skin.

Anae turns around and heads for the garage to get more rope.

There are not words to express how I feel right now. It's hard to believe I still possess the capacity for hope, but I must because my feelings are suspended for a crazy moment as I look up at him, this first moment we've had alone, and somehow still think maybe—just maybe—he'll turn this around.

He could be tricking her, right?

But the suggestion feels hollow even in my own mind. Watching them together, their strange ease with one another…. There's nothing that feels romantic to me on his end when he interacts with her, it's not like how he is with me, but there is definitely camaraderie. He may not love her—*I'll go to my grave refusing to believe that, apparently*—but they're friends. He likes her.

My stomach hurts so much, I almost wish I could throw up just to relieve the ache.

As if he heard my request and wants to make it easier for me to empty my stomach, Dare moves his hand off my mouth.

It doesn't go far. I hear the stiff leather crack as he cups my jaw and strokes my skin like he always has, only this time, with a leather barrier.

"Do you want it in your mouth or your pussy?"

His low murmur triggers a fresh round of tears. I'm hurt and angry and I want to lash out, but I also desperately don't want to die, so I control myself. This might be my last chance alone with him, and he's the only shot I have at getting out of here alive.

"Dare, please don't do this to me," I whisper, reaching up and touching his face tenderly, like I have all the nights we spent together. Like I did just last night after he had a bad dream. "Please. I love you."

He nuzzles my hand, still enjoying my touch. I guess at least I know that wasn't a lie.

"Please," I whisper, pulling him down to me so I can kiss him. "You don't have to do this."

"I don't know, mermaid. I've already come this far."

My heart sinks, then lifts back up because it feels like I have a chance.

"It doesn't matter," I assure him, caressing his face more desperately and shaking my head. "You can change your mind. You don't have to finish this."

He pulls back and caresses my face, watching me. "You've heard a lot I didn't want you to hear."

"I don't care," I blurt. "It doesn't matter. Please, just… Dare, I don't want to die. Please don't do this to me. Maybe it wasn't all real for you, but it was real for me. I *love* you."

His thumb moves deliberately across my cheek. His voice is so calm in the face of my tearful panic, it sends a chill straight down my spine. "Still?"

"Yes, still. Please. Please don't do this. Help me."

I stiffen as he pushes his gloved thumb into my mouth, but I let him do it. "You want my help, baby?"

Terrified and with tears still glistening in my eyes, I nod.

"You still love me?"

I nod again more desperately.

He leans in, trailing his lips across my jaw and making the hair stand up on my arms. "Even after all the twisted shit I've done to you?"

My heart is in my stomach, but I nod. "Yes."

His lips tug up as he pulls his thumb out of my mouth and leans back. He looks down at me, but there's no humor in his eyes. "I don't know if you mean that, mermaid. I think you're drowning again, but this time, I've done enough bad shit that you're willing to pull me down to save yourself."

"I do mean it," I say tearfully, disappointment swelling inside me because I know I'm running out of time, and I'm not getting through to him. He's still doubting me.

He'll never save me if he thinks I'll tell on him.

"Dare, I mean it. I don't want to get you in trouble; I just want to go home. Please…"

He pushes his thumb back into my mouth, pushing it deeper this time and gagging me. "I think I'll take your mouth. I haven't had it before, and if this is going to be the last time…"

"No, please, Dare." Tears spring to my eyes. "It doesn't have to be the last time. Please."

"That's it," he rumbles, watching a tear slide down my cheek. "Cry for me, baby."

I squeeze more tears out, not because he told me to, but because I can't stop them.

Dare moves my hands in front of me as Anae comes walking back into the room, and the last flame of hope burns out.

I didn't convince him, and now I won't get another chance.

"Loop it around her wrists," he tells her.

"Dare, please," I cry. "Please don't do this to me."

Anae smiles. "Ew, she's begging you?"

"Of course she's begging me."

She rolls her eyes as she winds the green rope around my wrists. "At least die with a little dignity, you dumb slut."

Dare smirks. "I don't know, I kind of like it."

Anae smiles faintly, but it's a tolerant, indulgent kind of smile like she finds his depraved comment charming. "You would."

The fact that his eyes glitter with shared amusement makes my blood run cold.

I feel hopeless and completely empty as Dare watches her tie the knot in the rope binding my hands together. I may have gotten one last moment with *my* boyfriend, but now I'm trapped beneath the weight of *hers*.

I stop begging even though he's not covering my mouth anymore. Dare's hand slips under my shirt and I feel the cool leather against my skin as he squeezes my breast.

Anae walks back over to sit on her throne and watch, but I don't care about her anymore. I don't care about any of it. He'd love it if I cried for him, so I don't. It's my final act of rebellion. Fuck him.

He must be annoyed by my silence as he fondles me because he gets rougher with my breasts, trying to get a reaction out of me. I don't even look at him.

"Damn, baby, you're right," Anae remarks. "She *is* a boring fuck."

My heart drops, but I don't bat an eye.

"I was going to take her mouth," he says, "but I have a feeling it won't be much fun." Pulling his hands out from under my shirt, he grabs my hips and turns me over. I feel a flash of fear because there's plastic beneath my face and it *would* be really easy to hold my face down and suffocate me, but maybe that would be better. Whatever sick shit they want to do to me, at least I wouldn't have to be here for it.

Dare adjusts his weight on top of me when I'm tummy down on the bed. He grips my hair with his gloved hand to hold me down where he wants me, and slides the other hand between my thighs.

This isn't the first time he's done this to me, just the first time I've called it what it is, I guess.

I close my eyes as he forces a gloved finger inside me. He pushes deep, working his finger back and forth. Violating me with it in front of her to get me ready for his dick.

I just want it to be over.

He pulls his finger out of me, but I feel no relief. I know what comes next.

Or what *should* come next, but I hear something that sounds like Dare ripping his glove off his hand.

"Hello?" he says in a tone that clearly isn't for Anae.

My heart slams forward in my chest.

Is he... *on the phone?*

"Help!" I shout. It's all I get out before Dare grabs my face so hard, slapping his still-gloved hand over my mouth in a clear command to shut the fuck up.

"No, that was... What do you need?"

My heart pounds.

Anae gets up and walks over, glancing uncertainly from me to Dare to see if he needs her help keeping me quiet. I try to cry out, but Dare's grip tightens painfully until I'm afraid he's going to cave in my jaw.

Please!

I still try to cry out for help. Maybe he'll break my jaw, but if someone hears me, it'll be worth it.

Because I'm trying so hard to be heard, Dare rushes whoever he's on the phone with. "All right, yeah. I'll be right there."

He ends the call and shoves the phone back in his pocket before leaning down and saying viciously, "What the fuck is wrong with you, huh?"

Is he serious?

I cry out as he releases my jaw and smacks it a little, rolling me over and shoving me back against the bed. He glares at me so coldly, fear sinks through my entire body.

He grabs a fistful of my shirt with his gloved hand, yanking me up off the bed and getting right in my face. "You want me to kill you right fucking now, you stupid little cunt?"

My body trembles but I can't speak. I'm too terrified.

That look in his eyes, the one I've seen when he's fucking me? I see it now, and I'm afraid I know what it is.

He wants to kill me.

He feels it right now, and maybe he feels the impulse when he's fucking me, too.

Of course, he's always curbed it before, but right now... he might not.

He lets go of me and I fall back against the mattress.

I can feel his irritation as he looks around for a moment, then climbs off me, and off the bed.

"What's going on?" Anae asks uncertainly.

"I have to fucking run home real quick. We need to do something with her. There's a key in a bowl on the counter in the kitchen. I need you to go grab it for me."

Anae hurries out of the room to do as he says.

Dare exhales with annoyance, cutting a dark look my way. He saunters back over to the bed, his dark eyes roaming my body before finally landing on my face.

I flinch when he leans close, thinking he might hit me, but he just grabs the plastic by my bound hands and rips a small hole in it.

"Stop fucking fighting me," he says lowly.

My eyes widen.

I'm confused, but he turns away to watch for Anae. She comes back and gives him the key.

"Thanks, baby," he says to her.

Hearing him call her that rips another hole in the lining of my heart.

"What's the plan?" she asks him.

"I won't be gone for long. Twenty minutes or so. When I get back, we'll finish her off. We'll do it your way." He opens the dark closet and slips the key into his pocket, then he grabs her by the throat with his gloved hand, pulling her close like he always does to me right before he kisses me.

The pain is too much to bear. I tell myself to just close my eyes. Don't watch. There's no point tormenting myself. But I have to see it. I can't look away.

She tips her face up just the way I would, the same fondness glinting in her blue eyes.

My bottom lip quivers, tears springing to mine.

He caresses her jaw like he does mine, and I hate myself for not being able to keep quiet as I draw a shuddering breath.

He smiles at her like he doesn't even hear me crying, and she smiles back.

But then, he lets go without kissing her.

"Come on," he says, "let's finish this."

My stomach twists as Dare walks over and grabs me, dragging me off the bed and helping me stand upright.

"I need you to change the plastic while I'm gone," he tells her, glancing at the bed. "She must have ripped a hole in it while I was playing with her. Can't risk getting fluids on the mattress when I fuck her. I'll take this sheet with me. The one on the couch, too, just to be safe. There's more in the garage, make sure you cover it all up while I'm gone."

"Okay," Anae says.

My heart beats funny, his words bouncing around my head.

The slow realization that... he just lied to her. He ripped that hole himself when she went to grab the key.

I look back at him and catch his gaze.

He holds mine steadily for just a second, but then he covers my mouth like he's afraid I'll say something stupid.

My heart starts to pound. Maybe I'm reading too much into it, but he didn't kiss her when he would have kissed me, and he just lied to her…

Is he on my side?

It's hard to imagine how he could be, but hope has its claws in me now and won't let go. Dare pushes me into the closet, Anae anxiously right on his heels.

"Why does the closet have a lock on it?" she asks.

"This is the model," he explains, grabbing me and pushing my legs out from under me, moving me so I'm sitting on the floor with my wrists bound and my legs curled up behind me. "My dad put a lock on it so he could store important paperwork and shit like that here without having to worry about people getting into it when they tour the property."

"Huh. That's smart. Good for us," she says, smiling faintly.

I look up at Dare as he takes a step back. His gaze rakes over me like it *is* the last time, and a wave of fear washes over me.

"When I get back, we'll drag her back to the bed. I'm not into this necrophilia bullshit of yours, but you have been pretty accommodating of all mine." He looks over at her. "How about a compromise?"

"What did you have in mind?" she asks.

"She needs to be alive when I start fucking her or it's a nonstarter. But maybe when my cock is jammed inside her pussy and I'm close to finishing… I let you strangle her. If she's dead before I'm done, I'm still gonna finish inside her, so you'll get your wish."

"Ooh, I like that," she says, her eyes lit with excitement. "Will you fuck me after?"

Dare smirks. "On the same bed, next to her body."

Anae sighs, gazing at him with such adoration, it makes

me literally sick. "You really are the best boyfriend ever."

CHAPTER 41
AUBREY

THE CLOSET IS dark and quiet.

It's the first sliver of peace I've had all night.

I'm not sure what's going on. I don't know if Dare was trying to signal me that he has something up his sleeve, or I'm clinging to clues that were never there because I need so desperately to hold onto something.

The things Anae said, even the things he said…

I don't know what to make of it all.

She said he only came for me to begin with because she told him to.

Thinking back to the beginning, I guess that would make sense. Dare was an ass after he pulled me out of the pool. It was only after that night he started being nice to me, and I didn't know why.

If that's true, when did it stop being something he was doing for her? The first time we kissed? Touched? When he made love to me?

Did it *ever* stop being something he was ultimately doing for her?

I guess if they pull me out of this closet and do the horrific shit they talked about doing to me, I'll have my answer.

I've been through so much tonight, I don't have much energy left. It feels like a reprieve leaning against the wall, waiting to find out my fate.

I hear Anae with the plastic on the other side of the door, so I know she's getting ready for his return. The bedroom is dark, so when lights brighten the room, I can see it beneath the crack under the door.

At first, I just see headlights and my heart drops.

If he came back, then I read it wrong. He's here to finish what he started.

But then I see the flashes of blue and red, and I start to cry —this time, with relief.

"What the fuck?" Anae mutters on the other side of the door.

I hear her moving around the room. I jump when she starts jiggling the doorknob, muttering, "Where's the fucking key?"

There's something in her voice. I don't know if it's panic or dawning fury, maybe a mix of both.

My whole body tenses and shakes as she yanks and pulls on the door before banging her hand against the wood. "He took the *fucking* key," she hisses.

He took the key so she couldn't get to me.

He *is* on my side.

I'm still afraid the door will buckle as she rages and yanks on it, screaming at me and calling me every name in the book.

She finally lets go of the door and goes silent, but I can hear her pacing. Suddenly she yells, "Answer your fucking phone, Dare."

There's a pounding noise on the front door.

"Open up. Police," a man calls through the barrier.

I'm saved.

I'm fucking saved.

I start crying, this time out of relief instead of fear.

Anae opens the door and tries to say there's been some mistake, but the cops aren't hearing it. I hear cuffs clinking and more shuffling, and then several pairs of boots on the floor outside.

"I'm in here," I call out.

The footsteps move closer. A man comes to the door and tries to open it, but since this door has a lock, it doesn't open. "You okay in there, sweetheart?"

"Yes," I call back, my voice shaking. "I'm tied up on the floor."

"Are you hurt?"

"No," I call back. "Just please get me out of here."

"I will," he assures me. "Hang tight just a minute, all right?"

He leaves and comes back with something that he jiggles in the door, and then it opens, and I start crying all over again.

A cop behind him snaps my picture, then the big, bald man kneels down to pull me out of the closet. "You're safe now," he tells me. "I've got you."

The first night I met Dare, I spent what felt like an eternity in the hospital.

This time, it's a police station.

I feel like an exhibit as I'm poked and prodded at. They ask a million questions I'm too numb to answer and take pictures of my body that make me feel cold. They collect my pajamas as evidence and give me a huge sweater and sweatpants to change into. They tell me my mom can bring clothes from home, but I ask her not to come.

I know she must be terrified, but I don't have the energy to look after anyone but myself right now, and I don't want

SAM MARIANO

her putting her health at risk just to come to the stupid police station.

They ask if there's anyone else I can call to pick me up. In fact, the officer even says, "What about your boyfriend?"

They think he's the hero in this scenario. After all, it was Dare who called the police and told them that when he went over to his girlfriend's house for a prearranged meeting, she wasn't there. It was Dare who had so thoughtfully and protectively put a tracker on my car after we had a scare with his unhinged ex-girlfriend threatening to cut my brakes because he needed to know exactly where I was if he ever couldn't reach me.

She'd faked his handwriting and tried to lure me to the beach behind his house because she knew I couldn't swim, but he made excuses, didn't take her threats seriously. He was beside himself, would have no one to blame but himself if something happened to me.

Thankfully, he called them so quickly after realizing I wasn't at home.

Thankfully, the police made it here before Anae could finish what she'd started.

In light of the heroism of my incredible boyfriend, the officer seems surprised when I shake my head. "No. I don't want him to come get me."

"All right. Is there anyone else you can call?"

I nod.

When Hannah walks into the station, I feel better immediately.

She feels like the bright, beautiful light at the end of a dark and terrifying tunnel. I don't know how I find it in me to smile, but I do at the sight of her face.

Her arms open to me immediately. I rush into them, holding her tight as tears sting behind my eyes. She hugs me back just as tightly, petting my hair calmingly and murmuring reassurances that everything will be all right, that I'm safe now.

I'm not so sure, but I don't care. Not right now.

When I'm done blubbering, I pull back and look at her. She's not tall like Dare, so I don't have to look up. "Will you take me home?"

She flashes me a smile. "Of course."

It's early morning, the sun just starting to rise in the sky. Hannah asks if I'm hungry, if I want her to stop anywhere and grab me something to eat.

I crack a smile. "I'd rather have one of your muffins."

"I'll make you a batch before I leave. You need to get some sleep. What a long, horrible night you must have had."

She doesn't ask for the details, and I don't want to talk about it, so I don't give her any. She must know Anae has been arrested and why.

It occurs to me she might think Dare was, too, since I called her to pick me up.

Because of the threats I know he's made, it occurs to me I probably should have told her. She probably came to pick me up thinking she didn't need to worry about him anymore.

"Dare's not in jail," I say, looking over at her.

She glances back. "Should he be?"

Definitely.

I nod. "But he isn't. And he won't be."

Her lips press together into a thoughtful little line but she just nods. "Okay."

When we get to my house, it's a crime scene. Police have been in and out of here taking pictures and collecting evidence.

The door closes down the hall. "Aubrey, is that you?"

"Yeah, it's me."

Mom's wearing a mask, but I can still see how her face crumbles at the sight of me. "Oh, honey," she says, rushing over to give me a hug.

I back up before she makes contact, holding up my hands. "Don't. I haven't showered yet."

Mom pulls back, looking inconsolable that she can't hug me. Hannah frowns, not understanding, so I explain.

"Go back to your room," I tell Mom once I've reassured her that everything is okay. "I know people have been in and out of here all morning. I'll… I'll clean the place from top to bottom, but I can't handle you getting sick on top of it. Please stay in your room until I can make sure the place is safe."

Reluctantly, Mom goes back to her room.

I need to shower, but I'm too tired and emotionally depleted. I don't know where I'll find the energy to clean up, but that's a problem for later.

My bedding is still wrinkled from Dare fucking me here before he kidnapped me. I'm a little mortified remembering that, but Hannah just straightens it out, then pulls the covers back so I can climb in.

She goes to get me something to drink and checks in on my mom. I thank her for the cold bottle of water, and I know I do need sleep, but I don't want her to go.

"Will you stay with me for a little bit?"

She nods. "Of course. I'll be here for a while, anyway. I have to make you muffins."

"No, I mean…" I rub the bed.

"Oh." She's surprised, but she smiles, nods, and then climbs into bed with me.

Once we're both snuggled up beneath the covers, I feel safe.

I know it's an illusion just like Dare was because he's still out there, and he'll be back. But for now, I feel safe with Hannah, and I just want to enjoy it.

"Do you wanna be the little spoon or the big spoon?" she asks lightly.

I smile. "It's up to you."

"You could probably use a big spoon today, huh?"

"I don't care. I'm just glad you're here."

"I'm glad I'm here, too," she tells me.

I smile, reaching out to touch her face.

She smiles back, and then I close my eyes.

It only feels like a moment that my eyes are closed, but when I open them again, it's much brighter outside and the house smells like banana muffins.

I'm groggy, but I roll over and check the time.

It's after two, so I drag myself out of bed, rubbing the sleep from my eyes as I stumble out into the hall.

More lovely smells hit my nostrils. I sniff the air, frowning with confusion as I walk down the hall and into a cloud of cleanliness.

Every single thing in my house has been straightened. The floors have been vacuumed or swept and mopped. Every surface shines, every messy pile of bills has been sorted and neatly stacked. Even the doorknobs appear to be shinier and brighter.

My mouth hangs open as I look at Mom sitting on the recliner with a bowl of soup I didn't make.

"What...?"

Hannah comes around the corner, an apron wrapped around her small waist, her hair tied back in a kerchief, and a mask on her face. "Good morning, sleepyhead," she says brightly. "I made soup and fresh bread. Are you hungry?"

I didn't think I was, but my stomach rumbles. "It sounds like it."

She chuckles and heads for the kitchen, turning on the

faucet and washing her hands at my sink. "I'll get you some-thing to eat."

"Hannah, this…" I look around again, at a loss. "You cleaned my whole house."

"It's not a big deal. Your house isn't very big." She freezes, horrified. "I didn't mean it like that. Your house is adorable. I just meant I'm used to cleaning a giant house, so this one was honestly no problem."

"You did not have to do that." I'm so grateful, I want to cry, but I've done enough of that for one day. "Thank you so much."

"Really, it was nothing," she says, reaching into a top cabinet for a bowl like she's lived here her whole life. "I wasn't sure what all they might have touched, so I just cleaned all of it."

I walk over to Mom, absently touching her shoulder. "Do you feel okay?"

Mom smiles and nods, putting her hand over mine. "You have the nicest friends. And this one can cook, too. This is the best soup I've ever had."

I smile, looking back at Hannah. "She's magical," I agree.

Hannah flashes me a smile. "I made your muffins, too."

"Remember how I asked you to marry me? Have you given any more thought to that?"

She laughs, her cheeks turning rosy.

Mom doesn't get the joke, but joins in anyway and inad-vertently ruins it. "I think Dare might have something to say about that."

Mom is only joking, but Hannah and I both stop smiling.

I let go of Mom's shoulder and join Hannah in the kitchen. "Thank you again," I say seriously. "This was beyond amazing of you."

"Really, it was no trouble at all," she assures me.

"Are you sure?" I ask, not because of all the work she did,

but because of the other things. "You won't get in trouble, will you? Does your stepmom know where you are?"

"No. It doesn't matter." I don't get the idea it's the truth, just that she doesn't want to talk about it. To change the subject, she holds out a bowl of soup with a thick slice of bread sticking out of it. "Careful. It's hot."

I accept the soup and the subject change, but as I sit at the table and eat the food she made for me, I start to think about all the reasons I should not have called her. It was selfish to do it, a moment of weakness because I was just completely fucking depleted. I'm always the one taking care of someone, and right then, I needed someone to take care of me.

But I shouldn't have asked that of her.

I know I've potentially put her in harm's way—in more than one scenario, even.

Hannah walks me down the hall to show me around the sparkling clean bathroom and tell me the load of clothes she washed is in the dryer.

Standing in the bathroom mirror, I think more about what she said. "Your mom doesn't—"

"Stepmom," she interrupts, shaking her head. "That awful woman is not my mother."

"Oh. Yeah, I'm sorry, I meant stepmom." I shake my head, feeling dumb. Hannah is rarely testy about things, so I feel even worse. "You said you clean your whole house. Don't they have maids?"

Hannah shakes her head, but the sparkle goes out of her eyes. "What do they need to pay someone for when they have me?" she asks lightly. "My dad left everything to her when he died because she was his wife, and he thought she would take care of me. She lets me live in my own house, but I have to effectively play housekeeper and wait on them hand and foot for an allowance."

"That's horrible. I'm so sorry, Hannah."

She shrugs, putting a smile back on her pretty face. "At least I've gotten efficient. Look how quickly I got this whole place cleaned."

I shake my head. Then I think about all the stuff she made for us today. I don't even think we had all those ingredients, so she must have bought them herself—and she's not rich like I thought, she just lives in a big house that was basically stolen from her.

I look down guiltily and feel the chain of my necklace move across my skin.

I touch it.

I'd forgotten that was there.

I don't know how after last night.

Anae's *trophy.*

I unhook it from around my neck. Hannah watches, instinctively putting her hand up to catch it when I offer it to her.

"What's this?" she asks.

"Dare bought it for me. It's from Dior, so it's probably expensive. Take it. Maybe you can sell it and get some money. You should have something for yourself."

"Oh, no, I can't take your necklace…"

"Please." I insist, closing her hand around it. "I want you to have it."

She looks up at me. "Are you sure Dare won't get mad?"

I shrug. "I doubt it. If he thinks I'd still want it after last night, he's crazier than I realize." Obviously, she doesn't understand what the pretty necklace reminds me of now, so I offer a brief explanation. "From what I've gleaned, Anae picked it out. Dare bought it for me, but told her she could have it as a 'trophy' after they killed me."

Hannah loses a shade of color. "What?"

"He didn't mean it, he was playing her, but…"

She looks at the necklace. "Yikes."

"Yeah, big yikes."

Sighing, Hannah says, "And here I thought Anae was bad."

"They're both terrible," I state honestly. "He's not better or worse than her, he's just smarter."

"Are you going to leave him?" she asks tentatively.

I offer a ghost of a smile. "I don't think I can."

Hannah's brow furrows and she looks down, absently shifting her weight from foot to foot. "I don't want you to stay in this relationship because of that threat he made, Aubrey. I mean, I'm sure you're not, but if you are… don't."

"We both know he wasn't bluffing," I state, meeting her gaze.

She shrugs. "No, he wasn't, but things are different now. He and Anae are definitely split up, and his threat itself wouldn't have been the worst of it, honestly. He knew Anae would torment me after the fact and make my life unbearable. She can't torture me if she's in prison."

That is true.

"So, he can't hurt me like he could have before. Coming for me might not even be worth it to him without Anae here to support the punishment. Maybe he'll just back off."

She clearly doesn't know Dare the way I do.

"That's not the only thing," I say softly, afraid of her judging me even though Hannah never has before. I swallow, then look up at her with my heart in my throat. "I don't know how I feel about him."

It feels like a shameful admission. If she were someone more callous, she might take one look at my traumatized ass and write me off as an absolute moron, but Hannah is compassionate all the way down to her bones. Rather than judge me, she grabs me and gives me another hug she knows I need.

"What you've been through with him… it's not normal,

and I'm sure it has been a lot to process. I don't blame you for being confused, or still feeling some attachment to him. He has messed with your heart, and he's so manipulative, I'm sure he was really good at it." She pulls back, still holding my shoulders, and meets my gaze earnestly. "But he is *abusive*, Aubrey, and I hope with all my heart you get away from him."

I nod because I know she's right, but I also know it's not that simple.

She doesn't know him the way I do.

Or, I guess, the way I thought I did.

I'm not sure what was real and what wasn't after last night. I've had thoughts, brief moments of clarity, where it hit me that maybe it doesn't matter. Real, fake—I should just walk away from it all, regardless.

And I know he won't *let me* walk away, but I'm actually *not* an idiot, and I've learned from watching my ruthless, psychotic, brilliant boyfriend mow over everything and everyone in his path to get his way.

Dare always has an insurance policy for himself, just in case he needs it.

This time, I made one for myself.

While I was being examined, I had a rape kit done.

I haven't decided if I'll actually report him or not. I need to talk to Dare first and find out the truth about some of the things I heard last night.

If I do go after him, I know it will be a brutal road for me. I know I'll be massacred in the court of public opinion, painted as the villain while he's propped up by his money, his status, his popularity. His general fucking handsomeness and all the things that, on the surface, make him look just fucking lovely.

I won't look lovely, but I'm the one who was hurt.

I know what's truth and illusion here because it's my

experience and I've lived it, but the world won't know. Baymont won't know. They'll make their judgments, and I know I'll be the one found guilty.

I don't know how I'll even make it through the rest of the school year here if I report their king for his actual crimes.

I'm also just not sure I want to.

But now I have the option.

Because some of the things Anae said combined with some of the things Dare himself has said put a question in my mind that wasn't there before: has he done this to other girls?

If I'm the first, it's my call.

But if I'm not? It doesn't matter how I feel, or how much more I will suffer for telling the truth; I will have to speak up.

AS SOON AS Mom is in bed for the night, I go to my room.

I don't feel safe there right now, but I wouldn't feel any safer in any other part of the house. The locks haven't been changed, and Dare got in last night with no signs of forced entry, so if he wants to get to me, he will.

I don't feel like putting myself through waiting for him to show up outside my window tonight, so before I get in bed, I unlock the window and crack it so he can just push it up when he gets here.

We haven't spoken so I don't know for a fact he will be here, but I'm expecting him.

My body feels tired, but I don't even try to go to sleep.

I wear a big baggy T-shirt and baggy, blue-striped sleep shorts. My hair is down, my face clean of make-up. I don't try to look cute for him. I don't want to.

I'm sitting on the bed on top of my bedding with my legs curled up, hugging my knees to my chest, when I hear the window open.

My heart drops instinctively at the sound of someone invading my bedroom, but of course, I know who the invader is.

Out of the corner of my eye, I see that Dare is dressed in a pair of fitted black sweats and a crisp white T-shirt with his jacket over it. He puts the window down and locks it, then turns back to face me.

I'm sitting in the dark, but he doesn't turn on the light.

I probably look like a creepy ghost girl in a horror movie. I kind of feel like one, too.

All day since Hannah left, I've felt hollow. Without her light, the darkness that surrounds me looms more heavily. Without her to distract me, I have all this heavy shit to occupy my mind.

Dare doesn't say anything at first, just walks over and stands at the foot of my bed.

He feels like a total stranger and the man I love at the same time, and the confusing thing is, right now, he's both.

"So," he finally says, breaking the heavy silence. "Last night was fun, huh?"

I know he isn't serious, but the absurdity of that word being used to refer to last night nearly tears the fragile thread my sanity is holding on by.

I look down at the bed instead of up at him. "Why does hanging out with you always have to be so dangerous?"

The bed sags beneath his weight as he takes a seat and touches my back. "Don't worry, you'll get used to it," he rumbles, doing his part to echo history.

I feel like I've lived a thousand years since that day on the beach with him. I shake my head, pulling my legs closer, and whisper, "What if I don't want to?"

"You don't have to." He leans in and kisses my shoulder through the fabric. "Come on, I was just kidding."

"Nothing about this is funny."

"You're right." He quiets for a minute. "I know last night was rough, Aubrey. I promise I'll never put you through something like that again. I just had to untangle a mess I was already in when I met you. This was the only way."

"Some guys break up with their girlfriends. You ruin their lives."

He looks at me, but I don't look back. "I had no choice, Aubrey. Anae is fucking crazy. She wasn't going to let go."

"I get that," I say, because I do. Anae is *clearly* a disturbed individual.

"There wasn't another way out. Believe me, if I could have ended it without putting you through all that, I would have. She would have come after you with or without me, but without me, I wouldn't have been there to stop her."

I nod. "Was it her idea or yours?" Finally, I meet his gaze. "Killing me, I mean."

His gaze is solemn. "I was never going to kill you."

"Could've fooled me."

"I had to fool you," he says seriously. "I had one chance, and I was already playing with a wild card. If she got it in her head that you weren't scared enough and you knew you weren't in real danger, she would have turned on me before I had the chance to turn on her."

I shake my head, looking down at my bed. "What an exhausting way to live."

"Tell me about it."

I look at the chipped polish on my toenails, unsure where to go from here.

Dare scoots closer.

"I know it's fucked up, Aubrey, but I *was* protecting you."

"I believe you," I say softly.

Like everything else he says to me, it's the truth, just not the whole truth.

Some part of me knows that, no matter what he'd say if I asked, some part of *him* enjoyed doing that to me. He liked kidnapping me and scaring me. He liked me tied up, crying and begging him not to hurt me.

There's a side of him I'll never understand, and never be fully at peace with.

Anae understood that side of him. She embraced it. Embraced all of him, even parts that terrify me, allowed him freedoms I could never bear.

And still, he chose me.

He could have done all the shit he wanted to do to me and even worse, and then he could have killed me and buried me, and gone right along with his life with her without missing a single beat.

He didn't get to be a hero this time, but he *did* still save my life.

Even though that side of him scares me, maybe I should be a little grateful that he's enough of a lunatic to convincingly play her like that and maneuver me out of harm's way.

Because he's right. She wanted to drown me that day at the beach, but thankfully, I didn't walk to the cave. Maybe it would have been over right there if I had.

If Dare would have simply broken up with her and started dating me, there's literally no reality in which she wouldn't have killed me.

Only this one.

It's a brutal, harsh reality, but I think he's right. I think it was the only way.

The room has been quiet for long enough that Dare decides it's safe to segue. "I had to talk to my dad's lawyer today."

My heart beats a little faster. "Oh yeah?"

He nods. I can feel him looking at me, but I keep my gaze down. "He's pretty hooked up in this town. Knows a lot of people."

"Hooray for him."

He misses one more beat, then delivers the shot he's been holding back. "Apparently, my girlfriend had a rape kit done last night, so… He wanted to know if there was anything we needed to get ahead of."

A chill sweeps over me. It lingers. I know it's not really cold in here, but I feel like all the warmth has been sucked out of the room, so I yank back the covers and climb under them.

A decent person wouldn't dare, but Dare climbs under them with me.

"Please don't touch me," I say before he has a chance to.

He sighs and laces his fingers together behind his head, looking up at the ceiling. "Are you planning to make a report?"

There's something chilling in the way he asks. He's not scared shitless the way I have been. He's not even mildly worried. Just… curious. Figuring out his next moves.

I feel colder now. I try to burrow deeper into the blankets.

I think about asking him to leave my room because despite his calm demeanor, I'm afraid of how this conversation could go very bad.

I shouldn't have to explain myself, honestly. He fucking raped me.

"Anae said you drugged me," I state.

"She did."

"Did you?"

I wait for him to deny it or make some excuse, but he doesn't. "Yes," he rumbles. "Twice. The first time I just gave you a crushed up Ambien. The second time I slipped you something stronger."

Wow.

My stomach aches, but I try to ignore it. "And then you…?"

"Yes."

I feel a bit sicker, but I ignore that, too. "Okay. Well. Then, I was raped."

"I didn't say you weren't. Just trying to figure out where we stand."

"Have you done this to other girls?"

"No," he says easily. "I didn't even know I was into it until I tried it with you."

"When? The first night I spent at your place?"

"Yes. And the night we had dinner with your mom."

"Why didn't you want me to be awake?" I ask quietly.

"I don't know," he answers. "I touched you a little bit while you were sleeping before we had sex, and then I wanted to take it further. The second time, you had technically said I could do anything I wanted to you that night."

"I didn't know I was saying it to a psychopath," I say flatly.

He doesn't have much to say to that.

After a moment, I say, "Since apparently I have to be very fucking specific, in the future, please do not ever drug me without my knowledge again."

"Okay. I won't."

I'm quiet for a moment, and so is he. Finally, I ask a question I'm not even sure I want the answer to. "Did you think about killing me last night? I get that it was a trap you laid for Anae, I believe you, but in the moment, while it was actually happening, did you think about it? Even for a fleeting moment."

"No."

I look over at him. "You swear?"

"I would never hurt you, Aubrey."

"You *have* hurt me, Dare."

"Fine, I would never fucking kill you," he says, irritated with me for even suggesting it.

Up until now, he has respected my request that he not

touch me, but apparently, that question pushed him past his limit.

He reaches over and grabs me around the waist, pulling me tightly against his hard body. Leaning close, he rumbles in my ear, "I fucking love you, Aubrey. Don't you get that by now? I would kill *for* you, but I would never hurt a hair on your goddamn head. I have ruined fucking lives to hold onto you, and I'd ruin more. The last thing I want is to lose you."

It's a little sick to feel so reassured by that, but maybe that's what loving him has made me: a little sick.

I turn in his arms so I can look up at him. He cups my face, and even though it's tender from the bruises he left there last night, it feels so good.

"I'm sorry," he says soothingly, leaning in to kiss my lips. "I'm sorry for all the shit I've put you through. I'm sorry for even giving you a reason to ask me questions like this, but I fucking love you. I need to know that you know that."

I close my eyes and sigh, lost for a moment in the reassuring strength of his grip as he pulls me close and kisses me. He kisses the side of my mouth and my face. He kisses my jaw around his hand, but he never lets go, never eases up.

"You're mine. You're fucking mine. It's forever, and I won't let anyone get in the way of that."

Finally, he claims my lips. He pushes me back on the bed, moving on top of me. I want to tell him no, not tonight, but then his hand slides up under my shirt and his tongue sweeps into my mouth. I can't speak, can't breathe air that isn't his, too.

To be loved so hard, so aggressively... it's frightening, but intoxicating, too.

I don't ask him to stop when he shoves his hand down the front of my ugly sleep shorts. I gasp against his lips as he teases my clit, stoking my pleasure until it's at fever pitch. I cry out and he covers my mouth with his, catching my cries and feeding on them as I come apart in his arms.

As my heart pounds in the aftermath, Dare wraps his arms around me and pulls me back into his relentless embrace.

"I love you," he whispers.

"I know," I whisper back.

CHAPTER 43
AUBREY

WHEN I WAKE up the next morning, my bedroom is bright, my legs are spread, and my boyfriend's face is buried between my thighs.

The sensation of his tongue on my clit sends a shiver of awareness straight through me and I moan softly, twisting my hips away from his beautiful head.

He pulls his mouth off my pussy to look up at me. "Good morning."

I stretch, twisting my body and bowing my back a bit. "Bold to wake me up with sex when we literally just had a chat about you casually raping me last night."

"What can I say? I'm a bold guy." He kisses my tummy, then looks up at me. "And you said I couldn't drug you. You didn't say I couldn't wake you up for breakfast."

"Ugh." I grab the pillow he slept on and throw it at him.

"A man needs to eat," he murmurs shamelessly, spreading my thighs again and latching onto my pussy.

He's doing good work, so I thread my fingers through his hair and close my eyes, enjoying this pocket of pleasure before we have to get back to the horrendous real world we're currently living in.

When he's done eating me out, and I'm lying in a sated, twisted, heavy-breathing heap, Dare pulls me into his chest and rests his chin atop my head.

"I have to go see my lawyer again this afternoon."

I frown a bit, nuzzling against him. "Okay," I murmur.

His grip on me tightens just a bit. "I need to know what you're doing so I can talk to him about it."

I'm still heavily fogged from that orgasm, but the realization sneaks through that this is perhaps the most twisted moment of our relationship. He's holding me, my heart still pounding from the orgasm he just gave me, asking if I'm going to impose legal consequences for the rape he definitely perpetrated against me.

I'm too distracted by the unsettling glimpse of reality to answer right away. He must take my silence as indecision because he starts talking again.

"I get it if you're not sure, but I want to make it very clear that in my mind, you and I are not on opposite sides. We are on the same team. I talked to Hayden about all this yesterday, and in the interest of shielding you from even more bullshit, he honestly believes it's in your best interest not to pursue it."

I crack a smile, but it's not really funny. "Your lawyer thinks I shouldn't report you for rape? Damn, what a hot take. I'm gonna need a moment to recover from all this shock."

"I'm serious." He pulls back a little to look down at me. "If you want to work something out that doesn't involve you trying to get me found guilty of an actual crime, we can, but I gave him an overview of the optics. You and I both know I'm the asshole here, but if you pursue it and put us on opposite sides of a court room, you're going to get torn apart."

That's a bitter little pill to swallow. I had already figured that out myself, but hearing him say it to sway me not to is…

unpleasant. "Right. That makes sense. Me getting torn apart for something you did."

"I'm not saying it's right, but that's the reality we're dealing with," he says, bringing a hand up to caress my face. His solemn brown eyes delve deep into mine. I get the feeling he wouldn't flaunt this ugly reality if I'd have just given him the answer he wanted already, but I'm making him by pressing the issue. "I kidnapped you, assaulted you, and left bruises on your body, Aubrey, and your own mother fucking loves me."

My stomach drops.

"So, how do you think the public would be persuaded to feel about it?"

I push his hand away, pulling out of his embrace and rolling away from him. "You can stop being an asshole, Dare. I'm not filing the report."

"I'm not trying to be an asshole," he says, rolling over in the bed so he can keep his gaze on me as I head for the door.

"Must be one of your god-given talents then," I state.

"Where are you going?"

"I have to pee."

I also have to get away from him before I punch him in the face.

Once I've made the trip to the bathroom, I decide to take a detour to the kitchen before I go back. Mom is still sleeping, so I don't want to make actual breakfast yet. I'm also not particularly in the mood to cook for Dare after the ugly shit he just said, so I grab us bottles of water from the fridge and two of Hannah's muffins before heading back down the hall.

I put Dare's bottle of water down on the end table nearest him.

"Don't look at me," I say, passing him his plate without meeting his gaze.

"But you're so nice to look at."

"I'm sick of you." I walk around the bed and climb up next to him.

"That's not true," he says casually, eyeing up the muffin like it's Inigo Montoya and he killed its dad. "Why have you brought me this?"

I glance over at him. "You said you were hungry."

He continues to eye it distastefully. "I don't like muffins."

My eyebrows rise and fall. I reach over and grab it off his plate, rehoming it on mine. "More for me, then."

He watches me take the first bite. "We should do something later."

"Can't. I need to spend some time with Mom tonight."

"Fine. Then I'll be over once she's gone to bed."

I pick a little piece of muffin off with my fingers, looking at it instead of him. I don't know if I want him to come over. I can't even decide if I want him to be here now, he just *is*.

But I also know if he wants to come, he will.

"You know, sometimes I might have other plans." I glance over at him. "Ones that don't include you."

He grabs the water bottle off the table and uncaps it. "Sounds boring." He takes a swig, then twists the cap back on. "Plans that include Hannah?"

"I know you're not in love with our friendship, but I like Hannah, and she's a good friend. If you won't be doing any more psychotic things to make her be like, 'hey, Aubrey, I think this guy's a danger to your general well-being,' then I don't see why you should have a problem with us hanging out."

"I can think of a few reasons," he murmurs.

I can hear the echo of unspoken words in the silence that follows. When he speaks again, all his good-natured patience is gone, and there's a dangerous edge to every syllable he utters.

"Do you remember when we first started hanging out and you told me you would never cheat on me?"

My stomach drops. It's the way he caresses certain words, wielding them like deadly weapons and framing me as his opponent. "Of course," I say uneasily.

"I want to reiterate now that you know more about me, I may have said it like I was joking, but I very much meant it when I said I would kill off the competition."

I pop a piece of muffin into my mouth so he doesn't notice I've lost my appetite, but as hard as it is to swallow, it might as well be sand. "I have told you several times now, Hannah isn't your competition."

Ignoring my objection, he goes on as if I haven't said anything. "And I understand that I was much easier on you then, and in some ways it probably feels like you're not even in the same relationship anymore. But you are, and maybe it's not entirely fair, but I will still hold you to all the promises that you made, and deliver on all of the threats that *I* made if I see a reason to."

This time, I don't speak. I know he isn't finished.

He takes the plate out of my hand and stacks it on the end table with his. He grabs my wrist and pulls my hand close, sucking my thumb and forefinger into his mouth in turn so he can lick off the brown sugar.

"It isn't a good idea to invite temptation into our relationship. I will never do it, and I expect you not to as well. I know you were only joking about being sick of me and joking is fine, but should you ever *actually* get sick of me, I would advise you to reflect on what made you love me in the first place and fucking bathe in it because I will never, ever let you go."

My heart stalls.

He grabs my bruised jaw, gently bringing my face close to his so he can kiss it. "I could detail what your life would look like if you ever cheated on me, how I would cut you out of the life you're living and transform my love into the metal bars that form your new home." He cups my breast through my shirt. "How I would strip away your will, ignore your *every single boundary*, and treat you like a toy, playing with you *exactly* how I want to without regard for whether or not you liked it."

I stiffen as his hand leaves my chest and comes up to wrap around my throat.

He kisses the side of my face again, tenderly, like the sweetest of lovers. "But I know you'll be more effectively moved by what I would do to *her*."

"Dare," I say, grabbing his wrist. "Please stop. I don't want to hear—"

"I won't be graphic," he assures me. "But you know some of the things I've done to you, and I *love you*. You witnessed what I've done to Anae, and I liked her, too." He lets go of my throat and leans away. "I have no fondness at all for Hannah."

It's hard to even think straight when he gets like this. All I can feel is fear and dread wrapping their hands around my throat the same way he does.

Dare grabs the plate he took from me.

I look over at him.

He lifts his eyebrows. "Would you like your muffin back?"

I shake my head wordlessly.

"No?" He feigns surprise, then takes a big bite. "Mm," he murmurs, watching my face. "It's sweet."

I swallow, not acknowledging his twisted bullshit, and move to crawl off the bed, but I don't get far. As soon as Dare sees what I'm doing, he grabs my wrist, yanks me onto his lap, and takes a bigger, messier bite.

He sets the plate aside and chews.

I refuse to look at him.

He grabs my jaw and turns my face toward his, indicating the corner of his mouth where there's just a bit of brown sugar. "Clean it off."

My stomach bottoms out. I know better than to fuck with him when he's in this mood, so I slide my arm around his neck and lean in.

His eyes close and he sighs with pleasure as I drag my tongue over the spot he pointed to, using my tongue to bring the sweetness to his lips. I lick his bottom lip, too, then push my tongue into his mouth, enjoying the bite of sweetness from this sordid little tasting.

Despite myself, arousal stirs between my thighs as he grabs me and makes me kiss him harder. I'm on top, but I'm not in control. My heart beats harder, our tongues tangling together, the tang of sweetness left behind as his hands tangle in my hair and he shoves me back on the bed.

There's no condom on his cock when he drives it into me, but I'm too caught up to care. My skin stretches to accommodate him so he slams into me harder. I claw at his back, crying out as he attacks my neck with his greedy, insatiable mouth.

The sex is mean and animalistic, but god, is it hot.

He pounds into me relentlessly, making me cry out and then catching my cries in his mouth again and again. He bites my lips and squeezes my tits until it hurts. Finally, he comes inside me.

His fingers dig into my hips when he comes. He holds them tight, forcing his cock deep like he wants to leave his mark on the darkest, most unreachable parts of me.

Afterward, he collapses on top of me.

I'm sick, so I curl close and kiss him. I play with his hair and touch his beautiful face, and when he whispers how much he loves me, I commit the worst sin of all: I believe him.

IT'S A LONG, exhausting day.

I have a shift at work, then a shower. Mom and I commiserate while I make dinner and she tries not to stare at my bruises.

If she thought about it, even for a few seconds, she might realize the hand that made them was too big to be Anae's. She might even think about when she has seen me with Dare, and his propensity for touching my face.

She must not think about any of that because when he starts texting me, there's not even a glimmer of doubt on her face.

He's right.

She fucking loves him.

And I get it. Her first impression of him was heroic. He made sure it was. First impressions are hard to shake, and Dare knows what he's doing.

I'm not as freshly traumatized tonight, so I put on one of the little pink nighties he bought me. I know Dare likes when I wear really girly sleepwear, and this one is comfy to boot.

I don't bother putting on panties before I climb into bed.

I'm actually so tired when I curl up, I think I might fall asleep, but when I try to, I'm wide awake.

Dare taps lightly on my window.

I didn't leave it open tonight, so I push back the covers and go over to let him in.

His lips tug up at the sight of me in one of my cute nighties. He must take that as a sign I'm in a Dare-friendly mood tonight.

He's still dressed for the day in jeans with a gray hoodie and a white T underneath. I watch him lock the window, then he turns back and looks down at me.

His gaze rakes over me. I can feel it glance across my mostly bare shoulders and collarbone, dip lower to graze my breasts.

He reaches for my waist and pulls me closer.

I lock my arms around his waist and look up at him.

He leans down and kisses me, a nice soft kiss. "You're a sight for sore eyes," he murmurs.

I smile, briefly laying my head against his firm chest and enjoying the safety of his arms encircling my waist. When I pull back, he catches my hand. I let it linger for a moment, but I'm tired. "Come to bed," I say, our fingers touching for another second before I drop his hand and climb up on my mattress.

Since he's staying the night, Dare strips down to his underwear before climbing under the covers with me.

"How was your day?" I ask once I'm snuggled up against him with his arms around my waist.

"It wasn't great," he says, stroking my hair.

A frown flickers across my brow and I glance back at him. "Why?"

His gaze is pensive like he's still working out how to approach it. "We need to talk about some stuff."

I roll on my back, still with his arms around me, so I can look at him. "What kind of stuff?"

"Legal stuff."

I sigh. "I don't suppose you're suggesting we do government homework together."

His lips tug up, but he looks sad. It's the only smile I've ever hated. "Nothing I can get the nerds on, unfortunately."

"What's wrong?" I ask gently, reaching up to caress his face.

He presses his hand against mine, trapping it against his skin. "I need your help with something, and you're not going to like it."

A wave of dread rolls over me. "What is it?"

"Did you talk to the cops today?"

I shake my head. "I'm supposed to go back tomorrow."

He nods, his thumb absently stroking my skin. "I fucked up a few things the other night. Part of it was because she was there, part of it was you. Working on my own, I wouldn't have made these mistakes, but when you do shit like this with other people, it's easy for things to go wrong."

I'll have to take his word for it. I've never committed crimes with anyone before.

"Anae rolled over on me. I expected she would, but the problem is... If they run tests on the clothes you wore that night, they'll find bodily fluids." His gaze drifts to the bruises he left on my jaw. "You have my fingerprints on your face. Maybe there were glove fibers in your mouth, or... inside you. Anae's telling them she didn't act alone, that I kidnapped and assaulted you, and if they investigate..."

"They'll find out you did," I say softly.

He holds my gaze for a moment, then drops it and nods.

If she goes down, he goes down with her.

How poetic.

"You got caught in your own trap," I murmur.

His jaw tightens, but he neglects to comment. "There's another option," he tells me. "Her mom's lawyer met with mine today. They said if you don't press charges, if you say it wasn't really a kidnapping and you went with her voluntarily but then shit went sideways, a lot of the charges can go away. She can plea down to a stay in a psychiatric facility, and she'll stop screaming about my involvement. They won't have any reason to run tests on your clothes, and since you're not going to do anything with that rape kit… As long as you maintain that I wasn't there when you go over your new statement tomorrow, this can all go away and I don't catch a charge at all."

My tummy drops and I frown. "You… want me to lie about everything?"

He shakes his head. "It's not what I want. It's what I need."

"Dare, I can't just—" I shake my head, vaguely disbelieving. "She wanted to kill me. If she gets out, she will try again."

"No, I know. Obviously, I wouldn't let that happen. I told the lawyers there was no deal if she got off completely. I don't want to go to fucking prison, but I'm resourceful, I'd find a way out of it. The deal I worked out still keeps you out of danger. Anae will be getting inpatient treatment hundreds of miles from here. She won't be back at school this year. She won't graduate. She'll actually have to do senior year all over again next year."

With Hannah?

"No." I shake my head. "I can't."

"Aubrey." He stares at me. "I know it's not what we wanted and it fucking sucks. I did all that work, you think I wanted it to go this way? But there's really no other option here. I'm your boyfriend; it's not unbelievable you'd lie to protect me. If they investigate Anae's claims, I'm completely fucked."

"So, I tell these lies, and she gets a slap on the wrist, basically? She helped kidnap and assault me, wanted to *carve* me like a holiday turkey *after* watching you rape me. She wanted to have me seduced and my heart broken over a goddamn *shirt*, and then she wanted to viciously kill me which she *actually tried to do,* and you really think what I should do is *lie for her* so this psycho fucking bitch doesn't have to serve time for her crimes? *Really*, Dare?"

His jaw locks. "I'm not saying it's ideal, Aubrey, but the alternative is that I go down with her. Is that what you want?"

"Of course it isn't."

"Then this is what we have to do. I did all this shit to protect you, and now, as unpalatable as it fucking is, I need you to do this for me."

This is so fucking *unfair*.

"She's *dangerous*, Dare."

He grabs me and pulls me closer to him. "I know Anae's unhinged, but I would never let her hurt you. I know this wasn't the outcome we expected, but this still accomplishes everything we need it to. By the time she gets out, we'll be off at college. We won't live in Baymont anymore. If she's still nursing a grudge and has the bad fucking judgment to come anywhere near us, I will get rid of her. I promise you that."

I shake my head. "She deserves to pay." I look over at him. "And maybe she can't hurt us anymore, maybe you're right. But what if she hurts someone else?"

I can see that he understands the enormity of what he's asking. He tries to make me feel better about it. "Hey, you never know. Maybe that time at the psych hospital will actually do her some good. She's probably better off there than prison, anyway. Prison would just teach her new tricks."

"It would contain her," I mutter. "Honestly, I am not Anae's advocate, and I don't care about her getting better. I just want her to be removed from the rest of society so she can't cause any further damage."

He takes my hand and brings it to his lips, luring me in with his big brown eyes. "But you don't want *me* locked away with her, right?"

I pout. "It depends on which day you ask."

He smirks, leaning over me and kissing my pouty lips. "Fuck, you know I can't concentrate when you do that."

"You want me to unleash all this literal evil on the world, and I hate it."

"Hey, you're doing your part to contain Baymont's evils," he teases, moving on top of me and kissing my neck. "Can you imagine all the damage *I* would do out there if I didn't have you to keep me occupied? You can't save everybody."

I sigh, tilting my neck. "I need to assemble a team."

"Someone call the Avengers," he murmurs biting my neck and likely leaving a brand new bruise on my skin. Immediately, he kisses the same spot, soothing the hurt he caused.

When he's done getting me all riled up with his kisses, he wraps me in his arms and pulls me against him. I close my eyes, enjoying the warmth and security of his embrace, but dreading tomorrow.

As if he can tell, he kisses my forehead. "Don't worry, mermaid. It'll all be over soon."

It's strange showing up at school Monday morning in Dare's car, but not having to worry about people seeing us.

They still stare—more than usual, as a matter of fact, but the reasons are different, and so are their attitudes.

It's all friendly smiles and treating me like I'm one of them now. Even the asshole who stole my picture off the ground and made that comment about me sucking a dick includes me in conversation as they chat on the quad.

There are whispers in the halls, rumors spreading like wildfire about Anae's arrest and Dare's speculated involvement.

When he saunters in with his arm wrapped around a new queen, no one questions the bruises on her neck or face, and no one dares say an unkind word about her. If the thought even passes through their minds that maybe he mistreats this one differently than he mistreated the other, no one mentions it.

I spot Hannah in the halls and give her a little wave, but I don't expect her to approach since I'm with Dare.

Surprisingly, she hugs her books to her chest and marches right up to us.

"Hi," she says.

I smile. "Hey."

Dare stares at her like she just threw a gauntlet on the ground in front of him, but doesn't offer a greeting of his own.

She's not paying attention to him, anyway. Her gaze is drifting from my face to my neck. "I have some makeup in my purse. I think I'm a little fairer than you, but I can try to cover those up if you want."

I tried before I left for school this morning, but I did a shit job and ended up washing all the makeup off. "Sure, I…" I pause, looking to Dare.

My heart beats harder when I realize I just instinctively looked to him for permission. I frown at the foreign instinct, but don't fight it. He's been so ridiculous about Hannah, I feel the need to. It might scrape my pride a little, but if it keeps her out of his crosshairs, then so be it.

Hannah notices the exchange, but doesn't remark on it.

"Go ahead," Dare says.

My cheeks warm. I grab Hannah's hand and haul her into the bathroom with me.

Once we're alone, she does murmur, "You have to ask his permission to go to the bathroom now?"

"No." I crack a tiny smile, but my cheeks are still warm with embarrassment. I watch her set down her books. "He has this notion that you and I like each other as more than friends, and he's being a full-blown lunatic about it."

"Oh." Hannah appears startled.

"Yeah, I know." I roll my eyes. "I'm just trying to avoid… stupid fighting."

Hannah nods with mock seriousness. "I, too, prefer only smart fighting."

I chuckle and she smiles back as she grabs a rectangular palette and a brush out of a little pouch in her purse. "Do you have a Mary Poppins purse? I swear, you have everything I need, every time I see you."

She smiles, lightly turning my face so she can get a better look at the bruising. "I like to be prepared."

She starts applying makeup and I start thinking about how I effectively screwed her over yesterday by changing my story. "Um… I wanted to say I'm really sorry."

Her gaze darts to mine, her confusion clear. "For what?"

"Well, the psycho boyfriend for one thing, but most recently… It's sort of my fault you're going to have to go to school with Anae next year. I don't know if you've heard yet."

"Oh. Yeah, I've heard." She smiles faintly, but it doesn't reach her eyes. "Don't worry about me. It would be my personal preference that the person who put these bruises on your face rot in jail for a good long time, but I'm sure you had your reasons."

The way she says it, it seems pretty clear she means Dare,

but she's not trying to shame me, so she doesn't come out and say it.

She sets the brush aside and uses her thumb to blend the edges. "You want me to get the hickeys, too?"

"Um, no, you can leave those."

"He really likes to mark you, doesn't he?"

"He really does."

"Must be because I'm so intimidating," she teases with a little wink.

I laugh. "Yeah, that must be it."

CHAPTER 45

DARE

WE'RE NEARLY to the cafeteria for lunch when a little blonde pixie flies over, grabbing my arm to get my attention, then letting go like she's afraid my evil might be contagious.

I would just keep walking and ignore her, honestly, but my much nicer girlfriend spots her little *friend* and stops. "Hey, Hannah."

I stifle the urge to roll my eyes, turning to face the girl.

She's got the bright-eyed look of determination as she looks up at me rather than Aubrey. "Can I talk to you for a minute?"

I hike up my eyebrows. "Me?"

Aubrey is similarly confused—but much more worried. "Him?"

Hannah nods. "Alone."

"Alone?" my pretty little parrot echoes. "I'm not sure that's a great idea…"

I'm sure it isn't, but I'm curious. "Sure." I drop my arm from around Aubrey's waist. She catches my hand before she lets go, giving me a wordless, pleading look, begging me to be nice.

I like it, so I lean in to give her a little kiss before I go.

Then, I follow Hannah into an empty classroom. "Interesting choice," I say, looking around the room lit only by a couple of cloudy windows. To up the scare factor, I reach back and close the door behind me. I lock it, too.

Her gaze flickers from the doorknob to my face.

I smile faintly, taking a slow step toward her. "You wanted to be alone with me. Now you are."

She takes a step back without meaning to. I can't imagine why she put herself in this position. She's clearly still afraid of me. I can see my threats ricocheting around inside that pretty little head of hers as she struggles to meet my gaze.

Her breathing is picking up with her fear. I can see her regretting this decision, but she doesn't back down from it. Instead, she lifts her gaze and meets mine.

I guess little Hannah found her courage.

"I want to talk to you about Aubrey."

"I figured."

"I know you and I don't like each other, and we never will. But we both care about her, right? So…" She looks down like it kills her a little to have to ask me for anything, but then she meets my gaze, hers softer and more pleading. "Please let me be her friend." She goes on quickly before I have time to tell her no. "I understand you're the gatekeeper now. You're in control. I get it. I'll play by your rules."

"Even though I'm an abusive, manipulative asshole?" I stalk closer.

She backs up. "My opinion of you hasn't changed, but it doesn't matter. I'm not suggesting you and I be friends. But I told you before I wouldn't help you trap her, and while I won't, I… I realize you'll never let me be in her life if I'm constantly fighting to free her. I won't interfere in your relationship. I just want to be there for her. It seems like being in a relationship with you will be hard on her. She at least needs a friend to help her through those harder times."

"That's the thing: it isn't. I can see why you think that because when you come around, she pulls away from me, and I have to fight to get her back where she needs to be, but that isn't what it's like between us when you're not around being a little troublemaker."

She looks at me, wholly unconvinced. "If you're starting down the same yellow brick road of absolute bullshit you've fed Aubrey, don't bother. I don't believe for one second that *you* are threatened by *me*. I am perhaps the least intimidating person in the whole universe, while you are... what you are."

I smirk at her kind way of wording that.

I also close in on her.

She grips the strap of her purse like it's a protective bubble she's trying hard to trigger, but her back hits the wall and no bubble emerges to keep me away.

"Understand this, Hannah. I will do whatever I have to do to keep you out of Aubrey's life. There isn't a line I won't cross. There was a moment in time when I thought I'd let you stick around because you are a glowing opportunity to control her. As protective as you are of one another, I could use you indefinitely. I could win every argument. I could play you off one another for the rest of fucking time and it seems like there's a bond of love between you that, even then, I would not be able to break. I believe that she would endure immense pain to protect you from me, and I believe you feel the same way." I touch her shoulder and watch her shudder, refusing to meet my gaze. "Can you imagine me turning down a gift like that?"

She swallows.

"And yet, I am. You're the perfect tool and I still won't use you. That should tell you that your pleas are falling on deaf ears." I catch her bottom lip with my thumb. She gasps and presses her head back against the wall to get away from it, but I follow, pressing harder on her lip, nearly forcing my way between them, but I stop just short of penetrating her mouth. "You can't be friends. I won't let you. And I won't change my mind, no matter how prettily you beg."

I pushed her a little far there. Her gaze darts to the door and I see her thinking about fleeing, but she makes no move to.

I drop my hand from her face. "I'm not sure what it is, but there is something profoundly incompatible about us, Hannah. I don't know if it's the balance of good and evil— perhaps we're just too far on opposite sides of the spectrum. Whatever it is, it feels impossible for us to exist in the same space without being at war with one another. You don't want to go to war with me. I will blow you up time and time again, and you'll keep coming back until there's nothing left of you because heroes are fucking idiots. You won't win. You won't succeed in saving her. All you'll do is make me hurt you both over and over again until you're gone. So, we're going to skip ahead to that part."

"But you don't *have* to hurt anyone. You say that like it's so inevitable when it isn't."

"But it *is*. We can't both have her. Someone has to lose, and it won't be me."

She glares up at me. "That won't work on me, Dare."

I cock my head curiously.

"Aubrey may have believed you when you played at jealousy, but I don't. I've watched from the sidelines while you were with Anae. You occasionally tossed out comments to make her feel special, like Milk-Bones to an eager pet after they performed well for you, but you've never been jealous. You said it yourself five seconds go—you know you're not going to lose her. You can't be jealous if you're not afraid of losing someone, that's not how it works. What is much easier for me to believe is that you know if you ask Aubrey to stop hanging out with 'the competition' for the good of your relationship, you don't come off sounding as controlling as telling her she can't have a friend she likes just because *you* don't particularly like her."

I smile. "See, that right there." I point at her. "That's why you can't be her friend. But, at the end of the day, my reasons don't matter. Maybe I am a manipulative bastard who knows how to get what I want. Maybe I just don't fucking like how much work I have to put in to pull her back in every time she sees you. Maybe I saw you cuddling my girlfriend who called you instead of me to pick her up and I didn't fucking like it."

Hannah shakes her head like I'm unbelievable. "Yeah, she didn't want to call you after you kidnapped and traumatized her. What a fucking shock, Dare. This is why she *needs* me. When you do crazy shit, I can be there to help pick up the pieces."

"Everything Aubrey needs, I will give her."

"No, you won't. You can't. You're not equipped for it." She shakes her head, that pleading look in her eyes again like she's just so desperate for me to understand. "If you're all she has, you'll lose pieces of her along the way."

"Then she doesn't need those pieces," I state simply.

"Are you honestly this selfish?"

"You can't really be surprised."

She shakes her head, looking down for a moment. When her gaze returns to mine, she tries one more time. "Please, Dare. I am literally begging you."

I touch her chin, keeping her gaze on me. "No." I move my hand, sliding it to the side of her neck. She stiffens, probably recalling the last time I had my fingers around her throat, but I don't let her look away. "I've laid all the necessary groundwork on Aubrey's end. I've been much clearer with you. Now, all that needs to happen is that you go away and let us live happily ever after."

"And if I don't?" she whispers.

My hand closes around her throat. "Then I stop being nice, and this war gets *bloody*."

I feel her throat work beneath my palm as she swallows.

"Maybe that's what you want," I murmur, my grip tightening.

Her hands fly to my wrist.

"You wanted my attention. Now, you have it."

I see the flash of fear cross her face. "No. No, I didn't want your attention, I wanted—"

"Sh, it's okay. You can admit it. It's just the two of us."

I lean closer and I swear she nearly bursts into fucking tears. "Please, stop," she whispers.

"I don't think you really want that." I lean down so my mouth is close enough for her to feel my breath on her lips when I whisper, "Do you have a little crush, Hannah?"

"You're sick," she hisses.

I smile, stroking her neck with my thumb while still holding on tight. "I can make you sick, too."

"Get your hands off me. You don't want to fuck me, you just want to scare me," she says, fighting the fear and trying to get back to seeing me clearly. A special talent of hers, and not one I can let her get a firm grip on right now, so I lean close and smell her hair. I hear her shuddering breath, a nearly silent squeak of horror as she listens to me breathe her in, my body pressed close so she can feel my heat.

"Are you sure?" I whisper. "You might think I'm bluffing, but how far are you willing to go to find out? Because, Hannah?" I look down at her. "I don't blink."

She looks up at me like I'm breaking her poor little heart again. Maybe I am.

She's so upset, so angry and wounded knowing there's not a shot in hell she'll win a game like this. Tears begin to glisten in her big blue eyes.

"There's more than one way to lose someone, you know."

My eyes narrow.

She swallows, still with my hand wrapped around her throat. "Maybe you think you can't lose her because you won't let her leave, but you're wrong. You can make her stop loving you. Maybe you can keep her as a prisoner after that, but you can only force her body to stay. You can't force her heart."

We're in waters murky enough that even Hannah with her unique abilities of perception can't tell whether or not I'm bluffing. "Maybe that's enough for me."

I don't know what I expect to see in her eyes, but it's not pity. "Then I feel sad for you."

I frown, letting go of her throat and taking a step back.

She holds my gaze.

For the first time, I'm tempted to look away from her, but I just swore I wouldn't, so I don't. "Your love for Aubrey is touching. Do what conventional wisdom tells you to and love her enough to walk away. I promise that if you don't, I'll make you both regret it."

She sniffles, swiping at her nose as I turn around to unlock the door and walk out.

Aubrey is waiting for me in the hall.

I smile at her to quell some of the anxiety she's clearly feeling.

She doesn't smile back. "What was that about?"

Before I can answer, I hear noise behind us and turn to watch Hannah rush out of the classroom and head down the hall in the opposite direction. Aubrey calls after her, but Hannah keeps going without looking back.

Good girl.

Aubrey, naturally, assumes this is my fault and turns to shoot me a dirty look. "What did you do to her?"

I grab her elbow and turn her away. "Nothing, we just talked."

She looks up at me, unamused. "She *ran* away, Dare."

"Our talk took longer than expected. She's in a hurry to get back to class."

Aubrey tilts her head and cocks an eyebrow, wordlessly expressing, "You expect me to believe that?"

I smirk, grabbing her pretty neck and pulling her in. "Honest. I was a teddy bear. We exchanged recipes."

"Recipes," she says flatly in disbelief.

I nod, a smile playing around my lips as I lean in to kiss hers. "Mm-hmm. We came to a gentlemen's agreement. We'll have a bake-off. Winner gets your heart."

Despite herself, she smiles. She rolls her eyes, too. "A bake-off? Well, I hate to tell you this, but if you challenged Hannah to a bake-off, I think you're going to lose."

I fit my hand over her jaw, lined up right along the bruises I left that Hannah covered up for her. Then I pet her pretty hair that Hannah braided and I cut off. "I don't lose."

She doesn't want to be charmed by my bullshit, but she is. "That's what you think," she murmurs against my mouth as I kiss her. "When is this bake-off? You don't even know how to bake."

"I guess you'd better teach me."

Eyes closed, she shakes her head. "You better enjoy your last days with me."

I smirk, biting at her bottom lip and sliding a hand down to cup her ass.

She lets me pull her into my side and wrap my arm around her waist, but she still turns to look back as I haul her farther from Hannah.

On second thought, I stop.

Aubrey stops looking back and looks up at me instead.

"You know what?" I say.

"What?"

"If my days with you are numbered, I had better make the

most of them."

She falls back into being playful when she realizes I'm still teasing her.

I take her hand and haul her out to my car.

She's wearing a sexy black top with a red skirt today. I stop her when she grabs at the door handle and take her panties off before we get in.

Aubrey lifts her skirt, spreading her legs just enough to give me a tantalizing glimpse as I drop into the passenger seat. She climbs in on top of me, straddling me and leaning over to pull the door closed.

I waste no time grabbing at the gold zipper of her top. It bares her shoulders and unzips like a dream so her tits spill free. "I love this shirt," I murmur, leaning in to kiss my way down her chest.

Aubrey smiles, her fingers tangling in my hair. "I should hope so. You bought it for me."

"I make such good decisions."

"Like 53 percent of the time," she says dryly.

I bite her nipple and she gasps, arching and pushing her tit against my mouth. I slide a hand beneath her skirt and she sighs as my finger slips into her.

When I met Aubrey, she would have been too afraid someone would see to take my cock in the front seat of a car, her shirt open and hanging off her body, my lips glued to her tits where anyone could see us.

Now, she cries out when she comes and doesn't even attempt to muffle the noise.

In the aftermath of her orgasm, she hugs me, her head resting heavily on my shoulder and my cock still inside her. I kiss the side of her sweaty neck, and her arm tightens around mine.

"I love you," she whispers.

"I know."

EPILOGUE
AUBREY

A SLOW SONG plays as I dance with my king.

It's not romantic like one might expect of the prom king and queen's solo dance, but it's soft and melodic, and just a bit sad.

I'm not paying much attention to the words, anyway. I'm more focused on the security of his firm chest pressed against my face, his strong arms locked around my body, the way my hips sway and Dare's greedy hand creeps toward my ass.

A smile tugs at my lips. "You better behave yourself."

"Who's gonna make me?" he asks lightly.

"The chaperones."

His hand slides over my ass and squeezes. "They better mind their business. If they think they're gonna stop me from grabbing your ass while I dance with you, they'd better brace for a shock."

"You're not allowed to ruin any lives on prom night."

"Oh, come on."

I shake my head. "Nope."

"You never let me have any fun."

I smile, tilting my head up so I can look at him. "You can

have all the fun you want with me when we get to our hotel room after this."

He cocks an eyebrow with interest. "*All* the fun I want?"

I reconsider what I'm offering. "*Some* of the fun you want."

He grins and leans down to kiss me. I tighten my arms around his neck and kiss him back. He lifts me off the ground, molding my body against his as the music stops. "We should just get out of here now," he murmurs against my lips.

At the mic, the principal—clearly wanting to cut off this public display of far too much affection—fumbles with the stand and says, "All right, let's hear it for the prom king and queen."

The spotlight is on us, so mercifully, Dare puts me down and takes my hand. The other students clap and then the crowd disburses, Dare and I walking away with complementary crowns.

"I'm thirsty," I tell him. "I'm gonna get a drink. You want anything?"

He shakes his head, holding onto my hand for a few seconds longer before letting me pull away.

I make my way through the crowd alone, smiling and offering a "thanks," in passing to three different people who stop to congratulate me on my win. Not that it was remotely a surprise. Juniors can attend, but only seniors can win prom king or queen at Baymont High, and Dare had no competition. My crown was earned by the simple virtue of being his.

After rumors spread all over the school about the crazy shit he may have been responsible for this year, the other nominees dropped out to avoid the possibility of landing on his bad side, so we don't even have a prom court.

It's a hollow win, but it doesn't matter much, anyway. High school is all but over, and it never meant much to me.

The prom theme this year is *The Wizard of Oz*, so I have to make my way through the emerald city to get to the drinks and snacks. There's no one else at the table when I get to it. I glance at the assortment of themed snacks, but only grab a see-through cup off the green sequined table. I reach for the ladle floating around in the punch bowl.

Before I can grab it, someone grabs my wrist.

I turn, startled.

My heart lightens when I see a familiar face I haven't seen in far too long.

"Hannah!"

She smiles back mischievously. "Hey. I can't believe Dare finally left your side. I've been waiting for an opening all night."

I chuckle, but glance over my shoulder just to make sure he isn't watching. I don't see him anywhere, so I turn my attention back to her.

"Wow, you look amazing," I tell her. She's wearing a red sequined dress that hugs her curves with her long blonde hair curled and pulled over one shoulder. Her lips are painted red to match the dress. "You're a sapphire, though?"

Generally, it's encouraged for students to pick prom clothes that match their houses. I'm not because Dare is onyx and he's my date, but if Hannah is here alone, she should be in a blue dress.

"Yeah, but my date's a ruby. He's around here some-where," she says, waving dismissively.

I crack a smile. "Sounds like true love."

"Fire up the horse drawn carriage," she jokes, looking me over. I'm wearing a tight black dress that showcases my cleavage and includes a sheer black cape. Given the prom theme and Dare's attraction to me in high heels, I also donned a pair of ruby red slippers. "What about you? You're not wearing emerald. I dig this evil queen vibe you've got going on, but it doesn't really seem like you."

"I'm the evil king's consort," I explain. "Adapting his vibe is pretty much mandatory."

"Ah, makes sense." She smiles, but I know she doesn't want to talk about Dare. "Well, you look sexy, so you definitely nailed the 'evil king's consort' look." Pointing at my head, she says, "You even have a crown now."

Dare's deep voice behind me melts my smile and causes Hannah to drop my wrist. Dare notices she was holding it and gives her a cool smile as he comes to stand beside me. "Is Cinderella trying to steal my girl again? I thought I'd gotten rid of you."

"Dare." I lightly smack him in the abdomen. "Don't call her that."

That's Anae's rude nickname for her, not his, and I don't appreciate him using it—especially to Hannah's face.

"I was just offering my congratulations to the queen," Hannah says mildly, indicating the crown on my head.

Dare's arm slides around my waist and he pulls me close. "*My* queen."

She gives him a knowing, narrow-eyed look. "Of course, your highness."

"Isn't that Anae's dress? Can't imagine she'd like you wearing it." Dare smirks, his gaze flickering over her outfit.

Hannah shrugs, looking down at the dress. "She can't wear it where she's at. She hated this dress, anyway." She grabs the material at her bust and looks at it. "It had a little bald spot over here somewhere. I glued on some extra sequins and fixed it for her, but she still..." She stops, seeming to realize she brought his gaze right to her boobs, and awkwardly drops her hand.

Dare's smile dissipates when he notices the necklace he bought me that I gave to her hanging from her slim throat. "Nice necklace."

Hannah touches it almost as if she'd forgotten she was

wearing it. Her cheeks turn rosy and she shifts her attention back to me. "Anyway, how have you been?"

"Good," I say, glancing at Dare as he shifts and lets go of my waist. I'm distracted keeping an eye on him, but I try to focus on Hannah. "Um, we're planning a trip, actually. After graduation, we're taking my mom with us to Italy for a couple of weeks."

"No way. That's awesome," she says. "How is your mom doing?"

I grin. "So good. It's been a long road, but her cancer is finally in remission."

"Oh my god, Aubrey. That's such good news. I hadn't heard. I'm so happy for you. Tell her I said… Actually, I don't know what you say to that, but it's fantastic news. Congratulations, I guess."

I laugh. I'm too happy not to these days. "Thanks. I will. How have you been?"

"I've been—" She stops and looks over at Dare. "Did you just take my picture?"

Dare shrugs.

I frown, confused when I look at his phone and see that he did.

What the hell?

"If you're gonna take a picture, you could at least take a picture of us both," I say lightly.

"Sure," he says easily. "Get in there, I'll take your picture."

He sounds a little too eager and it makes me uneasy, but I don't have any pictures with Hannah, and if he's giving this one his blessing, I might as well.

I leave his side and approach hers, feeling a sudden and no longer familiar wave of shyness as I try to figure out how to pose with her. She chuckles, as awkward about it as I am, and wraps her arm around my waist the way Dare does.

My heart lifts a little as I look up at him. His dark gaze is following every uncomfortable breath and I suddenly feel like this was a terrible idea.

I shake it off, though. I don't have to worry about Dare and Hannah anymore. Whatever conversation they had that day in the classroom, Hannah never really came around again after it. She liked photos and posts on social media from time to time to show we were still good, but we never actually talked.

Until tonight.

My chest feels tight. I tell myself there's no reason to be so nervous and flash a smile as Hannah and I pose for the picture.

Dare snaps it. Looks at it. Puts his phone back in his pocket.

I feel like I'm at the end of my first date and I don't know why. I try to shake the fluttery feeling, releasing Hannah and stepping away from her.

I drift back to Dare. He reclaims my waist, pulling me close, his gaze never leaving Hannah.

That feeling is back. The one where I think I've put her between his crosshairs. Why did I have to act so awkwardly around her?

"Anyway," I say, pulling Hannah's focus back to me. "We were just about to head up to our room."

Hannah smiles and nods with a polite, "Oh." She glances away as if searching for her date, but before she opens her mouth to politely get away, Dare speaks.

"You should join us."

My heart drops clear out of my body.

Hannah's eyes widen and she looks a little faint.

Dare smirks.

"Um, what?" I ask.

"You said I could have all the fun I wanted tonight, right?" he teases, looking down at me. "Maybe you can, too."

I can't speak or think or breathe. I'm afraid to move.

I don't know if he's messing with me or being serious. He has to be messing with me, right?

"I have to go," Hannah blurts before I can answer.

"Hannah, wait," I call, but she doesn't.

Dare's smirk spreads to a full-on grin as she hurries away from us. "Don't lose your shoe," he calls after her.

Once she's gone and I can draw a breath again, I smack him in the stomach. "What the hell was that?"

He shrugs. "She's fun to fuck with." He looks down at me, his dark eyes sparkling with mischief. "So are you."

"You weren't serious, right?"

"Of course not," he says, encircling my waist and pulling me tightly against him. "You know I don't share."

I don't know if I'm relieved or… something else, but I shake my head, still feeling a little breathless. "That was so mean. Why are you so mean?"

"You like it," he rumbles, kissing my jaw.

"No, I don't."

"Mm-hmm. At least a little bit."

I sigh with pleasure, my eyes drifting closed as he starts to kiss my neck. "You're a menace."

"I know."

"You're the one who belongs locked up in a tower where you can't torture any more innocents."

He grins against my neck. "Maybe you and Hannah can team up and take me on."

I can't resist. "Sounds like you wanted us to."

"Hey." He squeezes my side and I laugh. He turns me around and pulls me back against him, squeezing me around the waist and kissing the side of my head. "Let's get out of here."

Prom was hosted in the ballroom of a hotel by the beach, and Dare booked us a suite upstairs, so we don't have to go far. I take my heels off the moment we're in the door, and Dare picks me up like a caveman and hauls me laughing to the bed.

When we're both naked and sated and lying relaxed in each other's arms, I trace the lines of black ink covering his shoulder and bicep. When I met him, he only had the crow, but he's added to it this year.

When I asked why he got a big black crow inked into his skin, he said when he was growing up, his mother always told him the crow was a symbol of wisdom. When he started at Baymont High and they put him into onyx—Slytherin, if you ask Hannah, but actually the house that's supposed to stand for wisdom and loyalty—he thought the crow would be a nice representation of this period of his life.

Now, there's a mermaid wrapped around his bicep and a crown on the crow's head. His wings are open looking down at the havoc he seems to have wrought, but at the start of the year, he was looking at nothing. Now, he looks down at a busted clock, the glass splintered and bursting up toward him, the hands set to midnight.

I never asked him what that one meant.

It's cool, though. I like it.

I lean in and give it a little kiss.

I hear the pillow rustle as he turns his head to glance at the ink I just kissed. His gaze drifts to me, a relaxed smile on his face. The contented kind I don't see very often, but they're my favorite ones.

I reach up and caress his handsome face. "Did you have a nice prom night?"

He nods. "Did you?"

"I did. Thank you for taking me." Sighing, I tease, "I hope now that I'm your queen, I don't turn into a lunatic."

Dare grins, catching my hand and bringing it to his lips for a kiss. "You won't. You're not cut from that cloth."

I smile, resting my head on his chest and looking up at him, but my smile fades. "Are you glad about that?"

His brow furrows briefly like he didn't like that question, or maybe that it passed through my head. "Why wouldn't I be?"

I shrug. "I don't know. I'm a lot different from what you had before. I know you played a lot of different games with her. I guess sometimes I wonder if you ever get bored with me."

"No," he says, reaching down and stroking my cheek.

"Okay. Good."

"I would ask if you ever get bored with me, but I don't ask stupid questions."

I laugh, and he smiles. "Yeah, no. I don't know how anyone could ever get bored with you."

He smirks, grabbing me and rolling over so I'm underneath him. I spread my legs to make room for him—not to go another round, just so he can get comfortable on top of me.

Inevitably, once he is, though, he starts kissing and touching me. My body gets warm and he pushes a finger into me.

There's a knock at the door.

I gasp, and he pulls out of me.

A frown flickers across my face.

"Must be the room service I ordered," he says, sitting up on the edge of the bed and grabbing his underwear off the floor so he can pull them back on.

Oh, right.

I thought…

I shake my head of silly thoughts and smile up at my beautiful boyfriend, pulling the blankets up to cover my chest. "Room service. You spoil me."

He smirks as he looks back at me, then walks to the door in just his underwear because he's absolutely shameless.

He's shameless in the best way, though.

I won't say life with him is always easy and there have definitely been bumps along the way, but now that I've met him, I can't imagine doing it with anybody else.

He gets in your veins and poisons your blood. At first, you think you're just a little sick, but then you realize what you're infected with... it's severe, and there's no cure, and it never really leaves you.

Maybe it's corruption or liberation. I don't know if it's good or bad. I know it's intoxicating and addictive, and I can't even imagine a life without him anymore.

I knew he saved my life that night when he dragged me out of the pool, but I didn't know he was giving me a completely new one.

I guess, for all the bad she has done and will likely continue to do, at least Anae Richards did one thing right: she brought me to him.

The **Coastal Elite** world continues with ***Undertow***. If you didn't read it in the *Bully God* anthology, make sure you don't miss Hayden and Gemma's book! After that, you'll be all caught up and ready for ***Contempt***!

ACKNOWLEDGMENTS

First and foremost, thank you to May Sage for inviting me to take part in the Filthy Elites anthology! This story idea had whispered across my mind and I had the prologue written, but I didn't really have time to write it, so I shelved it and wasn't sure I would ever find time to get back to it. Now, that seems insane to me. I love this book so much—how could I not have written it? Coastal Elite wouldn't be the same world without this story as the foundation, and honestly, it probably wouldn't have been written if I didn't have that added motivation of not wanting to let you guys down. It really pushed me to finish the story even though I was totally exhausted. You kept me on track, whether you knew it or not, so thank you. :)

Also shout out to R. Holmes and Kayleigh King for inviting me to the Bully God anthology just before that. It was having two anthologies releasing one right after the other than initially inspired me to tie the stories together (though I planned to write *Contempt* for FE at the time) and then from there, the world grew, and it became a whole world/series that I fell head over heels in love with. When I love something that hard, I know it means my readers likely will, too, and honestly, Coastal Elite probably wouldn't even be a thing without my involvement in these two anthologies this year.

My readers, my beautiful, lovely, patient readers. I'm so glad you guys love Dare and all his depravity as much as I do! I can't wait to take you deeper into the Coastal Elite world. I just adore this world, it's dark and depraved and so much fun, and I'm so happy I get to take you guys into it with me. Thank you for always being so excited to dive into my words!

Melissa Derda, my wonderful PA. Thank you so much for all your help (and the great marketing copy because that Coastal Elite quote of yours is getting splashed across everything, hahaha). You are a fantastic human, and I'm so glad you stumbled across my books!

Amanda Anderson, your enthusiasm for Dare and Aubrey gave me life! Thank you for bringing me along on your reading journey and making me smile.

Thank you Beth Lewis Hale for lending me your eagle eyes and nursing expertise to iron out any little wrinkles I missed.

Issa Mireya Perdue for being such a hype queen! You never fail to get me excited, and you're just generally awesome. ;)

Clarise at CT Cover Creations, thank you soooo much for designing my spectacular alternate covers for this series! I had a great time brainstorming them with you and I'm so in love with the result!

Thank you to everyone who has helped share and spread the word about this book! I couldn't do any of this without you.

Sam
Mariano

ALSO BY SAM MARIANO

Contemporary romance standalones

Untouchable (dark bully romance)

Descent (dark billionaire romance)

The Boy on the Bridge (second chance bully romance)

Resisting Mr. Granville (steamy forbidden romance)

The Imperfections (forbidden romance)

Stitches (MFM ménage romance)

How the Hitman Stole Christmas (unconventional, a pinch of mafia)

Mistletoe Kisses (student-teacher romance novella)

Coming-of-age, contemporary bully duet

Because of You

After You

Forbidden, taboo romance

Irreparable Duet

If you're a **series reader**, be sure to check out her super binge-able Morelli family series! It's dark and twisty mafia romance, and the first book is *Accidental Witness*

Next in the Coastal Elite world…

The **Coastal Elite** world continues with ***Undertow.*** If you didn't read it in the *Bully God* anthology, make sure you don't miss Hayden and Gemma's book! After that, you'll be all caught up and ready for ***Contempt***!

ABOUT THE AUTHOR

Sam Mariano has a soft spot for the bad guys (in fiction, anyway). She loves to write edgy, twisty reads with complicated characters you're left thinking about long after you turn the last page. Her favorite thing about indie publishing is the ability to play by your own rules! If she isn't reading one of the thousands of books on her to-read list, writing her next book, or hanging out with her fabulous daughter… actually, that's about all she has time for these days.

Feel free to find Sam on Facebook (Sam Mariano's General Reader Group), Goodreads, Instagram, or her blog—she loves hearing from readers! She's also available on TikTok now @sammarianobooks, and you can sign up for her totally-not-spammy newsletter HERE

If you have the time and inclination to leave a review, however short or long, she would greatly appreciate it! :)